PENGUIN BOOKS

A PACK FOR SPRING

Growing up, Emilia wanted to be an author, therapist, and ice-cream stand owner. After eight years of being a trauma therapist, she checked off the second career on her list when she became a full-time author. Now all that's left is the ice-cream stand!

Emilia loves that writing romance allows her to explore worlds with guaranteed happily ever afters, cozy characters who love each other, and found families who overcome challenges together. She believes that everyone deserves to see themselves in romance, and she includes meaningful disability and mental illness representation in her stories.

When she's not writing, Emilia is probably embroidering, making pottery, napping with her dog, or reading romance books. An adventurer at heart, growing up in a multicultural Swedish-Iranian home instilled in her a love of travel and experiencing new cultures.

Other books by Emilia include the *Forbidden Duet* and *Cherished*, as well as her Empire of Royals Mafia series under her pen name, Emilia Rossi.

ALSO IN THE COZYVERSE SERIES

A Pack for Autumn by Emilia Emerson

A Pack for Winter by Eliana Lee

A Pack for Spring by Emilia Emerson

A Pack for Summer by Eliana Lee

A PACK FOR SPRING

EMILIA EMERSON

PENGUIN BOOKS

PENGUIN BOOKS

UK | USA | Canada | Ireland | Australia
India | New Zealand | South Africa

Penguin Books is part of the Penguin Random House group of companies
whose addresses can be found at global.penguinrandomhouse.com

Penguin Random House UK,
One Embassy Gardens, 8 Viaduct Gardens, London SW11 7BW

penguin.co.uk

First published in the United States of America by G.P. Putnam's Sons,
an imprint of Penguin Random House LLC 2026
First published in Great Britain by Penguin Books 2026
001

Copyright © Emilia Emerson, 2026

The moral right of the author has been asserted

Penguin Random House values and supports copyright.
Copyright fuels creativity, encourages diverse voices, promotes freedom
of expression and supports a vibrant culture. Thank you for purchasing
an authorized edition of this book and for respecting intellectual property
laws by not reproducing, scanning or distributing any part of it by any
means without permission. You are supporting authors and enabling
Penguin Random House to continue to publish books for everyone.
No part of this book may be used or reproduced in any manner for the
purpose of training artificial intelligence technologies or systems. In accordance
with Article 4(3) of the DSM Directive 2019/790, Penguin Random House
expressly reserves this work from the text and data mining exception

Illustrations by AlexBrushes and Anna Vaughn Jones
Book design by Silverglass Studio
Printed and bound in Great Britain by Clays Ltd, Elcograf S.p.A.

The authorized representative in the EEA is Penguin Random House Ireland,
Morrison Chambers, 32 Nassau Street, Dublin D02 YH68

A CIP catalogue record for this book is available from the British Library

ISBN: 978-1-405-98783-7

Penguin Random House is committed to a sustainable future
for our business, our readers and our planet. This book is made from
Forest Stewardship Council® certified paper.

*To the people who see us
especially when we're afraid of being seen.*

*And to the women who never made it out
and their daughters who did.*

AUTHOR'S NOTE

Welcome to Starlight Grove! If you picked up this book because of the super cute cover, I want you to know that this is a cozy, small town romance that's also *very spicy*. This book is for adults!

While this is a sweet, low-angst read, there is content that some readers may find upsetting. These are referenced as past events and include: brief mentions of the loss of a sibling to childhood cancer, deaths of parents, childhood bullying, discussions of a previous abusive relationship, and being cheated on (*not* by the MMCs). One character uses a mobility aid and struggles with feelings around his diagnosis/disability, and there are discussions of omegaverse-specific hormonal conditions. This book contains incorrect information about wild bunnies. Do not use this as a wildlife instruction manual! Lastly, there is an inaccurate depiction of a bearded firefighter. While this would not be permitted in our world, the Cozyverse has figured out how to get a tight mask seal with facial hair.

A Pack for Spring is part of the Cozyverse shared universe between Emilia Emerson and Eliana Lee. Our books can be read as standalones, but all take place in the charming town of Starlight Grove with shared characters.

This book ends in a happily ever after!

For more details about the spicy/adult content in this book, and to access exclusive bonus scenes, please visit emiliaemerson.com.

INTRO TO OMEGAVERSE

A Pack for Spring is a Why Choose Omegaverse.

Why Choose means that our female main character doesn't have to choose between her love interests for her happily ever after.

Omegaverse originated in fanfiction as MM (male/male) romance. It has evolved since then but remains a wonderfully queer-positive genre, which is reflected in the worldbuilding.

While every author has their own take on omegaverse, in general, it is an alternative world where society is composed of three designations: alphas, omegas, and betas. People are born into a designation, which influences their biology, personality, and instincts, but they do *not* shift into animals. Everyone has a scent that can change depending on emotions and stir up physiological reactions in others.

Cozyverse is our sweet, low-angst interpretation of the genre.

ALPHAS

Alphas are natural leaders, mostly male, and the most dominant designation.

Male alphas have knots at the base of their penis that swell during sex, allowing them to stay locked inside their partner. Female alphas have locks in their vaginas that serve a similar purpose with male partners.

When exposed to enough omega pheromones, particularly during an omega's heat, alphas can fall into rut, which is when they are overwhelmed by their instincts to sate and care for their omega.

Alphas can "bark," which means injecting their voice with a tone that omegas find difficult to resist. In this omegaverse, barks are used in trusting relationships where the omega consents to being put in a submissive state.

OMEGAS
Omegas are the rarest designation, and most are female. Typically, they are physically small and have a high need for physical touch. Omegas are often the center of pack life, the glue that holds the pack together.

Starting in early adulthood, omegas go into heat every three months. Heats last approximately one week, and during this time, omegas are ruled by their instincts. They have a strong urge to nest, gathering soft and cozy items into a bed for comfort.

Omegas must be knotted by alphas to avoid pain and physical harm during heat. If omegas want to prevent their heats, they can take a daily suppressant pill.

BETAS
Betas are the most common designation and what we would consider "normal" humans. They don't have strong scents and are least governed by pheromones, but they are not immune. Betas can be a part of packs, and alphas and omegas can bite them to form a bond.

PACKS
Polyamory is freely accepted, and many people form packs, or chosen families. Romantic and sexual connections between pack members can vary.

SCENT MATCHES
Scent matches are people who are uniquely compatible with each other and have strong reactions to each other's scents.

BONDS

Bonds are initiated by a bite and form a permanent emotional link between two people. Alphas and omegas exchange bites, whereas betas simply receive them to create the bond.

1
LUCY

I fanned my hands aggressively in front of my face to dry the tears welling up in my eyes.

My jaw clenched. This was ridiculous. I was about to turn twenty-nine, not ninety-nine. My life was *not* over.

A rogue tear dared spill down my cheek, and I brushed it away with a huff. My looming birthday, just three days away, was a painful reminder that I was entering the last year of my twenties without achieving any of the things I thought I would.

No doting pack.

No prestigious job at a fashion house.

No big city apartment.

Felix head-butted my leg with a loud *meow*, and I scooped him into my arms. He purred, the low rumble soothing as it vibrated against my chest.

"I'm just being dramatic. I'm a bright, young woman with my whole life ahead of me." My voice cracked, and Felix looked distinctly unconvinced. "How old are you, anyway?"

He half-heartedly swiped at my face. Hmm, maybe I wasn't the only one sensitive about my age. Felix had appeared in Starlight Grove eight years ago, right after Stanley became the mayor. Well, the mayor on paper. We all knew Felix was really the one in charge.

"You don't need to worry about aging, you magical immortal being." I kissed his forehead. "Do you want to come with me tonight? It should be fun."

His jaw parted with a massive yawn.

"Okay, Mr. Mayor. You can stay here and snooze."

I carried Felix over to his bed by the fireplace and tucked him in with one last chin scratch before turning to the large pile of clothes on my couch. I'd been putting off spring cleaning with the excuse that it wasn't *officially* spring for three more days, but it had gotten to the point where every time I needed to sit on the couch, I had to shove aside the mini mountain of clothes.

My phone vibrated loudly on top of the coffee table.

OLIVE

Your chariot awaits! We're outside

SUMMER

Ivy just picked me up! See you soon

"Why is it that no matter how early I try to get ready, I'm always running late?" I muttered.

By the time I located my jacket—a mauve peacoat I'd embroidered with gold flowers—most of my clothes were on the floor. Oh well, I would take care of that later. Probably.

"Bye, Felix! Have a good night!" I shouted over my shoulder as I raced to the door. In my distracted rush, my foot caught on the corner of a large box and I hit the hardwood with a graceless *thunk*. I blinked away my tears, telling myself it was definitely my stinging knees causing me to cry and not the fact that my very soul felt so *fragile*, like one more inconvenience would end me. I had a good life, so why did I feel so lost?

I slowly pushed myself up and rested my forehead against the door.

Get your shit together. You're stronger than this.

Except . . . sometimes I didn't want to be strong. But that was the problem, wasn't it? I needed to toughen up.

I drew in a deep breath and slipped out the door with a fresh determination and a soft smile plastered on my face. Tonight marked a new start. I was determined to make this last year in my twenties count . . . and hopefully find myself in the process.

A Pack for Spring

"Oohhh, it looks so pretty!" Olive leaned forward to get a better look at the festival through the window.

The two of us were squished in the back of the truck with Finn, one of Olive's alphas. Her other two alphas—Easton and my brother, Lars—sat up front.

She turned toward me, eyes bright and happy. "Have you been to this before?"

I shook my head. "Parisa said this is the first time they're having it here. Before they drove down to Boston to celebrate."

I'd met Parisa a couple of months ago at a networking event for local business owners. She owned a home goods boutique in the nearby town of Maple Glen. We'd hit it off and now messaged each other most days to chat about our lives and businesses and everything in between. The other day, she'd invited me to her town's inaugural Iranian New Year, or Nowruz, celebration.

Lars parked, and I pushed my door open, crinkling my nose at the horrendously loud *creak*. I threw my brother a pointed look. He loved his vintage Volvo truck, even though it had the bad habit of breaking down at inconvenient times.

"Don't give me that look," he grumbled.

I patted the truck's light blue frame. "I know Gustav has been good to you, but you do know Volvo has actually come out with cars this century, right?"

I jumped to the side to evade his shove.

"Hey!" Olive shouted. "Don't be mean to Lucy."

"But she insulted my truck!"

I laughed at how petulant he sounded.

"That's no excuse for violence." Olive sniffed and joined arms with me.

I stuck my tongue out at my brother as we headed toward the entrance of the Maple Glen fairgrounds. I'd been here a couple of times growing up when the traveling carnival came to town, but it had never looked like this. The air pulsed with vibrant music and laughter while kids ran circles around the food booths and the adults greeted each other with warm hugs and cheek kisses. Lines of orange and pink streaked across the sky as the sun danced lower, and the dozens of small bonfires scattered around the field made everything glow.

We stopped at the entrance to wait for the rest of our group.

"What's the deal with the fire?" Easton asked, tripping over his feet before slinging his arm around Olive's shoulders.

"Iranian New Year is the first day of spring, but tonight is the bonfire celebration and you're supposed to jump over a fire to symbolize leaving the old year behind," I said. When Parisa had explained it, something had clicked inside me. Maybe this was what I needed—a ritual to cleanse my life of all the bad energy and encourage new beginnings.

"Seems unsafe," Finn grumbled.

"You don't have to do it if you're scared," Olive said sweetly, and I snorted a laugh.

Finn and Easton had practically lived at my house growing up, and it was fun to see the wild boys I knew become overprotective alphas.

"Oh, they're here!" Easton said, waving his arms above his head.

Ivy and Summer skipped toward us with linked arms while Ivy's guys—James, Rome, and Logan—jogged to keep up. The transformation in Ivy these past few months had been so special. She'd always put so much pressure on herself with her teaching job, and seeing her relaxed and happy, doted on by her pack, warmed my heart.

Summer and Ivy half crashed into us, and we piled into a tight omega hug. The tension in my chest eased. No matter what happened in my life, I had my friends. I would be okay.

"I'm starving," Summer said once we pulled apart. "I can't wait to check out the food scene." She rubbed her hands together, a gleam in her eye. She had always been the foodie of our group, but it was even more true now that she was close to opening her bakery. Every meal was an opportunity for research.

We slung our arms around each other and headed into the festival, laughing as our shoulders bumped against one another. We hadn't gone far when someone shouted my name. I turned and my heart leapt when I spotted Leo Azad—Parisa's brother and my newest neighbor.

The storefront beside mine had become available this past winter when Ms. Ito retired, closing her long-standing gift shop that inexplicably specialized in socks with unique messages on them—I was currently wearing my "Jump Rope Is the Meaning of Life" pair. Summer had long been convinced that Ms. Ito was running a money-laundering scheme because there was no way her fancy sports car and designer bags were funded by socks. However she got her money, she'd decided to sell her shop and travel the world, accompanied by a string of attractive men. Leo had purchased it a few months ago and opened a thriving florist business.

The firelight danced across his warm skin as he approached. My eyes flitted down his body—only because he was wearing the black pants I tailored for him and the red shirt I'd embroidered with gold thread, *not* because I found his muscular thighs and arms distracting.

Luckily, Olive saved me from having to form actual words.

"Hey, Leo!"

"Hey, Olive. Your alphas staying out of trouble?" he asked, smirking as he glanced back at Lars, Easton, and Finn. Leo had been on the ocean rescue team that had saved Olive's guys when they crashed a boat in a storm last year.

"Mostly." Olive grinned. "They haven't even capsized a boat this week."

Finn pulled his omega to his side with a scowl. "Be careful, pretty girl." He leaned down and murmured something in her ear that made her cheeks turn bright red.

A pang of loneliness and jealousy seized my chest, but then Leo turned his attention to me. "Parisa said she'd invited you, and I was hoping you'd come." He rubbed the back of his neck in a nervous gesture that I found ridiculously endearing.

"I've been looking forward to it."

A stilted silence fell over us, and Leo shifted his weight onto his other leg. I bit my lip. I'd had a crush on the cute beta since our first meeting, when he came into my shop with an armful of flowers to introduce himself, but he always seemed uncomfortable around me. I would have chalked it up to social anxiety, except he seemed at ease and charming with everyone else in town.

"We're going to get dinner if you want to join us." I glanced over my shoulder and grinned when I realized Summer had snuck away and was already standing in line at a food stand.

"I told my family I'd eat with them," he said.

For the briefest moment, I thought he might ask me to join him.

"Here." He held out a small paper bag and I took it. "It's a mixture of fruit and nuts. It's supposed to grant wishes."

"Oh, thank you."

"Well, I hope you have fun. Nice to see you again, Olive." Leo turned around, moving stiffly like he couldn't get away from me fast enough.

I swallowed the lump in my throat. "You, too, Leo."

"That was weird," Olive said, cocking her head.

"Yeah, it was." Summer inched up beside me, a bowl of noodle soup in her hands. "Did something happen between you two?"

I shook my head. "No. He's always kind of like that with me."

"What, super awkward because he's clearly in love with you?"

I scrunched my nose. "What are you talking about? I'm not sure he even likes me."

"Lucy," Olive said, her eyebrows furrowed with reproach. "You can't possibly believe that. Everyone loves you."

My heart was too raw to have this conversation. I'd been nursing my secret crush for months, and I couldn't handle false hope.

I opened the paper bag and grabbed a handful of the nut and dried fruit mixture. "Let's get food."

Olive and Summer looked like they wanted to push it further, but Ivy put her arm around my shoulder. "Excellent idea. There's a kebab food truck over there that's calling my name."

I popped a pistachio in my mouth and made a wish.

A Pack for Spring

AFTER WE'D EATEN, I wandered through the rest of the booths, stopping at one with a goldfish tank. They were surprisingly mesmerizing as they swam around. Maybe I needed a pet.

"Lucy!"

The second Azad sibling of the evening bounded toward me.

"I'm so glad you're here!" Parisa engulfed me in a tight hug, her bright citrus scent swirling around me.

"Thanks for inviting me. This is all so cool."

Her eyes sparkled. "It is, isn't it? It's amazing to see my town show up and be so supportive."

A large alpha with brown skin and short-cropped black hair joined us. I didn't recognize him, but the possessive way he pulled Parisa to his side made it clear that he was one of her alphas.

"There you are," he said with relief. "Don't go running off again."

Parisa pursed her lips and shook her head. "Overprotective alpha. Amir, this is Lucy, the friend I was telling you about."

"It's nice to meet you." Amir's voice was deep and kind.

"Oh, and there's Sloane, my other alpha."

I turned to see a blond woman with a tray of food headed toward us. Amir took the tray from her when she got closer.

Sloane kissed her omega on the forehead and introduced herself. "Are you getting a goldfish?"

I peered back at the tank. "I'm trying to decide if Felix would eat it if I brought one home."

"I'm really hoping Felix is your cat and not your roommate," she said with a grimace.

I burst out laughing. "Yes, my cat. Well, not mine. He's too powerful to belong to any one person. He's Starlight Grove's mayor."

The two alphas stared at me, clearly trying to figure out if I was joking or not. I just smiled sweetly.

Parisa snorted. "Better not risk the goldfish's life, especially since they represent rebirth. Might be a bad omen if Felix eats it." She took my hand. "Come over here. I want to introduce you to my family." She led me over to a picnic table, her alphas following close behind.

"Parisa, azizam, come sit down." An older woman with curly gray hair held out her hand.

Parisa leaned down and kissed her on the cheek. "I want to introduce you to my friend. Lucy, this is my grandma, my Bibi."

Her grandma's eyes lit up and she reached out to take my hand, pulling me down to kiss my cheeks. "It is very nice to meet you."

"It's so nice to meet you," I murmured. This woman radiated warmth and immediately put me at ease.

"And this is my maman, Tara, and my baba, Mahmoud."

Her mom was stunningly beautiful, with golden skin framed by curly black hair and deep brown eyes. She drew me into a firm hug. "I've heard so many good things about you, Lucy, from both of my children."

My cheeks flushed. "It's nice to meet you, Mrs. Azad."

She patted me on the cheek. "Call me Tara, please."

Her husband stood and put his hand over his heart. "It's very nice to meet you."

I was surprised to realize Parisa's family members were all betas. I knew she hadn't grown up in a pack, but I'd assumed one of her parents was at least an alpha. It was exceptionally rare for an omega to be born to two beta parents.

Amir set the large tray of food in the middle of the table, where there were already several dishes.

"Join us, Lucy," Tara said.

"Oh, I've already eaten."

She waved off my protest. "Nonsense. You can always eat more."

"Don't argue with a Persian mom trying to feed you," Amir quipped as he took a seat and pulled Parisa down beside him.

I grinned. "Well, if you insist."

Being around this family felt like a warm hug. They were sweet and affectionate with everyone, including Parisa's alphas. Her father asked me questions about my shop, and it wasn't long before he'd set up an appointment to have me make a custom suit for an upcoming event.

"Where's Leo?" Tara asked.

I forced myself to keep my expression neutral, especially when Parisa's knowing gaze landed on me. She'd hinted heavily at how great she thought it would be if her brother and I dated, and my omega wholeheartedly agreed. But I'd experienced too much heartbreak to chase after a guy who wasn't interested, no matter how much I wanted him.

"I texted him where we were," Amir said. "Maybe he met up with someone."

A shock of bitter jealousy filtered down my spine. Met up with someone? I shoved a huge bite of chicken in my mouth to hide my reaction.

Bibi tutted and patted my hand. "Do not worry, azizam."

I raised my eyebrows, waiting for her to clarify her statement, but she just smiled.

"Are you going to jump?"

My heart skipped a beat at Leo's low voice and the gentle wave of his sweet cardamom scent. It was so intoxicating it made me want to wrap myself around his body . . . or at least steal his clothes for my nest.

It was on the tip of my tongue to ask where he'd been earlier, but I wasn't sure I wanted to know the answer.

"I was planning on it. I'm just a little nervous. Which is silly," I hurriedly tacked on.

"Nah, it can be scary if you've never done it before. Do you want help?"

"What do you mean?"

"I'll hold your hand as you jump. Keep you safe."

My cheeks flushed, and it had nothing to do with the heat from the bonfires.

"Okay." Sparks of electricity shot through me when his warm, strong hand surrounded mine.

He led me over to a bonfire—one of the smaller ones—and squeezed my hand. I tilted my head back to meet his gaze, my fingers itching to run through his dark curls.

"When you jump over, you leave all the burdens of the past year behind. They're burned away, and you enter the new year cleansed."

"That's what I want."

He nodded. "Together?"

"Together."

We took a running start, and it was only Leo's hand in mine that kept me from stopping when we approached the fire. I let out a little squeak and leapt. It only took a second, but when my feet hit the ground after clearing the flames, something had shifted inside me. The heaviness I'd been carrying, the grief at the unexpected ways my life had turned out, faded into the curls of smoke.

I beamed at Leo, but my smile faltered at the flash of pain on his face. He quickly masked it, but he was standing at an odd angle, with one knee slightly bent.

"Are you okay?" I asked.

He smiled, but it was strained. "Of course."

I opened my mouth to push further but completely lost my train of thought when he reached up and tucked a lock of my windswept hair behind my ear. It took everything in me to stop from jumping up and down at his attention. I perfumed, my scent filling the air, and I hoped his beta sense of smell wasn't strong enough to pick it up.

"You made it over," he said.

"Thanks for helping me be brave."

His fingers skimmed along my jaw. "You're always brave, Lucy."

Later that night, when I was curled up in my nest, his words echoed in my mind. *You're always brave, Lucy.*

It wasn't true, but for Leo, I wanted it to be.

2

LEO

I gritted my teeth as I parked in the alley behind my shop. I turned off my car and was engulfed in darkness. I didn't know if I should smash my head against the headrest or scream into the silence.

I had acted like such a fucking idiot tonight. When I saw Lucy sitting with my family, I'd hidden behind a booth and just watched. Because I lost my mind whenever I was around her. Because my family was sure to bring up the massive crush I had on her, and I wasn't ready for her to know yet.

I raised my hand to my face and breathed in deeply, trying to catch a hint of Lucy's scent on my skin, but there was nothing.

You're so fucking pathetic.

I squinted at the dark alley to make sure Lucy wasn't outside before grabbing my cane and getting out of the car. Pain shot through my knee like lightning, making my forehead break out in a sweat as I hobbled to the door and unlocked it. My heart sank as I stared at the staircase leading up to my apartment above the shop.

I should have used my cane tonight. Shouldn't have jumped over a bonfire with Lucy. Except . . . it was hard to regret when the sound of her laughter and the brightness in her eyes played through my head like the best movie I'd ever seen.

I limped into my shop instead of tackling the stairs to my apartment. I'd told myself I wouldn't use the air mattress in the storage room again, but here I fucking was.

I crashed down onto the bed and slipped a pillow under my knee. For a few moments this evening, I could pretend my life was good—no cane, one of my favorite celebrations of the year, and the beautiful girl I was obsessed with holding my hand. Now, as I laid back on a shitty air mattress, fully clothed because I was in too much pain to undress, reality came crashing back, dark and cold.

"Okay, that's it. We're stopping for the day." Cassie, my physical therapist, stepped back from the table, arms crossed.

"I can do more." My words slipped out through clenched teeth.

"No, you can't. Not without risking injury."

When I realized she wouldn't budge, I relented and pushed myself to a seated position.

"What's the plan here, Leo? The way you're going—refusing to use your cane, pushing yourself too hard—is going to end up with you in even more severe pain and using a wheelchair."

Irritation rose in me, sharp and defensive. "I told you when I started physical therapy that my goal was to walk without my cane by the start of spring, and now you're acting like I should just give up."

Cassie sat down on her rolling stool with a soft sigh. "There absolutely is a place for optimism in health care, and I don't want to take that away from you. But there's also a place for accepting the way things are. Your inability to accept your injury is going to make things worse in the long run."

I stared out the window, trying to breathe through my tangled web of emotions. A flicker of brown and white caught my eye. Felix, the town cat, smooshed his face against the glass, leaving a smudge in his wake. His eyes were locked on me. I gave him a little wave.

Felix had been the first Starlight Grove resident I met. When I'd entered my shop after getting the keys, I had unlocked the door to find him sitting on top of the checkout desk like he'd been waiting for me. I'd asked around town if anyone was missing a cat, but everyone was completely unconcerned. Apparently Felix, who was also inexplicably the mayor in a turn of events I still couldn't wrap my mind around, chose who he wanted to spend the night with, and everyone in town just accommodated him. After spending several days searching for the gaps or holes in my new building that were allowing the cat to enter my locked store and finding nothing, I'd given up. I'd gotten used to Felix randomly showing up, taste-testing new shipments of roses, and staring judgmentally at any man who came in and didn't choose the largest size bouquet to purchase.

I was pretty sure he'd doubled my profits.

With a flick of his tail, he marched away from the clinic.

Cassie cleared her throat and I reluctantly turned back to our conversation.

"Do you get where I'm coming from, Leo? I hope you know I'm on your side. I want you to succeed, but I'm worried about you."

I gave her a jerky nod and swallowed my anger. None of this was her fault. "Do you—" I took a breath. "Are you saying you don't think I'll get to the point where I can ditch the cane?"

Now it was her turn to gaze out the window with a deep sigh. I grimaced. Not a great sign.

"I think osteoarthritis of the knee is a chronic condition without a cure, and that the goal right now is to reduce your pain, increase your quality of life, and make it so you can hold off on having a knee replacement," she started. "I can't predict the future, but in my experience, you'll likely need a combination of meds, PT, and mobility aids for the rest of your life. But that doesn't mean your life is over or that you're doomed to be in this much pain. You can live a good life, Leo."

This wasn't new information. It was what my doctor had told me, what all the online forums said. But I'd been so determined to defeat the odds that I hadn't let myself imagine the alternative.

My cane leaned against the table, and I had the urge to set it on fire. My body had already cost me so much—my job in coastal rescue, my morning runs on the beach, and now my chance at landing the most incredible girl in the world.

"Just think about what I said, okay?" Cassie said softly.

I nodded, because what else could I do? I was tempted to ask her if she thought there was any chance that an omega could be interested in me with my cane. I'd asked Parisa what she thought, but she'd just rolled her eyes and said, "No one gives a shit about your cane besides you." Cassie might have a more objective omega perspective, but it didn't seem like an appropriate question.

She scheduled my next steroid injection while I wrapped a brace around my knee. I was so stuck in my head on my short walk home I forgot to turn down the alleyway behind my store. Instead, I continued down Main Street, stopping short when I spotted Lucy outside her shop door. Before I could drop and roll out of her line of sight, she glanced over.

"Hey!" A bright smile spread across her face. Her hair was in two braids and she was wearing light blue velvet pants and a matching top. I bet she'd feel so soft in my arms.

"Don't judge my wreath," she continued, and I realized she was adjusting a new floral wreath on her door. "It's a little wonky, and I probably should have just bought one from you, but I couldn't sleep last night and got sucked into watching about a million tutorials on DIY wreaths, and here we are."

A crease formed between my eyebrows. The wreath looked perfect, like everything Lucy did. She had a bad habit of tearing herself down.

Her eyes flickered to my cane, and I braced myself for her inevitable comments and the pity in her gaze. I'd successfully hidden it from her for *months*. Now all that effort was down the drain.

"And then I still couldn't sleep and I was hungry, so I watched a bunch of recipe videos on how to make the best pancakes. Have you had breakfast yet?"

My brain stuttered. "What?"

"Are you hungry? I was going to try out one of the new recipes."

Lucy wanted to make me pancakes. Lucy just invited *me* to her *home* and wanted to make me *pancakes*?

"I already ate," I blurted out.

Her smile faltered, but I was already unlocking my shop door.

"Gotta go do the flower arranging." I gave her an awkward wave over my shoulder as I slipped inside.

I sank to the floor, my heart pounding like I'd run a race. My leg shook from exertion, but my mind was too consumed by the omega next door to care.

I kept repeating the facts in my head like I was trying to solve a complicated word problem: Lucy + cane = pancake invitation?

Was it because she felt sorry for me, or did she actually want to spend time with me? My head fell back against my door with a *thump*, and I rubbed my hand across my face. I'd kept the gorgeous omega at arm's length since moving in, convinced I needed to wait until I permanently ditched my cane to ask her out. But now that future wasn't coming, and I didn't know what to do.

I opened my eyes and shouted when I found Felix sitting right in front of me.

"What the fuck!" I grabbed my chest, my heart racing. "How do you do this?" I looked around as if I would finally find the magical portal he was using to get into my store. "Also, what are you wearing?" My brow furrowed as I took in his rainbow-striped knit sweater and matching bow tie. He raised a menacing paw and bopped me on the nose. I guessed I deserved that. "I'm sorry, you just startled me. And your outfit looks great," I quickly added to appease him. Felix's expression stayed disapproving.

A miserable stone of regret weighed heavy in my stomach. "I've fucked up, haven't I?"

Parisa kept pressing me to ask Lucy out, but she didn't understand. Lucy was so far out of my league, it wasn't funny. She was beautiful, sweet, and talented. But more than that, she was an omega, which meant she needed alphas. Why would she waste time with a beta, especially a weak one like me, when she could get any guy she wanted?

But then . . . in my desperation to avoid disappointment, I had been the one rejecting *her*. Lucy had invited me to hang out so many times these past couple of months, and I had refused every invitation because I didn't want her to find out I used a cane.

In my quest to make myself worthy of her, I'd pushed her away.

I was at a crossroads. I needed to either stop pining after her and move on, or I could get over myself and try to court her, cane and all. And since the only way I'd be able to move on from her would be to literally slice out my heart, I was left with one option.

"Can you help me, Felix? You and Lucy spend a lot of time together. You know what she likes."

The cat puffed up, looking distinguished and even proud in his rainbow sweater.

I took a shuddering breath, desperately hoping it wasn't too late. There was no reason for her to give me another chance after I'd pushed her away so many times, but I would never forgive myself if I didn't try. For Lucy, I would risk it all.

3

LUCY

> **HOROSCOPE PISCES**
>
> Pisces, this is your year for all kinds of love! Embrace your sexy side, follow your intuition, and take the big leaps you've held yourself back from. If not now, when?

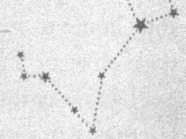

OLIVE ROLLED UP IN FRONT OF MY STORE—SUMMER, IVY, AND Felix in tow—in a golf cart exploding with flower garlands.

"Hop on in, birthday girl!" she shouted. Summer and Ivy cheered and blew noisemakers—the ones with the ribbons that unfurled when you blew into them. They were all wearing party hats, Felix included. I laughed at his grumpy expression.

Summer hopped out and placed a sash that said *Birthday Girl* across my body with a flourish before pulling me in a tight hug. "Come on! We have birthday shenanigans planned."

"I feel like the shenanigans have already started." I climbed into the passenger seat and Felix hopped onto my lap. "Isn't this Stanley's golf cart?"

"What the mayor doesn't know won't hurt him," Olive said.

Felix let out a loud *meow* and Olive's lips parted. "I mean the imposter mayor! The fake one! The *true* mayor is here with us and he told me it was okay to borrow it!"

"You might want to sleep with one eye open," Summer said in a stage whisper.

"Felix knows we all follow his rule of law." I gave him a forehead kiss.

"Birthday coffee for you," Ivy said, presenting me with a Beans 'n Bliss travel cup.

"Oohhh, yes. Thank you." I took a sip and gasped. "A pumpkin spice latte? But it's out of season!"

"Ella hooked us up," Ivy said with a grin, referring to the coffee shop's barista.

"She kept back a bottle of flavoring just for you." Summer pulled it out of a gift bag. "Just don't mention it to Lars or he'll break into your home to steal it. Anything that reminds him of his pumpkin spice omega." She batted her eyes exaggeratedly and Olive blushed, but I was laser-focused on the bottle of syrup. Every year when pumpkin spice lattes went out of season, I begged Ella to sneak me some.

"This is amazing. Thank you." I took another sip. The sun was shining and the gentle breeze carried the scent of flowers. It was the first day of spring, the start of the last year of my twenties, and I was determined to make it a good one.

Olive pulled away from the curb, causing all of us to grimace as we lurched down the street.

"Sorry, sorry!" she said. "I'm better at driving boats, but I'll get the hang of it."

"Now you don't have to worry about aging, Luce, since Olive will kill us all," Summer said dryly.

I glanced back in time to see Ivy elbow her, but as Olive hit the curb, I thought Summer had a point.

Felix batted at one of the flower garlands with his paw. I nudged him away to keep him from destroying them. "Did you all make these? They're stunning."

"Leo actually decorated the cart for us," Ivy said. "We ran into him last night mid-heist and he immediately offered."

"Not what I would call the behavior of someone who *doesn't like you*," Olive said in a singsong voice.

I pursed my lips, but I couldn't stop my stomach from exploding with excited butterflies. He did this for *me*? I hadn't seen him since he practically fled from me the other morning, but this rekindled all my sappy hopes that he returned my crush.

Well, maybe that was too far, but at least he didn't hate me. You didn't make beautiful flower garlands to decorate a stolen golf cart for someone you hated, right?

Olive turned down the road to the marina and I cocked my head. "What are we doing?"

"You'll see," she said coyly.

We all shrieked as the golf cart hit a speed bump.

"I swear, if that just messed up my pastries," Summer said through clenched teeth, clutching at a box that had been by her feet.

"Sorry!" Olive shouted.

"You're doing great," I reassured her, even as I tensed all my muscles as she took another sharp turn into a parking spot.

Summer peeked inside her box. "Phew, the pastries survived."

"Good." Ivy clapped her hands. "Let's get this party started."

I hoisted Felix into my arms, making sure not to bump his party hat as I got out of the golf cart. I wiggled happily when I saw my friends carrying gift bags. I loved presents and wasn't going to let my fear of being seen as shallow mess with me today. It was my birthday, damn it, and I was going to accept all the presents happily.

The boat, *My Sweet Olive*, came into view and my jaw dropped. Slung along the side was a huge banner reading *Happy Birthday Lucy* and a huge garland of pastel pink balloons.

"You did this for me?"

"Of course we did," Summer said, rolling her eyes. "We love you."

My friends ushered me over to a gorgeous table set up on the deck, complete with a floral tablecloth, colorful plates, and candles. I sat on the cushy seat and a mimosa materialized in my hand.

"You're spoiling me."

"As we should." Summer raised her class. "To Lucy, the sweetest, prettiest, and most crafty omega I know."

"To Lucy," Olive and Ivy echoed.

My cheeks turned pink with their praise, and I took a long sip of my drink. Summer opened the box of pastries, and I smiled when I saw it was filled with my favorite Swedish cardamom buns—the ones I couldn't eat anymore without thinking of Leo.

"I got the recipe from Frida, so hopefully they're good," she said, setting two of them on the plate in front of me.

I'd already eaten half of one by the time my friends took theirs. "They're amazing," I said around another huge bite. I held out a small piece for Felix, which he delicately took from my hand.

"Don't let James see you," Ivy said, cocking an eyebrow. Her beta was the town vet, who was growing increasingly stressed about Felix's diet. He'd done a presentation at the last town meeting that consisted of a series of slides labeled *Cat Food*, with pictures of kibble and cans of wet foot, and *Not Cat Food*, with pictures of cakes, hamburgers, and fries.

"I only gave him a small piece." I widened my eyes innocently, pointedly ignoring the fact that Felix was sneaking large bites of the pastry in my hand from under the table.

Ivy shook her head. "I saw nothing."

Summer dished up fruit salad into small bowls. "So, Lucy. Last year in your twenties. How are you feeling?"

"Well, I had three mental breakdowns yesterday, but I haven't had one yet today, so that's promising."

"No! Why mental breakdowns? My thirties have been my favorite decade so far," Ivy said.

The horrible urge to snap at my friend came over me. It was easy for her to say. She'd found her pack.

I took a deep breath. Ivy wasn't the one I was frustrated with. "That's good. Something to look forward to." My smile felt weird and plastic. "And in the meantime, I've been reading up on my Saturn return era."

"What's that?" Olive asked.

"It takes Saturn twenty-nine years to complete a rotation around the sun, so every twenty-nine years you're in your Saturn return, which signals a lot of big life changes." My friends looked just as confused as before, but I pressed on. "This is the year I'm going to find myself. I started making a list of what I want to do, like read my horoscope every day, see a fortune teller, get my aura photographed, and a bunch of other stuff."

"Oohhh, I love that! What did your horoscope say today?" Olive asked.

"I'm not sure because my newspaper hadn't arrived yet. Ever since Kevin took over the paper route from his sister, I'm lucky if I get the newspaper by lunch." And the *Starlight Tribune* did not have an online version.

"Wait, you're getting yours on the correct day? My last *Starlight Tribune* arrived *three days late*," Ivy said. "We ended up at a showing of *Love Under the Bleachers* at the movie theater instead of *Notting Hill*."

Olive snorted. "*Love Under the Bleachers* is a classic."

"Classily bad," Ivy groaned. "Although I did like the alien flash dance."

While Summer got up to demonstrate said dance, Olive put her arm around me. "Your Saturn return plan sounds fun, Luce. I'll come with you for any of it. I just hope you know that you don't need to find yourself. You're not lost."

I leaned my head against her shoulder. I'd known Olive for less than a year, but I couldn't imagine my life without her. No matter what she said, though, I'd been adrift for a while now, probably since before *they* came into my life, but certainly after they'd left it in flames.

But it was a new year, a new phase of life. I sent all my hopes for a fresh start into the universe, envisioning triumphing over the growing pains of my Saturn return and welcoming all the good surprises waiting for me.

4
LUCY

"Drumroll, please." I made a sound that bore a vague resemblance to a drum, and Felix gave me an unimpressed stare from his spot on my sewing chair.

"Hey, it's my birthday. You have to be nice to me." I scowled, but he just swished his tail. Whatever goodwill I'd gained from sharing this morning's cardamom bun apparently hadn't lasted to this afternoon.

"Okay, fine. You can save your enthusiasm for the big reveal." I reached into my large tote bag. "Ta-da!" I held up the outfit I'd sewn for him—a collared shirt with a strawberry print and matching hat and bow tie. "Now, I know you have a thing about the color red," I said, fending off his meows of protest, "but I promise it's all in your head. You look *great* in red, and I really wanted to make a dress with this pattern and you need an outfit to match. Plus, it's my birthday, so I should get my way."

Felix flopped to his side in a move I interpreted as resigned acceptance, and I beamed. "Thanks, Mr. Mayor. You won't regret it, and your fans will love it."

I got him dressed before hurrying into the back room and putting on my matching strawberry dress. I'd lain down for a quick nap after brunch and ended up sleeping way longer than I'd planned. I had to move fast to get to my moms' in time for my birthday dinner.

I drummed my fingers against my lips. "Where should we take pictures? It's too early in the season for the strawberry patch, but we could see if there are wildflowers in the field by the lighthouse?"

Felix meowed in approval.

"Great!" I grabbed my tripod and a basket, which Felix promptly jumped inside. I let out a grunt of surprise. Maybe James had a point—he was a bit of a chonk, but I didn't mind. It would help me build up my arm muscles.

I slipped out the back of my shop, walking down the alley that ran parallel to Main Street. No one knew about my secret social media project, and I wanted to keep it that way.

I peered around the corner as we got to the mouth of the alley. The nosy people in this town liked to appear out of thin air at the most inopportune times, but the coast was clear for now. I adjusted the basket and scurried down the dirt path to the lighthouse. When it came into view, bright white in the sunshine, I veered to the right into the large, overgrown field.

Felix jumped out of the basket and strutted ahead, confidently leading me. I skipped after him, my mood lifting with every step. It was our first warm day after a pretty brutal winter, and I was reveling in the warm sun kissing my skin and in doing one of my favorite things in the world. My social media account was a space just for me—where I could be playful and creative.

I let out a *whoop* when we came upon a large patch of blue wildflowers.

"Good job!" I picked Felix up under his arms and spun him in a circle. "You did amazing. And they even match my middle name."

My moms had been going through a bit of a hippie phase when they chose Bluebell for my middle name after the Swedish national flower. Two of my moms were Swedish—Isla, my biological mom who I called Lala, and Frida, my mamma. They insisted they wanted to give me a middle name that honored my heritage, but my other two moms—Jojo and my mom, Harper—admitted to me that alcohol *may* have influenced the selection of my middle name.

I spent a few minutes styling the basket with the props I brought—fresh strawberries, strawberry lemonade, and a pink quilt. I set my phone up on a tripod.

"Okay, I think we're ready. Do you want to sit in the basket?" I asked Felix.

He sniffed the props, gently picked up a strawberry, and held it in his mouth as he hopped into the basket. I squealed with excitement and joined him on the quilt. "Thank you for embracing the theme." I scratched his ears and he leaned into my touch.

I clicked my remote to take a series of pictures of the two of us. I'd never appeared in any of the photos I posted on Felix's account, but my birthday felt like a good exception. My secret account had grown faster than I'd ever expected—we were closing in on half a million followers. People loved Felix and all his outfits, but I still couldn't silence the voice in the back of my mind that said it was a frivolous, useless way to spend my time. Old voices echoed through my head—my school teachers, who told me I needed to *be more serious* and *apply myself*, and my exes, who had slowly cut me down until I didn't know how to trust myself anymore.

It was easier to just not tell anyone, then I could avoid their judgment.

I flipped through my camera roll and took a few more pictures of just Felix with the setup—the strawberry still held in his mouth.

"Okay, I think that's it!"

He released the strawberry and smacked his lips with a disgusted expression. I pulled a bag of cat treats from my tote—homemade by Summer because our little mayor had a refined palate—and gave him a handful.

While he munched happily, I lay on the blanket and looked through the photos, favoriting the ones I wanted to edit.

"People are going to be obsessed with these. See how good you look in red!"

Felix peered at my phone screen, but his expression remained unchanged.

"You know I'm right," I huffed.

Felix flopped over my chest, his body acting like my own personal weighted blanket.

"The next big holiday is Easter. We still have time, but I haven't had any sparks of inspiration yet for outfits."

Stanley had spent the past few town meetings teasing his new Easter Eggstravaganza plans that would apparently blow us all away—and once and for all settle the rivalry between Starlight Grove and Briar's Landing.

I closed my eyes, letting the sun warm my skin. "I'll come up with something good, don't you worry." The gentle rustle of the wind and birdsong swirled around me as sleep clung to the edges of my consciousness.

My vibrating phone jolted me back to reality. Shit, I was going to be late.

LARS

> Olive is having a hard time this afternoon. She's going to stay home with Finn and Easton tonight

I sat up, squinting against the sun as I looked over at the lighthouse cottage. Olive had seemed totally fine when she dropped me off at home after the birthday breakfast, but she dealt with depression that could come on fast.

OLIVE

> I think Lars just texted you but I'm soooo sorry. I really wanted to be at your birthday dinner but I had a meltdown this afternoon and my guys are making me stay home

LUCY

> I'm sorry about the meltdown 🖤 Can I do anything to help? And don't worry about it. We got to have our friend celebration this morning anyway!

OLIVE

> You're sweet but no, I'll be ok. Promise

I planted a kiss on Felix's forehead. "Olive's having a hard time. I think you should go keep her company."

His chest puffed up. He had moved in with Olive when she first came to Starlight Grove, and they had a special relationship.

He batted a paw at his bow tie.

"Oh come on, Olive will *love* to see you in your outfit. You should keep it on so you can show her." My friends might not know about my social media account, but they were very familiar with my hobby of sewing extravagant outfits for our mayor.

He sighed, nuzzled his little face against mine, and trotted off to the lighthouse. I watched him go, a pang in my chest at saying goodbye, but Olive needed him more right now.

I packed up my supplies and headed back to town, my steps heavy as I got back to Main Street. There must be something in the air today. This morning had started off so hopeful, but now I could feel a funk coming on. My too-sensitive heart felt tender.

"Lucy! Feliz cumpleaños, cariño!" I jumped as Marisol called out from her spot by the wooden fruit crates outside Mariposa Market. "Are you being properly spoiled today?" She pulled me into a hug and kissed my cheeks.

"I had birthday breakfast with my friends and I'm on my way to my moms' now."

"Sounds lovely, and that dress is stunning on you."

"Lucy! Mi querida, feliz cumple." Carmen swept out of the market. "Did you hear the news?"

"What's that?"

"The curse of the Beaufort House strikes again," Marisol said in an ominous tone.

My stomach lurched at the mention of the home my exes had rented. I'd never been *worthy* of moving in with them, but I had spent a lot of time at the house since they insisted my apartment was too cramped for all of us. Which might have been true, but the way they said it always made me feel small.

The Beaufort family had lived in the house back in the day—

they'd had three sons around my age but had left town when the parents' relationships fell apart. That was eleven years ago, and no one had rented the house for longer than a year ever since. During one particularly tumultuous stretch, there were five renters in the span of four months. It was at that point that we all decided the house was cursed.

It was one of the many red flags I'd ignored when I started dating my exes. I'd naively thought they would be the ones to break the curse, but they'd only made it ten months in the house before fleeing town in their egged cars.

"What do you mean? What happened to Mr. Smith?" I asked.

"Salvatore told me he delivered a very official letter to the house two days ago and now Mr. Smith is gone. Packed up in the middle of the night and left the key under the turtle statue on the porch." Marisol was practically glowing. She thrived on being the first person to spread town gossip.

"What was in that letter?"

She leaned forward, eyes sparkling. "Apparently, he was the heir to a Scottish castle."

"Psh, that's not what happened." Carmen selected a plum from the stand and handed it to me. "He got a last-minute job in Australia doing koala chlamydia research."

My eyebrows shot up. John Smith had only lived in that house for a couple of months and struck me as a rather dull person, but apparently I had judged the Scottish-Heir Koala-Scientist too hastily.

"No, no, no," Stanley said.

I jumped with a small scream. "Where did you come from?"

The human mayor adjusted the collar on his cream sweater and ignored my question. "Mr. Smith had to flee the country because the IRS was after him for tax evasion, which is further evidence that we need to have much stricter application procedures for anyone who wants to move to town."

"Eh." Marisol shrugged. "Our taxes just fund billionaires and genocide. Good for him for taking a stand for social justice."

Stanley's face grew red, and experience told me I had approximately three seconds to extract myself from this conversation before I was stuck listening to a long lecture about civic responsibility.

"Look over there! Did someone parallel park incorrectly?" I shouted.

Stanley turned, and Marisol and Carmen smirked as I sprinted away, not slowing until I'd turned the corner.

As I made my way to my moms', I wondered who would move into the Beaufort House next. Maybe I should enlist Felix to burn it down. It might be the only way to break the curse.

5

LUCY

IF I HAD ACCESS TO A TIME MACHINE, I WOULD HOP RIGHT IN, go back in time to the day last week when my moms asked me what I wanted for my birthday dinner, and tell past Lucy that she should not, under *any* circumstances, request frozen strawberry margaritas.

Not because they weren't delicious but because all four of my moms were currently tipsy and Jojo and Mom were well on their way to being drunk.

"I'm just saying, there's no harm in Lucy trying female alphas!" Mom half shouted, most of her margarita sloshing out of her glass. "It's not like she's had much luck with men."

I locked eyes with Lars, and he had the audacity to smirk at me. I drew my finger across my neck, but my death threat didn't faze him.

We'd finished dinner—my favorite fajitas from Señor Taco—and headed to the backyard for cake and presents. Lars got the fire going and we gathered around the firepit, wrapped in blankets, the string lights casting a gentle glow. Warmth from the flames kissed my skin and made it impossible to stop thinking about Leo—the way his hand had felt in mine, the exhilaration I felt jumping over the bonfire with him...

"Lucy doesn't need to be with alphas. She's a strong, independent woman," Jojo responded, her words slightly slurred.

"Well, omega health outcomes are better when they have a pack," Mamma said, tucking her short white-blond hair behind her ear. She was the most no-nonsense of all of us. She might not have always been the most warm and fuzzy parent as I was growing up, but she was fiercely protective.

I flopped back in my chair and sighed loudly. "Should I leave?

Seems like you don't really need me here for this conversation." My muttering was ignored so I pulled out my phone and opened the group chat: Felix's Feral Four.

> **LUCY**
> Help me. The moms are drunk and talking about how I desperately need alphas and Lars is being useless so I'm all aloneeee

> **OLIVE**
> I am SO sorry

> **LUCY**
> Not your fault. They're unstoppable

> **SUMMER**
> Your moms are hilarious

> **LUCY**
> ...

> **LUCY**
> You're dead to me

> **IVY**
> Hang in there, Lucy!

"No, don't misquote the research," Mom said, her usually loud voice raising in volume even more as pieces of brown hair flew from her messy bun. "That study showed that omega health improves specifically when they're paired with *female* alphas. And maybe that's the problem! Lucy needs a female alpha."

"So true," Lala said, curling up against Mamma's side. Alcohol always made her sleepy, something the two of us had in common besides our blond hair, blue eyes, and love of blankets. "Male alphas are the worst."

Lars scrubbed his hand down his face and let out an exasperated sigh. "You can't just say that. Not all male alphas are bad."

"Shh, honey," Mom said, waving her hand. "I'm the expert here as the only bisexual in the group, and let me tell you, knots aren't everything."

"Okay," he said, slapping his hands on his thighs before standing. "And with that, I'm going to head out. Happy birthday, Lucy."

He pulled me into a hug and I whispered "Traitor" in his ear, making him chuckle. When he pulled away, though, his expression was solemn.

"Thanks for sending Felix to the house. It means a lot to Olive." He cleared his throat, looking a little awkward. Lars was usually stoic except when it came to his omega.

"Of course." I squeezed his hand. "She'll be okay. We're all here for her."

He nodded and cast a look over his shoulder at our moms, who were still arguing about knots. "Good luck."

He jumped out of the way to avoid my shove and laughed as he crossed the yard. I eyed the gate. Should I also make a run for it? I loved my moms, but they could be . . . a lot. Since childhood, I'd carried around the sneaking suspicion that they secretly wished I was stronger and more independent. Instead, they'd gotten an omega daughter who made nest mood boards and fantasized about being spoiled by a pack.

"Let's change the subject." I sat back down and shoveled another bite of cake into my mouth. Mamma had made my favorite Swedish princess cake, and I was trying to decide how sick I'd feel if I ate a third slice.

"Good idea." Lala winked at me across the fire pit. Of all my moms, Lala was the one who understood me best. Probably an omega thing. "Do you have any weekend plans, honey?"

I nodded. Before my afternoon nap, I'd been scrolling social media and had come across a video of an omega who was solo-backpacking the Appalachian Trail. She talked about how restorative the forest was, how connected she felt to herself and the world, and something had sparked inside me. I wanted to feel like that. While hiking the entire Appalachian Trail was out, Starlight Grove was at the base of Solstice Mountain.

"I'm going on a hike."

My fork scraped against my now-empty plate. Fuck it. I was going for a third slice.

I glanced up when I realized my moms had fallen uncharacteristically silent.

Jojo cocked an eyebrow. "Oh?"

I nodded, shoving down the antsyness coursing through my body. "I want to try something new. Get connected with nature."

"We did the Thousand Step hike the other day," Lala said, referencing the popular nearby hiking trail. "I hadn't been in a while and was reminded how pretty the mountain is."

"No, I mean like real hiking." They still looked bewildered, so I added, "With camping."

Mom laughed but quickly choked it off when she took in my expression. "Wait, you're serious?"

That familiar prickly defensiveness rose inside me. "Yeah, I'm serious."

My moms exchanged looks.

"Is this something you read on a blog?" Mamma asked, her sharp gaze fixed on me.

"Yes, because I have no original ideas. It must have just been something I saw online," I snapped, ignoring the fact that she was correct. Damn her for knowing me so well.

"But you always complained when we went on hikes as a family," JoJo said. "You're not really the outdoorsy type."

"Do you have camping gear?" Mamma asked. "Have you done any research on how to do this? Are you planning to go with someone? Maybe Lars and his pack could take you."

A Pack for Spring

Frustration churned in my stomach and I leaned into the emotion to keep myself from bursting into tears. Why did everyone always think I was so inept? Was I really that bad at everything I did?

"Honey," Lala said. "I know the past year has been hard . . ."

"I was talking to Sandy," Jojo said, cutting her off. "She said her nephew found his pack on the Flame dating app. Have you tried that?"

"Maybe we should change the subject—" Lala started, but I'd had enough.

I jumped up from my chair, knocking it to the ground. "Are you serious? You can't even pretend to support me on my birthday?"

"Of course we support you!"

"Why would you say that?"

They were shouting over each other, but I shook my head.

"Yes, the support is crashing down upon me. You don't believe I can go backpacking, and your great solution for my life is for me to use the same dating app my exes used to cheat on me?"

"Oh, Lucy—" Lala said.

"Thanks for the dinner." I picked up the cake plate. There was still half a cake left, and I wasn't about to leave it behind.

"Wait, why are you upset?" A crease appeared between JoJo's eyes. "We just don't want anything to happen to you."

"We want to protect you," Mamma added.

My fists clenched, but I injected my words with a calm I didn't feel. "I know. It's just been a long day, so I'm going to head to bed." Before they could stop me, I crossed the yard and slipped through the back gate.

"Lucy, wait."

I let out a long sigh but turned to find Lala jogging after me.

"What?" I'd meant to sound sharp and snippy, but it just came out defeated.

"I don't like you leaving without a hug."

She wrapped her arms around me, enveloping me in her warm, earthy scent. I melted into her, carefully balancing the cake plate in one hand. Unwanted tears burned my eyes. I'd been able to keep them at bay when fueled by anger, but Lala always had a way of cracking me straight open.

"What's going on, honey?"

I shrugged. "It just feels like I'll never be enough."

Her lips parted. "What? How could you say that? You're always enough, Lucy. We love you so much."

"I know you love me. I love you, too. I just . . ." I trailed off. "Never mind. I'm just being dramatic." I forced a smile, but Lala still looked concerned.

She cupped my cheek and gazed intently into my eyes.

"Please," I said softly. "I just need some space."

Her shoulder dropped and a sad smile twisted her lips. "If that's what you need. I just hope you know we're always here for you."

When I got home, I stuck the cake in the fridge and crawled into my nest, fluffing the large velvet pillows so they formed a protective wall around my body. A shuddering sob shook my chest. Lala had warned me a while ago that my omega hormones would likely become harder to manage the longer I was without a pack, and they were hitting hard tonight. Even though plenty of omegas these days delayed getting packed up, my unique hormones made my omega urges all the more intense, even on suppressants.

My phone vibrated and I fished it out of my pocket.

SUMMER

> Hey are you ok? Did you survive your moms? I was teasing before but now I'm worried I hurt your feelings

LUCY

> You're sweet. I know you were just teasing

I paused, unsure what else I wanted to say.

A Pack for Spring

> **LUCY**
>
> My birthday's just hitting harder than I thought. I think I'm going to take a little solo trip this weekend.

> **SUMMER**
>
> Do you want me to come over? I tried making a croquembouche this afternoon and it ended up in a spectacular disaster, but it still tastes good

I squinted at the picture she sent of a lopsided stack of what looked like cream buns.

> **SUMMER**
>
> I have this Vietnamese rum we can soak it in
>
> Shit, it's a French dessert. We can soak it in champagne
>
> But I'm broke. New plan. Skip the dessert and head straight to rum

I choked on a watery laugh. I was being silly. I had the best friends in the world, and my moms, while chaotic, loved me so much.

> **LUCY**
>
> I love you. But I'm already in my nest and ready to sleep.

> **SUMMER**
>
> Do you really want a solo trip? I can come with you

The fact that she even offered when she was just weeks away from her bakery's grand opening made me want to burst into tears again.

> **LUCY**
> Have you seen that monstrosity you made??
> The bakery needs your focus!

> **SUMMER**
> You always have my focus if you need it

> **LUCY**
> I know. I just need a little time for myself and then I'll be back and ready to help you with the grand opening! Felix's outfit is going to be spectacular

I chewed my lip, wondering if I should tell her about my camping plans. But my moms' laughter echoing through my mind made me hesitate. I didn't want anyone else second-guessing my plans. I would take my trip, have a spiritual awakening, and return a new person.

I flipped back to the hiking videos I'd saved and started making a list of the supplies I'd need.

6
LUCY

> **HOROSCOPE PISCES**
>
> Saturn's return offers the gift of transition. Everything you have been working toward is within reach if you're brave enough to grab it. Be willing to release what's holding you back.

So. Camping.

What a magical experience of connecting with nature and my inner self. I'd never felt so centered and confident.

Ha. What an absolute fucking lie.

The second I had an internet connection again, I was going to send a *scathing* message to that omega backpacker.

Not really. I could never do that, but I was thinking it.

The incredible spiritual experience I'd envisioned, the one that would allow me to return home with a sense of certainty of who I was and what I should do with my life, had ended up being slow, clumsy, and muddy. I'd hiked half the distance I'd planned, the fading light forcing me to stop at a random flat area off the trail. My skinned hands and knees stung as I struggled for over an hour to set up my brand-new tent.

The alpha at the outdoor supply store had said this tent was a breeze to set up. He would also be the recipient of a vicious negative review I would never post. Although, he had warned me that my sneakers weren't sturdy enough for the hike I was planning, and since said sneakers were currently completely soaked through, he might have had a point.

My visions of starting a campfire and making s'mores before

writing in my new journal were replaced with cold, hard reality—huddling in my wonky tent, freezing as I shoved raw marshmallows into my mouth.

I pulled my brand-new sleeping bag tighter around me. Even sugar couldn't improve this situation. I missed my nest with the piles of pillows, blankets, and cloudlike mattress.

I closed my eyes and breathed deeply. Why had I thought I could do this?

You have to think things through, Lucy. Use that little omega brain of yours.

My heart ached with heaviness. I was used to being underestimated and told I was too impulsive. But a lot of times, my impulsiveness worked out. Years ago, I'd been walking down Main Street and saw that the old record store was officially vacant and available for purchase. I'd gone straight to Stanley, submitted an offer that same hour, and signed a contract the next day. Everyone had doubted me, and their worried comments that I hadn't thought my plan through felt like tiny paper cuts, but I'd forged ahead with all the confidence I could muster. My store had opened a couple of months later, and I'd had a steady stream of tailoring clients ever since.

But maybe my exes were right. I'd been lucky so far, but I couldn't go through life like a *flighty airhead*, expecting everything to work out in my favor.

A wet splat landed on the tent above me and I furrowed my brow. Surely that wasn't . . .

The skies opened and rain pounded loudly on the tent, which quickly started sagging under the weight of the water.

Of course.

I groaned and threw my arm across my face. Screw this. As soon as I woke up, I was going back home.

7
WILDER

I gripped my steering wheel until my knuckles turned white. I was fucking exhausted, coming off a forty-eight-hour shift—*forty-nine* hours after paperwork had trapped me after shift change. Living up the mountain suited me just fine, but mornings like this, with the pouring rain making the gravel road slick with mud, made me wonder if a house in town would be so fucking bad.

But I had my reasons to stay away.

A clap of thunder made me jolt as another gush of rain flooded the windshield. I squinted, as if that would make a difference. I was only five minutes from my driveway and didn't want to stop on an incline. With my fucking luck, I'd be washed straight off the mountain.

I continued inching forward until a flash of lightning illuminated something bright in the tree line. My heart started beating faster. I wasn't sure why, but after over a decade in firefighting and mountain rescue, I knew to trust my instincts.

I scanned the woods, every muscle in my body tense.

There it was again.

I let out a vicious string of curses when I realized what I was seeing—a young woman with blond hair and an oversized backpack was making her way down the mountain. She was drenched and her leggings were coated with mud. What *the fuck* was she doing out here?

I threw on the emergency brake just in time to see the woman slip. My heart seized as I watched her slide down the mountain almost in slow motion. Rain pelted me as I leapt out of my truck, leaving me instantly soaked, but my focus was fully on her. She'd managed to grab a tree branch, stopping her descent.

"Hang on!" I shouted as I grabbed a length of rope from the back of the truck. I tied it around my middle before securing the end to my hitch. I probably wouldn't need it, but mudslides could wash even the most experienced hiker off the mountain.

The ground shifted beneath me as I made my way to her. She was trying to get her legs under her, but her flimsy sneakers meant she couldn't gain traction. She fell back on her ass, rousing all my protective instincts.

My boots squelched, sinking into the mud as I quickly wove through the trees. When I finally reached her, I crouched down.

"Are you hurt?"

She jumped at another crash of thunder before tilting her head back. My entire world shifted and reorganized around me as her bright blue eyes met my gaze. She was the most gorgeous woman I'd ever seen, even with blue-tinged lips and chattering teeth.

"Hi," she squeaked. "Nice day for a hike."

Fuck, she was cute.

"Are you hurt?" I repeated.

"I twisted my ankle when I fell, but I think I'll be okay."

Her sweet voice was almost snatched by the wind, and I leaned forward to hear her.

"Can you help pull me up?" she asked.

I reached out my arm and she took it, her small hands clinging on tight. I carefully pulled her to standing, my other hand going to her side to keep her from falling. She tested putting weight on her injured ankle but immediately picked it up with a grimace.

"It's fine," she said quickly when I let out a low curse. "I can just hop."

Was it sprained? Broken? There was probably too much adrenaline pumping through her system to properly assess her pain level.

"Give me the backpack," I said gruffly, already moving to take it off her. My eyebrows shot up as I slung it over my shoulder. "This is heavy as fuck."

"Tell me about it."

I peered down at her, standing unsteadily on one leg, water dripping down her face. This girl needed someone to take care of her.

I glanced back at the road, clenching my jaw at the small river of mud and water rushing down the mountain. It wasn't a far walk to my truck—a couple dozen feet, if that—but I didn't trust her ankle to hold her.

"I'll carry you." I tugged on the rope around my waist, making sure it was still holding fast.

"I can walk." Another shiver wracked her body, and I was struck by the intense urge to bundle her up in front of my fireplace.

She tried taking a step, but her pained whimper made a low growl tear through my chest. I picked her up without warning. I didn't have time to convince her to let me carry her. We needed to get to safety before half the mountain washed away.

"Or I guess you're carrying me," she squeaked. Her chest was plastered to mine and her arms wound around my arms, clinging tight. Even with as cold, muddy, and wet as she was, she felt perfect against me.

I kept one hand on the rope and the other under her ass, supporting her as I took careful steps back to the truck. I swore when my boots hit a patch of mud and we slid a few feet down the side of the mountain. She tightened her hold on me, burying her face in my neck. I fought to get back on a stable patch of ground. I was not about to let her fall, especially when she was showing so much trust in me.

I grabbed a tree trunk for balance, the rough bark anchoring me as I inched back to the road. Fuck, would my truck even be able to make it the last bit to my house? I quickly ran through our various options. Only part of the road was flooded, so the truck still seemed like our safest option.

I opened the passenger door and reluctantly put the woman down on the seat. "My house is just a few minutes up the road."

She nodded, her eyes wide as I closed the door, untied the rope around my waist, and got in on the other side.

"Buckle up," I commanded.

Her frozen hands fumbled with the seat belt until I couldn't take it anymore. I reached over and got her buckled, wishing I had gloves to offer her.

"Hang tight," I said gruffly. "If we get stuck or start sliding, we'll leave the truck and walk the rest of the way."

Her eyes were wide as she nodded. I blasted the hot air, making sure her seat warmer was on high. My clothes were soaked and clammy against my skin, but it took a lot for me to feel the cold. This woman was tiny, shivering, and not remotely dressed for this weather.

I held my breath as I inched the truck forward. The wheels spun in the mud and dread seized me, but then we lurched forward. My arm automatically flew out to protect her, banding across her chest. Her sharp intake of breath brought me back to my senses, and I put my hand back on the steering wheel.

I eased the truck up the road, forcing myself to keep my eyes facing forward when all I wanted to do was check on her again.

I let out a sigh of relief when my driveway came into view.

"Almost there. You warm enough?"

"Starting to thaw."

I fiddled with the vents, making sure they were pointing at her, when a scent hit my nose. Bright and floral, with a note of mouthwatering sweetness that reminded me of picking plump strawberries, the juice dripping off soft skin . . .

Fuck. She was an omega.

My grip on the wheel tightened along with every muscle in my body.

Mine.

Her scent fanned the flames of the possessiveness my alpha had felt since I first laid eyes on her. Static filled my ears, and each ragged breath delivered more of her scent into my lungs.

I came to a stop in front of my cabin, mind whirling. I'd been so focused on the rescue, I hadn't thought about what came next.

There was no way we could get back down to town in the storm, and no conveniently located mountain hotel to take her to. She would have to stay with me.

An omega would be in my cabin.

Fuck my life.

"Thanks for rescuing me."

Her sweet voice pulled me out of my spiral. I took a deep breath and turned to face her.

"What were you doing out in this weather?" My words were too harsh, but images of her sliding off the side of my mountain flashed before my eyes and filled me with anxious rage.

"Oh, you know, just some camping and hiking. I'm Lucy, by the way."

She held out her hand. I stared at it, not trusting myself to touch her. She awkwardly lowered it. "What's your name?"

"Wilder," I grunted.

"Well, thanks for rescuing me, Wilder." She chewed her lip and glanced out the window. It wasn't even ten in the morning yet, but the storm light made it feel like night was falling. "I'm guessing getting back to town might be a bit tricky."

I turned off the truck. "You can come inside until it passes."

Before she could respond, I was back in the downpour. I sucked in a deep breath, filling my lungs with the smell of damp earth as I desperately tried to erase her scent from my memory. Her door popped open before I got to it, and I rushed over so I could carry her.

Only because of her injured ankle. Definitely not because my alpha was pushing at me to have the cute omega in my arms.

Lucy clung to me as I led us inside, only letting go once the front door was shut behind us. I glanced around my cabin, trying to see it through her eyes. I'd renovated it last year—rewiring the electric and updating the plumbing—but in terms of decoration it was . . . sparse. I had been more focused on making the old cabin livable, but maybe I should have gotten a throw pillow or something for the couch.

I toed my boots off. "I'll get you a towel."

I headed into my bedroom and stripped off my sopping clothes, leaving them on the bathroom floor. Did Lucy need something to wear? She had a backpack, but what if her clothes were wet? I pulled on sweatpants and a sweatshirt and grabbed an extra set for her.

She was still by the front door, dripping water on the floor, teeth rattling from the cold, when I returned.

I fought the urge to pull her against my chest.

"I got these for you in case you need them." I thrust my clothes at her, and she took them with shaky hands.

"Could I possibly take a shower?"

I swallowed hard at the image of the stunning omega in the shower, water dripping down her bare skin. I cleared my throat, ignoring my hard cock.

"Bathroom's down the hall. Clean towels are under the sink."

"Thanks." Her voice was an almost whisper as she started to shuffle by me. I shook my head and picked her up again.

"Are you going to be able to shower on your own?"

She froze in my arms and I squeezed my eyes shut. Fuck. Now it sounded like I was asking to shower with her.

"I'll be fine."

I nodded and set her down by the bathroom door. "Sit down in the tub if you need to."

"I will. Sorry for being such an inconvenience." She slipped into the bathroom and closed the door behind her.

Lucy was a temptation. A disruption to my carefully curated life. But I would never describe her as an inconvenience.

THE WOODSTOVE CRACKLED AS it radiated heat into the living room. I'd pushed the armchair close to the fire so Lucy could warm up after her shower. She'd emerged all pink and clean, her wet hair a darker shade of gold.

I'd touched her as little as possible as I wrapped her ankle, but her scent lingered on my skin and I couldn't bring myself to wash it off.

Her ankle was swollen and there was the start of a bruise, but I didn't think it was broken. I'd placed an ice pack over it and stacked a couple of pillows on the coffee table for her to elevate her leg.

I kept stealing glances at her as I prepared grilled cheeses and tomato soup. My alpha was fucking feral that she was wearing my clothes. Or rather, my sweatshirt, which was so long on her it acted like a dress, and wool socks.

And no pants.

No. Fucking. Pants.

When I'd spluttered, red-faced, at her bare legs and demanded to know why she hadn't put on my sweatpants, she laughed and pulled them on, easily fitting both of her legs into a single pant leg.

"How long have you lived here?"

My heart raced as I turned around to find Lucy sitting mere feet away on a kitchen stool, a blanket wrapped around her like a cape.

What the fuck? How did she sneak up on me like that?

She smiled and my scrambled brain struggled to process her question. "A year," I finally responded.

"Why haven't I seen you in town?"

Because I'm an antisocial bastard terrified of sweet little omegas.

I shrugged. "I'm at the firehouse when I'm on shift. Otherwise, I'm here."

"You work long shifts, right?"

"We do forty-eight/ninety-six. Two days on, four days off."

"That's pretty intense."

I grunted. Sometimes I even took extra shifts to cover for my guys. Our department was small, and it wasn't like I had much to do on my days off, anyway.

"Are you warm enough?" I asked, keeping my eyes fixed on the pan as I flipped the grilled cheese onto plates and dished up two bowls of tomato soup. I wasn't a chef by any means, but my mom had insisted I at least learn the basics so I could care for my future omega. My parents had remained confident that I would find love, even after I was kicked out of school and shunned by the entire town because my diagnosis made me a danger to society. Now that they were gone, there was no one left to believe in me. Including myself.

"Yeah," she responded softly. "Toasty warm."

I stole a glance at her face as I set the food in front of her. Her cheeks were rosy, eyes bright, and her soft smile made my chest squirm.

She hummed and did a little dance as she took her first bite. "This is amazing. Thank you so much. For everything."

My alpha puffed up at the compliment. "You live in town?"

"Yeah, I live above my shop. You might know it—Spring in Your Stitch?"

I drove down Main Street every time I headed to the fire station for a shift, but I did my best to avoid the stores. Besides the market and occasional take-out order from the local Chinese restaurant, I kept to myself. Although now that I thought about it, I bet Lucy's shop was the pink one with flowers all over it.

"You shouldn't tell strangers where you live," I grunted.

Lucy scrunched her nose and giggled. "Well, I know where you live and work, so you better be careful."

The idea of this omega being a threat to me made me grin, but my smile quickly fell when I realized *I* was the threat to her. Not that I would ever intentionally hurt her, but my inner alpha couldn't be trusted.

"If you have any clothes you need tailored or mended, drop them off at my store," she continued, oblivious to my inner turmoil. "I'm pretty sure saving my life entitles you to free tailoring services. Several of the firefighters come in regularly to have me tailor their clothes."

The thought of my guys—young, attractive, and moving around the world without my baggage—going into Lucy's shop ignited a vicious feeling in my chest that felt suspiciously like jealousy. I could imagine them fawning over her, trying to get her attention.

I ground my teeth. "I bet they do."

"It must be hard to be so tall and muscular you can't fit into regular clothing." She batted her eyes almost like she was *flirting*.

I lived in my uniform, work clothes, or sweats, but I was struck by the urge to buy new clothes just so I had an excuse for her to tailor them.

Stupid idea. And not conducive to my plan to stay far, far away from this omega.

A stilted silence fell. Lucy fidgeted with the cuffs of her sweatshirt—*my* sweatshirt.

"Do you want me to roll those up for you?" I blurted out the question before I could stop myself. Her lips parted and she glanced between me and the too-long sleeves.

"Never mind," I said, just as she responded, "Yes, please."

Her cheeks turned bright pink and she let out a forced laugh. "Of course, I can do it. Thanks again for lending it to me."

My chest clenched with regret as she rolled up the sleeves.

I focused my full attention on my food, doing my best to block out her mouthwatering scent. Once we were done, she got up and moved to grab my plate. I grunted and took the dishes out of her hand. She wasn't going to fucking clean up in my house.

"Go sit by the fire and elevate your ankle."

I caught her smile before she turned away.

8

LUCY

I WAS TRAPPED IN A ROMANCE NOVEL.

A dramatic mountain rescue followed by going home with a rough, hot-as-sin mountain man?

Romance. Novel.

I was curled up in an armchair by the woodstove, covered with a quilt that smelled of smoke, pine, and leather, just like the alpha sitting stiffly on the couch. His eyes were fixed straight ahead, giving me a chance to admire him. His dark hair was tied up in a bun and his firm jaw was lined with a beard. He was huge, probably the biggest alpha I'd ever seen. Tall and broad, with muscular arms and thighs, a wide chest, and a thick torso. I wanted to crawl over and curl up in his lap with his huge hands spanning my hips and waist, moving me wherever he wanted me...

The only issue was that Wilder seemed distinctly uninterested in me. He wasn't unkind, but his grunts, stony silence, and the fact he was sitting as far away from me as possible in the small living room made it clear he would prefer I wasn't here. My chest clenched with the familiar feeling of being a nuisance.

Lucy distracts other students by talking too much in class.

Lucy needs to work harder to apply herself.

Lucy struggles with codependence.

Finally, the silence stretched on so long that I couldn't hold myself back. "How did you get into firefighting?"

Wilder jumped, his eyes meeting mine like he was shocked I was still here.

Very flattering.

"Uh, I went to trade school and tried out a couple of things but none of them felt right. I saw a recruitment ad from the fire department in the paper. There was a big signing bonus—more money than I'd ever seen. I figured I'd give it a try. That was fourteen years ago."

"You must be good at it if you've stuck with it that long. Where are you from?"

"Western Mass. Did a short stint in Boston, but city life doesn't suit me. When the fire chief here retired, a guy I used to work with recommended me for the job. Still not sure why they hired me."

My brow furrowed. Most of the alphas I knew tended to be overconfident, but Wilder seemed almost down on himself. "Why shouldn't they hire you? You're clearly great at what you do."

A little thrill ran through my chest when his cheeks flushed. He rubbed the back of his neck. "I guess they were desperate."

"Do you like it here?" I leaned in, anxious for his response. For reasons I wasn't quite ready to examine, I wanted him to love Starlight Grove.

"I like being close to the ocean and living in the mountains."

Maybe not the glowing review I was hoping for, but liking the geography was a good start.

"How'd you get into sewing?" He wasn't looking at me when he asked the question, but I was thrilled he was keeping the conversation going.

"My mormor—grandma—taught me how to sew. She had this huge room with six different sewing machines and any supplies you could possibly dream of. She left them all to me when she passed away."

"Is that what you always wanted to do?"

I shrugged. "I liked sewing stuff for my friends and moms, but I didn't think it could be an actual business. I'd planned to enroll in community college after I graduated, but I didn't like school and didn't get great grades. When a storefront became available on Main Street a week after I graduated, I just went for it."

I braced myself for his judgment.

"Sounds like you made it work."

I swallowed hard, a smile tugging at my lips. "Yeah, I think so."

"You still like it?"

The standard answer I always gave was on the tip of my tongue, but that's not what came out. "I don't know."

He arched an eyebrow, prompting me to continue. "At first, I wanted to focus on custom clothes, but tailoring seemed like a safer and more straightforward way to earn money."

He frowned. "But it's not what you want?"

I shrugged, my chest tight. "I'm not really sure what I want anymore. I should have figured out my life by now, but I'm still just living in my hometown and running my small shop."

"Nothing wrong with that," he grunted, and it filled me with warmth. My cheeks grew even more heated when his gruff words made me perfume.

A low growl rumbled through his chest but was quickly cut off. He got up and moved to the window . . . to get away from my scent? The rain was still coming down hard and the pattering on the roof created a calm, soothing rhythm.

"I didn't even know it was supposed to storm today," I said.

He turned to face me. "Why were you out on the mountain without checking the forecast?"

I shrank back in my seat, fixing my eyes on the frayed edge of the quilt. If he had a needle and thread, I could reinforce the edge so it didn't fray further.

Wilder sat down again, but this time he was on the side of the couch closest to me. "Sorry. That was too harsh."

"Harsh but true. I should have paid more attention."

He sighed as he fluffed the pillows supporting my leg and adjusted the placement of the ice pack. My ankle barely hurt anymore, but I would happily sprain it again if it meant he would keep taking care of me.

"You could have gotten seriously injured if I hadn't come along. Did you spend the night on the mountain?"

"Yeah. I left yesterday morning and camped overnight."

"Why were you camping? Doesn't exactly seem like your thing."

"You're going to think I'm stupid."

"Try me."

I chewed my lip. Was I really going to tell this stranger what I hadn't told my friends and family? Maybe I would regret it, but I just wanted someone to know.

"I just turned twenty-nine and my life isn't what I thought it would be. I feel kind of lost." I shrugged like it wasn't a big deal, but the bitter edge to my scent gave me away. I hadn't brought my scent blocker with me camping since I didn't anticipate the whole *sexy mountain alpha rescue*, but I wished I had. Growing up, I'd loved the idea that my alphas would be able to sense my emotions through my scent, but in practice, it was pretty embarrassing. Especially since Wilder wasn't my alpha.

"I saw an omega online talk about hiking and it seemed so empowering. I've never gone camping before, but I thought connecting with nature could help me, you know, find myself."

God, it sounded so ridiculous when I said it out loud. After a miserable, sleepless night, I'd crawled out of my half-collapsed tent—the tent I'd abandoned on the mountain when the storm intensified. I'd tried to refold it to get it into my backpack, but after fifteen minutes of battle in the downpour, I'd given up.

I'd slipped down the mountain, growing colder and more drenched as I went.

"I guess I should have known I'd fail. Even without the unexpected weather, camping and hiking probably isn't my thing."

"I think it's brave."

My jaw dropped as my head snapped up. I searched Wilder's face to see if he was mocking me, but all I was met with was his steady, nonjudgmental gaze.

"What?"

"You went out of your comfort zone to try something new. That's brave."

This was the second time someone had called me brave in the past few days, and I fought the urge to burst into tears. For a long time, I'd felt like nobody really saw me. I had no reason to complain about my life—I had friends and family who loved me and were proud of me, which was more than a lot of people had—but it still hurt to feel invisible. I wanted to be chosen. Prioritized. And to not be constantly terrified of losing people's love and approval once they got to know the real me.

Wilder wasn't offering me anything. I wouldn't delude myself that this was the start of some big romance. But it still felt nice.

"Thanks," I whispered. "That's really kind."

"Not often described as kind," he grunted, which made me smile. Big tough alpha.

I leaned back in my chair, my omega feeling much more settled. "So, what do you do up here for entertainment?" The small living room was conspicuously lacking a TV or board games or . . . much of everything, really.

At his blank stare and silence, I let out an indignant noise. "You cannot possibly tell me that you sit up here for days straight and just, what? Grunt and chop wood?"

He crossed his thick arms, jaw set. "Fine. I will not tell you that."

I sat forward and the movement knocked the ice pack off my ankle. Wilder frowned. "Be careful." He moved it back, his fingers brushing my calf.

I perfumed again, and this time there was no ignoring it. My scent saturated the room like my omega was waving a bright red flag and shouting, "Take me, alpha!" I was about to apologize when Wilder abruptly got up and stalked out of the room. The back door slammed and my heart sank. Had my scent seriously driven him out into the middle of the storm?

"Well, I don't like your scent, either," I muttered.

I pulled the quilt more firmly over my body as I slumped in the chair. And I definitely did *not* breathe in more deeply to catch his scent off the fabric.

9
WILDER

The pounding rain blurred my vision as I swung my axe. The log split and landed on the drenched ground, absolutely useless for burning anytime soon.

Reasonable people didn't chop wood in the middle of a torrential downpour ... but then again, reasonable people weren't driven out of their home by a cute little omega who smelled like strawberries and sunshine.

My cock was rock hard, and even after thirty minutes away from her scent, I was still on the brink of rut. I snarled and slammed my axe down again and again until the slick handle slipped from my hands, the blade almost catching my leg.

I roared and slammed my fist against the metal shed covering stacks of firewood. The pain did nothing to cut through my haze, so I pulled my bottle of rut suppressants from my pocket with shaking hands. The bottle that clearly said not to exceed a max dose of one in twenty-four hours.

I popped the third one I'd taken since rescuing Lucy into my mouth.

I fucking *hated* this.

If I were normal, I'd be warm and dry right now, on the couch with the cutest omega I'd ever met. She was probably sweet with everyone, but in my fantasy, I was the one she wanted. As the temperature dropped further, cold air would creep into the living room.

Come here, sweetheart. Let me warm you up.

I'd pull her close to my side, her body fitting perfectly as she curled into my chest. My hand would tighten around her as her scent intensified and she let out a tantalizing omega whine.

Do you need me to make you feel good?

My hand under her shirt. Her bare skin like velvet against my rough callouses. Sliding down her stomach and hip.

No fucking panties. Only naughty omegas don't wear panties.

My forehead thudded against the side of the metal shed as I gripped my cock and imagined dipping my thick fingers into her tight, wet heat.

That feels so good, alpha. Don't stop.

The haze of rut gripped me as I thrust faster into my hand, clenching my jaw to keep myself from sprinting into the cabin and bending Lucy over my couch. I came with a low groan, the orgasm deeply unsatisfying.

A shudder worked through me as the rain washed away the evidence of what I'd just done. I stuffed my softening cock back into my pants as the suppressant finally kicked in, leaving me weak and dizzy.

A flash of lightning preceded an ear-shattering clap of thunder that made me jolt. Shit, the storm must be right on top of us.

"Wilder?" Lucy's shout reached me through the rain. She sounded scared.

My heart raced. Had something happened? My boots squelched in the mud as I sprinted back to the house. She was standing in the doorway.

"What's wrong?" I growled, every muscle tense and ready to spring into action.

Her eyes widened. "Sorry. I didn't mean to freak you out."

I closed the space between us. "What's wrong, sweetheart?"

Her lips parted and I realized what I'd just let slip. Her cheeks flushed, making her look even cuter, if that was fucking possible.

"I got worried you'd be struck by lightning," she mumbled.

I raised an eyebrow.

"I'm just being stupid. Sorry for interrupting." Her scent turned bitter, and before I knew it, I had moved both of us back inside the cabin. My hands were on her waist, squeezing and kneading. I didn't remove them even though our bodies were a hairbreadth apart and I was dripping water on the floor and all over her.

When was the last time I had been this close to throw a person over my shoulder? Except for the occasional emergency where I had to throw someone over my shoulder in a fireman's carry, I lived a life devoid of touch. A lump formed in my throat at how perfect she felt.

Another flash lit the room, followed by a clap of thunder. Lucy jumped and a soft whine slipped through her lips.

I gripped her chin. "You scared of storms?"

She tried to pull away, but I kept a firm hold on her, my fingers unwilling to let go.

"Sorry," she said again. "I'm usually fine with storms. I guess I'm a little jumpy after spending the night on the mountain."

I stopped myself from scolding her again for going out camping totally unprepared. I didn't have the right, but fuck, I wished I did.

"You must be cold," she said. "I'll get a towel."

Before I could stop her, she ran off to the bathroom, her bright scent surrounding me even in her absence. I adjusted my cock, which was half hard again, but my suppressants were doing their job of keeping me from falling into rut.

She came back with two towels. She handed me one before dropping to her knees and using the other to wipe up the water on the floor.

The most beautiful omega in the world was *on her knees* in front of me.

I let out a strangled noise and fixed my eyes on the ceiling. "You don't have to do that."

"I don't mind. I'm the one who made you come inside."

Her voice was so sweet. If I stayed here any longer, I would come in my fucking pants. I choked out some mumbled excuse and retreated to my room, where I definitely didn't strip off my clothes, jump in the shower, and jerk one out faster than any adult man had ever come before.

10

LUCY

"Aha!" I raised the pack of cards I'd found tucked in the back of a bookcase.

Wilder snorted. He seemed to have relaxed after he ran off to get changed. The storm was still going outside with some of the loudest thunder I'd ever heard, but I wasn't scared now that the alpha was inside with me.

"A pack of cards?"

"Our nightly entertainment." I skipped back over and sat as close to him on the couch as I could get away with. "Want to play?"

"I will if you sit your ass down like you're supposed to," he grumbled, elevating my ankle.

I grinned. "It's a good thing I'm here to add some fun to your life."

He shook his head, but the corner of his lips twitched in an almost-smile. I wiggled happily in victory.

"What are we playing?" he asked.

I split the cards to shuffle them, biting my lip in concentration as I tried that bridge trick thing. Half the cards flew onto the floor.

Oops.

"Well, I don't actually play cards that often, so I really only remember how to play go fish, war, or slapjack."

Wilder handed me the stack of cards he'd picked up off the floor. "I should have checked earlier, but do you need to get in touch with anyone? Let them know you're here?" he asked. "You can use my satellite phone. Reception is shit up here, especially when it storms."

"Oh, right. Thanks."

After a few long beats of silence, I glanced up. Wilder was looking at me with a stern, furrowed brow.

"Lucy?"

"Hmm?"

"People know you went camping, right? They'll be worried about you."

I didn't want to lie to him, but if I admitted the truth, he would think I was even that much more stupid.

"Lucy." His voice was deep, and it sent shocks of electricity through me.

"I might not have been *super* specific about where I was going."

He scrubbed his hand down his face with a long sigh. I braced myself, waiting for his criticism.

"You going to deal those cards?"

I blinked. "Oh. Yeah."

I fixed my eyes on the cards as I dealt them, not daring to look up until Wilder's fingers brushed against my cheek.

"Don't do that again, sweetheart. Your safety is important."

I swallowed hard. I wanted to hear him call me *sweetheart* for the rest of my life.

"I know it wasn't smart. I was worried my friends and family would tell me I wasn't prepared for camping and would try to talk me out of going."

"You don't say." His dry, teasing tone took away the sting of his words, even pulling a smile from me.

If I was still with my ex-pack, they would have gone on and on about how incompetent I was and how much I'd inconvenienced them by having to be rescued off the side of a mountain.

We're not prejudiced against omegas, but you have to admit—your behavior proves our point.

Can you not be so exhausting all the time?

I sent you a money request so you can reimburse me for my ruined muddy shoes.

But Wilder wasn't treating me like I was an inconvenience, and even his gentle scolding didn't fill me with shame.

"I might not be an expert hiker, but I am about to crush you in go fish."

He shook his head as he settled back on the couch. "Bring it."

11

WILDER

Lucy ended up crushing me in multiple games of go fish. She said it was because of her card-playing prowess, and I wasn't about to admit that the real reason was because her presence was so wildly distracting I couldn't focus on my cards for shit.

My cabin was usually quiet. Sometimes I turned on the staticky radio to fill the silence, but the shitty reception—especially during rain or snowstorms—meant I usually gave up on it. But Lucy filled the space with her constant joyful chatter. I'd learned she grew up in Starlight Grove with four moms and a brother. The more she shared, the more obvious it became that our lives were nothing alike. She loved her friends and participating in town events, while I'd purchased this cabin specifically to avoid social interaction.

The little omega made a content noise as she snuggled deeper into my chest. She'd drifted off a while ago, moving closer to me in her sleep until she was curled up against my side. I stayed frozen, unwilling to risk any movement that would wake her. I was fucking playing with fire. We could never be together, but in my heavily medicated state, I let myself soak up these moments.

Eventually, sleep pulled at me, and I knew my time was up. I gently shifted her until she was in my arms. She let out the cutest little disgruntled noise before blinking her eyes open.

"Time for bed," I said, my voice low.

Her arms wrapped around me and she rubbed her cheek against my chest. I didn't know if she was intentionally scent-marking me, but I knew with certainty that I would never wash this flannel.

I gently put her down on my bed, pulling the covers back and arranging a pillow to place under her leg.

"How's your ankle? Do you want more ice or pain meds?"

She shook her head. "Feels fine." Her words were slightly slurred and her eyes closed.

"Just shout if you need anything."

A line appeared between her eyebrows as she blinked her eyes open. "Where are you going?"

"I'm sleeping on the couch."

She shook her head and pushed up to a seated position. "No. I should take the couch."

Fuck no. "Lie down, Lucy."

"Wilder, you've already done too much for me. You worked a long shift and then had to rescue me. You need a good night's sleep."

"No."

"But—"

"The couch isn't safe. It's right by the front door."

She frowned. "So?"

"So, if someone were to break in, they would reach the couch first."

"Do you have many burglars making their way up the mountain during a storm?"

My traitorous lips twitched with the temptation to smile. "You're taking the bed. The storm should quiet down overnight, and I'll drive you back to town in the morning."

Her lip jutted out in a pout, but she laid back down. "You could always lie down with me," she murmured.

My cheeks flushed and my cock hardened. *Just do it.* My alpha was like a devil on my shoulder, tempting me to get in beside her. Terror seized me at the thought of it, at what could happen if we shared a bed. I let out a strangled sound as I stumbled out of the bedroom. I shut the door behind me, wishing it was made of metal so I would be completely locked out. My heart pounded, my mind swirled, and I clenched my fists. I couldn't stay here, mere feet from her. I had to burn off this energy.

I stormed out of the house again, heading back to the woodshed to chop more logs.

Morning light danced against my eyelids, and I groaned, my mind hazy with the fog of sleep. The few times I'd accidentally fallen asleep on the couch had taught me that thirty-six was too fucking old to sleep without a mattress. But as I shifted and stretched, I was shocked at how comfortable I was . . . the only exception being my painfully aching cock. It wasn't like morning wood was unusual for me, but this seemed extreme.

A soft little sound had me freezing. My eyelids flew open to discover the reason I was so comfortable. Curled up next to me on the couch, half on top of my chest, was a certain gorgeous omega. Her scent permeated everything—the couch, my sweatpants, the bare skin on my chest—and soothed my physical and emotional aches and pains.

How did she get here? She'd been fast asleep in my bed when I finally came back inside after splitting every single log in the woodshed. I had enough firewood to last me for the next six months. I'd taken a quick shower before collapsing on the couch and falling asleep almost instantly.

I closed my eyes and breathed in slowly. When I first revealed as an alpha, I'd dreamed of mornings like this, curled up with my omega and pack. My broken alpha had destroyed the future I'd dreamed about.

The longer I lay here, the more I risked. Well, the more *she* risked, even if she didn't know it.

"Lucy, honey. Wake up." I gently shook her shoulder, but she pressed even closer, slinging her thigh over my body so that it rubbed against my cock.

Fuuuuuck.

I cleared my throat. "It's time to wake up."

She whined and the sound rocked through me like fucking lightning. Her scent thickened as she perfumed, and the intensity of it clouded my mind.

Bite. Claim. Fuck.

I jolted, flying off the couch in my panic to get away. I was halfway across the room when I realized my hurried movements had pushed Lucy onto the floor. She landed with a startled *umph*. I tugged at my hair, horrified at what I'd done. In my desperate desire to protect her from harm, I'd hurt her.

A confused crease appeared between her brows and she looked around until her eyes landed on me. "Good morning." She pushed her hair out of her face. "This isn't where I fell asleep."

I fought the urge to rush to her side, check on her ankle, and cuddle her on my lap. I was too on edge to risk being too close to her, let alone touch her.

"Seems like you decided the couch was more comfortable at some point in the night."

Her cheeks flushed and she pushed herself off the floor. She cocked her head as she took me in. "Are you okay?"

"Fine." My tone was too brusque to be believable. "I just wasn't expecting to wake up with you on top of me."

Her face fell. "I am *so* sorry. I've been told I sleepwalk sometimes, so that must have been what happened. I never—" She cleared her voice, her lower lip trembling. "I'm sorry I made you uncomfortable."

She looked seconds away from bursting into tears. I was the worst scum of the earth, letting her believe she'd done anything wrong. As if waking up with her on top of me wasn't a fucking dream come true.

But it was better this way. Safer. She shouldn't want to be around me.

"It's fine. I'll radio the local weather station to make sure there haven't been any mudslides on the mountain, but we should be fine to head into town." She went to say something, but I cut her off. "Can you be ready in ten minutes?"

Her jaw snapped shut and she nodded.

I turned away and headed into the bedroom, closing the door securely behind me.

12

LUCY

HOROSCOPE **AQUARIUS RISING**

Aquarius rising, adventure is calling! Embrace your wild spirit by saying yes to new, unexpected opportunities. You never know where they'll lead.

I FLOPPED ONTO MY BACK WITH A FRUSTRATED SCREECH, THE aggressive sound of my vibrator still filling the room.

I switched it off. It was useless anyway.

An extraordinarily vivid sex dream featuring a certain muscular, gruff alpha with a man bun had dragged me from sleep at five this morning, which was exceptionally rude, not only because it was basically the middle of the freaking night but also because I'd been desperate for an alpha who wasn't here.

The alpha who had driven me back to town a couple of days ago in total silence.

He'd made me feel safe and cherished, but that was probably because he was a firefighter. It was his job to take care of stranded, woefully unprepared campers. I was the one who had spun our time together into a romantic fantasy.

My nest, usually so soft and cozy, felt like sandpaper against my hypersensitive, overheated skin. I'd been at it for *over an hour* and still felt just as unsatisfied as when I'd woken up. I rolled over to avoid the damp patch on the sheet beneath me.

You can't cry over unsatisfying orgasms, Lucy.

I threw my dildo with its large silicone knot across my mattress.

I'd taken an extra suppressant pill after Wilder dropped me off, but pharmaceuticals didn't stand a chance against him, which must be why these vivid dreams had woken me up for the past few nights. Well, that and I had secretly stolen one of his flannels from his laundry basket and couldn't stop pressing my face against it, breathing in his smoky, woodsy scent.

I was a glutton for punishment, but anytime I thought about removing the shirt from my nest, my omega lost her mind.

The only solution was to drive up the mountain and throw myself at the alpha.

Wait. No.

Drive up the mountain to bring him cookies to apologize for ... *everything*. Especially the nonconsensual cuddling. The only problem with that plan was that I didn't have a car or a license. Well, that and showing up at his door might be categorized as creepy, stalkerish behavior.

An idea sparked and I sat up, throwing off my blanket. What if I dropped cookies off at the fire station? Wilder's next shift started today, and bringing cookies there was less intrusive than showing up at his home, especially since he probably never wanted to see me again.

I winced as I got out of bed. My ankle was still swollen and throbbing. I hopped on one foot to my dresser, threw on a baby blue sweatpants suit, slid my feet in a pair of slippers, and headed downstairs. I scowled at the sunrise. It should be illegal to be awake this early. All of my friends were early risers. At least Ivy and Summer had the excuse that their jobs required it, but Olive got up early voluntarily so she could swim in the freezing cold ocean.

No one was perfect, I supposed.

I limped across the street to Summer's bakery. Opening day was still a couple of weeks off, but she'd officially moved in to the apartment above the bakery and spent her early mornings perfecting her recipes before doing her accounting job with Harry, Stanley's husband, in the afternoons. She was working too hard, but she said she needed the extra money and she also didn't want to abandon Harry during tax season.

I knocked, hoping she wasn't listening to the new Blissa Nova album too loudly in her big headphones. As I waited, I studied the new logo on the door—two dancing bánh mì wearing sunglasses and bikinis. It was over the top, ridiculous, and completely perfect.

A shadow moved inside and then Summer's panicked expression met my gaze through the glass. Shoot. Seeing me conscious at six in the morning was enough to make anyone think disaster had struck.

She opened the door, grabbed my arms, and dragged me inside. "What's wrong? What's happening?" Her voice was hushed as she ushered me back to the kitchen.

"Why are you whispering?"

"I don't know! Maybe you're being hunted by a monster with supersonic hearing."

"You've been reading too many of Olive's shifter romances."

Summer pinched my arm and I squealed, jumping away from her. "What was that for?"

She shot me a withering stare. "What was that for? Hmm, I don't know. Maybe because you disappeared this weekend, have been hiding away in your shop ever since, barely answering our texts, and now you're awake and dressed before eleven in the morning!"

I grimaced. "I didn't mean to worry you. I didn't have service for a while this weekend, and once I got home, I just needed some time to myself."

Summer huffed and washed her hands before returning to the stainless-steel countertop. A scowl was still fixed on her face when she shoved a scone into my hands.

"Here. I'm testing a new flavor."

Phew. I hadn't upset her too much if she was still sharing food with me. One time a couple of years ago, I'd borrowed her lip gloss without asking, which would have been fine except that I'd lost it. She had cut me off from baked goods for three whole days. Torture.

I sat down on a stool and took a bite. The scone melted in my mouth and I hummed. "Getting up early might be worth it if it means getting more of these."

"Great, you can be my assistant."

I wrinkled my nose. On more than a few occasions, Summer had texted at four in the morning after waking up, and I had responded by saying "Goodnight."

"Don't think you can get out of spilling what you did this weekend by sweet-talking my scones. Especially since I can scent an alpha on you."

The last bite of scone froze halfway to my mouth. Summer was focused on kneading the dough in front of her, so I risked a quick sniff of my arm. I'd spent the past few days plastered to the stolen flannel, but I didn't think the scent would stick to my skin outside my nest. But there it was, a gentle whisper of pine, simultaneously soothing and arousing. I swallowed down an omega whine.

When I looked up, Summer was staring at me with pursed lips. "Spill."

"You have to promise not to judge me."

"Lucy, when have I ever judged you?"

"Umm, how about that time I told you my dream was to be a circus acrobat? Or when I put whipped cream in my coffee? Or last year when I wore low-rise jeans and you said you'd rather go around pantsless than ever wear them again?"

Her lips twitched. "Yeah, well, that's because you deserved it. I promise not to judge you this time." She returned to her dough, weighing it out on a kitchen scale. "Unless what you did warrants judgment."

I snorted a laugh and reached for another scone. Summer tried to swat my hand away, but I was too fast. I scooted farther down the counter so I was out of reach. "I need to make sure it's worthy of a spot on the menu."

Summer tapped the palm of her hand with a wooden spoon in a slightly menacing gesture. "Start talking."

Every word fell like a stone, scraping against my throat as I forced out all my fears and worries about my life. For all her teasing, she didn't mock me as I described the disastrous camping trip, the alpha who instantly stole my heart, and the feeling of rejection I'd been left with. Once I finished, I felt lighter.

Summer grabbed my hand. Her skin was slightly sticky from the dough, but I didn't care. My hormone condition meant I craved touch even more than the average omega.

"I'm sorry you're having such a hard time with your birthday. You should have told me."

I shrugged, my eyes fixed on the uneaten scone clutched in my hand. "I was embarrassed. I should be stronger than this. I have such a good life, and it's not like I need a pack to function."

Her eyes softened. "No, but it's okay to want one."

"Too bad no one wants me." I said it as a . . . well, not quite a joke, but my tone was meant to be lighthearted and self-deprecating. But then my lip trembled.

Summer threw her arms around me and I hugged her back, breathing in and out slowly to stop from bursting into tears.

"I'm going to hunt down your fuck-boy exes. They won't know what hit them."

Maybe if you had been a better omega, you would have kept their interest...

No. Absolutely not, stupid inner voice.

I choked on a watery laugh. "It's almost a pity they moved. We only got to egg their cars that one time."

The luxury sports cars they gave more care and attention to than they ever gave to me.

"They didn't stand a chance against the curse of the Beaufort House."

"Sometimes I feel like I'm the one who's cursed."

Summer pulled away, moving her hands to my face and squishing my cheeks together. "You are not cursed. You're basically a Disney princess, and the reason it's been hard for you to find a pack is because there aren't many alphas good enough to be worthy of you."

"I'm not sure about that," I sniffed.

"Well, I am. And look, your presence summons all the animals."

Just then, something brushed against my leg. I looked down to find Felix. I patted my lap and he jumped up, snagging a bite of the scone before I could stop him.

Not that I would have, but I at least would have verbalized some sort of protest so the next time James interrogated me about our mayor's diet, I could tell him I'd done my very best.

I shoved the rest of my slightly smooshed scone in my mouth before Felix could polish it off.

"So . . . are you going to see Wilder again?"

My stupid heart leapt at the sound of his name. "He made it pretty clear he wasn't interested in me."

Summer and Felix made the same incredulous expression, but that was probably because I'd told her everything except for the whole *forcing him to cuddle with me* in the middle of the night. I pressed on. "But I thought I'd drop off some cookies at the fire station, as a thank-you for saving me."

"Ahh, the real reason you came over here this early."

I batted my eyelashes. "It's only because you're the best baker in town."

She let out an aggrieved sigh. "I *might* have a batch of Vietnamese coffee cookies that I can give you only because it's good advertising."

I was organizing the bakery's grand opening party. I'd already started on Felix's outfit, which was really the most important part, but I was also in charge of the invite list. "I'll make sure the firefighters come."

We spent the next half hour talking through all the details of opening day. When I grabbed the large box of cookies from Summer and limped to the door, I spotted Olive and Lars outside in a golf cart.

"Your chariot awaits!" Olive said, hopping out of the cart.

I looked around, confused. "What are you doing here?"

"Summer said you hurt your ankle and needed transportation."

I glanced over my shoulder and the omega in question blew me a kiss. I shook my head, but my heart swelled with how amazing my friends were.

"Why didn't you tell us you hurt yourself?" Lars was scowling, but he took the box of cookies out of my hand and set it in the golf cart. I did a double take when I realized Felix was already sitting in the driver's seat.

"It's just a sprained ankle. It'll be better in a few days."

"You've got to take care of yourself," Olive said. She wrapped me up in a gentle hug and I melted into her. I'd only been away from my friends for a few days, but so much had happened that it felt like a lifetime.

"You also need to respond to the group chat," she scolded.

"I will, promise."

"And there's karaoke coming up."

"Wouldn't miss it."

Lars groaned and pulled his omega to his side. "Easton won't tell us what he's planning, but he's practically skipping around the house so you know it's going to be terrible."

I grinned. "Terribly good." Easton went all out for his performances with *unique* song choices and elaborate costumes. I'd helped him source his drag queen costume for last month's performance inspired by Omegalicious Essence, the winner of last season's *Heat Street Drag Race*.

Olive coaxed Felix to the passenger side of the golf cart, and my brother boosted me into the vacated driver's seat. I patted Felix on the head. "You can drive as soon as you get your license."

"Don't even joke about it. Margaret's vision is so bad she would probably think he passed the driving test," Lars said, referring to Starlight Grove DMV's only employee who was approximately one hundred and twenty-three years old, give or take a few years.

"I'm assuming Stanley doesn't know his golf cart is missing?" I asked, turning the key.

"Nah. He added an alarm to prevent theft, but I took care of that," Lars responded.

I grinned. "Excellent. Thank you both for your help." I waved to Summer through the shop window.

I pulled away from the curb, driving down the quiet Main Street. There was a small early morning breakfast crowd at Beans 'n Bliss and Rosie's Cafe. Ella's shift didn't start until nine, and I felt like I was cheating on her if I got my daily latte from someone else. I would just have to power through without caffeine until then.

My heart started pounding the closer I got to the firehouse. "I'm being silly. It's not like I haven't been there before." I'd dropped off a large batch of cookies the day after the Firefighter Appreciation Festival last year to make up for Stanley's overzealous celebration that involved the gazebo catching fire. That must have been right before Wilder was hired.

When I pulled up to the curb, Felix hopped out and stretched before leading the way inside with a swish of his tail. The station was quiet. Most of the guys were probably still sleeping, like reasonable people, but Ezra was in the kitchen frying some bacon. He was a cute alpha who had asked me out shortly after moving to Starlight Grove a couple of years back, but my omega hadn't been interested. He'd taken it well, though, and we sometimes hung out with the same friend group.

"Hey, Lucy. Fancy seeing you here." Felix hopped up on the counter, and Ezra did a little bow. "Mr. Mayor. How kind of you to grace us with your presence."

"I brought cookies." I put the box on the counter and Ezra immediately opened it and popped one in his mouth, whole.

"Fuck, are these Summer's?" He grabbed another two.

"Don't eat them all," I scolded. "But yes. You're all coming to the grand opening, right?"

"We've got it on the team calendar."

"Great." I hesitated. "Umm, will you make sure Wilder gets some cookies?"

A slow smile spread across Ezra's face. "Oh?"

A Pack for Spring

Shoot. The firefighters were just as bad gossips as Marisol and Carmen.

"Nothing like that. He helped me with an injury, so they're just a thank-you."

Ezra's brow furrowed. "Are you okay?"

"Just sprained my ankle. Not a big deal." Although, it was throbbing more now. I needed to take some meds and elevate it.

Ezra glanced at his watch. "He should be in soon if you want to hang out."

But I was already hobbling to the door. "No, that's fine! Just don't eat them all before he gets here."

I pulled myself into the golf cart and flopped back in the seat. "We did it, Felix." I looked over and found him sitting primly beside me, a cookie secured in his mouth.

I shook my head. "I'm going to pretend I didn't see that."

13

WILDER

I walked into the firehouse, and for the first time since I started this job, I didn't want to be here.

I liked my work. The administrative tasks that came along with being fire chief could be tedious, but helping people gave me a sense of purpose and my guys were the closest thing I had to family. But today it took every bit of strength I had to stop myself from racing down Main Street to a certain sewing shop.

The past few days had been torture without Lucy. The cabin was drenched in her scent. Only the thirty-minute drive down the mountain prevented me from breaking into her home and claiming her. I'd gotten in my truck multiple times yesterday, but each time, I'd come to my senses before I got to town.

My alpha was furious that I was resisting the sweet omega, but I couldn't trust my alpha... couldn't trust myself. Firefighting was the only area where my alpha was useful. My strength, high pain tolerance, and heightened senses allowed me to make rescues others couldn't. The stack of cards from the people I'd helped throughout the years sat in my desk drawer. I pulled them out on the days my self-hatred mounted and I wondered what the point of me was.

The drawing from Teddy depicting me as a superhero leaping out of his burning house with him and his beloved bear, Teddy Jr., in my arms.

The letter from the elderly woman thanking me for saving her husband's ashes and their wedding album—the last things she had left of him—when her condo burned.

The card from the family whose home was taken in an electrical fire while they were on vacation, complete with pictures of their two dogs I'd rescued and fostered until the family had a new place to move into.

My alpha might be twisted and dangerous, but at least I was doing something useful with my life.

I put my stuff down in my closet-sized office and popped another suppressant. The attraction I felt for Lucy would fade and I could return to my normal, lonely life. I just had to control my alpha in the meantime.

"Morning, boss," Ezra called out with a wave of his spatula when I entered the kitchen.

The smell of eggs and bacon swirled around me, but there was something else, too. Something delicate, sweet, and floral. The hair on my arms stood.

"Someone dropped by with a present for you this morning."

My skin flushed hot and I held back a growl. Lucy had been here? With *Ezra*?

"What?" I snarled.

He chuckled and gestured to a large white box. I lifted the lid and was hit with another wave of the omega's scent.

"Lucy dropped off cookies as a thank-you for your help. She specifically told me to make sure there were some left for you."

A surge of possessiveness rocked through me. I picked up the whole box and stalked away.

"Hey! You have to share!"

Ezra's voice was cut off as I slammed my office door. There was no fucking way I was going to share a gift given to me by my omega.

I opened the box and spotted the card, carefully tucked into the side. My fingers shook as I pulled it out. It was a shockingly accurate drawing of a large, flannel-wearing man holding a blond woman in a storm. A speech bubble from her mouth read, "Thanks for the rescue!"

I flipped the card over to find a handwritten coupon for "Unlimited tailoring services for life at Spring in Your Stitch."

I opened my desk drawer and was about to place it on my stack of thank-you notes, but the thought of hiding it away, of shutting the drawer on this gift from the omega I could never have, was unbearable.

I left it propped up on my desk, and my eyes stayed fixed on it as I ate every last cookie.

14

LEO

I LEANED OUT THE FRONT DOOR OF MY SHOP. *Don't mind me. Nothing suspicious happening here.*

My heart skipped a beat when I saw the sign on Lucy's door was finally flipped to *Open*. Her shop had been closed for several days, and it had been torture to go so long without seeing her. I'd been tempted to text her, but I didn't feel I had the right to after I'd pushed her away. All I could do now was cling to the hope that she'd be willing to give me another chance to . . . to what? Be friends? I could barely admit it to myself, but what I really wanted was to court her.

I wouldn't delude myself into thinking I would be enough for her. Omegas needed alphas. But maybe I would be lucky enough to find some sort of place by her side, even as a beta . . . even with the cane currently in my hand as I crossed the street to Beans 'n Bliss.

Ella hooked me up with Lucy's latest favorite drink, which just so happened to be a strawberry cardamom latte with sweet cream. I tried not to let it go to my head that her favorite was a mix of both of our scents, but I couldn't deny the extra lightness in my steps as I carefully crossed the street, drink carrier clutched in my free hand.

I awkwardly pushed her shop door open with my shoulder. My beta sense of smell couldn't pick up scents like an alpha or omega could, but Lucy's floral strawberry was thick enough in the air for it to fill my lungs, soothing and arousing in equal measure.

Lucy was leaning over her checkout counter, a small frown creasing her forehead as she flipped through a stack of papers. At the gentle chime of the door, she looked up and smiled, causing a burst of butterflies to flutter through my stomach. She looked as beautiful as ever, maybe even more so because my eyeballs had been deprived of her beauty the past few days.

"Hey, Leo." She glanced down at the coffee carrier and chewed her lip. "Would it be presumptuous of me to assume one of those might be for me?"

I grinned. "Maybe I just really need caffeine this morning."

She jutted her lip out in the saddest little pout I'd ever seen and sighed. "I guess I'll just have to get my own . . ."

I shook my head and held out her latte—size large, because I wasn't about to skimp on courting gifts. "You know you have me wrapped around your little finger."

Her parted lips and wide eyes told me she, in fact, did *not* know. She reached out to take the drink and her fingers brushed against mine, the movement slow enough to be purposeful.

She took a sip. "I feel very spoiled this morning. I was waiting for Ella's shift to start before heading over."

"She had just arrived. She said she'd be in tomorrow for her fitting."

"I'm making her graduation outfit." She gestured over to a mannequin that currently held black suit pants and a vest with a subtle gray stripe.

"A suit?"

"Yeah. Ella's a badass."

"I didn't realize how much of your work was sewing custom clothes. I thought you mostly did tailoring."

An emotion I couldn't identify flashed across Lucy's face. "I mostly just make outfits for fun. I'm not a real designer."

I frowned. It was obvious how talented she was. She sewed most of her own clothes, which were always beautiful, and she'd made pieces for tons of people in town—which I knew because anytime someone wore one of her designs, they couldn't help but brag about it.

"Your stuff is amazing. My dad is excited for his upcoming appointment with you."

She smiled softly, the tension in her shoulders easing. "It's been so fun talking with him about all his ideas. Let me show you some of the fabric samples I got for him."

She came out from behind the counter, and my heart pounded as panic worked its way up my body because she was *limping*.

"Did you hurt yourself?" I choked out.

She glanced down at her ankle, lifting her floral pants enough for me to see the edge of a white bandage. "Oh yeah. It's just a sprain. I, um, went camping this weekend and ended up getting caught in that storm and twisted my ankle in some mud."

The storm this weekend had been one of the worst I'd experienced in the area. The torrential rain had started overnight and hadn't let up all Saturday. Lucy had been *camping* during it? If my knee wasn't messed up, I would pick her up right now and carry her around in my arms until her ankle was healed. I would go with her on her next camping trip and make sure she was safe. I would . . . well, pretty much follow her around like a lovesick puppy.

"You need to sit down."

She waved off my concern. "It's fine."

But I was already slinging my arm around her waist. My chest warmed with intense satisfaction at how perfectly she fit against my side. The top of her head brushed my chin, her soft, curvy body molded to the ridges of mine. Her scent bloomed, strong enough to overwhelm even my beta senses.

"You have to be careful," I said sternly. I kept my grip on her as the two of us awkwardly hobbled over to a table. We almost knocked each other over twice covering the short distance, and Lucy was giggling by the time she sat down.

Her eyes twinkled. "She is beauty, she is grace."

I inclined my head. "Thank you for the compliment."

She laughed, slowly shaking her head.

"You need to elevate your ankle." My brow furrowed as I got a better look at the ankle wrap. "Who wrapped that? It's not done correctly."

Lucy bit her lip. "That would be me. Guess I should have paid more attention to the YouTube video." She let out a self-deprecating laugh and I wanted to kick myself. I thought she'd gone to the local clinic and the doctor there had done a shit job, which was unacceptable.

It was also unacceptable for my omega to have to wrap her own fucking ankle, even if she wasn't mine.

"It can be hard to do if you're not used to it. You haven't gone to the doctor?"

"No, but someone looked at it." At my confused expression, she clarified. "The fire chief. He said it was sprained and wrapped it for me."

Wilder Everett was the fire chief. I'd met him a couple of times at Ocean Rescue trainings since he was the head of Mountain Rescue. He was a man of few words. Literally. I wasn't sure I'd ever heard him actually speak beyond the occasional grunt. But he had advanced training as an EMT, and I begrudgingly had to admit he probably knew what he was doing. "If it doesn't improve over the next few days, you should definitely go to the clinic. For now, will you let me redo the wrap?" A *brilliant* idea hit me. "I can do it every morning for you."

Her lips parted as she looked up at me, and my cock twitched at my deeply inappropriate thoughts. "It won't be inconvenient?"

Inconvenient? To spend my mornings with her? Try *dream come true*. "Nah, of course not. It's not like I have to go far to track you down."

"That would probably be helpful, if you don't mind. I can send you the video I watched this morning. Although, maybe it wasn't very good."

I chuckled. "I'm an EMT. It was part of the required training for Ocean Rescue."

Her cheeks turned pink. "I guess you don't need a video, then. But you do need a chair." Before I could say anything, she pulled out a second chair from the table, tipping it forward to dump the large box of bubble wrap off the seat and onto the floor. "For you." She waved her hand in front of it in a dramatic gesture. Damn, she was cute.

A Pack for Spring

I sat down and leaned my cane against the table. She glanced at it but didn't say anything. I wished I could read her mind.

I patted my good leg. "Put your foot up here."

She did what I asked and I froze. I did *not* think this through. Her foot was inches from my crotch. Warning alarms blared in my brain. *Don't pop a boner. She's going to think you have a foot fetish.*

A shiver ran through me when I gently touched her foot. *Get ahold of yourself. This is just another day as an EMT.*

"Did you hurt your leg?" Lucy asked.

My fingers faltered and my heart sank. Here it was. Time to face the music.

"Sort of."

I fussed with the wrap, ensuring the tension was just right. My eyes didn't leave her ankle as I started talking.

"I have osteoarthritis in my knee. My grandpa had it, and it started young for him, so I guess I was genetically predisposed. When I was a teenager, I tore my ACL, which strained my knee. The pain got worse the past couple years, but I ignored it." I had been so fucking young and stupid, believing I would be the exception and could just power through. "This past winter, I had an accident while doing Ocean Rescue and it pushed me to stage three osteoarthritis. The goal now is to prevent a knee replacement for as long as possible. And this"—I held up my cane, my face on fire—"is part of that."

Lucy moved her foot off my lap, and I was about to protest when she scooted her chair even closer to mine and grasped my hands. The heat of her touch and the strawberry sweetness of her scent eased my urge to run away.

"That's why you left Ocean Rescue?"

I nodded, fixing my gaze on her thumb softly moving across the back of my hand. Her fingers sported little red pinpricks from her sewing needles that matched my scratches from my early morning rose delivery.

"That really sucks." She squeezed my hands tightly. "Well, for you. It's pretty great for me."

I glanced up to meet her bright eyes. "Huh?"

"I get free flowers and medical care out of this deal. So honestly, pretty great."

Was . . . was she joking? I'd played out this scenario so many times in my mind. I had braced myself for the worst-case scenario—seeing her disgust and disappointment. Even my imagined best-case scenario had included a hefty dose of pity. I couldn't wrap my mind around her teasing smile.

"You're right," I choked out. "This is really great for you."

She wiggled her toes. "That wrap feels so much better. Thank you."

"Of course. I'll come back and redo it tomorrow morning for you."

"I'll provide the coffee and breakfast in exchange for your doctoring. What latte are you drinking?" Lucy asked.

"The same as you." I took a sip, gathering my courage before speaking. Before my accident, when I could ignore the twinges in my knee and my muscles were strong from daily workouts and Ocean Rescue drills, I wouldn't have been as anxious about asking Lucy out. Now it felt like jumping from a plane without a parachute.

"I will bring the coffee and breakfast," I said. "I can't have you supplying the food for our first date."

I held my breath. I was sure she would protest, say it wasn't a date, but then she smiled.

"If you insist."

When I was eventually forced to return to my shop because I apparently had to *work* and *take care of customers*, I felt lighter than I had since my accident. Lucy and I officially had a date tomorrow, and I was going to do everything in my power to make it special for her.

15

KING

My shoes created a steady beat on the pavement as I wove through the quaint streets of historic Starlight Grove. I usually ran on the longer trails along the beach and woods, but today's tight morning schedule meant I had to resort to burning off my energy as best I could before my meeting.

I pushed myself harder. I needed my lungs and legs to burn until the pain was all I could focus on.

I turned a corner and almost tripped over a fluffy creature sprawled in the middle of the sidewalk. My steps stuttered as I fought to avoid stepping on what I realized was a cat. The creature gave me a dirty look as if *I* had inconvenienced *him*, and I shook my head as I took off running again.

This stupid fucking meeting.

Negotiations hadn't even started and I was already tired of it all. The exhaustion was familiar—it had been my constant companion this past decade since my parents deteriorated and I had been forced to step in as CEO of their company.

I couldn't believe they'd been gone for two months. It would be a lie to say we'd been a close-knit family, but their absence still left an ache in my chest. Especially since their passing meant I was officially alone in the world. At forty years old, the family company was the only thing tethering me to their legacy—the family company I wasn't sure I wanted to keep.

I took a turn out of the neighborhood and the ocean opened up in front of me. My New York apartment had a wall of windows overlooking the Brooklyn waterfront, but it wasn't the same as being here by the water, the salt clinging to my skin. The ocean brought me back to the idealistic dreamer I was in my twenties when I was living in a shitty studio apartment, doing ocean conservation advocacy for pennies. I'd thought the past decade had killed off that version of myself, but maybe there was a bit of him left. I grinned as old memories of long hours in the nonprofit's shabby office flitted through my mind. It was easy to romanticize the late nights and packages of ramen a decade removed, but at least I'd felt like I was doing something meaningful back then.

I reluctantly turned away from the ocean and jogged back to the house I was renting. There were no hotels in Starlight Grove—apparently their mayor had banned any chain businesses within town limits—so the only thing my assistant had found was a short-term rental owned by a woman named Ms. Ito, who had decided to travel in her retirement. The furniture might not be my style and there were a bizarre number of boxes filled with weird-ass socks stacked around the rooms, but it was fine for a short stint and only a block away from Main Street.

The door creaked as I stepped inside. I was pressed for time and needed to make this a quick shower, but once the hot water was pelting my back, I found it hard to get moving. Everything felt so empty these days, like I was just going through the motions of my life. How had I ended up here?

"The recent storm made a mess of the coastline, which is why our housing developer has a plan for high-end luxury homes that balance aesthetics with durability."

"That's right. There are a lot of couples and families in Boston and New York who need a quiet retreat like this."

My dress shoes shifted on the sand beneath me. The real estate development company had insisted we come down to the beach so we could better visualize its plan for luxury homes on Maine's coast, but I felt like I was surrounded by a flock of overeager gulls in suits. Not that I could judge. This business meeting was my first time not wearing a suit since I started at the company. My assistant, Caroline, had forbidden me from bringing a suit or tie, saying it would be good for me to wear *normal people clothes* for once.

As if suits weren't normal.

"What are the plans to mitigate the environmental impact of the development?" I asked.

"Our firm has a strong record of compliance with the minimum standards set out by our federal and state environmental laws when it comes to air and water quality, along with the soil contamination," one of the gulls said.

My eyes wandered down the coastline. It was wild and rugged, one of the rare untouched areas of this part of the state. And I was responsible for deciding what happened to it.

"This is one reason we consistently attract luxury clientele. They love hearing about our innovative green building practices."

"Complying with the minimum standards set forth by environmental laws is innovative?" I asked.

Another gull piped up. "We find strong messaging largely relies on cohesive branding. There are no laws that prohibit us from using the terms 'eco-friendly' and 'green construction.'"

How inspiring.

I held my tongue as they continued their pitch, ending with a presentation in their office with blueprints and renderings of their proposed home designs.

"We worked closely with your parents to create these plans." The man's tone was friendly, but I sensed his underlying irritation. While I did understand his frustration—they were having to repitch me after almost having a closed deal—I wasn't going to sign off on the sale just because my parents had agreed to it. This deal had nothing to do with the company. After my parents passed, their lawyers had notified me that they owned a large piece of land on Starlight Grove's coast. They'd held on to it for forty-five years, but when Blackthorne Ventures approached them to buy it, they'd pursued the sale. They'd passed away before the final contract could be signed, so now it was up to me to approve the sale. It should have been a no-brainer. The land alone was valued at close to ten million dollars—enough money to be set for life.

Enough money to retire.

Dreams of no longer being the CEO of Empire Enterprises were tantalizing. I'd dedicated the entirety of my thirties to the company in a sad effort to win my parents' love. Something I'd never achieved and now never would.

I mulled over the sale on the short drive back to Starlight Grove's downtown. The faster I closed this deal, the faster I could head back to the city and to my normal life. But somehow, that didn't loosen the tension in my chest.

I slid into a parking spot in front of the coffee shop. When I first arrived in town a few days ago, I'd been a pretentious ass, assuming a shop named Beans 'n Bliss in a tiny town like this would have shitty coffee. I was wrong. I'd come every day so far—twice yesterday—and gotten whatever ridiculous latte the barista had suggested. I had yet to be disappointed.

My phone rang as I stepped inside. I glanced at the screen, planning to send the call to voicemail before I saw it was Caroline. I groaned internally before answering.

"Yes?"

"Oh good, you're already grumpy."

"What is it?"

Ella waved at me as I got to the front of the line. I fished a twenty out of my pocket and handed it to her. "Surprise me."

"You want me to surprise you?" Caroline asked. "Great, because that's why I'm calling."

"I wasn't talking to you." I stepped to the side as I waited for my drink.

"Too bad. There's a last-minute event in Boston tonight that you need to attend."

I frowned. "Caroline, I distinctly remember you yelling at me to take time off." I lowered my voice so no one around me could overhear. "You're the one who rented me this house in this bizarre small town."

"Yes, but this event is for charity." She pushed on before I could interrupt her. "It's a gala to raise money for childhood cancer research."

I clenched my jaw to stop myself from letting out a string of curses, because my assistant had me. She knew exactly what to say to manipulate me into saying yes, because I hadn't always been alone in the world. At one time, I had an older brother. My chest squeezed tight. Saint spent years of his young life in and out of the hospital before cancer took him from us, leaving my parents cold and broken. I had only been four when he died, so I barely remembered him beyond the pictures that had lined the halls of our home and the pointed comparisons my parents made between the two of us.

"Why can't I just send a donation?" I gritted out.

"Okay, so here's where it gets tricky."

I scrubbed my hand down my face. I wasn't going to like this. Ella called out my name and I picked up my latte—iced this time—and took a cautious sip. Sweet, fresh strawberry flavor hit my tongue, and I gave the barista a thumbs-up, juggling my phone and drink as I headed for the door.

"The event is an auction."

"Okay? I still don't understand why a donation wouldn't work. Cash donation or a weekend at the vacation house, whatever they want."

The cafe door swung open before I could reach for it, putting me face-to-face with a man with golden brown skin and dark curly hair. He arched an eyebrow, a teasing grin on his lips, and I realized I was blocking his way. I half stumbled as I moved to the side. He was a touch shorter than me, with lean muscles and a faint scent of something warm and spicy that identified him as a beta. He headed to the counter, and it was only as my lingering gaze trailed down his strong, broad shoulders and arms that I realized he was walking with a cane.

I blinked to clear my dazed mind and exited the coffee shop.

"That's why you have to be there. And I know you're going to say you don't want to do it, but it's for an important cause and will be good press. But you would have to leave Starlight Grove in the next three or four hours."

I glanced through the cafe window, catching one last look at the beta. Ella was handing him a full bottle of flavored syrup, which seemed odd.

"I don't have a tux with me," I said distractedly. "Wonder whose fault that is."

"Drat. This is why you shouldn't listen to me."

"Good advice. So I'm going to pass on tonight—"

"No, no! You can't do that. Surely there's a clothing store there where you can buy a tux."

"Oh yeah, I'll just head to the tux shop next door."

"They have one of those?"

"No, Caroline. They don't."

"Oh, we're being funny now, are we? All right, I'm looking at the map and there's a shop called Spring in Your Stitch that looks like a clothing store. Are you anywhere near that?"

I looked across the street to the shop my assistant just named. "No."

"Okay, great. So just go there, get a tux, and drive to Boston for the event. I've booked you a hotel room downtown since the date will take place tomorrow."

"What fucking date?"

Caroline let out a long-suffering sigh. "I love it when I talk and no one listens. The gala is an auction of eligible bachelors, and the winner gets to spend tomorrow with you. Nothing weird or sexual, of course. Just be your normal charming self and everything will go great."

"What the fuck?" I hissed, my hold on the phone tightening. "You want me to spend the day with a *stranger*?"

"They're going to be so appreciative. And there's no backing out now because I already told them you would attend. All the details are in your email. *Okaythanksbye!*"

KING

You are fired

CAROLINE

Better hurry up and get that tux!
Traffic might be bad getting into the city

KING

When you hire your replacement,
make sure to get one who's scared of me

CAROLINE

I hate to break it to you, but you are
one of the least scary people I know.

I'm calling Spring in Your Stitch to let
them know you're coming

The text contained a link. I clicked it against my better judgment, opening a website filled with faces of children with cancer and large graphics displaying statistics about the lack of pediatric cancer funding.

KING

This is emotional blackmail

I angrily sipped my latte as I crossed the street. My frustration only grew when I stepped into the shop, or, rather, *disaster zone*. The large room was filled to the brim with cardboard boxes, bolts of fabric, and those headless mannequin things with dresses on them. The walls were pink and covered with what looked like kids' drawings of a cat, and a large checkout counter sat at the back of the room, but it was empty.

How could someone run a business like this? I was ready to leave when I breathed in, filling my lungs with an intoxicating mix of flowers and strawberries that instantly calmed me. I took another sip of coffee, but the strawberry flavor paled compared to what I was scenting.

Just then, a woman popped her head out of the back room. She was wearing a flowing pink dress, and her blond hair was held back by a matching pink headband, but a few gold strands still fell in her face.

"Hey! How can I help you?"

I froze. She was the prettiest woman I'd ever seen. As she got closer, the mouthwatering sweet scent that filled the shop intensified. My heart raced. She was an omega.

She stopped in front of me and I realized how tiny she was—barely coming up to my shoulder.

"I need a tux." My head spun and I felt completely disoriented, something that hadn't happened in . . .

Ever?

I took a small step back, trying to clear my head. I was used to being in complete control.

"Oh!" Her blue eyes lit up. "Are you King? I'm Lucy. I literally just got off the phone with"—she glanced down at a ripped scrap of notebook paper—"Caroline. She said you'd be in soon, I just didn't realize she meant ten seconds later." She laughed, and the sound was so perfect it made my chest ache.

"Like I told her, I mostly do tailoring. There's a shop in Briar's Landing that sells formal clothes, but it sounds like you won't have time to get there and then to your event. You're in luck, though, because I actually have an old tux that someone donated that should fit you. I can do some speedy tailoring to get it to fit in time for you to leave for your event."

I held back my grimace. The chaotic shop and the promise of speedy tailoring didn't inspire much confidence. While I didn't want to go to this event, there would be cameras and I didn't want any humiliating photos to end up online. But I didn't have a choice but to follow Lucy as she led me into the back room, which was somehow

A Pack for Spring

messier than the front of her shop. There was a long clothing rack filled with rows of garment bags, but it was half blocked by a stack of cardboard boxes.

Boxes the omega was currently climbing on.

I let out a strangled noise and lunged toward her, my arm automatically banding around her waist and pulling her off the precariously stacked boxes.

"What are you doing?" Her voice was high-pitched and breathless, and her sweet scent thickened in the air. I quickly released her and stepped back before I did something ridiculous, like press my face into the graceful curve of her neck and lick her skin.

That would be inappropriate.

"Those aren't safe to stand on," I grunted. "You need to clean this place up and get a step stool."

Her smile stayed in place, but her shoulders slumped. "Yeah." She swallowed hard. "I can never seem to keep it organized for more than a few hours."

Shit. I didn't mean to embarrass her. "Just tell me what you need and I'll grab it for you."

With a bit of maneuvering, I snagged a black garment bag from the back of the rack and handed it to her. She partially unzipped it. "This is the one." Her eyes ran down my body, and I felt her gaze like a tangible thing. My cock twitched. Did she like what she saw?

"I think this will fit pretty well, actually. Put it on in the dressing room, and we can see what we're working with."

The dressing room ended up being a tiny corner of the shop, blocked off by a floral curtain. I gritted my jaw as I adjusted my half-hard cock to conceal it before getting dressed.

The tux was a bit old-fashioned, but I had to admit that Lucy had a good eye. It was baggy in spots, but at least I didn't have to worry about my thigh and arm muscles popping the seams, something that had unfortunately happened before.

Lucy clapped excitedly when I pushed the changing room curtain aside.

"Oh, it looks so good already. This is going to be a breeze." As she walked over to a side table, I noticed a flash of white on her ankle. It was wrapped with a bandage, and she was slightly favoring one leg as she walked.

"Did you hurt your ankle?"

She shoved a pile of fabric off the side table and let out a soft "Aha" as she found a weird pillow thing and strapped it to her wrist.

"It's just a slight sprain. I've been icing it."

"You shouldn't keep weight on it." Just because I ignored the variety of running-related injuries I'd obtained over the years, didn't mean this omega should.

She plopped down on the stool with a roll of her eyes. "Happy now?"

Oh, what a little brat. My alpha rumbled with the urge to dominate her . . . and take care of her.

"Ecstatic," I deadpanned.

She grinned. "If I had more time, I would adjust the jacket shoulders, but that's a much more in-depth process. I think hemming the pants and jacket sleeves will be enough to make you look passable for your event."

She scooted closer.

And closer.

Her scent was so thick I was seconds away from popping a boner, made even worse when I realized that, from my vantage point, I had a straight shot down the front of her dress.

Sweat prickled my forehead as I forced myself to think through every line of the Blackthorne Ventures boilerplate to distract myself.

Terms of inspection. Earnest money requirements. Historical city and county survey data.

Fuck. It wasn't working.

I couldn't stop myself from stealing another glance. She pulled a pin out of the cushion on her wrist and held another between her lips.

Those fucking plush, pink lips.

"That should do it for the pants." She pushed to standing and my hands automatically grasped her arms to steady her.

She beamed. "I just need to pin the sleeves. Then I'll hem everything and you'll be ready." She tugged on the jacket and arranged my arm how she wanted it. Her touch sent a shiver down my spine even through the layers of fabric.

"What's the event you're going to?" she asked.

"It's a charity gala. They're fundraising with an auction."

"Oohhh, a gala. I wonder what designers people will be wearing. Are you going to bid on anything at the auction?"

I shifted uncomfortably. "Apparently I'm going to be the one auctioned off."

Her expression transformed into an adorable little frown. "What does that mean?"

"They're auctioning off dates . . . or something." Fuck. I really needed Caroline to explain it again while I was actually paying attention. Did I have to give some sort of speech? Or get up on a stage?

Lucy laughed. "I can tell you're super excited."

I scowled, but her smile just widened. "I'm sure it won't be that bad. It's fun to meet new people, and I'm sure you'll be *very* popular."

My brain stuttered. Did that mean she thought I was attractive?

She moved on to the second sleeve. Shit. She was almost done. I usually didn't like being around people, but being around Lucy wasn't . . . terrible. A plan formed in my mind.

"Are you doing anything tonight?" I blurted out.

"Umm, I'm not sure. Missy said tonight's movie, *That One Time I Died and Reincarnated as an Alpha in a Medieval Princess Castle*, is a must-see, so maybe I'll go to the theater."

"I . . ." What the fuck did I even say to that?

"Apparently it's a scathing commentary on wealth inequality."

"Right . . . Well, if you decide to skip it, would you want to come with me to the event?"

She blinked up at me. "What?"

I let out a long groan, ruffling my hand through my hair that desperately needed to be styled after spending an hour on the windswept beach. "I need you to come and bid on me so I don't have to spend tomorrow with a stranger. You'll use my credit card, of course, not your own money," I quickly clarified.

"You want to buy yourself at an auction just to avoid spending time with someone you don't know?" Her tone was teasing.

"Yes."

She moved my arm from side to side as she inspected her handiwork. "But *I'm* a stranger."

"Yes, but if you bid on me, I can drive back after the event and move on with my life like this nightmare never happened."

Her eyebrows shot up and she burst out laughing. "Wow, you really know how to woo a girl."

"I'll pay you for your time."

She shook her head, a smile still playing on her lips. "You don't have to pay me. But I actually do have some errands to run in Boston..."

I waited with bated breath as she placed another pin in the jacket. When she didn't say anything, I added, "Caroline already booked a hotel room for me, but I was planning on driving back tonight. You could stay in the room and run your errands tomorrow."

She chewed her lip. "Are you sure? I won't be taking the room from you?"

I shook my head. "I have a commercial real estate sale I need to wrap up before I go back home."

"You're not here permanently?"

For the briefest moment, I was tempted to tell Lucy everything—how I wasn't sure what I even wanted out of life anymore. How deeply unfulfilling my work was, but how I didn't know what I would do without it. "No. I live in New York."

"Oh, that's a bummer. We have some fun festivals coming up—the Easter Eggstravaganza and my friend Summer is opening her bakery. You should come to the grand opening if you're still here."

I had only been in town for a few weeks, and I was pretty sure there had been a festival every other day, all of which I'd successfully avoided. Although . . . the image of walking around town with Lucy, my arm wrapped around her, feeding her cake at the bakery opening, flashed unbidden in my mind.

I bent my knees to make it easier for her to slide the jacket off my shoulders. *Do not think about her undressing you.*

I turned around to face her. "So, what do you say?"

She grinned and my heart skipped a beat. "Hmm." She dragged out the sound like she was intentionally torturing me. "It does sound like a fun adventure, and my horoscope did tell me to say yes to new opportunities . . ."

Horoscope?

"So yes, I'll go with you."

"Great. That's great. Thanks." I let out a slow breath. "Are you sure you want to drive separately?" For some reason, the thought of this omega driving to Boston alone made my skin crawl.

"Oh, I don't have a car. Could I ride down with you? And then I'll take the train back tomorrow."

A fucking train? Nope. Not happening.

"I'll arrange a ride back for you." I was sure Caroline could find a reputable car service.

Her scent intensified and she fidgeted with the edge of her skirt, her cheeks bright pink. "If you insist. Go take the pants off, and I'll hem everything and be ready in a few hours."

A gust of air hit my face when I left her shop twenty minutes later, but it did nothing to cool my overheated skin. As I made the short walk back to my rental, I was struck by the sensation that my attempt to make tonight's event simpler and more straightforward may have backfired spectacularly.

16

LUCY

> LUCY
> Which dress?

I sent mirror pictures of three dresses—all of which I'd designed and sewn in the past few months—to my friends. I wasn't sure why I'd made the gowns, since it was mostly a waste of time and money. I was a tailor in Starlight Grove, not a socialite in New York City. But right now, I was grateful I had these options on hand. Because it meant I would fit in at the gala, not because I wanted to attract King's attention.

Nope, not at all.

The first dress was covered with silver sparkles. It had a flowing, scooped neckline and a low-cut back. Sewing with the material had caused multiple late-night breakdowns, but the final result was so pretty it had been worth it.

The second was a floor-length floral dress with a structured corset top and tulle skirt. It was one of my favorites I'd ever made, but the pale green color lent itself more to a garden party, not a gala.

The last dress was definitely the most risqué. It was black with a tight, lacy top that hugged my curves through the hips and legs. The lace was see-through—not enough to reveal too much skin, but definitely sexy. I finished sewing this one last month. It had been a fun, creative project, but I never expected to have a reason to wear it.

SUMMER

I mean, you might be a little overdressed at the bakery grand opening, but I appreciate the support

LUCY

Ha ha very funny. I'm going to a gala tonight in Boston and I have to choose a dress in the next ten mins!!

OLIVE

Umm tell us more about this last minute gala??

LUCY

This guy came into the shop for a tux and needed someone to go with him and who fills a chair better than me?

IVY

That sounds like a date!

LUCY

No, not a date. Long story but I'm just doing him a favor and I needed to go to Boston anyway

SUMMER

This guy . . . is he hot?

LUCY

Can we focus on the issue at hand?! Which dress??

SUMMER

This is essential information to help us in our dress selection

OLIVE

How old is he?

Is he an alpha?

IVY

What's his name? What's the event?

LUCY

It's a charity event. Now I demand you tell me what to wear!

OLIVE

Shoot. Lars read my text over my shoulder

Finn is holding him back so he doesn't storm over to your shop to interrogate this guy

LUCY

This is not a date!!

OLIVE

He says you have to send us this guy's details if you don't want him to come over there

LUCY

His name is King. He looks like he's in his late thirties? early 40s? Idk!! And yes he's an alpha. He needed someone to come with him. That's it.

OLIVE

And is he hot??

LUCY
My brother needs to know if he's hot??

IVY
Isn't Lars out of town for a job?

OLIVE
Shhhhh

LUCY
Olive??

OLIVE
Ok well he didn't necessarily read it over my shoulder, but everything else is true

IVY
I love all the dresses but that last one is really hot

SUMMER
definitely that one! Make this hot alpha get on his knees for you

LUCY
...

I hope you know all of your outfits for the Easter Eggstravagazna just got 100000% uglier

SUMMER
That's fine. As long as you wear the third dress

I rolled my eyes but couldn't stop my smile. My friends were endearingly aggravating.

I looked out the window, my heart racing when I saw a fancy black SUV pull up to the curb. That had to be King. I did one last check of my hair in the mirror. I hadn't had time to put it up, so I'd added some loose curls and hoped that would be good enough. I tossed my makeup bag into my small duffel so I could finish getting ready in the car. Before I could second-guess myself, I grabbed the garment bag with the black dress and the one with the completed tux and half hopped downstairs, putting as much weight as I could on the banister.

King got out right as I locked the door, and I couldn't stop the thrill of pleasure that went through me when strode toward me. He immediately took my bags and held out his free arm for me to grab for balance.

Why was that so hot? The only reason my perfume didn't fill the air was that I had reluctantly applied No-NonScent Deodorant to mute my scent and lessen my embarrassment when spending several hours in the car with King. Besides, it was encouraged that omegas wear de-scenter at large events so we weren't a *distraction*. Which, *eww*, but I'd had enough of unwanted alpha attention in my life that I was perfectly fine avoiding more at this event.

There was only one alpha whose attention I wanted tonight.

My steps stuttered when King opened the passenger-side door for me. One time, I'd asked my exes why they never held doors open for me, and they told me if my arms were too weak to open doors, I needed to hit the gym. They'd made me feel ashamed for even hinting that I wanted some chivalry, and here was King doing it automatically when this wasn't even a date.

He even waited until I was settled in the luxurious leather seat before softly closing the door. I slumped back and fanned my face. It was a two-and-a-half-hour drive to Boston and I already had the urge to climb this man like a tree. This was going to be a loooong night.

Good thing I'd brought extra panties.

A Pack for Spring

King got in, quickly glancing my way before smoothly pulling away from the curb.

I fiddled with the radio, and he arched an eyebrow. "What are you doing?"

"Putting on my road trip playlist."

He muttered something under his breath and I grinned. It was going to be fun to get under this grumpy alpha's skin.

17

KING

I was in a hotel room with an omega, and my dick was about to punch a hole through my new pants.

I paced around the suite, as if that would help me burn off the electric energy coursing through my veins. Why did Lucy set me off like this? She'd talked the entire drive, alternating between singing along to her playlist, asking me what my favorite color was—something I hadn't thought about in a couple decades—and giving me in-depth descriptions of the outfits she had planned for the upcoming town festivals. By the time I pulled up to the Boston hotel near the gala venue, I knew more about sewing than I'd ever wanted to.

And I was utterly obsessed.

I hated small talk. And meeting new people. But Lucy was sweet, charming, and fucking funny. My cheeks actually hurt from smiling. For all my working out, my cheek muscles were apparently underused. I would have blamed my strong reaction to her as my alpha getting worked up because I was trapped in a small, contained space filled with her scent, but she must have put on some sort of scent blocker because no matter how hard I breathed in, there was no hint of her floral sweetness in the air. And that made me irrationally irritated.

Now I was a frantic, pacing mess as I waited for Lucy to get dressed in the bathroom because I didn't want her out of my sight.

The door opened and I quickly arranged my face into what I hoped was a neutral, almost bored expression. Better she didn't know how much she affected my alpha.

But then she walked into the living room and the earth stood still. The top of the dress was low cut and covered in lace. *See-through* lace. Her long, blond hair brushed the perfect curves of her breasts, and with each step she took toward me, the skirt's high slit exposed her bare leg. My mouth watered. I wanted to run my hand along her skin and bite her inner thigh, marking her so everyone knew who she belonged to.

Lucy exaggeratingly cleared her throat. "My face is up here."

"Zoned out for a second." Not sure who I was trying to fool because Lucy's smirk told me I was full of shit. "You look . . ." *Like the most gorgeous woman I've ever seen. Like I want to throw you down on this bed and ravage you. Like I don't want a single other person to lay eyes on you.* "Nice."

"Nice, huh?" She ran her hands along her hips. "I hope I fit in. I wasn't sure what the proper attire was for a fake date auction winner."

Hearing her say "fake date" left a sour taste in my mouth, especially since this event would be filled with rich, powerful alphas. Alphas who would love nothing more to steal her away from me. "The dress looks fine." My voice was harsh, and her expression fell.

Shit.

"I mean, it looks good. Great. You'll fit in fine."

What the fuck was happening to me? I might not like people, but I'd never been such a bumbling fool.

Lucy gave me a tight smile and I groaned internally.

"Do you have everything you need? The car's waiting outside." I'd put Lucy's bag inside the bedroom since she'd be returning here tonight.

Without me.

What if she wanted to bring someone from the event back with her? Fury flooded me, but before I could call off the whole event and keep her trapped here with me, she thrust her phone and a ziplock bag of makeup at me.

"Yeah. But can you hold these for me? I forgot to bring a clutch, and this dress definitely doesn't have pockets."

As if I needed another reminder of how the dress clung to her every curve. She lifted her skirt so that her heels wouldn't catch as she headed to the door.

Reality slapped me and I scowled. "Are you wearing heels?"

Lucy gave me a look that screamed *Duh*, and my palm itched with the urge to spank her.

I crouched down. "And you removed the ankle wrap. You're going to hurt yourself."

"What do you want me to wear? Sneakers?"

"They'd be better than those."

Her eyes narrowed. "If you think there's any chance that I'm leaving here in sneakers, well then . . ." She paused, furrowing her brow. "Then you are *wrong*."

I snorted. "I'm surprised I'm not bleeding after that cutting comeback."

She pursed her lips, but her expression quickly changed into something almost gleeful before smoothing out. "You're welcome to go without me," she said, batting her eyes and gesturing at the door. "I'm happy to stay here and order room service, and you can be auctioned off to someone else."

I snarled and closed the space between us, crowding her until her back hit the wall. Our lips were inches apart, and I gripped her chin between my thumb and forefinger. "You'll lean on me so you don't aggravate your ankle, and you'll tell me if it's hurting."

Her lips were parted, eyes wide, but she gave me a tiny nod.

I took a step back and extended my arm, which she took without argument.

This was going to be a long night.

"How are we playing this?"

I looked up from my phone. I'd pulled it out the second we got in the town car the event organizers had sent. Nothing on the internet could distract me from the omega sitting inches away, but I needed a moment to regroup after I'd almost kissed her at the hotel. Which was probably why I'd been typing random words into my notes app the past few minutes as we sat in traffic.

A Pack for Spring

"What do you mean?" I asked.

"Should we enter separately and pretend we don't know each other?"

I scowled. "Why would we do that?"

"To make the auction more dramatic."

"I don't care about drama. I just care about the night being over."

She nudged my side. "Come on. Live a little, Mr. Grumpy Pants. This is going to be fun! Free drinks, free food, lots of fun people-watching, and King, the businessman, being purchased at auction by a mysterious woman."

She batted her eyelashes, and I suppressed a smile.

"Whatever you say," I responded dryly. "But we're going in together. It will still be *dramatic* if my mysterious date bids on me."

She sighed. "I suppose I'll have to make do with that."

We neared the venue and my jaw clenched when I saw photographers lining the red carpet. Shit. Lucy was on the side closest to the curb.

"Wait there," I said once we came to a stop.

Before she could respond, I was out of the car. "Move," I snapped at the valet, who was about to open the door for her. His eyes widened and he stumbled back a couple of steps, hands raised in a placating gesture.

I opened the door for Lucy. She arched her eyebrows as she took my hand. She leaned in, standing on her tiptoes, and her lips brushed against the shell of my ear. "That was hot."

Fucking hell. Every cell in me responded to her murmured words. She was going to kill me before the night was over. She looped her arm through mine, leaning into my side and wearing a brilliant smile as we started down the red carpet.

The journalists salivated when they caught sight of her, and no wonder. She was the most gorgeous woman in attendance.

"Welcome Mr. King! Who is your date?"

"Mr. King! We hear you're going to be auctioned off tonight!"

Lucy waved at the photographers and of course, they lost their minds, turning their questions on her. She glanced up at me. "Aren't you going to answer them, honey?"

"No." I wrapped my arm around her waist and half carried her inside. Not that it helped because the second we entered the large atrium, every single man fixed his eyes on her. A low growl tore through my chest. Lucy jumped, but I kept her tight against me, my fingers digging in to her waist. Her practically *bare* waist because of the sheer lace.

"Why were they calling you Mr. King? What's your last name?"

"King is my last name."

"Oh! What's your first name, then?"

I didn't respond as I steered us through the large ballroom.

"Come on. What kind of fake date am I if I don't even know your name?"

I huffed, but it was all for show. Being around Lucy soothed the prickly anger and frustration I constantly carried around, leaving me . . . happy? Fuck, it had been so long since I'd felt like this I didn't know what to do about it.

"Sutton."

"Huh?"

"My first name is Sutton."

She beamed, her nose doing an adorable scrunching thing. "That's not even bad! Not as embarrassing as my middle name."

"What is it?"

"Bluebell."

A chuckle bubbled from my chest, and Lucy narrowed her eyes in outrage. "I didn't laugh at *yours*."

Without thinking, I leaned down and pressed a quick kiss to the top of her head. Even with her heels, she barely reached my chin. "Bluebell suits you."

She pursed her lips but couldn't hide the flush working down her neck and chest, drawing my eyes to her tits. I wanted to suck and bite them, cover her with my marks so all the assholes here knew they would never stand a chance.

I tore my gaze away. I never behaved like this. It must just be my alpha responding to her designation, but the excuse was like ash on my tongue. My assistant was an omega, as was my neighbor, and somehow I'd never had the urge to kiss the top of their heads . . . or bend them over the closest table and fuck them so everyone knew who they belonged to.

I kept my arm around her as we made our way through the large event space. The decorations were pretty standard for a party like this—white tablecloths, large floral centerpieces, and an excessive amount of glasses and silverware at every place setting. Easels were set up along the back of the room, holding large pictures of kids with quotes about how cancer research had saved their lives.

I averted my gaze, focusing instead on getting to our table. Three women and two men were already seated—none of whom I recognized—but Lucy let out a soft gasp.

My fingers tightened on her hip. "What is it?"

"That's Jacqueline Wu," she whisper-shouted. "I can't believe she's here. Oh my god."

"Who is she?"

Lucy's jaw dropped. "Only one of the top couture designers *in the world*. She looks perfect, of course. She's the one wearing the pale blue silk dress—it's part of her new spring collection."

There were three empty chairs at the table and I guided Lucy to the one beside the dress designer. She clutched my forearm when she realized what I was doing, her body practically vibrating with excitement. When was the last time I was that excited about work?

Oh, that's right. *Never*.

I unbuttoned my jacket and sat down beside Lucy, tugging her chair closer to mine and slinging my arm across the back of it.

"King," the alpha across from me said in a booming voice. "Good to see you."

It took me a second to place him. "Jack." I lifted my chin when I remembered he was one of the corporate lawyers who had helped with a company merger last year.

"I'm surprised you're here. We don't usually see you socializing." He grinned, his gaze turning to Lucy. "And who's your date?"

"I'm Lucy. It's nice to meet you."

"It's *very* nice to meet you. How did this one"—he jerked his head in my direction—"win such an amazing prize? You're clearly too good for him." Jack flashed me a shit-eating grin, and I imagined leaping over the table to strangle him. Before my possessiveness could get the best of me, Lucy put her hand on my chest.

"Don't let that grumpy exterior fool you. He's incredibly charming, especially when we're alone." Her tone was drenched with innuendo, and she leaned in to press a kiss to my jaw. The murderous urge I'd felt toward Jack vanished. I played with Lucy's hair, curling the ends around my fingers. Irritation flashed across the alpha's face, filling me with smugness.

Lucy turned toward the others at our table, effortlessly introducing herself and charming everyone in the process. She only faltered when she turned to Jacqueline Wu. My hand shifted to the back of her neck. I squeezed and the tension melted out of the omega.

"I'm a huge fan of your work. I've been following you since your blog days."

Jacqueline's eyes widened and she laughed. "Oh, wow. Not many can say that, which I'm grateful for. My early designs were *something*."

"They were amazing. I studied the Celina Tulle dress from your second collection for months when I was in middle school. It was all I talked about, so much so that my moms ended up banning any mention of the dress at dinner. My grandma helped me recreate it. My seams were crooked and the whole silhouette was a bit of a mess, but I wore it every single day during winter break."

Jacqueline looked taken aback but pleased. Lucy's sincerity was a breath of fresh air at events like this, when so many of the attendees were here to brag and posture.

"Do you work in fashion?" she asked.

"Oh, I just have a small tailoring shop in Starlight Grove."

I waited for Lucy to say more, to talk about the clothes she designed, but she didn't.

I tightened my hold on her neck. "Lucy is the best tailor I've ever seen. She tailored this tux for me in a matter of hours just this afternoon. And she sews. She made the dress she's wearing tonight."

Lucy squirmed in her seat, and I wished I could scent her so I knew what she was feeling.

The woman next to Jacqueline—I think she'd introduced herself as Susan? Sarah?—leaned forward. "You sewed that dress? The lacework is incredible. Who's the designer?"

"She is," I said, taking pleasure in bragging about Lucy, especially if she wasn't going to do it herself. It was a foreign concept to me—I'd grown up in a home where accomplishments were prized above all else. How fucking bleak was it that everything I'd achieved in life was motivated by my desire to win my parents' attention and approval?

The three women fell into an easy conversation about their predictions for summer fashion trends. I didn't understand any of it, but I was perfectly content to play with Lucy's hair and study her side profile. There were plenty of designers in New York City. Caroline could easily arrange meetings so Lucy could talk with all of them to her heart's content.

My hand froze against the omega's shoulder and my skin flashed hot and cold with the realization that I was envisioning spending time with her beyond this night.

I pulled my arm away and focused on the untouched salad in front of me like the wilted lettuce was the most fascinating thing in the world.

My life was in New York City, and by the way Lucy had talked about Starlight Grove on our drive, it was obvious that she belonged there. I didn't know how much longer I was staying in town, but I definitely was not in a place to start a relationship, let alone form a lifelong bond with an omega I met a few hours ago.

If Lucy noticed me pulling further into myself, she didn't let on as she effortlessly guided the table conversation as each dinner course was served.

"Ladies and gentlemen," a deep voice boomed across the large room, jolting me out of my brooding. "We thank you so much for attending tonight to support pediatric cancer research. The event we've all been waiting for, our bachelor auction, starts in five minutes! Bachelors, please make your way backstage."

Fuck. I'd been so captivated by Lucy, I'd forgotten why we were here.

"You ready for your big moment?" She leaned toward me and our arms brushed.

I cocked an eyebrow. "As long as you are."

She flashed me a gorgeous smile and lifted her numbered paddle. "I was born ready. Just remember to do a little twirl for me when you're up there." She winked, and I had the urge to pull her over my lap and smack her ass with the paddle.

Great. Now I was going to go on stage with a hard-on.

I brushed my hand across her bare back, desperate to have her scent on me as I got up from the table. Her little smile told me my move hadn't been at all subtle.

I waited with a group of six other men—all alphas—in the wings of the stage as the auction started. I recognized a few of them through business dealings, but none of us really knew one another. I couldn't see Lucy from here. Was she okay? That asshole Jack wasn't bothering her, was he?

I was second to last. When the assistant gestured me forward, I stalked out onto the stage. The lights cast the audience in shadow, and I squinted as I tried to spot Lucy.

"Here is one of New York City's most eligible bachelors, businessman Sutton King. He might spend his days as CEO of Empire Enterprises, but he certainly didn't get that body just from sitting behind a desk."

I scowled. What the fuck? The auctioneer was an old guy in his seventies who spoke in a croaky monotone. Catcalls rang out in the room, and I thought I caught Lucy's voice in the mix.

"We will start the bidding at five thousand."

I forced myself to stand tall and not fidget, but I hated not being able to see who was bidding on me. What if someone beat Lucy? Not only would I have to spend the day with a stranger, I would miss out on spending time with her.

The bidding hit thirty thousand, but it wasn't slowing down. So far, the top bid for the other alphas was thirty-five thousand.

The bidding hit forty, and there was a pause as the auctioneer waited to see if there were any other bids.

"Going once. Going twice . . ."

Hurry the fuck up.

"And sold! To bidder three hundred and twenty."

A relieved rush of air escaped my lungs. That was Lucy's paddle number.

I jogged off the stage and wound my way through the room until I got to our table.

"I won you," she said, a twinkle in her eyes.

In one swift motion, I pulled her up from her chair. I didn't care who was watching as I wound my fingers through her hair, using the leverage to tilt her head back to meet my gaze.

Her breath caught. "You didn't twirl onstage. I'm sure you would have had more bids if they had seen that ass of yours."

My lips twitched for the briefest heartbeat before they crashed against hers. Her taste bloomed on my tongue. She was all sweetness with an edge of something more, something uniquely hers that reminded me of the feeling of running full speed down a hill. Like plunging into something terrifying and exhilarating.

I forced myself to pull away. Her pupils were blown, her cheeks a delicious bright pink. My lips ran down the side of her face until they were right against her ear. "You were such a good girl, winning me, but it's time to go."

She nodded quickly and I wrapped my arm around her shoulders, keeping her pinned to my side as we strode to the exit. Multiple alphas cast me jealous glares.

Yeah, fuckers. She's mine. You never stood a chance.

18

LUCY

King pulled me out of the event room, but apparently I wasn't moving fast enough in my heels because suddenly, I was in his arms. I let out a shriek mixed with laughter as we stepped into the Boston night.

I wrapped my arms around his neck as he carried me bridal-style down the street toward the hotel. It wasn't very far, and neither of us were interested in waiting for a car.

My mind spun as I tried to make sense of King's change in behavior. The reserved, grumpy businessman had transformed into someone hot and passionate. Was he just that thrilled that the auction was over? Or was this going where I thought it was going?

He pressed his face into my loose curls and breathed in deeply. *Yep, this is definitely going where I think it is.* I squirmed in his arms as anticipation rocketed through me, sensitizing my skin. I hadn't had sex since everything fell apart with my exes. After their betrayal, I'd felt disconnected from that part of myself, but my time with Wilder and Leo had awakened it again.

The fear of rejection still clawed at my chest, but I wanted King, *craved* the pleasure he could give me, and I was finally brave enough to risk being vulnerable to get what I wanted. I ran my nose down his throat. He smelled so good, like the brightest orange blossom breeze mixed with the velvet night sky.

"I would say I can walk, but I don't want to," I murmured against his neck.

His chest shook with laughter. "Glad to know you approve of me carrying you."

As we headed down the block to the hotel, a huge cheer erupted and the door to a somewhat dilapidated hole-in-the-wall Irish pub burst open. A group of people wearing sports jerseys streamed onto the street around us, shouting and signing. King's hold on me tightened, but my chest bubbled with excitement. I loved a good party.

"Look at these two! Already dressed for a celebration!" shouted a man who looked to be around King's age with dark brown hair and glasses framing bright green eyes. "Come celebrate Ireland's victory with us!"

I poked King's chest. "Oohhh, let's do it. We can get a drink."

King's pained expression made it seem like I was asking him to jump in a vat of boiling oil.

"Come *onnnnn*." I injected an omega whine into my tone and took a chance when I trailed my fingers along his firm jaw. I was desperate for him to take me back to the hotel room and ravish me, but the sooner we got back, the sooner this night would be over. I wanted to drag out my limited minutes with this alpha. "You need some fun in your life. Besides, I won you, so it should be up to me."

"You won me with my money," he said dryly.

"Your money?" I tugged his credit card out from where I'd stuck it down my dress. His eyes lingered on the swell of my breasts, sending a thrill of satisfaction through me. "Not sure what you're talking about. I'm pretty sure this is *my* credit card, and I want to treat my date to a beer."

He shook his head, but he couldn't hide his smile as he headed for the entrance. When he crossed the threshold, I raised my arms and shouted, "Go Ireland!" The crowd cheered.

"Do you even know what team they're talking about?" King asked. His lips were right by my ear, which was the only way I could hear him as folk music and laughter swirled around us. The malty sweetness of Guinness hung in the air.

I grinned. "I don't even know what sport."

King's chest shook with laughter. We squeezed through the crowd until we got to the bar. He gently set me down on one of the few open stools.

The bartender spotted us right away. "We've got some newcomers!" he said in a thick Irish accent. "Welcome to Finnegan's. What can I get the pretty lady?"

I couldn't hear King's growl over the crowd, but I certainly felt it as he banded his arms around me, pulling me flush and tight against his vibrating chest. My panties were soaked with slick, and I doubted my de-scenter would last long if he kept this up. I was on the edge of losing control. I wanted him to cup my breasts, lift my skirt, and thrust his thick fingers inside me before bending me over the bar top and taking me.

Get it together, Lucy. I wasn't even into public activities, but I'd also never been around an alpha like King . . . or Wilder. They made my exes look like pathetic little-boy alphas.

The bartender's smile widened as his eyes flicked over my head to King and then back to me.

"What do you recommend?" I asked.

"A sweet omega like you might like a Nutty Irishman. It's sweet and creamy." He winked and King snarled.

I snorted at the name. "Who wouldn't love a Nutty Irishman? I'll give it a try."

"And for you?" he asked King.

"Guinness."

The bartender made a gesture like he was tipping an imaginary hat and started working on our drinks.

I patted the stool beside me, but King stayed standing, spinning me so I was facing him. His arms bracketed my body as he loomed over me with his muscular chest, potent scent, and stern expression. It was a move that could have left me feeling trapped, but all I felt was excited pleasure.

He leaned even closer, skimming his lips along my nose and cheeks. I shuddered as his scent overwhelmed me. "You're having fun toying with me, aren't you, baby?"

"Maybe."

He chuckled, the sound going straight to my core. "Enjoy your fun, little omega, because your ass will pay for it tonight."

More slick drenched my underwear, and I needed to be careful or I would leave a wet spot on the chair.

King's nostrils flared and he let out a low groan as he ran his nose down the side of my neck. Someone cleared their throat loudly behind us, pulling us apart, but not before I felt his tongue against my skin.

King caught the drinks the bartender slid across the glossy wooden bar. I had no idea what was in mine, but it was topped with whipped cream so it had to be good. I took a sip and hummed happily at the perfect blend of hazelnut and Baileys.

I turned and gave the bartender a little wave of thanks, and King's large hand landed on my thigh, squeezing tight. This level of possessiveness was definitely a red flag, but I couldn't bring myself to care.

King took a long drink of his beer, maintaining eye contact with me the whole time. My cheeks flushed hot and I sipped my drink to keep myself from saying something inappropriate. The air between us was charged with anticipation. When it got to be too much, I blurted out, "Let's dance."

I didn't give him a chance to refuse, grabbing his hand and pulling him onto the small dance floor in the center of the bar.

"Brat. You're supposed to be staying off your ankle."

"You can hold me up."

His arm banded tight around my waist, supporting most of my weight as he effortlessly spun me around to the beat of the music. I'd taken dance classes as a little girl, but I'd been more focused on chatting with my friends and flipping through the costume magazines to learn anything. But King? He moved like he'd done this a thousand times. We quickly caught the attention of the others on the dance floor, and they cheered as they formed a ring around us. I felt like we were Jack and Rose on the *Titanic*, dancing in our too-fancy clothes and having the night of our lives.

"Who knew you were so talented?" I laughed as he spun me

around again, my feet skimming against the floor. He tightened his hold, and that's when I felt it—his hard cock pressed against my stomach. I buried my face in his neck and breathed him in, his scent deep with arousal. He cursed and moved his hands to my ass, cupping hard before lifting me off the ground. The slit in my dress allowed me enough movement to wrap my legs around him as he carried me off the dance floor to the hoots and shouts of the onlookers.

He headed to a dark corner of the bar, his huge hands palming my ass. "Have you had your fun, baby girl?"

I perfumed, and there was so much slick between my legs now I was worried it would drip down my thighs. "Not if that means there will be no more fun tonight."

His hand trailed up my front, his fingers brushing lightly over my breast before collaring my throat. "Oh, the fun's just getting started."

19

KING

The hotel elevator opened and I carried Lucy inside. The walk back from the bar was a blur, my alpha instincts making me almost feral with how much I needed her.

She threw her head back and laughed as I pressed her against the elevator wall, her legs cradling my hips.

"So eager," she teased, but her little gasp as I ground my cock against her sweet pussy told me she was just as desperate.

"This fucking dress." My hands tightened on her hips and I ran my nose down the side of her face, breathing her in. Thank *fuck* her scent had returned. I wanted to forbid her from wearing de-scenter again, but the thought of others smelling her made me murderous. Maybe I could just forbid her from ever leaving my bed again.

The idea had merit.

"King." My name in her mouth, all breathy and needy, was *everything*.

"Were you trying to drive me crazy tonight, baby? Because you succeeded." I crashed my lips against hers, our tongues tangling together in an explosion of sweetness.

The elevator doors slid open and I jogged down the hall to my suite. No, *her* suite. I stopped at the door, my chest heaving. Shit. I was pretty sure we were on the same page, but I had to be sure.

"Our night can end right here if you want. There's no pressure."

Her blue eyes sparkled. "Hmm . . ." She drummed her fingers against my shoulder, and I growled with impatience. "Well, you have been drinking. It would be irresponsible for you to drive home now."

I'd had half a beer. I wasn't even close to being drunk.

"You're so fucking right. Safety first."

She ran her fingers through my hair, and I leaned in to her touch. "Coming inside is the smart thing."

I ground my cock against her. "Oh, I *definitely* want to come inside."

She blushed beautifully. "That was terrible."

"Mmm, yes it was." I kept a firm arm around her as I fished the room key out of my pocket and opened the door.

We'd been in this room just a few short hours ago, but everything was different now as I sat Lucy down on the bed and dropped to my knees. My thumbs brushed her inner thighs and came away wet with her slick.

"You've made a mess of yourself, baby girl."

She tried to press her thighs together, but my firm grasp kept them apart. "No hiding what's mine. Are you going to be a good girl for me?"

She bit her lip. "What if I want to be a bad girl?"

A thrill of pleasure went straight to my cock. I ran my hands down her calves and undid the tiny buckles of her heels, growling at the reminder that she'd defied me by wearing them. "I don't mind a naughty omega. As long as she knows that I won't hesitate to punish her for disobeying."

Her fingers dug into my shoulders and her scent intensified. Even when I returned to my dull life and this night was a distant memory, I'd never be able to erase the feel of her skin against my fingertips, the taste of strawberries on my tongue.

"Do you like that, baby? Do you want to play tonight?"

She nodded and I grasped her chin. "Words. I need to hear you."

"Yes. Yes, I want that." Her pupils were dilated, and each heavy breath was drenched with desire.

Everything in me screamed at me to hurry the fuck up, but I needed to make sure she understood what I was asking.

"You want me to take control?" I pushed up the skirt of her dress, revealing a tiny lace thong. "To spank you?" My fingers dug in to her lush thighs. "To use my bark? To fucking *own* you for tonight?"

Her lips parted with a moan. "Yes, please."

"So polite, so sweet. What do you say if you want to stop?"

"Like a safe word?"

I nodded.

"Red," she whispered.

"Good girl."

She inhaled sharply as I pushed her knees apart, revealing inner thighs glistening with slick. A rumble rocked through my chest as instinct took over and I buried my face between her thighs, lapping up her sweetness. She fell back on the bed with a moan, her legs parting farther as her fingers twisted in my hair.

I was drunk on her taste, her scent, and I needed more. She protested when I pulled away, trying to claw me back between her thighs.

"I love how fucking desperate you are for me." I encircled her ankles with my hand and lifted her legs in the air. "But you need to understand who is in charge." I landed two smacks on her ass to test her reaction. The scent of her arousal bloomed in the room, so thick I was dizzy with it.

"You like that? Your alpha putting you in your place?"

She shook her head but still whined when I released my hold on her. I chuckled. "Don't worry. I'm sure you'll rack up plenty of punishments tonight."

I pulled her to standing and turned her around, kissing a line down her neck and back as I loosened her dress, exposing more and more of her skin until she was completely naked besides her tiny lace thong.

"Lie down. I want to see you spread out before me."

I grabbed my cock through my pants, squeezing the tip to keep myself from coming as she crawled to the center of the mattress and rolled over, giving me a mouthwatering look at her bare breasts for the first time.

"I want to see you," she said as she cupped her breasts. "Take your clothes off."

I almost caved right then, but I managed to slowly shake my head as I pulled my jacket and bow tie off, keeping my other clothes on as I crawled over her.

"I thought we just went over who's in charge here." I gripped her chin hard, and her eyes flared with defiance and pleasure. She parted her lips, but I tightened my hold on her. "The only words I want to hear from you are *yes, sir.*"

Her inner struggle played out across her face as she wrestled with her instincts to submit with her desire to fight and assert herself. I saw the moment she made her decision.

"Yes, sir."

A deep purr vibrated in my chest, and I cradled her jaw as I pressed a hard kiss to her lips. "What a good girl." I pinned her hands above her head. "Keep them there unless you want me to stop."

Her lower lip jutted out into a pout. I wished I could say it had no effect on me, but fuck, my alpha wanted to spoil this omega. But even more, I needed to test her obedience, to make sure she actually wanted this before we fell deeper into the scene.

Her hands stayed exactly where I'd put them when I released her wrists. "That's it. Just keep them there and you'll get rewarded."

"Yes, please, sir."

My chest rumbled with satisfaction and I pressed my body against hers. "So fucking sweet." I punctuated each word with a kiss. I could stay here forever, tasting her, running my hands down her velvet skin, but I had so much more to explore and only one night to do it.

I worked my lips down her jaw and neck, lightly sucking on the curve of her shoulders and chest until I reached her breasts. They were heavy and pink-tipped, perfectly soft in my cupped hands.

"So fucking pretty."

I wrapped my lips around her nipple, sucking and swirling my tongue around the sensitive bud. When I bit down, Lucy let out a loud cry and her hands flew to my hair, holding me to her chest.

I released her nipple and cocked an eyebrow. "Where are your hands supposed to be?"

A Pack for Spring

Her eyes widened in realization and she quickly moved them back. "Sorry. Please don't stop."

I stared down at her, slowly drawing out my response to increase her anticipation.

"This is your one warning. Next time, I won't hesitate to punish you."

A flash of emotion crossed her face, something suspiciously like disappointment, and I held in my smile. Oh yeah, she was desperate for it.

I moved to her other nipple, taking it into my mouth and biting down harder than I had before. She cried out again, but this time she kept her hands where they belonged.

"Such a good girl," I murmured against her skin.

I was moving faster now as my control slipped. I pulled off her thong in one swift motion, leaving her completely bare before me. Her pussy was so fucking pretty—pink and puffy with arousal and adorned with a triangle of golden hair. She shuddered as I parted it with my fingers. Slick dripped from her entrance, and I was utterly lost in her perfection. I buried my face in her cunt, licking and sucking, drawing out her moans. Her slick tasted like fucking strawberries but also something even more complex—sweet and wild and all *her*.

I thrust two fingers inside her and her pussy fluttered, gripping them so tightly I moaned against her clit, imagining what she would feel like squeezing my cock.

I kept thrusting my fingers and working my tongue against her clit, overwhelmed by the primal need to make my omega come.

"King, I need—" Her plea was cut off by a scream as her orgasm crashed over her with shaking legs and a burst of slick. I licked and sucked, wringing every bit of pleasure from her before getting up.

Her dazed eyes met mine. "So fucking beautiful." I kept my eyes fixed on her as I slowly stripped off my clothes, my lips twitching as hers parted.

"Wow." She pushed up on her elbows, and her gaze lingered on my aching cock. I swore it fucking twitched under her attention. "Can I touch, sir?"

I steadied myself with a deep breath. Control. I needed it, craved it.

"You asked so prettily, but no, baby. You will take only what I give you."

I crawled over her, running my hands up her body until I collared her throat. Her eyes flared and I lightly squeezed the sides of her neck. I would *never* hurt her, but I savored her gasps and whimpers.

I ran the tip of my cock through her slick before pressing against her entrance, but instead of pushing in, I just held it there.

"Look at you, whining and making a mess of the sheets."

I was fucking dying to sink inside her, but seeing her squirm beneath me made the torture worth it.

"Please," she gasped.

I leaned over her, placing my lips close to her ear. "Beg for it."

She let out a sob and arched her hips, causing me to slip an inch inside her. A snarl tore through me and I pulled out completely before rolling her over and delivering several hard smacks to her ass.

"Who is in charge?"

"You."

"Are you sure about that? Because it seemed like you were trying to take control."

"I'm sure. Please. I'm sorry."

I drew back from her and she whimpered.

"Prove it. Present."

She hesitated before slowly pushing up to her knees. She glanced back at me, looking slightly unsure as she dropped her chest to the bed, leaving her ass in the air, presented perfectly for me. I ran my hand over her pale skin, although it wouldn't stay that way for long.

I leaned down over the bed so I could check in. Her eyes were brimming with tears, but they were tears of desperation and need, not of fear, and her scent was heady with arousal.

I stroked my hand down her hair. "You will take your punishment without complaining and without moving. If you can be a good girl for me, I will give you pleasure. If not . . ." I let my threat hang in the air.

"I'll be good. I promise."

I pressed a gentle kiss to her forehead. "Remember to say your safe word if you need it, baby. This is about you letting go, surrendering control, because it's what you need. But let me know if it gets to be too much."

She grasped my wrist. "Do you need it, too?" She bit her lip, her tone more vulnerable than I'd ever heard it.

"Yes, beautiful. I need this, too."

She let out a sigh of relief. "Good." Her lips curved into a smile, and I quickly captured it in a kiss.

"So fucking sweet. Now we have a punishment to deal with, naughty girl."

I stood behind her and delivered a hard smack to her ass without warning. She almost moved out of position, but her tight grip on the comforter kept her anchored.

I let out a dark laugh. "That was close, but you saved it."

My hand landed sharply on her other ass cheek, but she kept her position beautifully. I sank into the rhythm of the spanking, savoring her cries that turned to moans of pleasure. Her ass turned pink and heated under my palm, so I moved my strikes down to that tender sit spot at the top of her thighs. She clutched at the bedding, but she kept her ass presented to me, surrendering to the punishment.

I lost count of how many spanks I'd given her when she let a broken sob escape.

I immediately stopped and ran soothing hands over her skin. "Good girl, you did so well for me." I gently shifted her and gathered her to me as my chest rumbled with a loud purr. She curled her body around me, clinging to me for comfort as she came down from her endorphin high.

"Shh," I murmured, gently stroking her hair and running my hand down her back. "You're so fucking perfect."

She was boneless in my arms as I kissed the tears from her cheeks.

It had been a long time since I'd engaged in a scene like this—not since my days of being a member of a sex club owned by an alpha friend of mine from college. Throughout the years, my work days had stretched longer and longer until the job I quietly hated consumed my life, leaving no room for anything else.

But even back then, I'd never been this drawn to a scene partner.

"Have you learned your lesson, baby girl?"

She sniffed and nodded. "Yes, Daddy."

My heart stuttered to a stop as a riot of emotions rocked through me—confusion, pleasure, and deep satisfaction. Was she even aware of what she'd said? And why the fuck did I like it so much?

In one swift movement, I rolled us so she was beneath me, her hips spread wide around my body. This time, I didn't hesitate. I pushed inside her in one swift motion, and we both cried out at her tightness.

"Oh," she gasped. "It's too much. I can't—" Her words cut off with a moan as I rocked in farther. I was halfway inside her, my jaw clenched with the effort of not coming.

I brushed the hair out of her face. "Be a good girl for Daddy." I'd never said that before, but it felt so fucking right with Lucy. "You can take it. Just relax and let me in."

Her forehead softened. I pushed in farther, groaning at how obscenely she stretched around me. My knot was already swollen, straining to lock inside her tight little omega pussy.

"I'm going to fuck your pussy raw until you think you can't take one more orgasm, and that's when you're going to come again, but this time on my knot." I guided her trembling hand to where we were joined, wrapping her fingers around my knot. "It's barely half the size it will be when it locks inside you."

Her lips were parted, her chest heaving. Her grip tightened. "I want it."

"You want what, baby girl?" I skimmed my nose across her collarbone. When she let out a shriek of frustration, I pressed my smile to her skin. "Use your words." I injected my tone with an edge of alpha bark, compelling her omega to respond.

"I want your knot, Daddy. Please." Tears streamed down her face, and I couldn't deny her any longer. I pulled out before thrusting inside her so hard she moved up the mattress. I showed her no mercy as I kept going, no space to breathe or adjust to the sensations. All she needed to do was *feel*.

Her fingers dug into my arms, her nails leaving little crescent marks on my skin as she came again with a scream. I snarled in satisfaction as she rhythmically squeezed my cock. I wanted her to mark me, to imprint herself on my soul.

I lifted her leg toward her chest, opening her up wider as I continued thrusting in and out.

"Daddy," she whined.

"Shh, baby girl. I know you're sensitive, but I need another orgasm from you."

She shook her head, her eyes squeezed shut, her cheeks flushed red. I slapped her thigh, causing her to tighten around me even more.

"That's it. You can do it. Give me one more." I unleashed my full alpha bark. "Come for me."

We came together, my orgasm so fucking intense I almost blacked out. My knot pushed inside her, swelling to its full size and setting off another wave of pleasure for us both. Little whimpers escaped her lips, and I pressed kisses to her nose, cheeks, and forehead.

Once I came back down to reality, I curled my arms around her and rolled us so she was sprawled on top of me, still secured tightly by my knot.

"How are you feeling, baby?"

I waited, heart pounding, for her response.

"So good." Her words were slurred, her eyes shut, and her breathing slow. She was drunk on endorphins and utterly relaxed, which soothed the tendrils of anxiety in my chest that our scene had been too intense. I barely knew anything about Lucy, and certainly nothing about her sexual experience. But she'd taken it all in stride, showing no fear or anxiety.

"You were perfect," I murmured. "So damn perfect."

I ran my fingers through her hair and she let out a soft purr. I froze. I'd never heard an omega purr, let alone purr for *me*. She tightened her hold, wrapping her arms and legs around my body.

So fucking cute.

I resumed petting her hair, a responding purr rumbling through my chest before I drifted off.

20

LUCY

When I drifted back to consciousness, my teeth were chattering. I whimpered, confused and disoriented, when arms tightened around me.

"You awake, baby girl?"

King.

My lips parted with a shuddering breath, and I blinked my eyes open to take in an expanse of tan skin. I was draped over the alpha's chest, and when I shifted, I realized we were still locked together. My ass was tender, my muscles sore, my pussy practically split open on his knot, and I was confident I'd never felt pleasure that even remotely compared to what we'd just done.

His fingers ran through my messy hair, and I leaned in to his touch. "How are you?" His voice was low and soothing.

"Good."

Or at least, I *should* be good. Having sex with King one time had opened my eyes to a world I never believed existed. His dominance, his growls, the pleasure he gave me . . . I felt transformed. It had been the type of sex I'd dreamed of, that I'd read about in romance books, that I'd craved but never experienced. Sex with my exes had been lackluster, and I'd eventually just resigned myself to believing that's all there was to it.

Thank god King had proved me wrong. He had been stern and dominant . . . while also being gentle and attentive. Everything had been perfect, so why did I feel like I was about to crawl out of my skin?

He wrapped a soft blanket around me before slowly sitting up, keeping me firmly on his lap. He peered at me. "Are you feeling a little out of sorts, princess?"

My omega preened at the term of endearment, but the unsettled feeling in my chest persisted.

"I don't know why." My voice was hoarse, and King immediately grabbed a bottle of water from the nightstand. He held it to my lips and I didn't protest as I gulped it down—my arms were limp noodles.

"Have you ever done a scene like that before?"

Scene. I recognized the word from the BDSM romance books I'd read.

I shook my head.

He set the water bottle aside and drew me closer until my head rested against his chest. "That was probably too intense for a beginner," he murmured. "I'm sorry."

I frowned. I didn't want him to apologize. "But I wanted it. I liked it." *Let's do it again.*

I didn't say that part out loud. King hadn't promised me anything, and he was only in Starlight Grove temporarily. But my clingy omega was already dreaming of repeating our scene, this time in my nest so his scent would saturate everything.

"Sometimes after a scene, you can have what's called a sub drop. It can leave you feeling a bit shaky and vulnerable." He rubbed his cheek against the top of my head, scent-marking me. "Which is why I'm going to take care of you until you feel steady. Starting with a bath."

You need to take care of yourself, Lucy. Being an omega is no excuse for being dependent on us.

My exes' voices floated through my head, but I batted them aside. Fuck them. If I only had King for tonight, I wasn't going to refuse his care. I tightened my arms and legs around him as he stood, crying out as the movement shifted his knot inside me. Sparks of pleasure mixed with the stinging pain of my heated butt, and I was already on the verge of coming again.

He palmed my sore ass as he carried me into the bathroom.

"Ouch." I scowled and jutted out my lip, but he just chuckled.

"You earned that heated ass, baby. But don't worry, I'll rub some cream on it. In fact"—his nose skimmed my cheek—"you don't need to worry about anything right now. I've got you."

And I knew he did.

He turned on the bathroom light and I squinted against the brightness, but he immediately dimmed it. He carried me around effortlessly as he readied the bath. Once the tub was half full, he surprised me by getting in with me. His knot had loosened enough to move me off of him, but as he settled me in his lap, facing him, he seemed to be in no rush.

The heated water stung my spanked skin, but the pain quickly faded. I settled against him, staying in a sleepy fog as he massaged shampoo into my hair and ran body wash over my skin with firm hands.

"I could stay inside you forever." He sighed loudly. "But I guess I can't do that."

My lips quirked at how put out he sounded.

He slid out of me in a rush of cum. My omega snarled with displeasure, but King's movements were steady as he got me out of the bath, dried me off, and wrapped a soft robe around me.

He led me back to bed. "Lie on your stomach."

My pussy clenched and another burst of cum leaked out of me. I was tired and sore and still seconds away from bending over and begging him to take me again.

I stuck with lying down on the bed. The click of a bottle cap preceded cool lotion against my skin. I groaned as he gently rubbed it in, soothing the pain.

When he was done, he stretched out beside me. "How're you doing now?"

I smiled softly. "Better."

He drew me to his side, and the heat of his bare skin lulled me into a sleepy haze.

At least, until I jolted with awareness and rolled away from King.

"What's wrong?" he asked, sitting up and looking around the room.

"Did I . . ." I trailed off, my cheeks on fire. "Oh my god. Did I call you *Daddy*?" My endorphin-induced haze had conveniently made me forget that small detail, but my conscious brain definitely remembered.

King's lips twitched. "Yes, you did."

I pressed my face to the mattress. "Let's forget this ever happened. Sound good? Okay, great." I could only imagine the horror on my exes' faces if I ever made a slip like that.

King's deep, rich laugh filled the room, and he manhandled me back to his chest.

"I fucking liked it, baby girl. Now, be a good girl for Daddy and tell me what you want from room service."

"No amount of joint compound will hide that shitty drywall work. Whoever hung it must have been on their first day on the job. Or a kindergartener."

I snorted at King's track of scathing commentary. Who knew that the trick to getting the grumpy alpha talking was to put on a home improvement show?

"I thought your company did investment . . . *things*. Do you build the homes, too?"

"I should have you write our website copy." He chuckled. "We occasionally do some real estate investment, but it's mostly other investment *things*. I spent three summers framing new homes when I was younger, though."

I traced my fingers down his bare, muscular chest. He'd put his boxers on to get the room service, but he couldn't get more dressed than that when all he had with him was his tux. Which suited me just fine. Getting to take in his body with my greedy eyes made it easy to imagine him on a construction site, droplets of sweat dripping off his skin.

A Pack for Spring

My mind flashed to another hard-working, muscular alpha, and I swallowed hard. I'd done my best to push Wilder from my mind. I hadn't heard anything from him after I dropped off the cookies. It was fine. Totally fine. He'd already given me so much, it wasn't like he owed me any sort of thank-you or acknowledgment.

I just wished I could make my chest stop aching every time I thought of him.

"When was that?" I leaned over King and stole a fry from his almost-empty plate. He'd ordered way too much food, including my own side of fries, but food always tasted better when it was stolen off someone else's plate.

"That was after college."

"You didn't start working at your parents' company right away?" I'd asked him about his childhood and family during our drive down here, but he'd clearly been reticent to answer so I'd backed off. I wanted to know more about this alpha, to make sense of him.

He twirled a strand of my hair around his finger and tugged, sending a slight spark of pain through me.

"After college, I got a job advocating for ocean conservation. The pay was shit, so I took on part-time work with a building crew to keep myself afloat. I'd never done anything like that before, but they hired me on the spot since I'm an alpha. I spent that first year just carrying heavy boards for the guys until I proved myself and they taught me how to frame out a house."

"You did ocean conversation? That's so cool. I went through a marine biologist phase as a girl."

"I can see it now, sweet little omega standing on a boat as she charms all the animals in the entire fucking ocean."

I shook my head. "Not sure about that. That's more my friend Olive. She's the lighthouse keeper, and she grew up lobster fishing with her parents."

Shoot. Thinking of Olive reminded me that I should probably send my friends a sign of life, but I had no idea where my phone was and was way too comfortable to get up and find it. So I just cuddled into King, enjoying the weight of his arm around me as he complained about substandard tiling jobs.

"Do you miss ocean conservation?" I asked at the commercial break.

A little crease appeared between his eyebrows. "I'm not sure anyone's ever asked me that."

It was my turn to frown. "Why not?"

He shrugged. "I guess everyone assumed that I would work at the family company. The part they didn't understand was why I wasted my time doing nonprofit work instead of starting at the company right away."

"Doing what you're passionate about isn't a waste."

He kissed the top of my head.

"What made you leave your conservation job?"

Even though we barely knew each other, I caught the subtle tick in his jaw and tense set of his shoulders.

"My parents—mom and two dads, all alphas—started having health issues and couldn't run the company anymore." I hated the lost, far-off look in his eyes. "My brother was supposed to take over for them."

I wrapped my arms around his torso, my face pressed in the crook of his neck. "I didn't know you had a brother."

"I don't."

My throat tightened.

"He died on his tenth birthday. He spent most of my life in the hospital for cancer treatments while I was left at home with nannies."

Lars might have been annoying growing up, but the thought of losing him wrecked me. "I'm so sorry." My hoarse words were wholly inadequate.

His fingers ran through my hair. "I can't really miss him when I never knew him, but I miss the idea of having a brother. My parents were left with me, a four-year-old they didn't want."

I breathed in sharply. "What?"

"I was an accident, and they resented me for pulling their attention away from Saint—the son they actually wanted. Even worse, I had the audacity to not die from cancer. Unsurprisingly, I was never close with my parents, but when they had to step down from the company, I thought becoming CEO might be what finally made them proud of me."

He shrugged like it didn't matter.

We both knew how much it did.

"They're all gone now, anyway. Died within a few days of each other."

I moved slowly, like I was approaching a wounded animal, straddling his lap and curling myself around him as if my arms were strong enough to take his pain.

"They're the ones who missed out," I said. "They were too lost in their grief to see you. They should have done better. You deserve better."

His eyes squeezed shut and I worried I'd upset him until his arms tightened around me. I wanted to say more—how sorry I was that he gave up his passion to win the approval of parents who didn't deserve him—but I wouldn't be able to hide the rage I felt toward them, so I just pressed my lips to his throat.

We stayed like that until our slow breaths synched. His muscles eased. My eyelids grew heavy. As I drifted off, the huge alpha wrapped around me, I wondered what it would be like for all of us to live the lives we wanted, not the one we thought we should have.

21

LEO

9:45 A.M.
LEO

I should have asked what time I should come over.
I've gathered you're not a morning person

9:53 A.M.
LEO

Any requests for your latte?
Or should I ask Ella to surprise you?

Never mind, Ella said she knows
what you want better than you do

10:16 A.M.
LEO

You awake yet, sleepyhead?

10:24 A.M.
LEO

Char said blueberry pancakes
are your favorite, but I got some other
options in case you're not in the mood
for them this morning

>   10:36 A.M.
>   LEO
>
>   I'm at your front door
>
>   10:48 A.M.
>   LEO
>
>   You ok? I'm getting a little
>   worried

The ice in the two lattes had completely melted and the food was cold when I brought them into my shop and set them on the counter next to the bottle of latte syrup I'd convinced Ella to sell me yesterday. Lucy's shop listed its opening time as nine a.m., but I'd never seen her open right at nine. She usually ran ten to twenty minutes late . . . sometimes closer to an hour. But it was two hours past opening and she was nowhere to be found.

I hesitated, trying to decide what to do next. Maybe one of her friends had heard from her? Ivy would be at school, which left Summer or Olive. I decided to start with Summer, since her bakery was closer. If she wasn't there, I'd go to the lighthouse.

I grabbed my cane and crossed Main Street, heading down the block until I reached Suns Out Bánhs Out. I peered through the window and let out a sigh of relief when I spotted Summer. She was having an animated discussion with—I shifted to the side to see better—*Felix*. Well, it wasn't like I could judge. I'd had way too many one-sided conversations with the town mayor.

I knocked on the glass door and Summer waved me inside.

"Hey, Leo! Perfect timing. We need you to settle a debate."

"We?"

Summer gestured between her and Felix.

I cleared my throat. "Right."

"Felix thinks we should paint the inside of the store orange to match his fur, but I think we should lean more yellow to match the awning."

I glanced down at Felix and took a tiny step back at his expression. The phrase *if looks could kill* danced through my mind.

"Uhh." What do I do? *What do I do???* Yellow would fit the overall theme better, but I didn't want to give Felix a reason to suffocate me in my sleep, especially since he somehow possessed the ability to walk through walls. At least, I was pretty sure that was the most logical explanation for the other day when I'd walked into my bedroom and found him curled up on my pillow.

"I don't really know anything about paint," I said noncommittally. "I'm sorry for interrupting this, uhh, business meeting. I just wanted to see if you've heard from Lucy this morning."

"I actually haven't. I sent her a text earlier, but she didn't answer. I know she made it to Boston okay, though, so I assume she's just doing her errands before heading back. She always forgets to charge her phone."

"Boston?"

Summer cocked her head. "Yeah. It was a last-minute trip. Why? Do you need her?"

Yes. Desperately.

"No. I was just going to take a look at her ankle wrap and was worried when she wasn't in her shop." I tripped over a small stack of boxes on my way to the door. I blurted out an apology and gave Summer and Felix an awkward wave as I left.

Lucy was okay. That was all that mattered.

She'd had to go to Boston last minute and just forgot about our date. It was just a miscommunication, not her rejecting me because I was a beta or used a cane.

Unless . . .

Had she changed her mind because my suggestion for a date was coffee and wrapping her ankle? It had seemed like a brilliant plan to ease Lucy into dating, but I should have gone all-out.

It was fine. I would track her down once she got home and check in, and I wouldn't be all pathetic about being stood up.

I headed back inside my shop, slamming the door closed behind me.

22

LUCY

King pulled up to my shop and I was smacked in the face with déjà vu of being in exactly this spot a few days ago with Wilder.

I'd woken up in King's arms. We'd had slow morning sex and room service pancakes before heading to Boston's fabric district. I'd expected the alpha to be impatient as I dug through bins of fabric, but he didn't complain or roll his eyes once. Whenever I found a hidden gem, he held out his arm so he could carry it for me.

Shopping always put me in a good mood, but it had never felt like *this*, like I was practically walking on air. I'd fantasized about this for so long—being spoiled and cherished by an alpha even while doing something mundane.

It was only after shopping that things started going downhill. We grabbed lunch in Chinatown, but King was on his phone the whole time. I brushed it off as him being busy with work, but things did not improve when we got back in the car. He responded to my attempts to start a conversation with terse answers until I finally gave up. We sat in silence, the sick feeling in my chest growing with every mile.

Did he regret what we did? After how vulnerable he'd been last night, sharing about his family, I'd deluded myself into thinking he might want more from me than just sex.

He put the car in park.

"I had a good time, Lucy."

Lucy. No longer baby or princess.

I nodded. "Me, too."

Here it came.

A Pack for Spring

"I'm not sure how much longer I'll be in town, and I'll be busy with this real estate sale..."

He trailed off and I swallowed the hard lump in my throat at the obvious rejection. This was fine. I could be a cool, casual omega. New year, new me and all that. Maybe twenty-nine would be the year of attachment-free hot sex. Wasn't that what your twenties were for, anyway?

I pasted on a smile. "I'm glad we met and that I could help you with the event." I pulled the door handle. "Maybe I'll see you around before you go." *Oh god, did that sound desperate?* "You know, because it's a small town," I added quickly. "Thanks for helping with my fabric errands." I pushed the car door open.

To my dismay, King got out and popped the trunk. Duh. My bags. I went to take them, but he scowled. "I've got them."

I held my front door open, and he set the armload of bags inside. I'd just had the best fucking sex of my life. I should be orgasm-drunk and happy, but I was on the verge of tears. How did other people do one-night stands?

Not everyone gets as attached and needy as you do.

Right. That.

He hesitated and my chest filled with a burst of hope. Had he changed his mind? My cheeks heated when I realized no, I was just *blocking the exit*.

I scooted aside with an awkward laugh. "Give me a call if you need me to bid at another auction."

Unlikely. Mainly because I realized we hadn't exchanged numbers, but also because I was sure women were constantly throwing themselves at him in New York.

His eyebrows knitted together. "Lucy..."

"Oh, wait. Do you have my phone?" I'd given it to him before the gala and had completely forgotten about it.

"Shit. It must be in one of the tux pockets."

Our first stop of the day had been to purchase him an outfit at the hotel gift shop, which meant he was currently a walking advertisement for the Boston Red Sox between the branded sweatpants, sweatshirt, and baseball cap.

He'd grumbled about the outfit until I'd told him he looked hot.

I followed him outside as he grabbed the garment bag. Luckily, Main Street was uncharacteristically empty, so I didn't have an audience for my heartbreak.

King fished my phone out from the inside pocket of the tux jacket. "Sorry about that."

My phone was dead, which was not shocking since my battery lasted for all of five minutes. I was sure I had a flood of messages in the group chat demanding updates, not that I had any to give besides:

Lucy: 0

Heartbreak: 2

He returned the garment bag to the trunk.

"If you want to wear the tux again, I could do a more thorough tailoring job. Although, I'm sure you have lots of custom tuxes in New York. And tailors. I could always mail it to you if you don't want to come back here." *Oh my god. Where's an anvil falling from the sky when you need one? Did anvils even exist anymore?*

"Oh, uh, I'll let you know about the tux."

I nodded too vigorously. "Yes, good idea. Well, drive safe. You know, the three blocks to your rental."

"Are you okay?" His voice carried the same tenderness it had when he was inside me this morning, and I couldn't handle that.

"Me? I'm fine! I hope you have a good rest of your evening."

He opened his mouth for a moment but then snapped it shut. He ran his hand through his hair as he looked away.

"You, too, Lucy. Take care of yourself."

I closed my front door so I couldn't pathetically watch him drive away. I trudged upstairs to my apartment, leaving my shopping bags strewn on the shop floor. My ankle was mostly better, besides the occasional twinge, especially after King insisted I elevate and ice it last night and this morning.

A Pack for Spring

I flopped down in my nest and plugged in my phone. It was almost eight p.m. and I needed to get something to eat and catch up on my emails, but all I really wanted was to rot in bed and nurse my tender heart. How was it possible that I hadn't dated anyone for over a year and now, in the span of a few days, I'd gotten overly attached and then subsequently rejected by two alphas?

My phone screen flickered on and I unlocked it to find a barrage of messages and a calendar alert for tonight's town meeting.

I groaned. I attended all the town meetings, but maybe it'd be okay to skip this one...

A sick feeling gripped my chest as I opened my messages.

Oh no.

OH NO.

I sat up, heart pounding, as I read text after text from Leo. How could I have forgotten our date? He'd gotten coffee and breakfast for us, and I had stood him up. I was the worst person in the world.

I clutched my phone and ran downstairs. My chest was heaving by the time I got to Leo's door. The inside of his shop was dark, but I knocked anyway. I called his cell, but there was silence after just one ring. Had he screened my call? I pulled back my phone and realized it had died again. Apparently, charging for all of thirty seconds wasn't enough.

Was Leo upstairs? Or maybe he'd gone out for dinner? I looked up and down Main Street, but most of the shops were dark. They closed early on town meeting nights...

Wait. The town meeting.

Leo usually attended them.

I took off, sprinting down the street as fast as I could.

23

LUCY

My shoes slapped against the sidewalk as town hall came into view. One of my life goals was to never run—I was more of a strolling omega—but the large clock on the building told me I was late. So not only was I the worst person ever, I was also going to be treated to a Stanley lecture. The last time I was late to a town meeting, he'd spent ten torturous minutes lecturing me about the importance of punctuality. In front of everyone.

My breaths were ragged as I ran up the town hall steps, through the front door, and down the corridor to the meeting room. I braced my hands on my knees to catch my breath. I needed to navigate this next part carefully so Stanley didn't notice my entrance.

I cracked the heavy door open just a smidge and it let out a loud screech. *Nooo.* This was going to give me away. *Tomorrow I'm breaking in and spraying WD-40 on these hinges.*

Okay. New plan.

I dropped to the floor on my stomach and slowly pushed the door open until there was enough space for me to squeeze through. I inched forward slowly, fully aware of how absolutely ridiculous this whole situation was. Any pride I possibly had was left on the dingy carpet.

Even if people noticed that the door was open, they wouldn't be able to see me. That was, unless they were the hot beta sitting in the otherwise empty back row. Staring straight at me.

The moment I was clear of the door, I crawled to the last row of seats and popped up to take the chair next to Leo, whose mouth was hanging open.

"What the hell—"

"Lucy Andersson-Spring!" Stanley's exclamation cut Leo off.

No, no, no. That can't all have been for nothing.

"Yes, Stanley?" I batted my eyes and smiled innocently.

"The meeting started eleven minutes ago. I cannot believe you'd choose to be late. *Again*."

My lips parted with a sharp gasp and my hand flew to my chest. "After your compelling speech about punctuality? Never. I've been here since the meeting started."

Stanley pursed his lips. "I didn't see you."

"She came in with me," Leo said.

My heart squeezed. He was defending me? Did that mean he didn't hate me?

"What?" Stanley spluttered.

"Lucy and I were talking before the meeting." Carmen smiled mischievously from her seat on the stage beside Stanley and gave me a wink.

"Can we get back to the topic at hand?" Hank, the grouchy bookstore owner, grumbled.

Stanley shot me one more narrow-eyed gaze before jumping back into the meeting agenda.

I let out a long sigh and slumped in my seat. "Thank you." The only threat Stanley posed to me was the ability to bore me to death, but my omega still preened at Leo's protectiveness. She wanted to curl up in his lap and rub her scent all over him. But first, I had to apologize.

"You're welcome," he said, lips quirking into a smile that made me lose track of all my thoughts. "Your entrance makes a lot more sense now."

I swallowed hard and grabbed his hand. "Leo, I am so sorry about this morning. My phone died and I just got back and plugged it in and saw your messages. I totally forgot about our date. I don't expect you to forgive me or give me a second chance, but I just need you to know how incredibly sorry I am."

He blinked, looking somewhat dazed. Then he did something

that made my world flip on its axis. He entwined his fingers with mine and squeezed. "It's okay." He ruffled his messy curls with his other hand. "I thought maybe you changed your mind because my date idea wasn't very good."

I swallowed hard. "Never. Lattes and pancakes make the perfect date." His easy forgiveness was disorienting. Shouldn't he make me work for it? Instead, he settled back in his seat, keeping my hand firmly in his.

"What did I miss?" I leaned into his shoulder.

"It was a solid five minutes of Stanley arguing with Carmen about the rules of order for the meeting. Then Felix popped in, stole his gavel, and ran off. So nothing much, really."

I grinned. I loved this crazy town and how easily Leo had fallen into step with all of us.

"People, pay attention!" Stanley shouted. He resorted to banging his fist on the podium since he was gavel-less. "Last year, Briar's Landing hid ten thousand Easter eggs in comparison to our measly nine thousand. This year, we've set an ambitious goal, but I trust we will all rise to the occasion!" He raised both arms in the air in victory.

"How many eggs do you want to hide?" Carmen asked with a dramatic sweep of her bright pink kaftan. "Last year almost ended in disaster."

"That will *not* be happening again. Easton has a lifetime ban on attendance." Stanley glared at the alpha, who had one arm slung around Olive's shoulders, an easy smile on his face.

"Just try and stop me," Easton said. "I will be the egg hunt champion once more!"

Stanley's face was turning red. "Town ordinance thirty-seven point nine states that the mayor of Starlight Grove has the power to ban any town citizens from official town gatherings if they pose a threat."

"Last I checked, Felix hadn't banned me from any festivals," Easton said smugly.

Stanley's face turned redder at the reminder of who we thought of as the true mayor. "I will not hesitate to unleash the full power of the law on you! Tread carefully, or you'll find yourself in jail."

"We don't have any cops," Marisol shouted from her seat. "Or a jail." Tittering laughter broke out across the room, and it took Stanley a few minutes to regain control.

"People, we need to be united. Do you want Briar's Landing to defeat us?" This had a sobering effect. Starlight Grove town pride ran high when it came to our festivals.

I nudged Leo. "I hope you didn't move here to be a secret undercover operative with the express purpose of sabotaging our Easter Eggstravaganza."

"You mean did I come to Starlight Grove months ago, rent a building, set up my apartment, and start a whole flower business for the express purpose of undermining the Easter egg hunt?" He leaned in close, hypnotizing me with his warm brown eyes and dark lashes. I swayed closer, drawn in by his sweet scent swirling around me. "You caught me. But now that you know my secret, what will I do with you?"

Arousal shot through me, and I bit my tongue to hold in a whimper. I wanted to kiss him, crawl into his lap, strip down, and...

I broke eye contact and scooted away before I did something embarrassing. Leo was *potent*.

His low chuckle made my cheeks heat, but my embarrassment transformed into satisfaction when he shifted in his seat, adjusting the bulge in his pants.

"How many eggs are you proposing?" Carmen asked again.

Stanley walked over to a poster board on an easel covered by a faded floral bedsheet. "This is the plan!" He whipped the sheet off and the poster fell flat to the ground.

"Stanley is not having a good night," I said out of the side of my mouth.

Leo squeezed my hand. "I would be more sympathetic, but last week he came into the flower shop and made me show him every single variety of flower I had in stock to prove I wasn't running a black market exotic flower ring."

"Well, are you?"

"Oh yeah. But my illegal exotic flowers are under a secret trapdoor in the back."

Could he be any cuter?

"You better stay on my good side now that you've given me the power to destroy you," I said.

"I'm pretty sure you've always had that power."

What did that mean?

Now it was his turn to break eye contact, fixing his attention on Stanley, who managed to put the poster back on the easel with a shouted "Ta-da." I scrunched my nose as I read the poster's title: *Starlight Grove's Path to Egg Hunt Domination*.

"Twenty thousand eggs?" Carmen exclaimed. "Stanley, be reasonable."

"You cannot be *reasonable* and expect to win," he shot back.

"Why is your poster written in Comic Sans?" Summer called out.

I stood up slightly and spotted her and Ivy in the row in front of Olive and her guys. I waved and Summer turned, immediately scowling as she held up her phone, pointed at me, and dragged her finger across her throat.

I blew her a kiss.

A loud argument broke out about proper font usage for official town posters.

Leo leaned in. "Maple Glen's town meetings were never this entertaining."

"Honestly, this is pretty tame. He hasn't even insulted Briar's Landing's mayor—"

"We will not fail! We will not stumble! We will once and for all defeat Claude Fumble and prove that Starlight Grove reigns supreme!"

"There it is," I said dryly, and Leo snorted.

"Who is Claude Fumble?"

"It's actually pronounced *Foom-Blay*. He's the mayor of Briar's Landing. He and Stanley have a major rivalry going on, so they trade incredibly mild insults."

The rest of the meeting centered around talking Stanley down from placing a bulk order for twenty thousand plastic Easter eggs and what prizes would be offered for the winner of each egg-hunt division.

Stanley was finally talked down to eighteen thousand eggs and the meeting came to a close.

"Shoot," I muttered.

"What?" Leo asked.

"I haven't started Felix's Eggstravaganza outfit." I rubbed my eyes. With my custom orders, the craft night event I was planning, and my house growing messier and messier, there never seemed to be enough time in the day anymore.

"I like the idea of a cat having an official dresser. But I'm sure he'll understand if you don't have time to make him something."

It was on the tip of my tongue to tell Leo about my secret social media account and how the fans would riot if they didn't see Felix in costume, but I stopped myself. I couldn't imagine Leo ridiculing me like *they* had, but my fear held me back.

"I take my job as his dresser very seriously."

Leo smiled. "I'm sure you do."

Somehow, the space I'd created between us had disappeared. His thigh was firmly pressed against mine again, and I swore his eyes flitted to my lips.

"Are you doing anything now?"

"What?"

Why was I so nervous? He'd already said he'd forgiven me, but I was still braced for rejection. My recent track record was less than stellar. "Would you like to have our date now?"

"Yes," he blurted out. He ruffled his hand through his hair again and his scent intensified. "I'd like that."

I grinned. We were both trying and utterly failing to play it cool. My omega was practically dancing. I didn't want to get my hopes up yet that this date would lead to anything else, but after months of trying to get Leo to hang out with me, I would take whatever he offered, even if it was just friendship.

"Do you want to go to the diner?" he asked. "I bet Char could be convinced to make pancakes for dinner."

People were filing past us now to the exit, throwing curious looks our way. Summer and Olive walked down the aisle super slowly, clearly trying to get my attention while Ivy physically pushed them along. She was definitely getting a fancy latte delivery at school tomorrow.

"I have half a cake at my place that Summer made. I could grab it and we could find a spot to sit at the park or on the beach?" The diner was always crowded after a town meeting, and I would prefer to avoid the comments Leo and I would get if we showed up together.

"I'm honored you would share your cake with me."

Don't think dirty thoughts.

I stood and flipped my hair. "Who said I'm sharing? Maybe this is a Bring Your Own Cake date."

Leo shrugged. "Sitting with you and watching you eat cake is still a great use of my evening."

Ahhhh! How was I supposed to act normal after that?

He reached down and grabbed his cane off the floor before standing with a pained grimace. My heart ached for him and what his osteoarthritis had cost him. He seemed to be happy running his shop, but I couldn't imagine how I would cope if an injury stopped me from sewing.

"Is your knee hurting?" I asked softly.

He cleared his throat. "It's just stiff from sitting for so long."

"Can I help? Do you need medication or something?"

His eyes shuttered and he shook his head. "No, it's fine." His words were clipped, his scent bitter. Oh god, he was obviously sensitive about this, and I'd made it worse. Regret sat heavily in my stomach. Was he going to cancel now?

"We should get going." He gestured for me to go ahead.

He wasn't canceling! I hadn't ruined everything! And now I was determined to do everything I could to make him smile.

We were among the last of the stragglers to make our way outside. The sun had set, and there was a chill in the air.

"There are some benches in the town center, and the string lights are really pretty. How about I run and grab the cake and meet you there? That path there is actually a shortcut to the town square." My voice was high pitched with anxiety. I didn't want to make it too obvious that I was trying to prevent him from having to walk too far. If I had a car, I would offer to drive him.

Leo's jaw clenched. "Yeah," he finally answered. "Sounds like a plan."

My smile felt slightly wobbly. "Okay, meet you there in a minute!"

"Wait." His hand closed around my bicep. "What about your ankle? You shouldn't be running around."

"It's feeling a lot better. I promise." A brilliant idea struck me, and a real smile spread across my face. "Actually, wait. I have a solution that will keep me off my ankle."

His eyebrow cocked. "Oh?"

"You'll have to wait and see. Just stay here and I'll be back."

He nodded and I took off jogging for the second time today, because apparently I would break my no-running rule for Leo.

24

LEO

Lucy took off running down Main Street and I barely resisted the urge to smash my head against town hall's brick exterior. I'd been rude and defensive about my cane when she was just being sweet.

I stared after her like a lovesick puppy. I had no idea what she was planning, but I was sure it was a ploy to keep me from having to walk. Which I should appreciate, but *I* wanted to be the one taking care of her. Unfortunately, I didn't have a choice tonight. I'd tweaked my knee earlier while unloading a flower order, and it screamed in agony as I half collapsed onto the town hall steps.

It was probably a good thing Lucy wasn't here to witness that. Omegas needed strong partners. At least, that's what I'd always been told.

Designations had never been a big deal growing up. Everyone in my family was a beta except for Parisa, a rare omega born to beta parents, but things changed once my classmates started revealing as alphas in high school. It only got worse in college. I'd roomed with three alphas—guys I'd been friends with for years—until they'd decided to form a pack without me. They left me to live alone my sophomore year in a tiny single room. I eventually dropped out to work with Ocean Rescue full-time.

I'd been told more than once that omegas didn't want or need betas. Even though I'd rolled my eyes at the obvious alpha-centric propaganda, I'd apparently internalized the messaging more than I'd thought.

A golf cart came careening down the road, pulling me from my morose reminiscing. I gritted my teeth as the driver let out a whoop and started doing doughnuts in the middle of the empty street. Where was Stanley when you needed him? Starlight Grove's human mayor was over the top with his ordinance enforcement, but this person was going to hurt themselves if they didn't slow down.

After another doughnut, the golf cart sped toward me. I squinted as I tried to make out the shadowy figure driving. My jaw dropped for the second time this evening when the streetlight glinted off of Lucy's gold hair.

A burst of laughter escaped my chest when she pulled up in front of me, eyes bright and cheeks pink.

"Woo! That was so fun! Jump in, Leo."

"I didn't know you had a golf cart."

"I don't. This is Stanley's."

"He let you borrow it?"

"Nope. Now enough stalling." She patted the spot beside her.

She was right—I was stalling. I was pretty sure I had about a fifty-fifty chance of dying if I got in, but apparently I didn't care because I was already halfway into the passenger seat.

"You can hold this." She plopped a white box on my lap that I guessed contained whatever remained of the cake after her erratic driving. "You ready?"

I tightened my hold on the box. "Umm, we don't need to—"

My words were cut off as Lucy accelerated the golf cart. I swore and threw an arm across her so she didn't fall out. She just laughed and patted my arm.

"How is this thing so fast?" I shouted.

"My brother hot-wired it and installed an extra-powerful battery."

She took a sharp turn around the corner and I hung on for dear life.

"Stanley wanted a turbo golf cart?"

She just grinned, and I shook my head, amusement lighting up my chest. "And you look so innocent."

"Looks can be deceiving." She winked.

We passed the fire station and kept going. There wasn't much out this direction besides the ocean.

"Where are we going?"

"One of my favorite spots in town. I discovered it when I was little and ran away from home."

We turned onto a narrow dirt path I'd never noticed before. The golf cart's headlights barely illuminated the road ahead, and I was almost taken out by a low-hanging pine branch.

"Why did you run away from home?" I asked, desperately needing to distract myself from our imminent demise. I lunged to knock away another branch that almost got Lucy in the face.

"I had a flair for drama when I was young."

I bit my lip to hide my smile. Lucy had retained her flair for the dramatic into her adulthood. Two town meetings ago, she'd gotten into a heated argument with Stanley about the importance of having period-appropriate costumes for the school's production of *Little Women*. Now I knew more about the history of zippers than I ever needed to, but I could listen to Lucy talk forever.

I let out a strangled noise as we hit a divot. The cart lurched and the cake almost flew off my lap. I clutched the cardboard box in one hand and my cane in the other.

"What made you run away?" I asked through clenched teeth.

"I watched a documentary in school about whales being kept in captivity and how awful it is for them, and I didn't think my family was taking the issue seriously enough. I decided to hold a protest in town—I made a poster that said *Free the Whales*, complete with hand-drawn illustrations—but my moms said they were too busy to join. After I walked up and down Main Street a couple times, I got bored and decided to run away."

I could imagine it—a tiny Lucy with her handmade sign and righteous indignation.

"I would have joined your protest."

"Yeah?" Her lips curved into a smile.

"Yeah."

A matching smile appeared on my lips even as my knuckles turned white from trying to stay on the golf cart. We were going uphill now, squeezing through a narrow tunnel of trees. Finally, we emerged into a small clearing at the top of a cliff overlooking the water. The Starlight Grove lighthouse was to our right, its beacon illuminating the water, and the town twinkling below us.

Lucy parked. "Cool secret place, right?"

"It's beautiful." Without the hum of the golf cart, I could hear the gentle crash of ocean waves below and the occasional hoot of a bird. I stretched my arm along the back of our seats, wishing I was brave enough to pull her into my side. "Do you come up here with your friends?"

She shook her head, her eyes fixed on the horizon. "I've never brought anyone up here."

My heart stuttered, and the rejection I'd felt this morning evaporated into the night air. "I feel very special, then."

"You are." She tentatively leaned back until she brushed my arm. That little touch was enough to set me on fire. The more I got of Lucy, the more I craved her.

I took a chance and twirled the ends of her hair around my finger. "What happened when you ran away?"

"I stumbled upon the dirt path and kept walking until I found this spot. I decided I would just live in the woods to punish my family for not taking me seriously. But eventually, I got hungry. By the time I got back to town, I was sunburned and cranky. Marisol saw me pass by, and she pulled me into the market, fed me a sandwich, and listened to me cry about the whales." She gave a little shrug. "And then I headed home."

"Your moms must have been relieved when you got back."

She let out a broken laugh. "I thought they'd be crying and apologize for not caring about the whales upon my return, but they hadn't even noticed I was missing. To be fair, it felt like I'd been gone for days, but it was only a couple of hours. See, dramatic."

I frowned. "It's not dramatic to care about things." Lucy spoke positively about her family, but it didn't sound like they were all that supportive. "I thought you were close with your moms?"

"Oh, I definitely am. I go over to their house all the time, and I know I can always count on them and Lars. I just . . . sometimes it feels like they don't always understand me. Maybe it's a designation thing. I've had really strong omega traits since I was little, and it made me really sensitive. I think it was confusing for my alpha moms. But my mormor—grandma—was an omega, and she lived down the street. She always said I took after her." She fell silent as she gazed out at the waves. "She passed away when I was ten. Actually, the whale protest was shortly after she died. It was a hard time for all of us, and I think what I really wanted was for her to show up here and tell me everything was going to be okay."

This time, I didn't hold back as I curled my arm around her shoulders. She melted into my side.

"I'm sorry. I can't imagine losing my Bibi."

"I enjoyed meeting her at the festival. Have you always been close?"

I nodded, my cheek brushing the top of her head. "Definitely. Parisa and I went to her house after school every day when we were little. She's the one who got me into growing flowers. We spent so many hours together in her garden in Iran."

"Mormor is the one who taught me how to sew. She left me all her sewing machines, and that's what I used to start my store."

We lapsed into a comfortable silence, and with every passing moment, Lucy relaxed farther into me.

She trailed her finger along the box in my lap. "Should we eat some cake?"

I snorted a laugh. "I'm not sure how well it survived the treacherous journey."

"Ugly cake is still cake. And I haven't eaten dinner, so I'm not picky."

"You need to eat dinner." My words came out in a stern tone I didn't recognize. Everyone in my life knew me as laid-back Leo, but Lucy seemed to bring out another side of me.

She gestured at the box. "Uh-huh. Dinner."

I shook my head. This girl. "I guess I'm going to have to make sure you eat real food tomorrow."

"Whatever you need to do," she said primly.

Lucy pointed my phone's flashlight at the box as I opened it, revealing a cake that looked absolutely perfect.

"And you were acting like my driving was bad." She pulled out two plastic forks from her small purse.

"I plead the fifth."

She elbowed me, laughing, and dug in. I followed, my eyes widening as the taste of fresh mango burst on my tongue. I immediately loaded my fork with another bite.

"Summer made this?"

"Isn't it amazing? She's been in recipe-testing mode as she finalizes her bakery menu, and I've definitely reaped the rewards. I'm organizing the grand opening. You should come." She nudged my side in a touch that was so casual and perfect it made my heart ache.

"If her other baked goods taste like this, I'll be there every day. By the way, was the whale movie you watched *Dark Depths*?"

"Yes! Have you seen it?"

I chuckled. "You could say that. I also watched it as a kid, and it kind of shaped the trajectory of my life. The first time I saw it, we were still living in Iran. My parents had just told me we were moving to the U.S. and I was furious about it, especially since Bibi couldn't come with us."

"She couldn't? Why not?"

"Her husband, my grandpa, was a horrible man. He was barely home, but when he was, it was a nightmare." My jaw clenched as old rage rushed through me. "My parents wanted to bring her with us, but she couldn't leave the country without his permission, and he refused to give it."

Lucy squeezed my hand. "That's horrible."

"My parents refused to leave her at first, but my mom is a midwife and was offered a fellowship in Maine to further her research into rural maternal health. It was an amazing opportunity for her, and they also wanted to ensure Parisa had access to whatever opportunities she wanted." I swallowed hard. "My mom was terrified of leaving my grandma behind. I don't know what Bibi said to convince them to move, but she's pretty impossible to say no to."

"How did she get over here? Did her husband change his mind?"

I shook my head. "No, we got lucky because he died like a month after we moved here. Maman was on the phone with our family in Iran the next day to arrange Bibi's travel."

"I'm so glad you have her."

"Me, too. But anyway, when I found out we were moving, I was upset. I didn't want to leave my friends or home, but Baba told me we were moving to a coastal town and promised we would go whale watching."

"Did you?"

I grinned. "Oh yeah. I even convinced my entire family to go on an Alaskan cruise the summer after my senior year so we could see the whales. I toyed with being a marine biologist for a while, but I barely passed my science classes freshman year of college, so I went into Ocean Rescue instead. I figured it would keep me close to the sea."

"I wanted to be a marine biologist for a while, too. Funny how things turn out."

"Yeah, it is." And for the first time in a long time, I thought my life had turned out okay if it brought me to this moment in time.

We were down to the last bite of cake.

"You finish it," I said.

"I'm super full. You take it." She leaned back and patted her stomach.

I shook my head. My upbringing would not allow me to take the last bite of cake. "It's yours." I nudged the box her way.

She sighed and speared the final bit of cake with her fork. But instead of eating it, she brought it to my lips. Now I was torn between the hospitality my Iranian culture demanded and the desire to do anything to please this omega.

After a moment of hesitation, I wrapped my hand around her wrist and took the last bite of cake off her fork. My eyes had adjusted enough to the darkness to see the general outline of her features, but as her scent bloomed around us, bright and happy, I had the urge to aim the flashlight at her face to fully see her expression.

"Can I ask you a question?" she asked softly.

"Of course."

"Is there anything that helps your knee pain? Not that you have to talk about it if you don't want to," she hurried to add.

I tightened my hold on her. "I'm sorry I snapped earlier. I'm still getting used to needing a cane. I thought it was temporary, and I recently found out it's more of a long-term thing. So that's been hard." She squeezed my hand and I let out a shuddering breath. "My doctor keeps trying to refer me to pain management, but I haven't decided yet if I'll go."

"Why wouldn't you?"

Because it feels like accepting defeat, like giving up.

"I guess I've been in denial."

She hummed and I braced for her to tell me I was being silly and that, *of course*, I should go.

"If you change your mind, I'd be happy to go with you."

My heart stuttered, and a slow smile split my cheeks. "I may take you up on that, azizam."

We had swayed so close her face was inches from mine.

"What does that mean?"

My fingers trailed down her arm. I was lost in a haze, completely mesmerized by Lucy. She smelled like wildflowers and strawberries, like *home*.

"Sweetheart," I murmured. "Is that okay?"

"Yes." She brushed her lips along my jaw. "Call me that as often as you want."

My hand tangled in her hair. She shivered and I drew her closer. "Are you cold?"

She shook her head, her nose skimming against my short beard before she cupped my face. Our lips were a hairbreadth apart, so close I could practically taste her.

"Leo." Her whispered murmur was sweet and soft and needy.

I closed the space between us, groaning as my lips pressed against hers. We moved together like we'd been doing this all our lives. I tugged her closer, closer, closer until she was straddling my lap.

"Your knee?" she asked, breathless between kisses.

"I'd rather chop it off than have you move."

She laughed, but the sound was cut off as my hand went to her jaw, my tight hold urging her to open for me. My tongue dipped into her mouth, and she was sweeter than I'd even imagined, like the honey and rose of my favorite Persian cake.

"Fuck." My hands gripped her hips. "You're perfect." I palmed her ass, pulling her flush against my hard-on.

She let out the most precious omega whine as she ran one hand through my hair and wrapped the other tightly around my neck. "You smell so good," she said between kisses.

I puffed up, ridiculously proud that the sweetest omega in the world liked my scent. I hugged her tighter to me and wondered why the fuck I'd held myself back from her.

LUCY PARKED THE GOLF cart in a space outside our shops, but neither of us moved.

We'd kissed at the top of the cliff for what felt like seconds, but was closer to an hour. I wanted more—to dip my fingers into her heat and fuck her until she came, to lick up the slick coating her inner thighs, to sink my cock into her heat—but I held back. Lucy deserved more than our first time being outside in the dark... and I was pretty sure Stanley might actually lose his mind if we fucked in his golf cart.

When her teeth started chattering from the cold, I'd reluctantly moved her off my lap so we could head back to town.

She tangled her fingers with mine. "Thanks for giving me a second chance to have our date."

"The first of many."

The streetlights illuminated the pink of her cheeks and the brightness of her smile. I wanted to invite her inside, to pull her into my bed. We didn't even have to do more than sleep. I'd be perfectly content to just hold her.

Reality crashed down on me. The pain in my knee, which had been easy to ignore when she was on my lap, was now so intense I knew I wouldn't make it up the stairs. Our first night together would not be on my shitty storage room mattress as I alternated applying ice and heat to my knee.

I reluctantly walked her to her door. "Are you going to leave the golf cart here? It feels like we should hide it."

"Good to know you're willing to be an accessory to any crimes I commit," she said with a toss of her hair.

"Of course. Although, if you need to dispose of any bodies, we might need some help lifting them."

She grinned and leaned in for a kiss. "I might know some people who would help. But for now, it'll be fine parked there."

She unlocked her door and lingered for a moment before saying goodnight and slipping inside.

25

WILDER

The sun was shining, Beans 'n Bliss was bustling, but none of that registered in my mind because Lucy was back.

My heart raced as she propped her shop door open with a brick—a pink brick with flowers painted on it because *of course* Lucy wouldn't use a plain, boring brick as a doorstop.

She stood, and a huge smile curved her lips as she looked in my direction. She waved, and for one beautiful, time-stopping moment, I thought she'd spotted me through the Beans 'n Bliss window.

Reality crashed back, harsh and cold, when I realized she was waving at the lighthouse keeper, Olive, who was crossing the street with a dark-haired alpha at her side.

I held in a snarl as they all hugged. How dare another man get close to *my* omega?

Fuck.

Not mine.

"Wilder? Are you okay? Wilder?"

I jerked my gaze to the barista in front of me. Her brow was creased. "Is something wrong?"

I shook my head, the movement stiff and jerky. "I'm fine. Black coffee, please." I paid, stuck a few crumpled bills in the tip jar, and moved to the side.

Ella's concerned gaze followed me. I couldn't blame her for worrying about my sanity. I'd come in four times yesterday, hoping each time to catch a glimpse of Lucy, but her shop had stayed closed.

It was the first day I'd gone without seeing Lucy since she'd dropped off the cookies, and I fucking hated it. The angry, possessive beast clawing in my chest had kept me tossing and turning so much

A Pack for Spring

that being called out at three a.m. had been a welcome distraction. It had turned out to be a false alarm with a young family's carbon monoxide detector, but we'd thoroughly checked their house to be safe. Their two-year-old girl had immediately latched on to me, so I'd completed my checks while she sat on my shoulders, her tiny fists wrapped tightly around my top knot as she made fire engine sounds.

My guys had gone to bed when we returned, and I'd shut myself away in my office with the excuse of being behind on paperwork.

Ella called out my name, and I grabbed my coffee from the bar. My very unnecessary cup of coffee, seeing as I'd single-handedly drunk a whole pot earlier this morning, but going to Beans 'n Bliss was the only way I could see Lucy without being a total creep.

Although, staring at her through the coffee shop window might be somewhat questionable behavior. My alpha's fixation on her was just further proof that I was right to stay away.

Lucy was still talking to her friends. The dark-haired alpha had a casual arm slung around Olive's shoulder, making my insides burn with white-hot jealousy—not because I wanted the lighthouse keeper, but because I wanted that easy intimacy she shared with her mate.

I stayed at the window until Lucy's friends left. She lingered outside her shop, an unreadable expression on her face, before disappearing inside.

In another life, I'd bring her coffee. Wrap her in my arms.

But that wasn't my life.

I took a bitter sip of coffee and returned to the firehouse.

26

LUCY

> **HOROSCOPE PISCES**
>
> Pisces, the universe wants you to know that stealing golf carts is strictly prohibited by town ordinance 72.3, subsection V, under the vehicular code of Starlight Grove, which carries a sentence of up to three hundred hours of community service. The stars are watching.

THE TASSELS OF MY SILVER DRESS BRUSHED AGAINST MY THIGHS and my sequined cowboy boots clicked against the sidewalk as I crossed the dark parking lot to the post office, or rather, to the secret karaoke bar in the post office basement.

Our mailman, Salvatore, had proposed starting this karaoke bar several months ago at a town meeting. Stanley had immediately shut down the idea, saying that a karaoke bar violated no fewer than thirty-seven town ordinances. To no one's surprise, the karaoke bar had still opened, in full defiance of our human mayor. The real twist was which townsperson had secretly pushed through the appropriate paperwork: Harry O'Sullivan, Stanley's husband. Not only that, according to Summer, Harry had even given Sal the seed money he needed to open the bar.

Right now, the bar only opened a couple times a month. A few days before karaoke night, we would all get a pink flyer advertising a gutter maintenance service, and the date and time of the next karaoke night was revealed in Gutter George's phone number. The subterfuge made it all the more thrilling, and for the first time, we didn't have to drive to Briar's Landing or Maple Grove for late-night entertainment.

It was usually a highlight of my week—a time to let loose and hang out with my friends—but tonight, I was dreading it. And not because Easton had insisted tonight's theme should be *A Good Old-Fashioned Country Throw Down*, but because my friends had been trying to pin me down and make me spill everything that had happened the past few days. When I'd turned down their offer to meet for lunch today with the excuse that I was behind on custom orders, there were many threats of kidnapping if I didn't tell them everything at karaoke.

I wanted to talk to them, to get their thoughts on everything, but I'd held back because I was embarrassed. I'd been rejected by two alphas back-to-back, and while Leo hadn't rejected me, part of me was scared I'd jinx our relationship if I said out loud how happy I was.

I pushed the basement door open, revealing a large space with an eclectic blend of vintage armchairs, couches, and coffee tables facing the small stage at the front. Dozens of disco balls hung from the ceiling, casting a glittering glow on the room, and Dolly Parton's "9 to 5" blasted from the speakers.

I turned toward the bar but stopped with a startled shriek. Olive and Felix blocked my way with matching stern expressions.

"Hello," I said brightly. "You two look cute." They were wearing matching cowboy hats, and Felix wore a belt with a large western buckle around his waist.

Olive wagged her finger. "Don't even try to distract me."

I scratched Felix under his chin and grinned. "I might be convinced to tell you everything if I get a drink or three in my system."

"That can definitely be arranged."

Olive adjusted her hold on Felix and linked arms with me. James was leaning against the bar, which meant Ivy must be close by. He waved when he saw us, but his smile transformed into a frown when he spotted Felix.

"Have you two been feeding him people food?" the vet asked, crossing his arms.

Images of the peanut butter and jelly sandwich I'd given him for lunch cha-cha'd through my mind.

Olive and I shook our heads.

"We would never do that," she said.

"We were at the presentation," I added. "The cat food versus people food one."

James narrowed his eyes, and I had to bite my lip to keep from laughing. He made an *I'm watching you* gesture before grabbing the drinks Salvatore set down on the bar.

Once James was out of sight, I crouched down slightly to look Felix in the eye. "You're going to get me in trouble."

"Who are you in trouble with?"

I spun around to see Ivy leaning against the bar where her man had just been.

She raised an eyebrow in a move that would make any third grader fall in line. "Besides us, of course."

I groaned and rested my head on the bar. "I just got here, and I've already been scolded by three people."

"Make that four." Summer squeezed in beside me and signaled to Salvatore. "We need a jumbo pitcher of frozen strawberry margaritas."

I leaned against her shoulder. "You're going to scold me, too?"

"Only if you withhold the dirty details of you and the beta," she said. "Besides, you're getting off easy. I wanted to follow you and Leo after the town meeting, but Ivy wouldn't let me."

"Stalking is not appropriate," Ivy said.

"Tell that to Easton," I said.

"What about Easton?" Olive hopped up on a stool, Felix perched on her lap.

"Summer wants to adopt his stalking tendencies," I said.

Olive grinned. "I wouldn't recommend it, but it did work out for us, so who knows?"

Ivy went to say something, but Summer waved her hand. "No, enough chitchat. I saved a table for us in the corner." She grabbed the huge pitcher of margaritas and jerked her head toward the table.

A Pack for Spring

We squeezed onto a plush velvet couch, and Summer filled our glasses to the brim. Felix hopped onto my lap and tried to stick his face into my drink.

"Absolutely not." James swooped in out of thin air, grabbed Felix, and carried him away.

We burst out laughing at Felix's dramatic meows as he extended his arms to us over his abductor's shoulder.

"All right, we all have our drinks, so now you're going to spill," Summer said.

"You sure you don't want to do some karaoke first?"

She scowled. "Stop stalling. On my way here, Marisol, Carmen, and Harry all stopped me to ask what's going on with you and Leo. Do you know how hard it is for me to be out of the loop with town gossip, especially when it pertains to my friend?"

"Yes, so hard for you," I deadpanned.

"You don't have to tell us if you're not ready," Ivy said, except she spoke at the same time as Olive, who said, "If you don't give us all the details right now, I'll die."

I almost choked on my drink. "Fine. But no telling the town gossips."

"Start with the party you went to with the mystery alpha," Summer demanded. It didn't escape me that she hadn't agreed not to gossip.

I told them how King had come into my shop and asked for my help to get him out of the auction, along with everything that happened afterward. I left out of a few of the more salacious details—including the whole *Daddy* thing—ending with our unceremonious parting.

Summer tenderly squeezed my hand. "How do you feel about not seeing him again?" She was bright and loud and didn't take life too seriously, but I knew the side of her she rarely showed to others—the tender, sensitive side that felt responsible for those she loved.

I shrugged. "I knew he wasn't offering a relationship and I did it anyway, so I only have myself to blame."

"Lucy," Olive said softly. "That's not how it works. You're allowed to be upset about it."

"Yeah. I just . . . what's wrong with me? Why does no one want to form a pack with me?" I kept my eyes fixed on my margarita glass. "First Wilder, now King?"

My friends wrapped their arms around me, squeezing tight and holding space for me to just feel. When we finally pulled apart, I dabbed my eyes with a cocktail napkin.

"Nothing is wrong with you," Ivy said. "Nothing at all. Relationships are hard and complicated."

"You're one of my favorite people," Olive said.

"What she said," Summer said gruffly.

"Thanks."

"Where's King staying, by the way?" Olive asked, sounding suspiciously innocent.

"Why do you ask?"

"No reason," she said.

"Uh-huh. You can't TP his house."

She just smiled.

I pursed my lips. "He's renting Ms. Ito's place."

Summer's eyes widened. "Did he say if she left any sock inventory? Tofu chewed a hole in my favorite dancing cupcake socks and I have to find a replacement pair."

I could only imagine King's reaction to four omegas showing up at his rental and demanding to look through the house to find possible hidden socks.

I took another long sip of my drink to soothe the lump in my throat. "Funny enough, I didn't ask about sock inventory while we were fucking."

Now it was Ivy's turn to choke on her drink, and Summer slapped her on the back.

"Okay, let's get back on track," Olive said. "What's going on with you and Leo?"

I chugged the rest of my margarita, and Ivy poured me another as I told them everything—Leo wrapping my ankle and asking me out, me standing him up, and our golf cart excursion.

"This is good, right?" Ivy asked. "It sounds like he's interested in a relationship."

"Yeah, I think so." I'd felt so secure with Leo when we were on the cliff, in our own world. In the light of day, I struggled to believe he really wanted me after he'd given me mixed messages for months. "I guess I'll just have to see how it goes."

One of Ivy's alphas, Rome, set a large platter of appetizers down on the table. "Make sure you girls have some food on the side of your alcohol." He leaned down, gripped Ivy's chin, and gave her a kiss worthy of the final scene of a romance movie. When he pulled back, Ivy's cheeks were bright pink.

Rome gave his omega a final caress on her cheek before walking over to the booth where Logan was firmly holding Felix to his chest in air jail.

Summer fanned her face. "Whew. That was hot."

"Wait," I said, turning back to my friends. "Was I cheating on Leo by being with King?"

"Huh?" Olive cocked her head. "You and Leo weren't officially together when King asked you to the gala. Besides, wouldn't he assume that you have alphas courting you? Omegas need packs."

I drummed my fingers against the table. She was right. Even now, I didn't know where Leo and I stood. He hadn't officially said he wanted to court me. Was this just fun for him? "His parents are betas, though. What if he doesn't understand pack life?"

"Isn't his sister an omega?" Ivy asked. "She has a pack, right?"

I let out a sigh of relief. "You're right."

"And you can just ask Leo the next time you see him. Have a little define-the-relationship chat," Olive said.

Summer and I crinkled our noses, making Olive and Ivy roll their eyes. How nice it would be to feel that secure, all loved-up with their packs.

"I'll talk to Leo," I said. *Eventually*. In my experience, serious relationship talks always ended in disappointment.

Thankfully, our conversation shifted to plans for our upcoming events—the craft night I was planning, Summer's grand opening, and the Easter Eggstravaganza—until we were interrupted by Easton hopping onstage to uproarious cheers.

The rest of the night unfolded in a margarita-induced haze, coming back to me in flashes the following morning as I nursed my coffee and aspirin.

LUCY

> Did I really get up onstage and sing Jolene or did I dream that?

SUMMER

> You and Felix sang an impassioned duet

IVY

> I slept until nine this morning. NINE. My guys thought I was dying

> Also did Easton do a dramatic strip show to "I will always love you"?

OLIVE

> I would say that was a fever dream except I woke up beside him this morning and he was completely naked except for a hot pink boa covering . . . well, things

SUMMER

> tbh I don't remember anything after Harry and I performed Devil went down to Georgia

LUCY

I'm pretty sure finding out that Harry plays the FIDDLE was what finally broke my brain and made me pass out

IVY

I'm too old for karaoke night. I'm going to need five business months to recover

SUMMER

I can give you a week

I signed us up for next week's karaoke night. The theme is boys vs. girls and we have to win

LUCY

I'll practice my Spice Girls cover

Another message came in—this one from Leo.

LEO

Good morning, darling. How're you doing?

Darling. I melted.

LUCY

Karaoke night tried to take me out

LEO

Was it the karaoke or the alcohol?

LUCY

I plead the fifth.

> Do not expect me to look pretty this morning for our coffee date

LEO

> You're always beautiful, pretty girl

> But that's why I was texting. I have to cancel. A friend of mine is doing flowers for a wedding in Vermont today and their assistant is sick. They asked if I could drive down to help them

> I'm sorry

My omega pouted, but this was not rejection.

LUCY

> Don't apologize! Will you be back tomorrow?

LEO

> They need help with flowers at the after-wedding brunch too so I probably won't be back until Monday or Tuesday. Could I take you out for dinner on Wednesday?

I glanced at my calendar app and chewed my lip.

LUCY

> I'm actually hosting a craft night on Wednesday. This first one is invitation only as I work out the kinks.

> Would you want to come?

> I'd love having you there

I squealed and tossed my phone after the last text left me feeling flayed open, but when it vibrated, I couldn't curb my curiosity.

LEO

> I am honored to get an invitation to such an exclusive event!! I'll be there

Warmth rushed through me as I smiled like a fool. I loved that neither of us were trying to play it cool.

LUCY

> Yay!
>
> I hope the wedding goes well
>
> Are you going to be ok? Like with your knee?

The second I sent the text, I cringed. I didn't want him to think I was questioning how capable he was. I just hated the idea of him hurting.

LUCY

> I hope that's ok to ask
>
> I obviously know you're an amazing florist. And you're super strong.
>
> Big arm muscles

LEO

> Tell me more about these big arm muscles

LUCY

> Don't fish for compliments
> I'm sure you own a mirror

> **LEO**
> I'm glad you like my big arm muscles, pretty girl.
>
> And you can ask me anything. My friend knows about my knee so I'm sure they'll yell at me to take it easy.
>
> Thanks for your concern

> **LUCY**
> Always

My body might feel like I'd been run over, but my smile refused to leave my lips as I slowly rolled out of my nest, feeling wanted and cared for.

> **LUCY**
> Leo! I can't believe you did this

> **LEO**
> Did what, pretty girl?

> **LUCY**
> Don't even pretend. Pizza Pete ratted you out. Thank you for my dinner 🖤

> **LEO**
> I need to make sure my girl eats more than cake

> **LUCY**
> Cake is a perfectly acceptable dinner
>
> But thank you. It means a lot

27

LUCY

> **HOROSCOPE PISCES**
>
> In your quest to find answers to life's big questions, don't forget that sometimes the simplest thing to do is cast your eyes up.

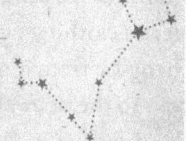

I CURSED AS MY THREAD SNAPPED *AGAIN*. I WAS WORKING with a new fabric and couldn't get the tension set correctly on my sewing machine. I'd spent yesterday morning nursing my hangover, not starting on this order until the late afternoon. I'd sewn until two in the morning and started back up again at seven.

"I'm never taking another rush order again," I muttered to the empty room. My hands shook as I brushed my hair out of my face. It was midday and I hadn't eaten since Leo's surprise pizza delivery last night—a pizza I'd eaten between bouts of happy tears. I couldn't believe he'd done that for me, especially while he was busy working.

I stood with a groan. I needed sugar, but I'd eaten the last of my gummy bear stash yesterday and I didn't have to stand in front of my open fridge with unseeing eyes to know there was nothing in there for me to eat.

I grabbed my sweater on my way out the door and headed toward the diner when a horrible sound stopped me in my tracks. I whirled around, looking for the source. There it was again—an anguished yowl.

"Felix!" I spotted his brown, orange, and white fur among the budding leaves in the tree above. "What are you doing up there?"

He continued his pitiful meows, his claws digging in to the tall branch to keep from falling. I looked around for help, but the street was empty. Where was everyone?

"Can you make it down if you go really slow? I'll stand right here in case you fall." I held out my arms, but his panicked noises intensified.

"Shit, shit, shit. Okay, plan B. I'm going to get the ladder."

I flew back into my shop for the large metal ladder Lars had gifted me for some unknown reason when I first opened. I'd exclusively used it as a clothing rack, but now was its time to shine. I tossed the outfits hanging from it onto the floor. By the time I dragged the bulky ladder out to the sidewalk, I was a dizzy, sweaty mess.

I leaned it against the tree trunk. "All right. I can do this. Easy peasy." I squinted up at Felix. Had the tree grown taller in the past two minutes?

I wiggled the ladder to make sure it was sturdy. "Here goes noth—" The base slipped and the whole thing crashed to the ground, smacking my shin in the process.

"Fuck!" That was going to leave a bruise. I blinked away the tears. There was no time to spare for crying. "Plan C it is. I'll be right back, Felix! Hang on!" I shouted the words over my shoulder as I took off for the firehouse.

Two things quickly became clear—first, I'd forgotten to put on real shoes and my slippers were not made for sprinting, and second, today was the opening day for the farmers market in the town square. At least that explained why Main Street was empty.

People waved and shouted at me as I squeezed through the crowded booths, not stopping until I burst into the fire station. I doubled over, gasping for air as black spots danced in my vision.

"Lucy?"

Wilder jogged across the lobby, brow furrowed.

"Felix. Stuck in a tree." I squeezed the words out of my overworked lungs.

"Felix? The cat?"

"Please help. He's crying. Can't come down."

Ezra poked his head into the entryway, and I had a vague memory of the two of us singing a rousing duet of "Barbie Girl" at karaoke. "What's going on?"

Wilder growled and shifted closer to me. "Get the truck ready. We'll need the ladder." His hand was on my back as he guided me into the garage. "I'll boost you up."

"I get to ride in the fire truck? That's so cool."

A boyish smile flashed on his face, and it was so disarmingly charming, my brain ceased to function. Then his hands were on me—huge and strong as they grasped my hips and placed me into the passenger's seat.

"Want me to drive, boss?" Ezra asked.

"I got it," Wilder snapped. He rounded the truck and got in the driver's seat while Ezra hopped in the back with a smirk.

The moment Wilder shut the door, his deep pine scent flooded the enclosed space, decadent and perfect. *Oh no*. I clenched my fists, trying to summon the intense panic I'd felt moments ago to stop myself from perfuming, but Wilder's scent was too soothing.

"Where did you see Felix?"

I breathed through my mouth. "He's stuck in a tree outside my shop."

Ezra leaned forward. "Felix? Fuck. This is our most important mission yet."

Wilder grunted and pulled onto the road. Even with my stress and exhaustion, I felt a thrill at being in an actual fire truck.

"Are you going to honk the horn?" I asked.

"The road's empty."

My shoulders slumped.

He gestured at the steering wheel. "There are two horns. The loudest one is by the pedals, but there's another one here. Have at it."

I squealed and leaned over, brushing against the alpha's thick slab of a chest as I stretched to reach. The horn was loud and satisfying, and I laughed. "I feel so powerful."

Wilder muttered something I didn't catch, but before I could ask what he'd said, we pulled up outside my shop. As I pushed the truck door open, Felix let out a loud *meow* and started slipping. I shrieked and hopped out—the pavement sending a shock through my feet as I landed—and ran to the base of the tree.

"Be careful," Wilder snapped. "You should have waited for me."

"He's going to fall!"

Felix clung to a branch, his chunky body dangling precariously in the wind. I stood underneath him with my arms extended while Ezra and Wilder got their ladder out of the truck. Wilder arched an eyebrow as he moved my abandoned ladder to the side and set his up in its place.

"I know you weren't fucking going to use that," he said.

I smiled and batted my eyelids. "Of course not."

His chest rumbled as he climbed up the ladder. I definitely was *not* distracted by the way his muscular arms and thighs strained against his uniform as he climbed.

When he was within reaching distance of Felix, he plucked him from the branch, tucked him unceremoniously under his arm, and climbed back down.

"I believe this belongs to you," he said gruffly.

I hugged Felix to my chest. "That wasn't a good idea, was it?" I cooed. "Let's not do that again." He flopped back in my arms, purring and looking no worse for wear. "Say *thank you* to the nice firefighters for the rescue." But Felix wasn't having it. He pushed out of my arms, landed nimbly on the ground, and strutted away.

"Glad he's not too traumatized," Wilder said dryly.

I shook my head. He was likely more embarrassed than hurt, but I'd check him over and give him extra treats and cuddles later. "Well, *I'll* say it. Thank you for the rescue. Again."

"At least this one was less dramatic."

My cheeks heated at the reminder of our first meeting. Being this close to him made it clear my massive crush hadn't magically subsided. I wanted to run my fingers through his hair. Wrap myself around him. Scent-mark his neck and sit on his . . .

Ezra came over and rested his arm on Wilder's shoulder. "Rescuing the mayor. All in a day's work."

I laughed and shook my head, but my smile turned strained as my body was hit by an intense wave of fatigue.

The world spun around me.

"What's wrong?" Wilder moved in front of me, his hands resting on my shoulders. "Lucy?"

"I'm fine. Just need to sit down." Blackness encroached on my vision.

"Fuck." Hands urged me to the curb. "Head between your legs, sweetheart." Wilder's voice reached me like it was coming through water. He gently rubbed my back as I curled over my bent knees, breathing deeply.

"Drink this." Ezra placed a bottle of water in my hand and I took small sips. My skin was clammy, but my vision was slowly coming back.

"Should we take her to the hospital?" Ezra asked.

A whine slipped through my lips. I cleared my throat. "No. I'm fine."

"Get me the pulse ox and blood pressure monitor," Wilder said.

I slowly lifted my head. "I don't need the hospital."

Wilder cupped the back of my neck, and his touch felt so good it made me want to purr. "I'm going to check your vitals. If I think you need to go, you'll go."

His stern tone made me equal parts irritated and aroused, and the flare of his nostrils told me he could tell. I shut my eyes again in humiliation. I kept perfuming around Wilder even after he made it clear he wasn't interested. Why would he be, when he only ever saw me at my most helpless?

Ezra dropped to his knees beside me and placed the pulse ox on my finger. He went to put on the blood pressure cuff, but Wilder tore it out of his hand and slid it up my arm himself. He grunted once he got the reading.

"A bit low. When was the last time you ate?"

"Last night," I mumbled.

Wilder made a noise in the back of his throat. "Right. You"—he gestured at Ezra—"get back to the station. I'm taking my lunch break."

"You don't have to stay here with me," I said after Ezra drove away. *Please don't leave.*

No matter how hard I'd tried to be stronger and more independent, I still craved being spoiled and taken care of.

"Why haven't you eaten since last night?"

Uh-oh. He sounded mad. I curled in on myself automatically. My omega hated disappointing him.

"I've been busy with work. I was on my way to get food when I saw Felix."

"Not good enough." He stood and held his hand out to me. "Do you need me to carry you?"

"Where?"

"The diner."

I could already hear the gossip that would spread if Wilder carried me down Main Street. Carmen and Marisol might faint from excitement.

I took his hand and stood. "I'm okay." My limbs were still weak, but the world had stopped spinning. Wilder grunted and kept my hand firmly in his as he led me down the street.

28

WILDER

I KEPT A CAREFUL EYE ON LUCY AS WE WALKED TO THE DINER, my hand hovering inches from her back so I could catch her if she passed out.

She'd better not. My heart couldn't take it. Even now, I was fighting the urge to pick her up and whisk her away to my cabin, where I'd wrap her up in blankets and feed her.

That's called kidnapping and is illegal, the angel on my shoulder pointed out unhelpfully.

Who gives a fuck about the law? Do whatever you can to keep our omega safe. The devil on my shoulder made a lot of sense.

We headed inside the diner without further incident and settled into a corner booth. Lucy was pale and her hand shook as she took a long drink of water. I got up and grabbed her a straw, but what I really wanted was to hold the glass for her.

I'd done my best to stay away, but every glimpse of her through the coffee shop window pushed me closer to breaking. She'd sealed her fate when she ran into the fire station . . . when she came to *me* for help.

Our server—an omega named Rosie—came over, but my alpha couldn't have been less interested in her. "Hey, guys, welcome in. What can I get you?"

Lucy stared unseeingly at the menu and my alpha urged me to take control, but I couldn't because I didn't know what she liked. Irritation flooded my veins.

"You go ahead." Lucy glanced up at me.

I shook my head. "You go first, sweet girl."

"Are you doing okay, Lucy?" Rosie asked.

"I'm just tired." Her smile was strained. "I'll do the veggie burger and fries, please."

"Cheeseburger for me, thanks."

Lucy fixed her eyes on her glass of ice water as she created a tiny whirlpool with her straw. I wanted her eyes on me, but at least this gave me the opportunity to study her. Her hair was in two braids, tied at the ends with ribbons that had strawberries on them, matching the pattern on her shirt and pants. She looked fucking adorable. If she were mine, she would be in my lap right now. It wouldn't matter that we were in public. I wanted my omega touching me at all times.

She caught me staring, and I quickly looked away.

She wasn't mine, *couldn't* be mine, but staying away from her was unbearable. My life had been *fine* before meeting her. It might have been dull or lonely, but at least it was uncomplicated. Nothing about the omega in front of me was uncomplicated.

Ever since that fateful storm on the mountain, my dreams had been consumed by Lucy. In the nightmares, she was in danger and I couldn't save her. I'd seen her fall off a cliff and be swept away by the undertow as I stood helplessly frozen. The worst ones, though, were when *I* was the danger she couldn't get away from, when she ran from me in the woods and I caught her, throwing her down on the ground like the monster I was.

Dangerous creature.

Twisted alpha.

Shouldn't be allowed in a decent society.

My jaw ticked as the voices of angry high school parents and teachers echoed in my mind.

"How's your day going, cat rescue aside?" she asked, breaking the heavy silence.

"Fine."

"Right. Well, that's . . ." She trailed off like she didn't have the energy to generate a response to my pathetic nonanswer.

Come on. *Conversate.* "What have you been working on?"

"Just some custom orders."

A heavy feeling settled low in my stomach. When Lucy had been at my cabin, she'd barely stopped talking. I wanted that again, for her voice to form the soundtrack of my life.

"Are you sure you're okay? I should take you to the hospital."

I looked around to track down Rosie to tell her we needed our food to go but froze when a gentle hand closed around mine.

"I'm fine, I promise. I just feel bad for taking up your time. If you need to go back to work, I'll be okay."

She was smiling, but her eyes were so fucking sad.

"I want to stay." I dragged in a deep breath. "I've missed you."

Her lips parted, and I might have thought she was upset if it weren't for the sweet burst of her scent—wild strawberries and flowers and sunny days lying down on the forest floor. Nothing in my life could compare to the satisfaction I felt when I made Lucy happy.

"Thanks for the cookies, by the way," I added.

She beamed. "Did you like them?"

"I ate them all. Pissed off the guys."

"Well, I'll have to bring more for the guys, then."

I grunted. *I* should be the only one she brought cookies to.

"You should come to the grand opening of Summer's bakery," she continued. "It's in a few weeks."

I'd noticed the *Coming Soon* sign in front of the bright yellow bakery on my many drives past Lucy's store. "Might have to do that."

Rosie dropped off our food. I waited for Lucy to start eating before I took a bite of my burger.

"What custom orders are you working on?" I asked, hoping I could tempt her into conversation. This time, she brightened and started telling me about the custom suit she was making, the outfits she had designed for Felix, and the craft night she was planning.

As she was talking, she placed her pickle spear on my plate. I locked eyes with it. I hated pickles, but Lucy had given it to me. Was this some sort of omega pickle ritual? I couldn't risk upsetting her, so I stabbed it with my fork and choked it down.

"Craft night is actually in a few days. The past couple weeks have been so busy it totally snuck up on me. I'm kind of nervous about it."

"You have no reason to be nervous." I would destroy anyone who dared say anything bad about her event. "What kind of craft are you doing?"

"It's a beginner embroidery project." She chewed her lip. "You should come. If you want."

I blinked. Lucy was inviting me to craft night. I must have passed the pickle test.

"Not sure I'd be any good at embroidery." I stared down at my huge, scarred hands.

"It's just for fun. You don't have to be good at it."

Her big blue eyes were all hopeful, and I refused to snuff that out. I would just have to take extra rut suppressants before the event to keep her safe from me. Even now, my alpha was pushing me to grab her.

Pull her onto my lap.

Scent-mark her.

Knot her.

I had no idea how to handle this. Being away from Lucy felt like slowly dying, but being close to her felt like courting disaster.

Maybe you'd become desensitized to her if you spent more time around her.

Fuck. I was weak.

"I'll be there."

I was playing with fire, but I couldn't regret my words because the smile on Lucy's face would stick in my mind for the rest of my life.

29

KING

I WAS HAVING A MIDLIFE CRISIS. OR SOME SORT OF BREAK from reality. That was the only explanation for why I was walking into a flower shop to buy a gift for the omega I was *not* starting a relationship with.

I'd been in yet another meeting with Blackthorne Ventures—hopefully one of our last before we finalized the sales contract—and their office flower arrangements had taunted me the entire time. Apparently my alpha was so desperate and starved for Lucy's scent that a sad approximation of it was enough to give me a hard-on.

So instead of driving back to my empty rental, I'd turned onto Main Street with no concrete plan or strategy. All I knew was that I needed to see Lucy again, and for once in my life, I was following my instincts.

An explosion of colorful flowers greeted me inside, carefully organized into buckets lining the shelves and the floor by the checkout desk. Their scent hung heavily in the air, but it was mixed with something else . . . something warm and spicy.

A man came through the door behind the counter. "Hey! Sorry, have you been waiting long? I was dealing with a delivery out back."

My heart skipped a beat. It was the beta I'd seen in the coffee shop—the tall, muscular beta with golden brown skin, curly black hair, and dark eyes that made me lose my train of thought.

"I'm Leo." He held out his hand.

"King." I took his hand and a surge of the floral, spicy scent washed over me, making my mouth water.

Leo's eyes flicked down my body, sending sparks through my stomach. Was he as affected by me as I was by him?

I released his hand and he cleared his throat, running his hand through his curls. "How can I help you?"

"I need flowers."

Leo chuckled when I didn't elaborate. "You're in the right place. Any particular type of flower or arrangement style?"

"Uhh." I looked around, eyes wide, until he took mercy on me.

"I've got premade arrangements, which are good if you're wanting to leave with something today."

I followed him to a large table filled with vases. I stared at them, feeling like I was being forced to do a calculus problem. Except I was good at calculus.

"So . . . you make all of these?"

Leo covered his chuckle with a cough. "I make the arrangements, yeah. Some of these are flowers I've grown in my family's greenhouse, some are supplied by local farms, and I partner with two ceramic artists who make the vases." His fingertips trailed gently over the flowers, and I imagined what his touch would feel like on my skin.

"Sounds like you found your calling."

He cocked his head, meeting my gaze with his deep brown eyes. "I guess I did. I never expected to be doing this, but maybe the universe knew what I needed more than I did." He rubbed the back of his neck with a laugh. "That probably sounds stupid."

"It doesn't."

His scent intensified and I almost swayed toward him before shaking myself back to reality. What was I doing? I was here to get flowers for Lucy.

I cleared my throat. "So I just select one of these vases?"

"What? Oh, yes. Who are you getting them for? Is it a special occasion?"

I glanced toward the wall that separated us from Spring in Your Stitch. "Do you know Lucy?"

His eyebrows raised. "Of course."

"Well, umm, the flowers are for her, so if you have any idea of what she likes . . ."

"These are for *Lucy*?" He took a step away, and I caught a burnt edge to his scent.

"Yeah. Is that a problem?"

"I'd go with these," he said, avoiding my question. He picked up a large, irregular vase that was shaped like a newspaper with *Starlight Tribune* written on it. I didn't really get it, but it was filled with flowers in all different shades of pink, which felt like something Lucy would like.

"Here, let me take that." He gave me an odd look when I took the vase from him. I didn't know why Leo walked with a cane, but there was no reason for him to carry a large, bulky arrangement when I could do it for him.

We headed back to the checkout counter. Leo did not meet my gaze as he inspected the arrangement, picking out a few flowers he found flaws with.

"So how do you know Lucy?" he asked, trying and failing to sound nonchalant.

My alpha bristled as I finally caught on to what was going on—*he liked her*. Possessiveness burned hot in my chest.

"We met not too long ago." *I've been inside her. Felt her pussy squeezing my knot.* "She came with me to an event in Boston last week."

"Ahh, I see." Leo punched in my purchase on the computer, and I tapped my credit card.

"Thanks for stopping in," he said in a clear dismissal.

"Thanks for the flowers. I'm sure Lucy will love them." I was laying it on thick, but I couldn't stop myself. I expected some sort of snarky response, but he just turned away and walked through the back door, slamming it shut behind him and leaving me with a strangely hollow feeling in my chest.

My odd interaction with Leo left me shaken as I exited the shop and stood in front of Lucy's door. Was this a bad idea? Spontaneity was not my forte, and I doubted she'd be thrilled to see me. I was pretty sure I'd upset her when I dropped her off after our night together. She deserved better . . . but maybe I could give her better.

There was nothing saying I couldn't extend my stay in Starlight Grove. Nothing waited for me in New York besides my office.

I pushed the door open, and Lucy stuttered to a stop in the middle of the room. Her arms were filled with bolts of fabric. My lungs greedily dragged in her scent, settling my emotions and making my cock twitch.

"Hi." I took a few slow steps toward her.

Her eyes were wide. "Hi?"

"Do you need help with that?"

"No." A bolt of fabric fell from her arms and hit the floor with a loud *thud*. She glared at it like it had personally betrayed her.

I put the vase on a side table before gathering up all the fabric in my arms. "Where do you want this?"

"I don't need your help."

"Humor me. It will make me feel useful."

She huffed and gestured for me to follow her into the back room. "You can just put it there."

"On the floor?"

She crossed her arms. "Is that a problem?"

"Of course not." I set everything down, stacking them as neatly as I could.

"What can I help you with? Do you need another tux?"

My chest twinged at her frosty tone and the confirmation that I had hurt her.

I stepped toward her. She stepped back.

I growled. My alpha saw it as a challenge. I kept advancing until her back was pressed against the wall, her chest heaving as I caged her in.

"King," she whispered.

"I love my name on your lips. It sounds so fucking good, baby."

Her scent deepened with arousal, but there was still an edge of anxiety in her eyes that I was desperate to erase.

"What are you doing here?"

I had no business touching her, but I couldn't stop myself from cupping her jaw and running my thumb along her cheek. "I'm here to see you. I brought you flowers."

"I don't understand."

"I can't stop thinking about you and our night together. I couldn't stay away anymore."

Hurt flashed across her face, and I furrowed my brow in confusion. Why would that make her upset?

"You're here for another one-night stand, then? Can it still be called that if it's not just one night?"

I snarled, tightening my hold on her chin and forcing her to meet my gaze. "I am not here for a fuck. I'm here for *you*."

"What—what does that mean?"

I opened my mouth and shut it again. Shit. What did it mean? This was why I didn't fly by the seat of my pants. My life was planned out, orderly and predictable. Relationships were the opposite of that. I'd used my work as an excuse to push people away the past decade, and once I'd hit forty, I'd resigned myself to staying single. But . . . maybe I could do this. Court Lucy. At least until she realized I wasn't nearly good enough for her.

She sighed and pushed her hand against my chest. I took a reluctant step back.

"King, if you don't even know what you want, this isn't . . ."

"Just hold on one second."

She chewed her lip and I freed it with my thumb. Touching her mouth was the ultimate temptation, but I resisted kissing her. She needed to know I was interested in more than just hooking up.

"I don't know how to do this, baby. My life has been a mess the past few months, and nothing has made sense until that night with you." My hand shifted to her throat. Her eyes flared. "Can I take you out on a date tonight, princess? Let me spoil you like you deserve, and we'll figure the rest out."

She shook her head and my heart dropped.

"I can't tonight. I'm setting up for a craft night I'm hosting tomorrow. But . . . I could add an extra chair for you if you wanted to come."

My heart skipped a beat. I possessed absolutely no artistic talent, but I didn't give a fuck. Lucy was giving me an opening.

"I'll be there."

Her lips quirked as she tried to hide her smile. "Okay. I'll see you then."

"Let me help you set up."

"What?"

"For craft night." I looked around. "Do you have more things to carry around?"

"You don't have to do that."

I lightly squeezed her neck. "I was an ass to you the other day. So yes, I do. Put me to work."

She perfumed and I knew I had her.

I spent the next hour moving furniture and large boxes of fabric, scolding Lucy whenever she tried to lift something heavy. That's what I was here for. My alpha preened under her gaze and I had to stop myself from taking my shirt off to better show off my muscles.

By the time we wrapped up, Lucy was smiling as she chatted excitedly about the event. Her sweet "See you tomorrow," paired with a kiss on my cheek, meant I was practically floating as I headed home.

30

LUCY

> **HOROSCOPE PISCES**
>
> Pisces, our dreamer. Celebrate the romantic, passionate parts of you, but don't forget to pair your dreams with action.

OLIVE, SUMMER, AND IVY BURST INTO THE SHOP WITH ARMfuls of bags.

"The craft night crew has arrived!" Summer shouted. "I'm ready to perfect my stabbing skills."

"Please stick to stabbing the fabric only," I said as I placed a small pack of needles by each place setting.

"Stanley is coming, so no promises." She smiled sweetly as she placed a gorgeous tiered cake on the snack table while Olive and Ivy unloaded seemingly endless food containers. I'd hired Summer to cater the event and should have expected that she'd go overboard.

"This is way too much food," I protested.

"No such thing," Olive responded. "Easton is coming and he said he's starving."

Summer snorted. "I should have baked a second cake."

"Wow, Lucy, you did an amazing job cleaning the shop," Ivy said, looking around with wide eyes. "I've never seen it like this."

My cheeks heated, not because of her shock—everyone knew organization was not my thing—but at the reminder of *how* it had gotten like this. Whenever I tried cleaning on my own, I inevitably got distracted and suddenly four hours had passed and I was on the floor surrounded by sheets of paper and pressed flowers. But with King's help, I'd gotten it done in a fraction of the time.

And when I came downstairs this morning, I thought I could still catch a trace of his scent.

"I liked the mess." Summer squeezed me into a tight hug. "But I guess this is better for events."

"I suppose I'll have to keep it clean if I do more of these."

"People are going to be banging down the door to schedule with you." She rested her head on my shoulder and I stroked her hair.

"You okay?"

She hummed. "Just tired. I keep waking up in the middle of the night with ideas for the bakery menu and recipes I need to tweak."

I returned her tight hug. "You have to take care of yourself." Not that I had room to talk. I kept a notebook by my bed with all the sketch ideas that came to me in the middle of the night. "I appreciate you coming tonight, even though you're so busy. It means a lot."

"Anything for you, babe."

I chewed my lip. "I just hope people have fun."

This event had emerged out of the burnout I was feeling lately with tailoring. There was absolutely an art to tailoring, but it had never been my passion. The tiny voice in the back of my mind, the one my exes had almost completely stamped out, whispered that it was time for me to finally produce my clothing line, the one I'd been dreaming up since I was sixteen. But I was terrified of failing because it would confirm that I wasn't actually capable of doing something serious. I didn't have a college degree, had never done a fashion internship, and had no formal training. Maybe that was the next step I needed to take. I could apply for internships or classes or *something*. Except that would mean leaving Starlight Grove.

Olive joined us, squeezing me into a tight hug on my other side. "It's going to be amazing. I'm super excited to learn. Come over here, Ivy. It's group hug time."

Ivy laughed as she put down the chips she was pouring into a bowl. I closed my eyes as my three friends squished me hard among them. How could I even think of leaving *this*?

When we finally broke apart, Summer flopped down in a chair. "Who's coming tonight?"

I pulled up the attendee list on my phone. "We've got Marisol, Carmen, Stanley, Harry, Olive's guys, Ivy's guys, Naomi, Ella, and Lina. Oh, and Wilder, King, and Leo." I mumbled that last part so it took my friends a second to process what I'd said, but once they did, it was mayhem.

"What?" Summer shrieked, jumping up from her chair while Ivy and Olive gasped dramatically.

"I'm glad we're going to be super chill about this," I deadpanned.

"Forget being chill! Tell us everything." Olive's eyes gleamed with excitement in such contrast with the reserved, standoffish omega who had moved to town a few months ago.

"I thought they might like to come, so I invited them." My tone was light and breezy as I unnecessarily straightened a stack of paper. It was no big deal that the guys were coming. I *definitely* hadn't imagined them getting along so well that by the end of the night, they declared their undying love to me, decided we should all be a pack, and carried me to my nest to ravage me.

Nope. Definitely wasn't thinking anything like that.

"I didn't know you were talking to King again. How did I miss that?" Olive asked.

My cheeks heated. "He actually stopped by yesterday." My eyes flicked to the large floral arrangement in the center of the food table. "And brought me flowers."

Another loud round of squeals and jumping followed, and this time, I couldn't stop myself from joining in.

"What did he say when he brought the flowers?" Summer asked.

"He said he couldn't stay away." And that we'd *figure the rest out*, whatever that meant.

Ivy squeezed my hand. "I'm so happy for you. Are they officially courting you?"

The anxiety monster who lived in my chest reared its head. "Not officially."

Summer waved her hand dismissively. "That's just a formality. Mark my words, you'll be courting by the end of the night."

It was ten past seven and my attendees were gathered around the table, drinks and snacks in hand.

Everyone except the absent Leo, King, and Wilder.

I snuck away to the back of the store to check my phone, clinging to the hope that the guys had all texted me and the notifications had somehow been swallowed.

But there was nothing.

My palms grew clammy at the realization that Leo and I were the only ones who had actually exchanged numbers—we'd done it right after he moved in next door. How was it possible that I had spent the night with Wilder and slept with King and didn't have their numbers? I chewed my lip. I could text one of the firefighters to ask for Wilder's cell, but was that too stalkerish?

Stalkerish and clingy. But what if something had happened to them?

I sent Leo a text checking in.

An arm around my shoulder made me jump. "Don't worry. I'm sure they're just running late," Ivy said.

I smiled. "Yeah, probably."

She gave me a little squeeze. "Come on. You can catch them up when they get here."

31

KING

I FLIPPED THROUGH THE HUGE STACK OF LEGAL PAPERS IN front of me, my irritation growing with every passing second.

I shut the folder and leaned back in my chair. The gathered members of Blackthorne Ventures shifted uncomfortably as I stared them down. Good. I wanted them on edge.

"Where is the environmental impact report?" I asked.

"Is it not there?" the CEO asked, an over-the-top look of confusion on his face. "That's so strange." He looked at the company lawyer. "Do you know what happened with that?"

"It must not have been finalized before the secretary printed the documents, but we do have it."

The CEO nodded. "I was sure it was something like that. Kristen's nice to look at but isn't always the sharpest." Several of his coworkers joined in with his laughter.

I wasn't smiling.

"What I recommend is that we sign this contract tonight, since we're all here," the lawyer said. "With the understanding that we'll add the environmental impact report as an addendum later.

How stupid did they think I was?

I steepled my fingers, the picture of calm even as every muscle in my body was lined with tension. "I can wait while you get the complete report." I was in no rush to close this deal now that I had a reason to stay in Starlight Grove.

The CEO spluttered. "Kristen has gone home for the night. There's no one to print the document."

My jaw clenched and I made a mental note to have Caroline reach out to Kristen and offer her a job. She deserved better than working with these assholes. Besides, stealing their assistant would piss them off, which was just the cherry on top.

"Oh, I'm sure if you all put your minds together, you can figure out how to work the printer." I gave them my practiced corporate smile—utterly bland with a sinister edge.

They spouted off excuses. I tuned them out.

Did they have the environmental impact report but wanted to hide what it contained, or had they never commissioned it, assuming I wouldn't notice it was missing?

Either way, I was not the right person to fuck with.

I glanced at my watch, startled when the face read seven-thirty. My chest tightened, and my leg started bouncing before I could stop it. Lucy's event.

Shit.

I was late and didn't even have her number to let her know.

She consumed my thoughts, infiltrated my dreams, and now these assholes were encroaching on my time with her. This meeting should have finished over an hour ago, but every single point of the contract had turned into a long, drawn-out battle.

"Do you have somewhere you need to be?" The CEO's smug tone made me bristle.

I adjusted my jacket sleeve and held his gaze until he cleared his throat and looked away.

"So, gentlemen, are we going to track down this report?"

32

WILDER

I TUGGED AT MY SHIRT AS I LOOKED IN THE MIRROR, WISHING I owned something nicer. I spent all my time either on shift or in the mountains, so it wasn't like I needed a suit or even a button-down, but it didn't feel right to go to Lucy's event in a flannel shirt and jeans.

I would never be Prince Charming, but it'd be nice not to feel like an ogre next to the pretty little omega.

I tied back my hair in a topknot and forced myself away from the mirror.

Get your shit together. It's going to be fine.

I would just tell Lucy I needed her help with my wardrobe. Actually, that was perfect. It would give me a real excuse to spend more time together. Except . . . that was exactly what I shouldn't be doing.

I snagged my bottle of rut suppressants on my way out of my bedroom. The max dose listed was one pill a day. I'd been taking two a day ever since meeting Lucy, and that was barely enough. I'd kept my alpha under control the other day at the diner, but yesterday at the grocery store, I'd been practically huffing the cartons of strawberries before realizing what I was doing.

I swallowed hard as I imagined turning feral during craft night, my alpha taking over until there was nothing of me left besides instinct. My self-loathing returned full force. What if I hurt her? I wouldn't deserve to live.

The smart thing to do would be to text her and say something came up. A fire emergency. Shit, I could even set something on fire to make it more realistic.

But texting her would mean I'd have to admit that I got her number from Ezra.

I hung my head in my hands and groaned. I was officially losing my shit.

Tonight would be fine. We wouldn't be alone. She would be safe.

I popped open the tiny orange bottle and took my third suppressant of the day before grabbing my keys and the box of chocolates I'd gotten for Lucy. I'd spotted them at the market and they brought back memories of all the chocolates my dads had given my mom. They would grow almost giddy when they found an especially unique box of chocolates. When I was younger, I hadn't understood why it made them so happy to give her presents, but I did now. I would bring Lucy presents every day just to see her smile.

I locked the door behind me, but in my rush to get to my truck, I stumbled on the porch steps and face-planted hard in the dirt. I landed on the chocolates, the corner of the box stabbing my stomach.

Fuck. Luckily, besides my stinging palms and sore chin, my pride was the only truly injured thing.

I pushed myself off the ground but immediately collapsed again. My arms trembled with exertion, my muscles too weak to hold my weight.

The world spun around me in a haze of green and brown. My last thought before the world turned dark was how I'd wasted all that time getting ready just for my outfit to get covered in dirt.

33

LEO

"Leo, my love, what are you doing here?"

I groaned as Bibi entered the greenhouse, a large basket hanging off the crook of her arm. I'd parked around the corner from my family's house and practically crawled through the edge of the yard so they didn't see me, but I should have known she would discover me. Nothing got by her.

"I'm just here to check on the peonies, Bibi." I'd been helping her in the greenhouse for years, but this was the first time I was growing flowers to sell on a larger scale. For now, I sourced them from a small farm in Maple Glen, but I hoped that eventually the majority of the flowers in my shop would be home grown.

I crossed over to where she was standing and kissed her cheeks before reaching out and taking her basket out of habit, even though *I* was the one with the cane while she walked perfectly in her old age.

"What's wrong?" She peered at me, her gaze too knowing.

"Nothing."

She hummed and patted my cheek. "Help me pick my herbs, azizam, and then we will have tea."

"I don't have time for tea."

Her narrowed eyes said it all: *There is always time for tea.*

I sighed and followed her around with the basket as she hummed the tune of a lullaby. It brought me back to the sunny afternoons we spent together in Tehran, flipping through old horticulture and gardening books as she told me stories of her childhood when she helped her parents harvest roses to make rose water.

She finished picking her herbs and gestured for me to follow her to the house.

"Bibi, I'm not good company tonight," I tried again.

She made a dismissive noise and that was that. She was the matriarch of our home, one of my favorite people in the entire world, and she would not be denied.

I opened the back door for her, gesturing for her to enter first. The scent of familiar spices—saffron, cumin, and cardamom—hung in the air.

"Leo, I didn't know you were coming home tonight." Maman beamed as she crossed the kitchen and pulled me into a tight hug.

"Did someone say Leo?" Baba's voice boomed across the house, and moments later, he entered the kitchen. His face lit up and he squashed Maman and me between his large arms. "My son, your presence brings us great joy."

I didn't want to be around anyone this evening. Or rather, there was one person I wanted, but she didn't want me back. But being surrounded by my parents put me more at ease. There was no doubt I belonged here.

We fell into an easy rhythm created over countless evenings of family dinners. I served Bibi tea, Maman made tahdig, and Baba handled the kebab. Occasionally, Maman and Baba exchanged concerned looks when they didn't think I was looking, but they didn't push me to talk.

We gathered at the table, but the warmth of the food and conversation couldn't quite touch the ice-cold lump that was my heart. Baba doted on Maman like usual, adding food to her plate without her asking and refilling her tea glass. I'd grown up surrounded by so much love, but now I was left without anyone to give it to. And that hurt.

I withdrew into my head, half listening to my family's conversations. Maman was working on a large rural maternal health grant, and Baba was planning a greenhouse expansion. Bibi was unusually quiet, but the mischief dancing in her eyes had me bracing.

I was trying to decide if my stomach would stretch enough for me to eat seconds when she spoke up.

"Azizam, next time you come for dinner, bring Lucy."

"Yes, you must," Maman added a little too quickly, growing my suspicion that they had previously discussed this. "She's *so* lovely."

"And talented," Baba added with perfect timing, like this was a skit they were performing. "She emailed me progress photos of my suit, and I am definitely going to be the most handsome man at the award ceremony."

"When you pick up the suit, you should invite her to dinner," Bibi said.

They stared at me expectantly. *Was I saying how much I loved my family? Because I take it back.*

"We're not really . . ." I trailed off because what was there to say? She chose someone else over me. An alpha.

"Not what?" Maman's eyebrows knitted together.

I shoveled a huge bite of rice into my mouth to buy me some time. I didn't want to lie to them, but I was embarrassed.

Everyone stared at me while I chewed. Slowly. Only the sound of the front door broke our staring contest, but the distraction was not welcome because there was only one person it would be.

Sure enough, my sister strode into the room wearing an embroidered pink headband I knew she'd gotten from Lucy. I held back a groan. All I'd wanted was to spend the evening alone, wallowing in my depression, but now I found myself caught in an Azad-woman ambush. Damn my family for having healthy communication skills.

Parisa greeted everyone with hugs and kisses before sitting down beside me.

"Who sent out the bat signal?" I asked under my breath.

She snorted as she picked up the glass of tea Baba poured for her. "Bibi was the first to text. Maman's text came twenty minutes later."

Yep. Classic.

"But when Baba texted, that was when I knew something was going on."

My eyes widened. Baba did *not* text, which meant my attempt to hide my dark mood from my family had failed miserably.

"I'm surprised your alphas aren't here. Don't they break out into hives if they're more than three feet away from you?" I was being an asshole, trying to goad her into changing the subject, but she didn't fall for it.

"They're worried about you, too, Le-Lo." She traced her finger along her glass, her scent turning acidic.

Aww, fuck. I couldn't stand seeing my little sister sad, especially when she pulled out my childhood nickname. My full name was Alireza, but Parisa's baby babbling had transformed it to Le-Lo, and once we moved to the U.S., I'd claimed the nickname Leo. It was an easier name for my classmates to pronounce, but it also just felt more like me. Besides, my sappy side loved the reminder of a chubby toddler Parisa chasing her Le-Lo around.

I wrapped an arm around her shoulder. "I'll be okay, Ri-Ri." Her lips tugged up at her own childhood nickname.

"But what happened? Is it Lucy?"

The rest of the table had fallen suspiciously silent. I sighed, but it wasn't like anything I shared would stay secret.

"We went on a date after the last town meeting."

Maman's eyes brightened and Parisa let out a little squeak.

"But it's not going to work out." I took a sip of tea as if it would keep my words from scraping the insides of my throat. "An alpha came into my shop yesterday to buy Lucy flowers."

"Who?" Parisa asked.

I shrugged. "I don't know. Last week, Lucy and I were supposed to have our first date and she stood me up. Turns out, she was in Boston with this alpha."

"She stood you up?" Maman's lips turned down in a fierce frown. "I thought she was better than that. At least you know now. Don't waste your time on inconsiderate people who don't appreciate you."

"She's not inconsiderate." I grimaced at the bite in my tone and forced myself to loosen my jaw. "She made a mistake and she apologized. But she didn't tell me about this guy, and obviously something is going on between them."

Maman's scowl persisted, but Parisa looked confused.

"Okay... and? If she apologized for standing you up, I don't understand the issue. It sounds like she's building a pack."

The fire of my righteous indignation spluttered and then extinguished.

I had been so caught up in my self-pity and insecurities, I'd forgotten one of the most basic facts about omegas. Of fucking *course* Lucy needed a pack. I'd discarded my hope of being part of a pack so thoroughly after college it hadn't even dawned on me that Lucy would consider having me as part of her pack alongside the handsome alpha. King. I'd been drawn to him from the moment he entered my store. When he'd talked about Lucy, I hadn't just felt rejected by her—I'd been *jealous* that I couldn't have him, too. Instead of asking Lucy about any of this, I'd thrown a pathetic fit and stood her up for her craft night when she'd told me she wanted me there.

My hand shook as I pulled out my phone. I'd put it on *Do Not Disturb* so I could sulk without interruptions. Looking at the bright screen now only made me feel worse. Lucy had texted me two hours ago.

I had let her down.

"You really think so?" I asked softly.

"Yeah, Leo. She needs a pack and she would be lucky to have you. Any omega would."

I swallowed hard. "Probably not anymore. I was supposed to go to an event she's hosting tonight."

"What are you doing here still?" Bibi asked, tossing her hands in the air.

Maman hopped up from the table. "Bring her food."

"Yes, good idea." Baba jogged after her to the kitchen.

My brow furrowed. They'd met Lucy for all of a few minutes and were already this obsessed? Actually, yeah. That tracked. She had that effect on everyone.

Moments later, I was being pushed out the door, multiple glass containers of food in my hands and my family's shouts of encouragement following me to the car.

34

LUCY

"Lucy, cariño, the embroidery goddess is not on my side tonight." Marisol waved her embroidery hoop in the air and I grinned. Always the flare for drama.

I helped her untangle her thread before walking around the table to check on everyone's progress. I'd played a game with myself when selecting the pattern option for tonight, guessing which attendee would choose what pattern. I'd been spot-on with one exception—in a shocking turn of events, Stanley had chosen a custom pattern I'd designed of Felix wearing a bow tie. The cat in question was sitting on the table next to Stanley, closely supervising his work.

"You've done a good job organizing this," Stanley said as he effortlessly completed stitching Felix's tail.

"Wow, thanks, Stanley." Praise from our human mayor was rare.

"Although, you do not have a prominently displayed event permit or evacuation route."

I pursed my lips. There it was.

Harry patted his husband's hand. "You're off the clock, babe."

"The mayor is never off the clock," Stanley grumbled.

Harry winked at me, and I hid my smile behind my hand as I moved to help Easton and Lars.

"How's it going, big brother?" My lips twitched at the tangled mess in front of him.

"This is worse than when you made me play with your Barbies," he grumbled with a scowl.

I rolled my eyes. "That's weird because I remember you begging me to play with you."

"As if," he huffed. He did a double take when he looked at Olive's flawless embroidery of a mermaid tail emerging from ocean waves. "How is yours so fucking perfect?"

My friend grinned and met my gaze, but I quickly looked away. I couldn't handle the concern and pity I knew I'd find there. The way I'd avoided Ivy, Summer, and Olive's pointed stares all evening should win me an Olympic medal.

At first when the guys didn't show, I'd been concerned that something had happened to them, but as the minutes ticked by, the truth became clear: None of them wanted to spend time with me.

How could I have been so stupid? My twenty-ninth year was supposed to be about me and my personal growth, but so far I'd spent it obsessing over men. I'd deluded myself into thinking my horoscopes were telling me to say yes to romance, and now I was left with a broken heart and only myself to blame.

Finally, mercifully, the event came to a close. All I wanted was to bury myself in my nest and cry myself to sleep. Was that too much to ask? Yes, apparently it was because my friends were packing up their things at sloth speed, and Olive and Ivy gestured for their guys to wait outside.

"Thanks for coming," I said brightly, busying myself with putting away the leftover food. "I think people had fun."

"Lucy." Olive's gentle tone brought tears to my eyes, which just made me irritated. My mental breakdown wasn't scheduled to start for another ten minutes.

"Whew, am I tired. I think I'll leave cleaning up for tomorrow." I silently willed my friends to move to the door. *It's right there. Go. Go. Go.*

"Are you okay?" Olive took a hesitant step toward me.

My lips were frozen in an unnatural smile. "Me? I'm totally fine."

"Did they text or anything?" Ivy asked.

I squeezed my eyes shut and shook my head. I knew my friends wouldn't judge me, but standing here, all pathetic and rejected, when Ivy and Olive were packed up and happy? I died a little on the inside.

"What fucking assholes," Summer snapped. "We will get our revenge."

"Yes, revenge." Olive nodded sagely. "We'll recruit Felix to help."

Ivy, our peacemaking rule-follower, looked briefly conflicted, but when she caught my gaze, she nodded. "No one hurts our Lucy."

I swallowed the hard lump in my throat as my friends all squished me into a group hug.

"Breakfast at the diner tomorrow," Summer said, her tone leaving no room for argument. "For plotting and pancakes."

"I bet we can convince Char to make those strawberry cheesecake ones," Ivy said, clearly trying to make me feel better.

It was working. I loved those pancakes.

"Sounds good. I'll see you all in the morning." My smile was wobbly as we hugged one more time.

A few minutes later, I was in my nest and ready for my breakdown, but instead of crying, I found myself going on my phone and looking up fashion internships. Most of the application deadlines had already passed for summer and fall internships, but several had waitlist forms that I filled out just for the heck of it.

My heart was a pained, aching lump in my chest at the thought of leaving. Starlight Grove was my home—the holder of my childhood memories and the place I'd hoped to grow old. But I refused to wallow my life away.

And I was done begging people to love me.

35

LEO

By the time I got back to Starlight Grove, it was after ten and Lucy's store was dark.

My heart pounded as I got out of the car and peered through her shop window. Nothing.

I knocked on the door but was unsurprised when no one came. Even if Lucy could hear me from upstairs, why would she answer? She hadn't answered any of my calls on my drive over.

I pressed her contact name again, my heart sinking with every ring. My forehead thudded against her door.

I had messed up over and over again with Lucy, but no more. She had no reason to forgive me, no reason to give me yet *another* chance, but I wouldn't give up this time. She might decide she didn't want to be with me anymore, but it wouldn't be for my lack of trying.

36

KING

I slid into a parking spot near Lucy's store and took a deep breath. Even though I told myself that shit happens and Lucy probably hadn't even noticed I didn't attend craft night, guilt clawed at my insides. Yesterday, it had seemed so important to make Blackthorne Ventures squirm. My parents had drilled into me the importance of never showing weakness, and leaving that meeting would have been weak. But when I'd driven past her dark store on my way home last night, I wondered why I was holding on to their values when they had been three of the most unhappy alphas I knew. I'd been so desperate to win their love and attention that I'd spent my entire life doing what I thought would make them happy—including leaving a career I loved. And where had that left me?

Lucy made me happy. The unsettled feeling I'd carried with me for years vanished when she smiled at me.

And I had let her down.

I got out of the car and stopped abruptly when I saw a huge alpha standing in front of Lucy's shop, his arms crossed. His hair was tied up in a bun and he wore work pants and a long-sleeved black shirt. I pulled myself to my full height as I approached. What the fuck was he doing outside Lucy's shop? Was he bothering her?

As I got closer, I realized the sign on the door read *Closed*.

I ignored the alpha as I peered through the window. The shop was supposed to open at nine, but there was no sign of movement inside.

I turned to find the alpha scowling at me. My jaw ticked. "Are you waiting for Lucy?"

A Pack for Spring

He lifted his chin in affirmation but said nothing.

I fought the urge to roll my eyes. "Do you know when she opens?" I could get her coffee and breakfast while I waited. In my experience, gifts were the way to earn a woman's forgiveness.

Before he could answer, Leo emerged from his shop, a massive bouquet in his arms. He stopped short when he saw us, his eyes flicking to the sign on Lucy's door.

"Lucy isn't in?"

"Apparently not. How long have you been here?" I addressed my question at the mountain of an alpha.

"Twenty minutes." His voice was rough, like he didn't use it very often.

"Oh," was Leo's only response. "It's Wilder, right?"

He lifted his chin.

"This is King." Leo nodded at me.

I didn't give a fuck about introductions. "Did she order flowers?" I asked Leo.

"Um, no."

The three of us stood awkwardly, avoiding eye contact, until the beta spoke.

"Are you two courting Lucy?" There was a fierceness to his tone that set me on edge.

"So what if I am?" I said at the same time the other alpha grunted. Seriously, did this guy know how to form words?

Leo's grip tightened on the flowers, but he didn't back down. "Well, I'm courting her, too."

My alpha bristled, but I also found his assertiveness attractive.

"Were you at craft night?" I asked.

Leo looked unsure for the first time. "Ah, no. I couldn't make it. You?"

"I had work," I muttered.

We both looked at Wilder. I swear if he just grunted . . .

"Something came up," he said.

"Wait." Leo's eyes widened. "We were all invited to craft night and didn't go? Shit."

This was worse than I thought. Lucy must be really upset.

Leo's big bouquet of flowers taunted me. "I'll be back," I muttered, heading across the street to Beans 'n Bliss, refusing to be shown up by the hot beta.

37

LUCY

> **HOROSCOPE PISCES**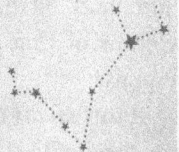
>
> Pisces, our compassionate spirit. Your sensitivity is your strength. Keep your eye out for the vulnerable, and see how you can lend a hand!

I WRAPPED MY ARMS AROUND MYSELF AS I TRUDGED INTO THE tree line at the base of the mountain. I wasn't going hiking again—I wouldn't repeat that mistake—but I needed to get away.

Golden, early morning light streamed through the tree canopy. I swallowed around the lump in my throat. All the enthusiasm and excitement I'd felt about last night's class had been quickly snuffed out with Wilder, Leo, and King's absences.

Just because you're an omega doesn't mean you get to act spoiled. Not everything's going to go your way all the time.

Stop crying. You're always crying.

Maybe you need to up your suppressant dose if you're going to be this emotional all the time.

I sank down on the forest floor, wishing my omega wasn't so . . . much. I only had myself to blame for how I was feeling. I'd let myself get infatuated *again*. I'd started dreaming of nests and heats and being spoiled by a pack *again*. In the midst of my fantasies, I'd ignored the waving red flags that clearly communicated that these guys weren't really interested in me.

The sounds of the woods washed over me, and dappled light through the trees danced against my closed eyelids. Tears spilled down my cheeks and I buried my face in the sleeves of the baggy sweatshirt

I'd pulled over my pajamas—the ones covered with illustrated Felix faces.

There were so many things I needed to do today—clean up my shop, get caught up on my invoices and expense reports, and muster up the energy to put on a good face at breakfast with my friends—but I just wanted to stay here and ignore reality. The Felix's Feral Four group chat had already been inundated with messages this morning "just checking in." The fact that I usually slept in bought me a tiny window of time to pull myself together before they demanded a response.

A tiny *squeak* made my muscles tense. I lifted my head and checked my surroundings. Was that a mouse? A chipmunk?

There it was again.

Whatever it was, it sounded upset. I rubbed my temple. If I was smart, I would scoot out of here before I got attacked by some rabid woodland creature, but I was not smart. I got on my hands and knees and peered through the underbrush until I locked eyes with a tiny baby bunny.

"Aww, hey cutie. Are you waiting for your mama?" I wished I had my phone so I could take a picture. I stayed still, not wanting to scare it, but the more I looked, the more concerned I grew. The bunny's eyes were open, but it was lying on its side and barely moving. I had no idea what normal bunny behavior was, but something about how it was positioned had me worried.

I slowly crawled closer and pushed aside the leafy branch that was half covering the bunny, revealing a gash on its hind leg.

"Oh no," I whispered. I looked around as if a bunny ambulance would appear out of thin air. "I feel like I'm not supposed to touch you, but I also can't leave you." What if the cut was infected? I hesitated a few more heartbeats, wishing again that I had my phone and could look up what to do.

The bunny let out another tiny squeak and its eyes started to close. Panic shot through me. "I'm sorry if I'm doing the wrong thing," I murmured as I gently picked it up. I tucked it against my chest, careful

A Pack for Spring

not to bump the injured leg, and headed back to town as fast as I could. "I'm going to take you to James, and he'll fix you right up. I know, I don't like going to the doctor, either, but he's really nice. I promise."

The town was starting to wake up by the time I hit Main Street. Shops were opening, many of them already sporting Easter-themed decorations and signs for the Eggstravaganza. A few people called out to me and waved, but I didn't stop. Whisker's Vet Clinic was all the way at the end of the street, and the walk felt endless.

I passed my shop on the opposite side of the street and did a double take when I saw Wilder, King, and Leo standing outside my door. What were they doing? At least I had confirmation that they were alive.

"Don't worry. You're my priority, little cutie. Men are the absolute worst. Unless you're a boy. That doesn't count."

I kept my head down, hoping they wouldn't spot me, but I wasn't that lucky. I quickened my pace, ignoring the steady pounding of their footsteps.

Wilder got to me first. "Where have you been?"

The question stopped me in my tracks, and I whirled around to face him. "Where have *I* been? What kind of question is that?"

His eyes widened at my tone, but I kept walking. The clinic was in sight. *Please be open. Please.*

"Lucy, wait," Leo called out.

King jogged to my side. "I got you a latte."

I glanced over at him. *What?*

He ruffled his hair. "Look, I know you're upset, but let's just talk about this."

"What are you carrying?" Wilder asked, his long legs easily keeping up with me.

"A bunny. Since you're here, open the door for me and then go away."

"Did you say bunny?" King asked.

Wilder pulled on the clinic door. "It's locked."

Panic rose in my chest. The bunny wasn't moving much, and I

was terrified I was too late. "I don't have my phone. Someone needs to call James."

King whipped out his phone, but then the door opened, revealing a confused Naomi. I almost cried with relief.

"Is James in? I found an injured bunny."

"He just got here." She ushered me inside. The guys followed for some inexplicable reason.

James popped his head out of the clinic's kitchen, a Beans 'n Bliss mug clutched in his hand. "Hey, Lucy. What's up?"

I jumped when King and Wilder growled, their scents intensifying as they moved closer to me. What the fuck was going on?

"I found this bunny in the woods and its leg is injured."

James's easygoing expression turned serious as he led me into an exam room and placed a towel on top of the metal table. "Set the little guy down."

I very gently placed the bunny on the towel and hovered close as James examined it. The bunny let out a little squeak, and a relieved breath rushed out of me. It was still alive.

"Poor girl. You've been through it, haven't you?" James said softly.

"She's a girl?"

"She is. I would guess she's just shy of three weeks old. Was she alone?"

I nodded, on the verge of tears. "Did her family leave her?"

"No, no. At this age, they can hop around and are usually weaned and not relying on mom. But this girl's injury has stopped her from doing that. She's dehydrated and hungry."

"What about her leg? Will she be able to hop around again?"

James hesitated, and I was seconds away from losing my shit, when a warm, comforting hand gripped my neck. I let out a shuddering breath at Wilder's touch.

"I can give her pain meds, clean the wound, and suture it, but we need to start her on antibiotics right away. Bunnies are prone to infection."

A Pack for Spring

It wasn't lost on me that he hadn't answered my question. "Will she be able to live a normal bunny life?"

James grimaced. "I certainly hope so, but this isn't my area of expertise. I'm pretty sure there's a bunny sanctuary nearby. Let me check with Naomi if we have their info."

He headed out of the room, and I lay my head on the examination table so I was eye level with the bunny. She was breathing hard, but her eyes were bright and her nose was twitching. "You're such a survivor, sweet girl. We'll get you all fixed up."

"She is very cute." Leo rested his arms on the table. I scowled, hating his stupidly delicious cardamom scent, his floppy curls, his sexy golden skin, and how all of that made my omega want to purr.

Wilder leaned down on my other side. Heat radiated off his body, and I was *not* remotely tempted to press myself against his skin.

He ran a finger down the crown of the bunny's head. The contrast of his huge hands doing something so gentle did something to me.

"What a sweet girl you are."

How was I supposed to resist that deep growl? And why was I jealous of a bunny?

King leaned down on the other side of the table. He was unfairly attractive—perfect hair, chiseled jaw, and a delicious, earthy scent with edges of orange blossom. Being surrounded by these men made my skin flush. My body felt electric and alive, and I groaned when my perfume filled the room. Traitorous omega hormones. I needed to stock up on No-NonScent Deodorant because this was just embarrassing. They'd shown me loud and clear last night that they were not interested in me. At least, not interested enough to make me a priority, and I deserved more than that.

"Her ears are a little lopsided," King said.

I fixed him with my withering stare. "Don't say that. Her ears are perfect."

His eyes widened, but his response was cut off when James returned.

"Good news. I got the bunny sanctuary on the phone, but they can't pick her up until tomorrow. They gave me some care instructions, though, so we'll do our best for her here until then."

The bunny snuggled into my palm and my heart exploded. I didn't want to leave her here. Did they even have a cozy place for her to sleep? Would she get scared?

"Or . . . you could take care of her until then?"

James's eyes were gentle as he looked between the bunny and me, like he could read my mind.

"Would that be okay?" I asked hoarsely. "I want her to get the best care."

"I think so. It will at least be quieter at your place. The owner of the rescue recommended we give her goat's milk since we don't have any bunny formula."

I chewed my lip. "Does the market have goat's milk?"

James frowned. "I can text Marisol and ask. If not, there's a specialty grocery store in Briar's Landing, I think."

"Oh my gosh," Leo said. "My grandma bought some goat's milk the other day for a dish she was making. She might still have some. I'll call her." He stepped out of the room and I had to hold myself back from shouting "Don't go."

"In the meantime, let's get this girl the pain meds she needs and clean up this wound," James said. "Do you want to help me hold her, Lucy? I could also get Naomi in here if you don't want—"

"I'll do it. Just tell me what to do."

I stayed close to the bunny, and Wilder and King stayed close to me as James squirted pain meds into her mouth.

Leo popped back into the room. "She's got some. It's about a half hour drive, so I should be back in an hour."

My jaw dropped. What was happening?

"You don't . . . I mean, are you sure?"

Leo's expression softened. "Of course. It's no problem."

He turned toward the door but let out a pained noise as he stumbled and dropped his cane. His hand slammed against the wall to stop himself from falling.

"Leo!" I lurched toward him but King got there first. He gripped Leo's upper arm, firmly stabilizing him while I leaned down to grab his cane.

"Thanks," he mumbled, not meeting my gaze.

"Are you okay? Do you need to sit down?" I asked.

"No, I'm fine."

I took a small step back at his harsh tone.

"I'll drive," King said.

Leo jolted. "What?"

"My car is parked a couple of blocks down. I'll get it and drive you."

"I'm perfectly capable of driving," he snapped, jerking his arm out of King's grip.

The small room filled with the burnt scents of stress and aggression, and I let out an unintentional whine.

James cleared his throat. "I should mention that wild bunnies have big fear responses. They can actually have heart attacks if they get too scared, so let's all take a deep breath."

Oh my god, she could have a heart attack? That was not going to help me calm down.

Wilder gripped the back of my neck again. "Everything's going to be fine. Leo, go with King." Before Leo could protest, Wilder spoke over him. "I know you can drive, but King's car is closer and time is of the essence."

Wow. Wilder was *commanding*. Not what I expected of him, but I liked it.

"Umm, okay," Leo said, looking confused at his own agreement.

He and King seemed reluctant to leave, casting me long glances before closing the door behind them.

I turned back to the bunny while James tended to her wound. I didn't realize I was crying until Wilder wiped my cheeks.

"She needs a name," he said in his deep, gentle voice.

I nodded. "What about Blossom?" The name popped into my mind and felt right. It wasn't until after I spoke it out loud that I realized I might have been inspired by the remnants of King's orange blossom scent lingering in the air.

"Blossom. That's a great name," James said as he finished closing her wound. "If you want to hang out in the lobby, I can show you how to feed her the goat's milk once the other guys are back." He lined a small box with a towel and placed her inside.

I carried it out to the lobby, feeling like I was holding the most precious thing in the world.

38

WILDER

Lucy, Blossom, and I sat down in the lobby. I spilled out of the tiny clinic chair, pushing my thigh flush against hers.

I needed to create space between us, especially since I hadn't taken any suppressants after last night's shit show. When I'd finally regained consciousness, cold and stiff on the ground, I'd half crawled inside and passed out on the couch.

You need to move. Stand up. Step over. Sit down. Any minute now.

Lucy glanced up at me, her eyes wide and watering. Could she sense the turmoil churning inside me? The danger she was in?

A piece of her hair fell in her face, and before I realized what I was doing, I tucked it behind her ear. My thumb caressed her cheek before I pulled away. "Are you okay?"

She nodded, but her heartbreaking sniffle ruined me.

I softened my voice. "Blossom is going to be fine."

"Yeah."

A couple of people trickled in for their appointments with the vet. Lucy's eyes stayed fixed on the bunny.

"I'm sorry I missed craft night." I'd practiced my speech the whole drive down the mountain, but now that I was in her presence, all the words flew out of my head. "I wasn't feeling well."

My excuse sounded so fucking feeble, but it wasn't like I could tell her the full truth. *Sorry I didn't come. I was passed out on the ground like a fucking idiot after overdosing on rut suppressants, which are the only thing keeping me from going feral and attacking you.*

Lucy's eyes flashed to mine, a little crease between her brows. "Are you feeling better?"

"Yeah."

We lapsed back into silence, and I wanted to smash my head against the wall. This was my chance to have Lucy to myself, and I was wasting it.

Leo's question swirled through my mind—*Are you courting Lucy?* I recognized him from the joint Ocean and Mountain rescue trainings. I assumed his cane had something to do with why he wasn't at the last one.

Well, I'm courting her, too.

Fuck. The thought of sharing Lucy filled me with white-hot possessiveness, but then . . . could I stay in her life if I were part of her pack? I would always have to keep myself at arm's length, would never be able to have sex with her, but if the other guys were there to protect her from me . . .

Would it be better to have a place in the periphery of her life, or would that just cause more pain? Would I be able to see the other guys with Lucy without killing them, especially knowing I could never touch her like they did?

Leo seemed . . . fine. I couldn't say the same about the pretentious alpha. King.

The door opened and the two men in question stepped inside. I held in a snarl as their eyes immediately went to my omega. A gentle touch pulled me up short. Lucy squeezed my wrist before standing.

The entire time James was showing Lucy how to feed Blossom, I could still feel the ghost of her touch on my skin.

It was everything I could never live without.

As we followed Lucy out of the clinic and slowly walked back to her place, I knew one thing for sure: I would do anything to conquer my fear, my jealousy, my fucking *instincts*, if it meant staying in Lucy's life.

She hesitated outside her shop. "Um, well, thanks for the help, I guess?"

"Can I take you out for breakfast?" King asked.

Leo and I scowled at him.

"*I* was going to ask if you wanted to go to breakfast," Leo said. "Also, I got you flowers."

Before I could say that I also wanted to take her to breakfast, Lucy spoke. "I already have breakfast plans."

"What about lunch?" I blurted out.

She scrubbed her hand down her face, her exhaustion clear. I wanted to wrap her up in a blanket and hold her in her nest. My cock twitched at the thought and I took a small step away.

"I can't—" She swallowed. "I can't deal with this right now. I just . . . Thanks for the help." She took the bag of supplies and closed the door behind her.

39

LEO

"So . . ." I trailed off, my eyes locked on Lucy's closed door. "That could have gone better."

The alphas were silent, but their bitter, twisted scents said it all.

I ran my fingers through my messy curls and faced them.

Wilder and King had matching crossed arms, clenched jaws. A wave of insecurity hit me—they were so tall and broad and *alpha*—but I refused to let it drown me. Lucy was too important.

"We should talk."

Wilder lifted his chin in what I assumed was agreement.

"Fine. Where should we go?" King asked.

I gestured at my shop. I wanted to stay close to Lucy.

We shuffled inside.

More awkward silence.

The alphas seemed even more lost than I was, so it was up to me to start the conversation. That was okay. I'd thought things through on the drive and knew what I wanted.

"When you came into my store to get Lucy flowers, I thought you were together," I said, gesturing at King. "I didn't go to craft night because I was jealous. I should have handled it better, and I won't make that mistake again. I'm not letting Lucy go, so the question is, are we going to court her as a pack? Or are you two stepping aside?"

They growled and I bit my lip against my smile. Alphas were so easy to provoke.

"Lucy is mine," King snapped. "I had a work meeting last night that went long, but I'm not going anywhere."

"Guess you're stuck with me, then," I said, cocking an eyebrow.

His gaze on me was so heated it almost made me blush. We'd

driven to my family's home in near silence, King's orange blossom scent and the crackle of tension in the air the only thing passing between us. Maybe I was imagining it and this was all one-sided. Either way, now was not the time to let my attraction to the hot alpha distract me.

I turned to Wilder.

He cleared his throat. "Didn't expect I'd ever have the chance to be with an omega."

"Why not?" I asked.

He shrugged. "Reasons."

King groaned. "For fuck's sake, can we all agree to speak in full sentences?"

I held in a laugh at the alpha's dramatics, but Wilder apparently didn't find it funny. He squared off with King.

"I don't owe you shit."

King took a step toward him. Alpha pheromones filled the air, making me both stressed and aroused. *No time to examine that.*

"Let's tone it down." I stepped between them. "Wilder, are you joining us in courting Lucy?"

He lifted his chin.

"Okay. If we're going to do this, we need to show her we're serious about her, and that we can be a pack. If that's what she wants," I tacked on.

"How are we going to do that when she won't talk to us?" King asked.

I'd thought this through already. "Lucy is close with her friends. We're going to ask them for advice."

40
LUCY

7:02 A.M.

OLIVE

Good morning! How is everyone doing today?

IVY

I'm doing well. Thanks for asking.

SUMMER

I am also well. How are you, Lucy?

8:41 A.M.

OLIVE

Lucy? Are you ok?

SUMMER

She's probably sleeping like all of us should be

But I'm drinking a double espresso this morning so I'm ready to murder those insensitive assholes

IVY

Summer

SUMMER

> What? This is me being a good friend. Assholes who stand up our friend deserve to perish

OLIVE

> We discussed taking a more subtle approach, remember?

SUMMER

> You discussed it. I didn't agree

9:57 A.M.

IVY

> Omg Lucy!! James just called me

> Lucy brought in an injured baby bunny to the clinic!!

SUMMER

> What?? How did I miss this?? MY BAKERY IS ON THE WAY TO THE VET

OLIVE

> Is the bunny ok?

SUMMER

> This is why I need to set up cameras to notify me of any movement on the street!

OLIVE

> Where did you find the bunny?

SUMMER

I hate not being the first to know important information!!!

OLIVE

I want to see the bunny

IVY

That's not all. She was accompanied by LEO, KING, AND WILDER!!!!

SUMMER

THAT'S IT. BREAKFAST IS HAPPENING NOW. GET YOUR BUTT OVER HERE.

OLIVE

Bring the bunny!!

"LUCY!" IVY WAVED AT me from the table in the corner of the diner.

I carefully set my bag down on the table.

"Did you bring the bunny?"

I grinned at Olive's look of pure desperation and gestured at my bag. "See for yourself."

They all leaned over and gasped at the tiny little bunny curled up on the plush piece of velvet I'd folded on the bottom.

"Oh my gosh! She's so cute," Olive cooed. "What's her name? Is she doing okay?"

"Her name's Blossom, and I think so. She drank some goat's milk before passing out. James stitched up her leg, so hopefully she has a full recovery." I couldn't handle anything less.

Summer brushed a gentle fingertip across Blossom's ears. "Where did you find her?"

"In the woods."

"Lucy," Ivy said, her voice full of reproach. "You weren't hiking again, were you?"

I pursed my lips. "No. I just went on a walk to clear my head." I jumped when Felix hopped up on the chair next to me. "Where did you come from?"

"He insisted on coming with me," Olive said, taking the seat beside the mayor. "He would not be dissuaded."

Felix put his paws on the table and peered into the bag. "Um." I grabbed his body. "You're not going to eat the bunny, are you?"

Felix fixed me with a withering stare before turning back to Blossom, a purr bursting through his chest. He didn't look particularly hungry, so I loosened my hold.

"Do you have a new best friend?" Olive asked, scratching his ears.

"Just don't let Stanley see her or he'll start having ideas about how she'll feature in the Easter Eggstravaganza," Summer said.

"That would be so cute! I have to make her a little Easter bunny outfit." My heart sank. "Except the wildlife rescue people are coming to pick her up tomorrow."

Everyone at the table looked as dejected as I felt, Felix included.

"Do they have to take her?" Olive whispered.

I nodded, throat tight. "James said wild bunnies can't be domesticated. I probably shouldn't have brought her here. I don't want to stress her, but she looked too sad for me to leave her behind."

"She doesn't look stressed," Ivy said as Blossom let out the most adorable little squeak before falling back asleep.

"Good morning, ladies." Char came over, notepad in hand. "And Felix, even though the last time you were in here I distinctly remember telling you to stay out."

"What did Felix do?" Olive put her arm around him, squishing her face against his.

"He stole one of Stanley's blueberry pancakes. Snatched it clean off his plate and ran away."

The four of us looked at each other and Summer shrugged. "Eh, who's to say the pancake didn't fall off the plate? Moving on."

Char snorted and took our orders before doing a double take at my bag. "Is that—" She shook her head. "Never mind." She muttered something about omegas as she walked away, and all of us laughed.

"I'll give you a bite of pancake," Olive cooed to Felix. He gave her sad eyes and she huffed. "Fine, two bites."

I grinned. Olive couldn't refuse Felix anything. Not that I could, either.

Char dropped off our drinks and I stirred creamer into my coffee, doing my best to ignore the conspicuous silence that had fallen over the table.

"Sooo . . ." Olive said.

Summer huffed, clearly having exhausted her patience. "What's going on with you and the guys? Did they tell you why they didn't come to the event?"

I shrugged, my heart still aching. "Wilder said he wasn't feeling well, and Leo got caught up with a family thing. I'm not sure about King."

"Why didn't they let you know right away? Did their phones simultaneously break?" Summer's tone was scathing.

"Wilder and King didn't have my number. They were waiting outside my store this morning when I walked by with Blossom on the way to the clinic. I was a bit distracted so we didn't really talk. It's not like they actually owe me anything."

"They owe you human decency and basic consideration." Olive and Felix crossed their arms at the same time, both looking murderous.

"We'll egg their cars and TP their homes," Summer said. "I'm sure Easton will help us."

"My guys will, too," Ivy added.

My lips quirked. "Even Rome?" Rome and Ivy were both sticklers for the rules.

"He cares about you. All my guys do. This whole town loves you, Lucy."

"I appreciate it. But I just want to move on."

"But . . . revenge." Summer sounded so disappointed it almost made me smile.

"We'll find someone else to get revenge on, I'm sure," I said.

Char delivered our food—four orders of strawberry cheesecake pancakes—and Olive mercifully asked Summer how the bakery grand opening was coming along. Summer launched into a long discussion on the pros and cons of industrial bread ovens, drawing the attention away from me.

I immersed myself in the conversation with a smile I didn't quite feel. Ivy's words replayed in my mind. I knew the town loved me, but I couldn't help but wonder what they really thought behind my back.

Lucy, so flighty and unserious. That must be why she can't land a pack.

As soon as I finished eating, I started gathering up my things. "I've got to get going."

Ivy frowned. Our breakfast dates usually stretched for hours until an exasperated Char kicked us out. "So soon? Why?"

"I got behind on some custom orders with the workshop and everything, and Blossom needs some quiet."

"Are you sure you're okay?" Olive asked softly. "It's okay if you're not."

"Thank you. I'll be fine." I leaned down and gave her a hug. Ivy and Summer joined in, squishing me among them, until I pulled away with a strained smile.

I picked up the bunny transport bag and headed out the door, Felix slipping outside with me.

"Are you hanging out with me today? I don't have a new outfit ready for you yet, but we could brainstorm for the Eggstravaganza."

He flicked his tail, leading the way as we crossed the street. I hadn't been lying to my friends—I had a ton of work to catch up on—but as I walked into the shop, I knew I didn't have the energy for any of it. My omega was crushed by rejection from the guys she'd already claimed as hers.

I headed upstairs to my nest. Some omegas slept in a normal bedroom and just used their nests for heats, but my omega instincts had always been . . . intense. Without a pack, being in my nest was the only thing that settled me.

I filled another syringe with milk for Blossom, and the three of us curled up in the middle of the plush velvet pillows.

"You are the cutest in the world," I whispered to Blossom as she ate. Felix's paw landed on my arm, his claws slightly digging in to my skin. "And you're the handsomest boy."

He purred and settled in beside me.

Once she was done eating, Blossom made a few tentative hops. Her leg was already looking much better. Felix and I watched her, mesmerized. After a few minutes, she hopped back to me and curled up in the crook of my neck. Everything I'd read about wild bunnies said that they were scared of people, so I had no idea what to make of her behavior. All I knew was that I wasn't ready to say goodbye.

Felix curled up against Blossom's other side, nuzzling his face against her little ears before falling asleep. I carefully pulled out my phone and took a selfie of the three of us. If these were the only moments we would have together, I wanted to remember them.

41

LEO

"You just have the most stunning flowers. I keep telling my grandson to come get a bouquet for his girlfriend. That is, if they stay together. I'm always telling her she's too good for him, but she won't listen."

"That's very nice, Mrs. Cassini," I said. King gestured wildly behind her, and I shot him a look. What was I supposed to do? Throw Starlight Grove's oldest resident out of my shop?

"Well, it was nice to see you—" I started.

"She's just so lovely and my grandson is quite useless. Are you single? I think you'd like her."

King let out a loud, strangled noise.

"Are you all right, dear?" Mrs. Cassini fixed the alpha with her piercing gaze.

"Actually, I think I'm having an allergic reaction. Leo, you should probably take me to the hospital."

The wild look in his eyes really sold his story.

Mrs. Cassini gasped. "Oh no. What are you allergic to?"

"Flowers," King deadpanned.

I masked my laugh with a choked cough. "That sounds serious. I'm sorry to cut our visit short, Mrs. Cassini. I hope you have a good rest of your day."

"You, too, dear." She leaned in. "Keep an eye on that one. Doesn't seem to be very bright."

I nodded sagely. "I certainly will."

We held our breath as she took her bouquet and left the shop.

King let out an exasperated sigh. "Fuck, I thought she'd never leave. Where's Wilder?"

The door swung open, revealing the alpha in question.

"Ready?" he asked.

I'd been ready to track down Lucy's friends right away, but Wilder had gotten a call about an urgent issue at the fire station. Part of me wanted to track down Lucy's friends without him, but that wasn't right. If this was going to work, we had to commit to being a pack.

King had stayed with me at the shop, a move he may have regretted when Mrs. Cassini arrived and proceeded to talk nonstop for thirty minutes about town gossip.

But now we were ready.

"So . . . where do we go?" King asked.

"Let's check Summer's bakery."

Wilder grunted, which made King groan. I chuckled and led the way down the street. I kept a firm grip on my cane, not wanting to risk falling again. Earlier today when I fell, I'd snapped at Lucy again. That was unacceptable. I needed to get my shit together, because so far it wasn't my cane pushing her away—it was my insecurities.

My lips twisted when we found Summer's bakery empty.

"Maybe she's getting coffee?"

We headed back down Main Street in the direction of Beans 'n Bliss. The coffee shop was bustling but no omegas to be found.

A *meow* caught my attention.

"Hey, Felix. You staying out of trees?" Wilder asked, surprising me with his loquaciousness.

The cat flicked his tail at us before strutting to Rosie's Cafe. "I guess we can check in there," I said.

King opened the door, and I immediately spotted three of the four omegas who made up the Omega Overlords—Lucy's name, not mine. Olive, Summer, and Ivy were huddled together in a booth in the corner, deep in thought. Their eyes widened when they saw us.

"Hey. Do you have a minute?" I asked.

Olive smiled, Ivy cocked her head, and Summer narrowed her eyes. "That depends."

"This is King and Wilder. We want to talk with you about Lucy."

A Pack for Spring

Summer made a disgruntled *tsk* but gestured for us to sit. She was clearly the ringleader here.

We faced off with the omegas.

"Well, speak." Summer crossed her arms. Ivy and Olive followed suit.

"You probably don't know who I am," King started, "but Lucy and I—"

"Went to Boston for an event, and you"—Olive gestured at Wilder—"saved her when she was hiking in the woods. And all three of you stood her up at craft night. We're Lucy's besties. Of course we know your crimes."

Wow. Olive was a little scary.

"Right." King was clearly taken aback. "Well, we wanted your advice." He glanced at me, eyes wide with panic.

"We know we messed up," I said. "And we need your help on how to apologize to Lucy and win her back."

"Win her back?" Ivy asked. "I wasn't aware you ever had her."

I swallowed hard. She was right.

"We know she's too good for us. But if she's willing to give us another chance, we want to court her," Wilder said.

Well, he didn't talk much, but when he did, he made it count.

The omegas looked at each other, some secret conversation passing among them.

"All right," Summer said, sitting back in the booth like she was presiding over her subjects. "We'll help you, but if you hurt our friend again, we will destroy you."

"Understood," King said. Wilder and I nodded.

"Lucy believes in signs," Summer said.

Now it was our turn to look at one another.

"What?" Wilder asked.

"Signs, like from the universe. She reads her horoscope in the newspaper every morning, so I would recommend starting there."

"Start where? With horoscopes?" I asked.

Olive's lips quirked into an almost smile before she nodded sagely.

"Yes. You should read your horoscopes every morning and follow the universe's advice. If you're meant to be with Lucy, the universe will show you the way."

I locked eyes with the guys. They were fucking with us, right?

"We were more thinking of getting date ideas or something," I hedged.

Ivy shrugged. "You can ignore our suggestion. I'm sure you can figure it out on your own. That's gone really well so far."

"Do you have any other suggestions?" King asked.

"Nope," Olive said.

Summer flipped her hair over her shoulder. "Why would you need more than the wisdom of the entire universe?"

I opened my mouth and then shut it, finding myself lost for words.

Wilder stood from the table. "We will take your advice." He stalked away.

"Umm, right. Thank you," I said as I followed him.

Wilder was retying his bun outside the diner, the movements highlighting the muscles in his massive biceps. The alpha was undoubtedly hot, but he didn't do anything for me. Not like . . .

King joined us outside the diner.

"That was interesting," he said.

"Not really what I expected them to say." I racked my brain, trying to remember if Lucy had ever mentioned horoscopes to me.

"Do you think they're messing with us?" King asked, glancing back through the diner window.

"Yes," Wilder said.

My eyebrows shot up. "You don't think we should do what they suggested?"

"Didn't say that. They're fucking with us, but that doesn't mean they're wrong."

"What the fuck does that mean?" King asked.

Wilder let out an aggrieved sigh. "Lucy talked about her friends for hours when she was at my cabin. If they say this is what we should do, we do it."

A Pack for Spring

"Makes sense to me," I said.

"All right," King said.

"I have to cover someone's shift today," Wilder said abruptly. "Meet you at the newsstand tomorrow morning at eight."

With that, he stalked off.

"It might be hard for him to work today since he's already used up his quota of the words for the entire day," King said dryly, making me chuckle.

A swirl of questions tornadoed through my mind. We all wanted Lucy, but were these alphas actually interested in becoming a pack or would they eventually try to push me out?

One thing at a time. We were united in our goal to court Lucy, and that would have to be good enough for now.

42

KING

Leo was already at the newsstand when I arrived the next morning. He was leafing through the paper, giving me the chance to take him in without being noticed. His olive-green T-shirt stretched across his lean chest, and my heart fluttered at the way his curls fell over his forehead. I swallowed as my eyes raked down his body. His dark jeans clung to his thighs and ass and were cuffed at the bottom. That detail, along with his leather work boots, gave him an air of effortlessness that I could never achieve but was wildly attracted to.

I'd realized I was bisexual in college after a string of drunken nights forced me to confront that it wasn't the alcohol that made kissing guys so much fun. I'd never taken it farther, but now I couldn't stop thinking about the sexy beta.

He glanced over his shoulder and did a double take when he caught me staring. His expression transformed into a smirk. "Morning."

"Good morning. Thanks for getting the paper."

"Of course. I've actually never read the horoscope section. Now we just need . . . oh, there he is."

Wilder jogged down the street toward us.

"Morning." Leo waved at the alpha. "How was your shift?"

"Fine."

I rolled my eyes. "Let's get this show on the road."

It had been a while since I'd read a physical paper, but I didn't think it was normal for the horoscopes to take up a full spread.

"I looked it up and I'm a Libra. Seems like a missed opportunity for me to be a Leo, but I guess that's not how the universe works," Leo quipped. "What signs are you?"

"Uhh, how do you know?" Wilder asked.

Leo grinned. "It's based on your birthday."

The top of the paper had a chart. My January third birthday made me a Capricorn, and Wilder's November twelfth made him a Scorpio, whatever that meant.

I finally found the appropriate horoscopes.

> ## HOROSCOPES
>
> **LIBRA** sun, lover of beauty! How could you ever express your appreciation? The ladies at the Groovy Bookclub need someone to serve them tea and snacks. They'll appreciate the help (and the view).
>
> **SCORPIO,** feeling like standing strong in your independent spirit today? Well, there's a one-man job just for you. The gutters at Spring in Your Stitch haven't been cleaned in a while, and the forecast calls for rain! Get to cleaning.
>
> **CAPRICORN,** you've always been so ambitious! Today, ignite that same ambition in the town's youth. The stars urge you to head to the kid's career day happening at the elementary school. Don't forget your presentation!

"Huh." Leo looked up from the paper. "I didn't expect them to be so..."

"Specific?" I added dryly.

A low chuckle rang through Wilder's chest, making my jaw drop in shock. This was the first time I'd seen him emote.

"Those omegas are definitely fucking with us," he said with a grin. "We've got our tasks for today. I'm on shift for two days starting tomorrow morning, but I should be able to get away to meet you here at the same time tomorrow."

Before we could respond, the huge alpha walked away, whistling.

"I guess I'm hosting a book club today," Leo said, his grin matching Wilder's. "Hope you have a career day presentation ready."

I groaned. "Want to trade?" Why couldn't the universe tell me to clean Lucy's gutters? Or better yet, her shop—not just because it would give me the chance to be close to her, but also because the state of her store stressed me the fuck out.

"Nah, we can't piss off the stars." He handed me the newspaper. "I'll see you tomorrow morning, if not sooner. Have fun at school." He winked and headed down the street. My eyes stayed on his ass for much longer than appropriate.

I folded up the paper and headed to Beans 'n Bliss. If I was going to be around children, I needed an extra large latte.

The coffee shop was bustling this morning, but it fell silent when I walked in. I thought I was imagining things until I stepped up to the counter and Ella fixed me with a vicious glare.

I glanced over my shoulder to make sure she was actually looking at me.

She was.

"Good morning?"

"Hmm," she said, raising her eyebrows. "Good for some."

"What?"

She exhaled loudly, like I was inconveniencing her. "What do you want?"

What the fuck? Every other time I'd been in here, the young barista had enthusiastically regaled me with detailed updates of her favorite K-drama.

"Is everything okay?" I asked against my better judgment.

Ella crossed her arms. "I'm very busy, so if you're not going to order . . ."

"Right, well, I'd like an extra large iced latte with strawberry cold foam. I also want to pay for Lucy's coffee in advance."

She paused her angry tapping on the checkout screen. "What?"

"Whenever she comes in, I want to make sure her order is free. I could buy a gift card that you keep for her?"

"Oh. That's . . . nice." She grabbed a gift card and wrote Lucy's name on it. "How much do you want to put on it?"

"Let's start with two hundred."

Her jaw dropped. "Dollars?"

I nodded. "Just let me know when she's running low and I'll put more money on it."

"I . . . okay."

I stared at Lucy's shop through the coffee shop window. Leo had told us she liked to sleep in and never opened her shop on time, but I couldn't look away. I didn't know how it was possible to miss someone I barely knew, but my chest ached at her absence.

Ella called my name. When I went to grab my latte, the barista fixed me with a piercing glare. "You know you can't just win Lucy over with lattes, right?"

I swallowed hard. "Yeah, I know."

Her words stuck with me as I headed out of the shop. The few brief relationships I'd had were more acquaintances-with-benefits situations. There had been no depth to them, and any mistakes I made could be fixed with gifts or money. But Lucy was so much more than that.

I started walking in the direction of the school only to stop short when I spotted a white-haired man crouched down by my car. He was holding a measuring tape with a cat by his side. The cat placed his paw on the measuring tape, and the man nodded before standing.

"Excuse me? This is my car. Is there a problem?"

The man scribbled something on his clipboard. "You are in violation of town ordinance twenty-four point two, subsection C, which states that all cars must be within six inches of the curb when parallel parked."

What? I prided myself on being an exceptional parallel parker. "I've always heard you should be within a foot of the curb. How far away am I?"

He thrust a parking ticket at me. "Six and a half inches."

"You're giving me a ticket because I am *half an inch* too far from the curb?"

He crossed his arms. "Rules are rules. I understand you *visitors* don't always understand how things work in our town here, but it is my job as mayor to ensure no one causes problems."

Oh. Lucy had told me a lot of stories about the town mayor during our road trip. I dug deep to suppress my irritation and turn on the charm.

"I'm King. You must be Felix," I said, holding out my hand.

The man scowled. "What? No, I'm Stanley O'Sullivan. That is Felix." He gestured at the cat.

My brow furrowed. I could have sworn Lucy had said the mayor's name was Felix.

"My mistake. I apologize, Mayor O'Sullivan. I'm certainly not here to cause problems. Since I wasn't aware of the parking ordinance, maybe—"

Stanley cut me off with a dramatic flourish of his clipboard. "Ignorance of the law is no excuse." As he marched away, I swore he muttered, "And you've caused enough problems."

I glanced down at the cat. "Well, that could have gone better."

I HELD THE SMALL Post-it note with the map the Starlight Grove Elementary School receptionist had drawn to help me get to Ms. Winter's classroom. It wasn't until I stepped inside that I realized Ms. Winter was *Ivy*, Lucy's friend. She slapped her hand over her mouth when she saw me, stifling her laughter.

Oh yeah, the omegas were all in on this. While I struggled to find the hilarity of this situation, it would take more than this to scare me off.

"Okay, class, our guests are here!" She clapped her hands to get the attention of the horde of small children. "First up, we have Mrs. Isla Andersson-Spring here to talk about her job as a graphic designer!"

Time stopped as I slowly turned my head. Sitting in the back of a classroom was a petite blond woman who bore a striking resemblance to my omega.

Welcome to my nightmares.

"Then we'll hear from Mr. King about his, uhh, work."

She clearly had no idea what I did, which I might have found funny if I wasn't trapped in a room *with one of Lucy's moms*.

Thankfully, the classroom of children prevented her from doing more than narrow her eyes as she passed me on the way to the front of the room. I took her chair in the back, my anxiety only growing as she delighted the class with her presentation on logo design. She showed different logos she'd made and had the children vote on which version was their favorite. There was much screaming and passionate debate.

I shrank down in my tiny chair. How the fuck was I supposed to follow that?

"Thank you, Mrs. Andersson-Spring! I'm sure you've inspired many budding graphic designers today. Next up is Mr. King."

I walked to the front of the class to a smattering of applause.

"Hello." I gave an awkward wave. "I'm the CEO of Empire Enterprises in New York City."

At that, several children perked up.

"You live in New York City?"

"How tall is your house?"

"One time my dad took me to New York and we ate a hot dog from a cart!"

"Have you ever gotten a hot dog from a cart?"

The children stared at me, riveted.

"Um, yes. I have." Not in a long time, but I had to admit those hot dogs were damn good.

"What do you get on your hot dog, Mr. King?"

"Ketchup, mustard, and relish," I responded. If all of their questions were this easy, this would be a breeze.

"Mustard?" a child squealed. "I hate mustard!"

"I love mustard! But only the yellow one."

"All mustard is yellow!"

"No, it's not! Some is orange!"

"Orange and yellow are the same!"

I sought Ivy, desperate for her help, but she and Lucy's mom just sat in the corner, smiling. I had been abandoned.

"So you work at a hot dog stand?" a redheaded girl asked.

I scrubbed my hand down my face. "No, I'm the CEO of a big company."

"Oh." She looked so disappointed I was tempted to change my career.

"What does a CEO do?" another child asked.

"I have meetings with clients, look over contracts, and make big-picture decisions about the fiscal direction of the company."

The children's eyes glazed over and one boy in the front shouted, "Booooooringgg."

"Tanner, let's keep our words respectful," Ivy chided.

"What did you want to be when you grew up?" another child shouted.

I was fucking sweating. How did I turn this around? "Um, well, I worked in ocean conservation for a while."

"I like the ocean!"

"What's a conservation?"

"It's where you play music! My mom told me!"

"That's a conservatory," Ivy said. "Conservation means to protect something. So ocean conservation is . . ."

"Protecting the ocean!" the children shouted in unison. Well, that was mildly cute.

"Fish James comes from the ocean!" A girl pointed at a fish tank in the corner containing a betta fish.

Excellent. Time for me to shine with my trivia knowledge. "Betta fish actually live in freshwater, not the ocean."

Tanner crossed his arms. "So you don't care about protecting Fish James?"

Last year I negotiated a two-hundred-million-dollar merger. That was leaps and bounds less stressful than this. "Conserving freshwater habitats is also very important to me," I said seriously.

Tanner narrowed his eyes but then he nodded.

Phew.

"Did you protect the ocean from sharks?"

I chuckled. "Nah, we worked to protect everything inside the ocean, including sharks. I actually swam with sharks once."

The kids gasped.

"Did it eat your arm?"

"No," I responded dryly. "I still have two arms. I was in a big cage underwater to protect me, but most sharks are actually really peaceful. Sometimes they attack people, but we have to remember that the ocean is their home."

"Ms. Winter, can we swim with sharks?" a girl shouted.

"Probably not, Madison," she said, receiving a resounding round of "Boo"s. "But remember, we have our field trip to the New England Aquarium in a few weeks."

The children cheered. "Mr. King, are you going to come to the aquarium with us?"

"Oh, no, I don't think—"

"We do need chaperones," Ivy said, an evil glint in her eye.

The children cheered.

When I left the classroom a while later—Lucy's mom at my side and a form confirming me as a field trip chaperone folded in my pocket—I wondered how my life had gone so off the rails so fast. But if I was honest with myself, I'd had more fun talking about ocean animals with Ivy's class than I ever had at my "boring" job.

I held the door open for Lucy's mom and we stepped outside. I tried not to squirm under her piercing gaze.

"Ivy says you're important to Lucy, but my daughter hasn't said anything about you." She cocked her head. "So, are you? Important?"

I opened my mouth and closed it again.

"I hope to be."

She hummed. "Lucy deserves the world. If you plan to give her anything less than everything, you should step back now. Because while I might seem very intimidating, I have three alphas who wouldn't hesitate to destroy you."

With a sweet smile and flounce of her hair, she walked away.

43

WILDER

I SCRAPED ANOTHER CHUNK OF LEAVES OUT OF LUCY'S GUTTERS and thanked the universe I hadn't been commanded to do something *social* to win over my omega. Manual labor was much more in my wheelhouse.

"Umm, what are you doing?" My heart leapt at Lucy's voice. She squinted up at me from the sidewalk, and time stopped because my girl's eyes were red and puffy.

I was down the ladder in an instant, leaning down to cup her face. "What's wrong?"

Lucy's plush lips parted, but no words escaped. She was wearing a soft yellow dress decorated with green vines. She looked perfect except for the fact that she was fucking *crying*.

"Tell me who hurt you, sweetheart, and I'll take care of it." A rumble rolled through my chest as protectiveness surged through me. Lucy was pure sweetness, and she moved through the world giving that sweetness to everyone she met. I would be the one to shield her from the world's harshness.

Her cheeks flushed a gorgeous pink. "Nobody hurt me." At my growl, she continued. "I have to bring Blossom to the wildlife rescue people and I'm sad to say goodbye." She laughed, but it was a hollow sound. "It's my fault for getting too attached. I do that a lot."

It was only then that I noticed the small bunny curled up on her arm, her nose twitching gently in her sleep. "Nothing wrong with that," I said gruffly. And I meant it. "She looks happy with you."

A sad little smile twisted her lips. "She's made both of us happy." I glanced down and realized Felix was sitting by her feet. "I hope I've taken good care of her, but I need to do what's best for her."

Irrational hatred for the wildlife rescue rose in me. "I'll come with you."

She blinked. "Oh. You don't—"

I didn't let her finish her sentence and instead put my hand on her back and guided her down the street to the clinic. She glanced up at me, confusion filling her bright blue eyes, but I had no explanation to offer for my behavior.

"What were you doing on the ladder?" she asked.

"Cleaning your gutters."

"Why would you do that?"

Now it was my turn to be at a loss for words. "It needed to be done."

"Riiiight." She peered at me like she was trying to figure me out.

James was already in the lobby when we arrived. He greeted us with a smile, and I had the urge to smack the expression off his face. I'd never cared about being charming, but now I wished I had the beta vet's easy appeal.

"You're right on time," he said, gesturing at two women who looked to be in their sixties standing by the check-in counter. "This is Mable and Iris from Maine Wildlife Rescue."

"It's nice to meet you. I'm Lucy." She glanced up at me. "And this is Wilder, who is here for . . . reasons."

I snorted and Lucy flashed me a smile that made my breath catch.

Iris clasped her hands together when she caught sight of the still-sleeping Blossom. "She looks like she's doing well."

"I think so." Lucy's voice was steady, but the slight burnt edge to her scent gave her away. I rubbed my hand down her back before I realized what I was doing, my alpha desperate to soothe her.

James opened a door to a small exam room. "I'll take another look at Blossom's leg to make sure it's healing well before we send her to her new home."

All of us filed into the room. My bulk made it a tight squeeze, but I wasn't about to leave Lucy's side.

She set Blossom down on a towel and the bunny immediately hopped back to her. Mable and Iris exchanged a surprised glance.

"You're okay, cutie," Lucy crooned, gently stroking the bunny's tiny ears. "James is just going to check your leg."

But Blossom just burrowed closer to her.

"How long has she been acting like this?" Mable asked, eyes wide.

"Like what?" Lucy asked, glancing back at the women. Just then, Felix startled all of us by jumping onto the exam table. I hadn't even seen him enter the room. The cat stood over Blossom, his fluffy paws bracketing her on either side.

"So... cuddly," Iris said, bewildered.

"Oh. She's been like that since I brought her home. But that's not weird, right? Wouldn't she want to cuddle instead of being alone?"

Iris squeezed past me so she could get closer. "It is rather odd, actually. Wild bunnies stay skittish around humans, even at our rescue. She actually might be a domesticated variety who got out. Sometimes it can be hard to tell them apart, especially when they're little. Let's take a look at her."

Blossom was wrapped around Lucy's wrist so tightly she had to be pried off.

"Well, it looks like her leg is much better." Mable chuckled. She inspected the bunny until she saw something that made her eyebrows shoot up. "Well, that makes sense. Blossom here is indeed a wild bunny, but she's exceptionally rare." She handed her back to Lucy, who tucked her to her chest. "Blossom is an omega."

Lucy's jaw dropped. "What? I didn't know bunnies could be omegas."

"Most people don't. The first research paper confirming the existence of omega designations in bunnies and rabbits was published just a few years ago."

Mable's eyes were bright with excitement. "This is incredible. We haven't had a documented case of an omega bunny in New England because they usually die really young."

"Why?" Lucy breathed, holding Blossom even closer.

"Wild bunnies tend to be pretty solitary, and omegas need packs. Luckily, Blossom found hers." Iris looked between Lucy and Felix.

"We're her pack?" Lucy's scent was a riot of emotion, and I couldn't stop myself from wrapping my arm around her shoulder. She leaned into my chest and her scent settled.

"It seems that way. What would you think about keeping her? If you can't, we can still take her, although I worry that without a pack—"

"She's staying," Lucy blurted out. I hadn't realized how much tension she was holding in her body until it released. Her shoulders loosened and a radiant smile spread across her face. "It sounds like you're stuck with me, Blossom. Is that okay with you?" The bunny did a sleepy stretch and then flopped back down to sleep.

"This is amazing," James said with a clap of his hands. "Could you show me how you identified Blossom as an omega in case I run into this situation again?"

Iris gently took the bunny from Lucy and launched into an animated discussion with James and Mable about the latest research.

"Are you happy now?" I murmured to Lucy.

She beamed. "Yeah."

"She's lucky to have you." Fuck, I sounded like such a sap, but seeing Lucy happy was everything.

Mable and Iris gave Lucy instructions for the bunny's care and promised to keep in touch. When we finally left the clinic, Felix purring as he strutted ahead of us, the energy couldn't have been more different from our way there. Lucy was practically bouncing, her gold hair caught in the wind as she told Blossom all about the nest they would make for her.

When we got to her place, she hesitated as she glanced up at me. "Thanks for coming with me."

When I kept standing in silence like an idiot, she continued. "Um, and you don't have to clean my gutters. I'm sure you have lots to do. Are you working today?"

"No. My next stretch starts tomorrow." I took a step forward.

Slowly raised my hand. When she didn't move away, I ran my fingers down her arm until I captured her hand. "I didn't explain myself well yesterday. I need you to know I would have come to craft night if I could have."

She squeezed my hand. Her blue eyes were equally stunning and piercing, leaving me with the distinct impression that she could see straight through me. This was when I should tell her everything about my diagnosis and why we could never be truly together like an alpha and omega should be, but the words got stuck in my throat.

"Wilder, I . . ."

"You don't need to say anything, sweetheart. Just know that I'm here for you, and I'm going to keep being here until I win back your trust."

Her lip trembled and she looked away.

"Can I give you a hug?" My words came out rough and broken.

She let out a shuddering breath and fell into my arms. I wrapped them around her, being careful not to crush Blossom, and kissed the top of her head.

Later, once her gutters were clean and I was back in my cabin, I could still scent her on my shirt.

44

LEO

I PUSHED OPEN THE DOOR TO THE BOOKSTORE AND WAS IMMEdiately confronted by Hank's withering stare. I hadn't interacted much with the bookstore owner, but he attended every town meeting and definitely won the award for the grumpiest person in town. Although King and Wilder might give him a run for his money.

I waved awkwardly. "Hello, I'm helping with the book club today."

His eyes flicked down to my cane. Hank used one as well, and I braced myself for the inevitable commentary. *Why on earth would you be using that? You're too young for a cane.*

He grunted. "You know Olive?"

"Um, yes."

The old man's expression softened the slightest bit. "In the back."

Huh. Maybe Hank was all right.

I wove through the aisles to the meeting room, which contained tall stacks of books, a table with food, and a circle of comfortable chairs—one of which was occupied by Felix wearing a blue pinstriped bow tie.

"Are you here for book club?" I asked him.

"Hey, Leo."

I jumped when Olive popped out from behind a large bookshelf. For a second, I'd thought Felix had spoken to me.

"Hey, I'm here to serve tea and snacks?" My words came out as a question, and Olive couldn't quite suppress her giggle. Wilder was totally right—the omegas were orchestrating all of this. Not that I minded. I would jump through whatever hoops necessary to win Lucy's trust.

"The rest of the group should be here soon. They're going to be *so* excited you're here."

THE MEMBERS OF THE Groovy Book Club were *thrilled* to have a new ~~victim~~ member. Attendees included Carmen, Marisol, Char from the diner, her omega Rosie, and Missy, who owned the movie theater. Oh, and Jo, who was *one of Lucy's moms*. Which could have been fine except that *of course* Marisol and Carmen immediately told her everything—about my interest in courting Lucy and my absence at craft night. My cheeks burned with embarrassment as I served the food and refilled everyone's drinks.

Once the book discussion started, I found myself without much to do.

"Come join us, Leo," Olive said, a mischievous glint in her eye.

Who knew the sweet-looking lighthouse keeper was so evil?

I rubbed the back of my neck. "I haven't read the book."

Carmen dismissed my objection with a wave of her hand. "Certainly never stops me from attending. Sit down."

Well, okay then.

The only available chair was the one currently occupied by Felix. The room fell silent as I stood in front of him. I stared at his sleepy eyes, begging him to move via telepathy. *Please don't make me look bad in front of my crush's friends and mom. Please please please.*

Felix gave a slow, luxurious stretch and scooted to the side of the seat. I squeezed in beside him. He just secured himself a lifetime supply of unlimited treats.

I stroked his ears as the chatter picked back up.

"What I liked best about this book was how amazing the male characters treated their omega. They *always* show up whenever she needs them," Rosie said.

Olive nodded. "Totally agree. So much of being a good pack mate is being present."

Felix purred lazily on my lap as I suffered through my well-deserved hazing. The women eventually grew more relaxed with playful teasing and inside jokes. By the time the gathering came to a close, I'd received an official invitation to attend next month's book club—a great honor, according to Marisol.

I stayed behind to clean up. Jo was the last to leave. "I hope I see you around, Leo." She winked and headed out.

"Wow," Olive said. "That was a glowing endorsement."

"It was, wasn't it?" I grinned. "Have I won you over, too?"

She hummed. "That remains to be seen. But this was a good start."

I held my head a little higher as I left the bookstore.

45
LUCY

LALA

So I had an interesting career day experience. Ivy had another presenter today—an alpha

MAMMA

What alpha?

LALA

Oh, his name is King and apparently he's trying to court Lucy!

JOJO

Another one??

LALA

What do you mean?

JOJO

Leo was at book club today and he's trying to court Lucy.

MOM

I thought that big alpha I saw cleaning her gutters today was someone she hired, but NOW I'M HAVING SECOND THOUGHTS

The onslaught of messages in the family group chat interrupted the sewing tutorial I was watching. I groaned and sat up in the tub, the scalding water sloshing around me. I never brought my phone with me when I was taking a bath, but I'd finally decided what I wanted to sew for Felix and Blossom for the bakery's grand opening, and it meant learning a new technique. I thought I could finish watching the tutorial while soaking.

Critical error, apparently.

I dried my hand before picking up my phone, squinting at the messages as if that would somehow make them make sense.

LALA

> Lucy! How could you keep this from us? Did you know, Lars?

LARS

> Why would I know?

> Although Olive has been extra scheming lately

MAMMA

> What's going on, Luce? Are you with these alphas? You need to bring them to dinner

MOM

> I'll make my new risotto

JOJO

> Leo is such a cutie. Can't wait to have him be an official part of the family

Oh dear god.

A Pack for Spring

> **LUCY**
> Ok ok everyone needs to settle down
>
> We're not together so no risotto necessary
>
> Although feel free to bring me some

LALA
Whatever you need to tell yourself, cutie.

I huffed and opened Felix's Feral Four group chat.

> **LUCY**
> Whatever schemes and plots you're enacting, you need to stop

OLIVE
What are you referring to?

> **LUCY**
> Don't even pretend! I know King went to Ivy's class today and Leo went to Olive's book club! And I now have clean gutters for the first time in . . . ever

OLIVE
Who doesn't love education, literature, and home maintenance?

SUMMER
I am shocked and hurt that you would accuse us of something like scheming and plotting

LUCY
Very convincing

IVY
Are you mad at us?

LUCY
No, not mad. I know you're trying to be helpful. I just . . . I don't know. Maybe romance just isn't in the cards for me

SUMMER
I'm never one to say give men a chance, but these guys really want you. That doesn't mean you have to say yes to them, but maybe they'll be able to prove to you that they're worth taking the chance

LUCY
What else are you plotting?

SUMMER
Us? Plotting?

LUCY
Fine. Keep your secrets.

46

LUCY

HOROSCOPE PISCES

Pisces! Today is the perfect day to hop hop hop into the life you want. Also, a great day for the town to claim a decisive victory over Claude Fumble for all time!

THE EASTER EGGSTRAVAGANZA WAS WELL UNDERWAY. As usual, I'd been fighting against time to finish not only Felix's and Blossom's costumes but also all the bunny ear headbands for the kids taking part in the egg hunt.

Well, all the kids plus Easton, who was currently leading the charge.

"Into the breach! We must catch every last egg!" He pointed his blow-up sword in the air and a swarm of children cheered and ran into the field by the lighthouse, followed by Stanley shouting about the *proper decorum for official town events*.

I'd gotten here early to hand out the headbands, which was why I knew that King, Leo, and Wilder had helped Stanley set up before being assigned booths to run. I pointedly ignored them, even though my omega was practically whining in desperation to get to them.

She needed to pull her shit together.

At least there was one perk of getting here early—I was one of the first people to go through the food line. Summer had made bánh mì and Vietnamese coffee cookies, Harry was representing his Iowan culture with his famous Snickers salad, and Carmen brought a variety of Dominican dishes.

I spread out my quilt on the edge of the field. Olive and Ivy were tucked away with their packs and Summer was busy with the food, so Felix and Blossom were keeping me company. I'd done a photoshoot with them earlier and the post already had a hundred thousand likes. People were flipping out over Blossom's debut on the social media account, and I'd already gained a lot of new followers. The only drawback was that the larger my account grew, the more likely it was that people in my real life would stumble upon it. I needed to get over my anxiety and just tell people.

Felix batted at his floppy brown bunny ears while Blossom sat serenely with her pink bow.

"Leave your ears alone, Felix. You look amazing."

He let out a sassy *meow*, snagged an entire bánh mì from my plate, and trotted off.

I shook my head. "Boys, am I right?" Blossom twitched her nose and I leaned down to kiss her forehead. "It's okay. I was prepared." I pulled out the secret bánh mì I'd slipped into my dress pocket.

After I'd eaten, I laid back on the blanket with Blossom curled up beside me. The sun danced across my closed eyelids until everything went dark. I opened my eyes and let out a startled scream when I found Parisa looming over me.

"Well, that was quite a welcome."

I clutched my pounding chest. "Sorry. I wasn't expecting someone to practically fall out of the sky on top of me."

She grinned and sat down on the blanket. Her hair was pulled up in two curly space buns, and her beautiful maroon jumpsuit reminded me of one I'd designed for my currently imaginary clothing line, except mine was fall-themed with velvet material and long sleeves.

I propped myself up on my elbows. "I didn't know you were coming."

"I wasn't sure I'd be able to because my heat ended just a couple days ago and my alphas are always super protective post-heat." She rolled her eyes, but her smile gave her away. My heart ached with longing—to be cared for, even fussed over—and my gaze wandered to my guys.

No. Not my guys.

The guys.

"But I finally convinced them I'm not a fragile little flower, so here I am and ready for gossip," she continued.

"Hmm? What gossip?"

"*What gossip*, she asks." Parisa pointed at Blossom and then gestured at Wilder, King, and Leo at their respective booths. I bit my lip.

"Well, this is Blossom. She's an omega."

Parisa gasped. "We come in bunny, too?" She reached out and stroked Blossom's ears. "Oh my goodness, you are the sweetest little baby. I love you so much already, yes I do."

Blossom yawned and flopped on her side, immediately falling asleep. Parisa laughed. "How do you get anything done? I would stare at her all day."

I grinned. "That pretty much sums it up."

A loud cheer across the field pulled my attention. I had to purse my lips to keep from laughing once I saw the source of the commotion. James had wandered over to King's booth, and now they were both surrounded by a group of children chanting "Fish James! Fish King!"

Parisa snorted. "Okay, spill. What's going on with you and them?"

I aggressively plucked blades of grass. "I don't know. We're not together, but they want to be. Except, they weren't interested in me until I stopped being interested in them. It's just about the chase. I'm sure they'll lose interest soon."

"You really believe that?"

I shrugged.

"Lucy." Her tone was full of the familiar reproach I frequently heard from my friends when I said something they didn't like. "That's not true. Leo has had a crush on you from day one. Obviously I can't speak for the alphas, except that Bibi told me Leo brought an alpha home because they had a goat's milk emergency. I thought she was having a stroke because what the hell does that mean?"

My lips twitched in a smile. Okay, that was pretty funny. "They were getting goat's milk for Blossom. Thank Bibi for me."

"I don't think goat's milk delivery is the behavior of people who are just in it for the chase."

I hated how hopeful her words made me feel. I didn't want to be hopeful—it just led to me being disappointed. "Maybe I'm just meant to be single forever." Oh god, that sounded extra pathetic even to my ears. "Sorry, I'm just in a weird mood."

She squeezed my hand. "Courting is hard. I'm here for you if you want to talk about it, and don't feel like you have to hold back on complaints about Leo, either."

I grinned because I had told Olive the same thing after she bonded with Lars. "I might take you up on that." I glanced down to check on Blossom, and my heart stopped when I didn't see her.

"Do you see her? Blossom?" I scanned the blanket and surrounding area. Panic drenched my voice. I was scared to move in case I crushed her.

"She was right here." Parisa stood and carefully walked the perimeter of the blanket while I got on my hands and knees and ran my hands over the material. When we still didn't find her, Parisa and I lifted the blanket to check underneath it.

Still nothing.

Nausea churned in my stomach and I felt dizzy with fear as I looked out into the crowded field. Her leg had only just gotten better. What if she got hurt again?

Parisa gripped my shoulder and squeezed. "We'll find her."

Just then Stanley walked by, megaphone in hand. Acting on pure instinct, I grabbed it from him. "Attention everyone!" My voice emerged from the speaker tinny and crackly but loud enough to grab everyone's attention. "Blossom the bunny is missing. Look down when you walk so you don't step on her."

A Pack for Spring

Everyone froze and looked at the ground except for Wilder, whose eyes went straight to me. Waves of his alpha protectiveness reached me from across the field, and seconds later, he abandoned his booth and carefully made his way over.

He pulled me into his arms without hesitation and I half collapsed into his chest, my fingers clutching his flannel shirt.

"We'll find her, sweetheart." He gently pried the megaphone from my hand. "Everyone gather round. We'll section off the field in a grid pattern, and everyone will be responsible for one section."

I sniffed and pulled away from his chest, taking in the small crowd gathering around us. Summer and Olive squished me between them, King's concerned gaze was fixed on my face, and Leo was speed-walking toward us, the tip of his cane sinking into the field with each step. There was a pang in my chest. He shouldn't do anything to aggravate his knee.

Wilder divided the field, assigning each section to a pair of searchers.

"King, come with me," he said. "Leo, stay here with Lucy."

My fingers dug into his arm. "Wait, what area should I search?"

He leaned down and cupped my face with both hands. "You and Leo stay here. There's a good chance Blossom hasn't gone far and will come back here."

I wanted to argue, but he didn't give me a chance. He pressed a firm kiss to my forehead and took off with King.

"Come here, darling." Leo held out his arm to me.

I shook my head. "I need to look for her."

He snagged my hand and pulled me close. "Where did you last see her?"

"She was right here." I dropped to my knees and gently unfolded the quilt for the millionth time.

Leo lowered himself to the ground beside me with a low groan.

I grabbed his arm. "Be careful of your knee."

"I'm fine, but I won't say no to your hands on me." He threaded his fingers with mine and squeezed.

"What if we can't find her?" I whispered. "Omega bunnies can't survive on their own."

"Come here." He pulled me to his side and stroked my hair as I rested my head on his shoulder. "She's off having a little adventure, but I'm sure she'll be back in your arms soon."

I shook my head. "I'm a bad bunny mom."

His hold on me tightened. "Don't say that. You're the one who saved her. I saw Felix over by the fruit stand earlier. I'm assuming his outfit is your doing?"

I appreciated Leo trying to distract me from the clawing panic making me feel like I was going to crawl out of my skin.

"Yeah. He's a good sport to put up with me."

"He's lucky to have such an incredible personal dresser. Did you make Blossom an outfit?"

I sniffed. "I just sewed her a bow because I didn't know how she'd feel about wearing clothes. She seemed to like it, but maybe I should have made her something more elaborate."

Leo pressed a kiss to the top of my head. "I'm sure she loves her bow. She's already Easter themed, anyway. I bet if you posted your Felix outfits online, people would be obsessed."

I froze. Did he know? I pulled away so I could see his face but found nothing but sincerity there.

"I actually have a social media account for Felix." My voice was almost a whisper, the words scraping against my throat as I waited for his judgment.

His face lit up. "Yeah? Can I see it?"

I opened my account on my phone, my heart hurting when the picture I took of Felix and Blossom this morning popped up on the screen.

"Oh my god!" His jaw dropped as he scrolled through my latest posts. "This is incredible. Look at how many followers you have. I mean, I shouldn't be surprised. Everything you do is amazing."

I swallowed hard. Did he really mean that?

"Baba seriously will not shut up about getting his suit, and it's

A Pack for Spring

making me jealous. I'll have to cross my fingers and hope I'm worthy of getting on your custom clothing waitlist."

The corner of my lips curved. "I do have a long waitlist, but the good news is, I can be bribed."

His low chuckle tickled my cheek.

I scanned the search area. King was leading a group of children who were carefully scanning the ground, and Wilder was crawling on his belly underneath the food table.

"How did Stanley recruit you three to be volunteers?"

"The universe told us to."

I crinkled my nose. "Huh?"

He shrugged. "We're following the commands of our daily horoscopes. Today it said it was critical for us to report to Stanley as Easter Eggstravaganza volunteers."

Before I could make sense of what he'd said, a huge smile broke out across his face. He gave me a tight squeeze. "Look over there, pretty girl."

Wilder was walking toward us, a cardboard berry basket in his hands. "We found her!" He waved his arm, and everyone in the search party cheered.

I jumped up and sprinted toward him, skidding to a stop to see a snoozing Blossom lying amid the blackberries, her mouth and paws stained dark purple.

My legs buckled, and Wilder's firm arm wrapping around my waist was the only thing keeping me upright.

"She's okay?" I choked on a sob.

"She's perfect."

I scooped Blossom into my shaking hands and tucked her to my chest. King and Leo were soon by my side, enveloping me in their embrace. I didn't care that I was supposed to be keeping my distance or that our hug would be gossip fuel for the town or that Easton had stolen the egg hunt championship crown and was being chased by all the town children. All I cared about was soaking up their comfort, and the tickle of Blossom's nose against my skin.

AT THE END OF the festival, the guys—Felix included—walked me home. Blossom had been a happy little bunny the rest of the day, delighting the kids with her cute little hops, but I was still a bit of a wreck.

"Thanks for your help today. I'm sorry I got so emotional." My cheeks heated and I couldn't look Leo, King, or Wilder in the eye.

They had been nothing but sweet to me, but I was still braced for sly, cutting remarks.

Leo ran his fingers down my arm in a tender caress. "You never have to apologize for feeling." He glanced at Wilder and King before continuing. "We didn't do a good job explaining ourselves the other day. We want to court you, which means we want to be with you in all of life's moments, even the painful ones."

He lifted my chin, his thumb brushing against my lips. "I'm so fucking sorry for letting you down, azizam, but I'm all in. Nothing you do will scare me away."

King pressed close to my side. "What he said."

"Agreed," Wilder added.

Leo let out an exasperated sigh. "I say all of that for you two to say ditto?"

A smile tugged at my lips as I slowly shook my head. "They're alphas. What can we expect?"

King twisted his fingers in my hair and tilted my head back. "Brat." His voice was filled with affection, and I shivered with pleasure.

Wilder's chest was firm against my back. "What do you say, sweetheart? Will you give us another chance?"

My omega was shouting at me to say yes, and my chest ached with the urge to give in. But I couldn't shake the loneliness I'd felt at craft night, and my determination to do this year differently.

"I don't know." My words came out in a hoarse whisper. "It's not that I'm mad or holding a grudge against you all. I'm just not sure a relationship is what's right for me." I squeezed my eyes shut, waiting for them to lash out or just walk away, but they pressed closer.

"It's okay to not know," Wilder said gruffly.

King gripped my chin. "Just as long as you're okay with us not giving up."

I chewed my lip. "You'll get bored."

Leo snorted and pressed a soft kiss to my forehead. "You're not getting how serious we are about you, but you will. Can we come inside? Keep you company?"

Yes, please. I don't want to be alone.

I took a deep breath. "I think I need some space. If that's okay."

I hated saying it, but I knew it was the right move. My emotions were running high right now. I needed a chance to figure out what I really wanted.

The guys looked disappointed but didn't argue.

"Of course." Leo enveloped me in a tight hug. "Just remember, you never have to be alone if you don't want to be."

Then it was King's turn. He leaned down, his lips a soft whisper against my cheek. "I put my number in your phone. Use it whenever you want, for any reason." My senses were awash with sweet, crisp floral citrus.

Wilder took his place, fixing me with a stern look. "We're here for you, sweetheart." He scratched Blossom under her chin. "You take it easy on your mama. You gave us all a scare today."

Heart officially *melted*.

We shared one last group hug and then I slipped inside and headed straight to my nest, wishing I could have stolen their shirts to take with me.

47

LUCY

> **HOROSCOPE PISCES**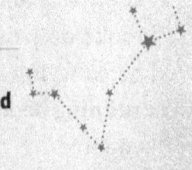
>
> Pisces, you beautiful, hopeless romantic! Some love connections are written in the stars ... and others need a little help. Head down to the community center this Friday night. It's time to find your perfect match!

My legs burned as I climbed the winding staircase to the top of the lighthouse, but I didn't slow. I was on a mission.

I pushed the door open and the wind caught it, slamming it against the building. Well, that entrance was a bit more dramatic than I intended, but that served my purposes. I stood in the doorway, one hand on Blossom snoozing in the little sling I'd made for her and the other on my hip.

My friends looked at me, their eyes wide.

"Um, hi?" Olive said.

"What is this?" I held up the partially crumpled invitation I'd found in my mailbox this afternoon.

Summer squinted. "It looks like a piece of paper."

When I fixed her with my withering stare, she continued, "You see, there are these things called trees and you can chop them down and use the pulp—"

Ivy covered Summer's mouth. "What is it, Luce?"

I let out an utterly nonintimidating omega growl. "Don't pretend you don't know! This is an invitation to tomorrow night's speed dating event."

A Pack for Spring

Olive grinned, but at my indignant expression, she schooled her face. "Oh, is there a speed dating event?"

I met her exaggeratedly innocent expression with a scowl before taking a seat.

When I'd called an emergency meeting of the Omega Overlords, Olive had suggested we come to the lighthouse for cocktail hour. A tray of drinks sat in the middle of the table and I grabbed one, not caring what was in it.

"Don't even pretend to be innocent. Marisol, Carmen, and Felix stopped me on my way here and told me not to worry about speed dating night because they had everything under control."

Summer waved an airy hand. "That could mean anything."

"They were wearing their fortune-telling costumes and told me my men had *very illuminating tea leaves*."

Olive burst out laughing. "I'm sorry, but Carmen and Marisol kidnapped me last week. They took me into their mystical backyard shed and served me the worst tea I've ever had in my life. If the goal was to punish your guys, I think that achieved it."

Summer cocked her head. "What did your tea leaves say?"

"Apparently I was a mermaid in a past life."

"Makes sense," she responded.

I shook my head, but I couldn't stop my smile as all my righteous indignation bled out of me. I loved my friends more than anything. "You're all ridiculous little meddlers. I don't want to punish them. I just . . ."

"Just what?" Ivy asked gently.

"I just wish the presents and volunteering and stuff were things they were doing because they wanted to, not because they're being told to."

"We didn't tell them to get you presents," Olive said.

I blinked. "What? Really?"

"We've simply assisted the universe in nudging them in the right direction," Ivy said. "But they've done the rest."

"Oh." I took a sip of the cocktail. It was sweet and citrusy, and it reminded me of King. "Are you sure?"

Olive squeezed my arm. "Promise. And we wouldn't have helped them if we didn't think they were serious about you."

"We needed to see how committed they actually are," Summer said. "And they've spent *hours* with Stanley in the past week. That shows determination."

She arched an eyebrow and I grinned. She wasn't wrong.

"So what presents did they give you?" Olive asked, waggling her eyebrows.

Knowing that the gifts were something the guys did on their own made me feel all warm and melty inside, but old insecurity rose inside me. "I swear I'm not super materialistic." I chewed my lip. "It's not like they *have* to get me gifts."

My friends looked puzzled. "It's not materialistic to want presents," Ivy said.

I scoffed. "Not according to my exes." My words slipped out without permission. I tried my best never to speak of them out loud.

"Fuck themmmm," Summer said. "They deserve worse than they got."

"True. But egging their cars was satisfying." Especially since they'd cared more about those cars than they had me.

"I get that it's hard, though," Olive said. "The first time my guys took me to Nest Wonderland, I struggled with letting them buy me things. But they do it because they want to, not because they feel obligated. They know it makes my omega feel special, and it makes them feel all proud of themselves for providing for me."

"Don't let your exes ruin this for you," Ivy said gently. "I know what it's like to come into a relationship with insecurities, and it's okay to be hesitant. But sometimes it's worth the risk."

I swallowed hard. "Yeah, maybe you're right."

"Of course we are," Summer said. "So, what did they give you?"

My shoulders loosened and I took another sip of my drink. I'd been busy with work this week, so I hadn't seen much of the guys. It scared me how much I missed them, but they hadn't made me feel forgotten for even a minute.

"King left a gift card at Beans 'n Bliss, so all my lattes are free." Ella had practically jumped up and down when she told me. There was nothing quite so exciting for a teenager than being a part of a romantic scheme. "And I had a new spring wreath on my door one morning. Every day, I've gotten food deliveries for lunch and dinner." I hated cooking, so not having to worry about making food, especially when I got sucked into a sewing project, was a dream come true. "Also, I've had a new package at my door every day with things for my nest."

That last one made my cheeks flame red because giving an omega nesting items was something you only did if you were really serious about courting them. It was an intensely personal thing for an omega, and I was really picky about what I brought into my nest. Somehow, everything they'd sent was perfect. There had been huge soft blankets, cute throw pillows in the shape of strawberries, and clothes. *Their* clothes, drenched in their scents. I'd actually cried when I opened this morning's delivery. There was a huge flannel that smelled like Wilder, a T-shirt so worn and soft I never wanted to take it off from Leo, and a button-down shirt that clearly belonged to King. I'd put all three of the shirts on at the same time and ran up to my nest. I'd looked like a huge blob of fabric, but I didn't care. I'd actually whined when I had to take them off to come here, but I'd left them safely tucked in my nest for my return.

"I love getting things for my nest." Ivy practically had stars in her eyes as she rested her chin on her hands with a sigh.

Summer gazed out at the ocean, an air of sadness around her, but she smiled when she caught me looking. "It's good to make your guys work for it, but you're never obligated to say yes, no matter how much time and energy they put in."

I leaned over the table and squeezed her hand. She wasn't a hopeless romantic like me, but it was still hard to be an omega without a pack.

I knew King, Wilder, and Leo would respect my decision if I told them I wasn't interested. But . . . I didn't want to do that. I'd spent the past few days thinking and processing, and I kept coming back to one simple truth: I wanted to say yes to them. Spending the rest of the Eggstravaganza with them after the Blossom scare had given me a glimpse of what pack life could be like with them—Leo teasing King as they made eyes at each other, Wilder being grumpy and gruff except when he gentled his voice to talk to Blossom or me, and all of them casually touching me any chance they got.

The lighthouse door opened, and Easton emerged in a waiter's uniform, carrying a tray of appetizers.

"Good evening, beautiful ladies," he said in an over-the-top French accent. "Some refreshments, courtesy of ze chef."

"Wow, what excellent service," Ivy said. "I didn't know you spoke French."

"Oh, yes. Hablo bon francais."

He set the tray down on the table with an exaggerated flourish, revealing artfully arranged Chinese food appetizers that were definitely from the Red Lantern, Summer's family's restaurant.

"Thanks, baby," Olive said.

Easton leaned down and gave her a heated kiss. "Anything for you. Are you warm enough?"

"Toasty warm."

He gave her one more kiss and headed back downstairs.

"Oohhh, fortune cookies," I said, snagging one off the tray. "Summer, are you still writing these, or have you passed the torch to your brother?"

She flipped her hair. "As if anyone could live up to my fortunes."

Ivy and Olive snagged cookies, too, and we cracked them open.

"The goats have read your diary. They know all," Olive said.

"Well, that's mysterious," I said. "How did the goats learn to read?"

"Don't ask questions," Summer said with a wave. "I might have had a National Geographic show on in the background while writing these."

A Pack for Spring

"The hierarchy will collapse at brunch," Ivy read out. "That sounds promising."

I looked down at the small slip of paper in my hand. "Be open to new opportunities. You never know how the universe will surprise you."

"Oh my gosh, a normal one," Olive said. "It's meant to be!"

Summer cleared her throat. "Turn it over."

I snorted as I read the second part of the fortune. "The surprise will be meteors."

Ivy snagged a dumpling with perfect chopstick form. "It's actually meteorite."

"Thanks, Ms. Winter," Summer said dryly before fixing her eyes on me. "So . . . what are you going to do?"

I speared a dumpling straight through the middle with a chopstick, ignoring Summer's distressed groan. "I guess I have to seize every moment before the meteorites take me out."

"You're going to speed dating?" she asked.

I bit my lip. "You know it's the night before your grand opening."

She dismissed my concern with a wave. "I'll make sure to have plenty of caffeine on hand in case you have a *long, hard* night."

Olive and Ivy burst out laughing, ignoring my narrowed eyes.

"Ugh, fine. I'll do it. I'll go."

They cheered, and Blossom stuck her head out of the sling and squeaked.

"I'll watch the baby for you tomorrow." Ivy leaned over to scratch Blossom's chin. "James will be thrilled to hang out with her."

I guess I'm doing this.

Please be nice to me, universe.

48

LUCY

I was walking down Main Street toward the community center when a golf cart pulled up beside me.

"Your slightly late chariot awaits!" Leo declared. He looked way too good in a dark green suit and white shirt that was unbuttoned enough to be deliciously slutty. "Unless you just want to stand there and eye-fuck me?"

I pursed my lips at his cocky grin and rounded the cart to hop into the passenger's side. "Just making sure you weren't a serial killer."

He curled a lock of my hair around his finger. "That's good, pretty girl. Safety is very important."

His floral cardamom scent was strong, practically hypnotizing me as I swayed forward. "Hi," I murmured.

"Hi." He ran his nose down the side of my cheek. The tension and uncertainty I'd carried with me since we last parted melted away. Leo's arms felt like home.

His hand shifted to my neck, his grip firm and confident as his lips found mine. The evening air filled with my perfume until we were a perfect blend of wildflowers, cardamom, and berries. I'd considered wearing de-scenting deodorant tonight, but the vain part of me wanted my guys to be taunted by my perfume all night. That might also have influenced my outfit decision—a floral miniskirt paired with a blue sweater that hugged my curves.

Leo's fingers trailed up the bare skin of my thigh and he groaned. "Are you trying to kill me, joonam?"

I didn't know what *joonam* meant, but his voice was low and reverent and I wanted to hear him say it again.

"Maybe," I said against his lips. "Is it working?"

His hand squeezed my leg and I was moments away from begging him to move it higher when he pulled away.

"We have an event to go to." He shifted in his seat and I smirked when I realized he was subtly trying to adjust his cock.

"Or we could skip it."

He shook his head as he pulled away from the curb. "I'm pretty sure Wilder and King would hunt us down and kill me, which would leave speed dating night without any hosts."

My eyebrows shot up. "You're hosting?"

"I've learned not to question the wisdom of the tea leaves," he said, just as we passed Marisol and Carmen standing outside the market. They gave me an enthusiastic thumbs-up.

Leo was all smiles, seemingly unbothered by the town's shenanigans or my hesitancy.

My quickly crumbling hesitancy.

His warm hand surrounded mine for the entirety of the drive, which was about three times longer than usual with Leo's snail pace.

"You drive like Ivy," I said as he finally turned into the community center parking lot.

"She must be an exceptional driver."

I snorted. "I was going to say *boring*, but sure. Exceptional works, too."

"Just let me know who in town drives like you and I'll make sure to never get into a vehicle with them."

I fixed him with a glare, but he just grinned as he grabbed his cane and got out of the golf cart.

I hopped out after him. "Thanks for picking me up."

He wrapped his arm around my waist and pulled me flush against his chest. "I'll steal Stanley's cart for you anytime, azizam."

How did he make that sound so romantic?

The second we were through the community center door, King and Wilder were on us. I laughed as they squeezed me between them.

"What took so long?" Wilder grumbled.

I pressed my face into his neck, breathing in deeply. "Did you miss me?"

"So much, sweetheart."

"I missed you, too," King said, sounding incredibly disgruntled as he tried to steal me away from Wilder.

I spun out of their reach. "No fighting over me. I have to get in there and find a date."

I laughed as their growls followed me into the main room.

Tables were set up in a horseshoe shape. Some attendees were at a coffee station in the corner, but most were already seated. There seemed to be an unusually high number of firefighters in attendance.

"We have to get things started." Leo's arms surrounded me from behind and I leaned back into his firm chest.

"I guess I'll find a seat, then."

King crossed his arms, a glint of murder in his eye. "Or you can stay here with us."

"But where's the fun in that?" I laughed as I headed to the tables, making sure to add an extra swing in my hips.

Ezra caught my eye and gestured at the empty chair across from him.

"Hey, Lucy."

Before I could respond, Leo called everyone to attention.

"Welcome to speed dating night." The sweet florist glared at Ezra as he spoke. "We're going to get started."

He nudged King, who sighed and started reading off a piece of paper in a dull monotone. "We are thrilled to have you all here tonight. Love is like a song's gemstone." He turned to Leo and Wilder. "Who the fuck wrote this?"

"Just keep going," Leo urged.

"We invite the wisdom of the universe into this room to ignite sparks of loving mystery . . . Okay, no," King said, shaking his head. I bit my lip to stop myself from laughing. "Here's what we're doing. Everyone has five minutes to talk. After the time is up, the gong will sound. If you're on the inside line of the tables, stay where you are. If you're on the outside edge, you'll move one spot to the right. Everyone got it?"

Wilder, whose expression looked exactly like Felix when he was denied dessert, hit the gong.

Ezra choked out a laugh. "This is priceless." He pulled out his phone and snuck a picture of his boss. Wilder caught him and flipped him off, but when his eyes landed on me, his face softened.

I blew him a kiss.

"Everyone clear on what's happening?" King asked. "Okay. Go."

I turned to Ezra, grinning. "I think they have a future emceeing events."

The firefighter shook his head. "At least the boss didn't have to speak. He might have to string together two whole sentences in a row. I'm pretty sure he got through an entire shift last year with just grunts."

Hmm. Wilder certainly couldn't be described as chatty, but he talked plenty with me.

"What are you doing here? Is it firefighter night or something?"

Ezra's eyes glinted with mirth. "Nah, but a little birdy told us the boss was leading speed dating night and we had to see it for ourselves." He leaned in across the table. "Also, we have a betting pool."

"Betting on what?"

"On when you and the boss will make it official. So if you could hold off for another two days, that would be *great* for me."

I pressed my hand over my mouth to stifle my laugh as I glanced over at Wilder. He looked seconds away from killing his entire team. "I should be offended by that, I think."

Ezra stretched, showing off his muscular arms. He was cute and charming, but he didn't give me butterflies. I hoped he found someone soon. He'd make a great partner.

"Nah, it's all in good fun. But seriously, make him wait for two more days. It's good for him."

"What makes you think he's even interested in me?" It didn't sound like Wilder was chatting about romance at the fire station.

Ezra snorted. "I'm very smart, Lucy. The signs might have been subtle—how he guarded the cookies you brought with his life, how he's taken time off for the first time since he started so he could do things for you, how he almost beat me up when I mentioned your name..."

A throat cleared, and Ezra's smile widened. "Subtle, subtle hints." Wilder stood behind him with his crossed arms and a menacing expression on his face.

"Time's up," he snarled.

Ezra leaned back in his chair, the picture of ease. "I haven't heard the gong."

Wilder's scowl deepened and he waved at Leo, who immediately clocked what was happening and rang the gong.

"Now fucking move."

I shivered at the command in his tone, but Ezra was unaffected. He locked eyes with me, smiling widely as he grasped my hand and kissed it.

Wilder shoved him out of his chair.

"That was rude," I scolded. "Are you okay, Ezra?"

Wilder gripped my chin. "You don't look at him. You look at me."

"Don't worry about me, Lucy. I'll survive." Ezra grinned as he sat down in the next seat. The alpha who was supposed to take the spot in front of me started to say something, but at Wilder's expression, he fled across the room.

"I didn't know the hosts of speed dating also participated." I tried to sound stern, but in reality, I was melting on the inside at my alpha's show of possessiveness.

"I'm not participating," he said, sounding distinctly disgruntled. "I'm just preventing these assholes from getting any ideas."

I grinned. "And what ideas are those?"

He leaned forward, his scent washing over me, all wild and earthy and hypnotizing. "That they have any chance with you."

I shivered at his dominance. My omega wanted him to throw me over his shoulder and carry me away from here to ravage me. But instead of begging him to do just that, I forced myself to lean back in my chair, creating space between us. I'd already forgiven the guys for craft night, but the vindictive part of me wanted to draw out his suffering just a *tiny* bit more.

I looked around. "Don't they? There are a lot of attractive options..."

Wilder's growl was partly obscured by the loud ring of the gong. I glanced to my right to see who my next partner was and laughed when I saw King blocking the way. Aggression rolled off him in waves, turning his scent bitter, and it made me feel... secure. Cared for. My exes' jealousy never felt like this. If we went out and they thought someone was looking at me, I was the one who got the blame.

Of course they're looking. You look like a slut in that skirt.

How had I ever thought the way they spoke to me was okay? It started with sly "jokes" and passive-aggressive comments that left me feeling confused and guilty. I'd carried around shame that I had done something wrong for so long, but Wilder's and King's current scowls didn't make me feel that way at all. Instead, I was bubbling with happiness and feeling distinctly *wanted*.

Wilder leaned over the table and kissed my forehead before letting King take his seat.

"Hi, Daddy," I said.

Ezra guffawed from two spots down the table, and King's eyes darkened.

"Are you having fun, baby girl?"

"Yeah, I am."

A heartbreaking smile spread across his face as he leaned forward. "Good. Have your fun now, because you'll be paying for it later. We're all going home together after this." When I didn't respond, he arched an eyebrow. "Say *yes, Daddy*."

"Yes, Daddy," I said, my voice breathless.

"And tomorrow, Easton is coming to your store to take measurements for new shelves."

"Wait, what?"

His eyes softened. "I love your store, baby girl, but you'll be able to work more easily if it's organized."

"I know I should be better about keeping things neat..."

King grasped my hand, running his thumb across my skin. "No. You are busy running your successful business, but now you don't have to do it alone."

Hearing King call my store successful was almost as big of a turn-on as the way he kept full eye contact as he lifted my hand and pressed a kiss to the inside of my wrist. My skin was electrified, and my panties were damp with arousal.

"Should we clear the room, or can you two keep it in your pants for a few more minutes?"

I jolted at Leo's voice. My eyes flicked over King's shoulder to see the hot beta smirking at us. King huffed and stood, conveniently keeping his hand in front of his crotch. Leo snorted as he sat down, propping his cane against the table.

"Wait." I leaned forward. "That's new." I hadn't noticed it earlier, but instead of his usual beat-up black cane, he had a gorgeous wood cane with a floral pattern made from gold inlay. It looked like art, just like the man holding it.

"It was a gift." He cocked his head toward King.

I looked between the two men, cataloging the blush on the alpha's cheeks and the loose set of Leo's shoulders. I'd never seen him this at ease when talking about his cane and that, more than anything, made me feel like this could work. That *we* could work. My guys had been working together all week like a pack should. They'd done it for me, but also maybe for each other.

Also, there was clearly something between King and Leo, and I was fucking thrilled about it. Pack life for me had always meant family—one filled with unique, individual relationships but connected by deep love and care.

"Azizam, what's wrong?" Leo cupped my face and I realized I was crying.

I let out a wet laugh. "Nothing, I'm just being sappy. I can't believe you've done all these things the past couple of weeks."

"There's nothing we wouldn't do for you."

"I would accuse you of exaggerating, but you volunteered for Stanley, so you must be telling the truth."

Leo grinned. "So true. Although, it's been pretty fun to get to know everyone in town. And pretty priceless to see those two"—he jerked his head at Wilder and King, who were currently standing next to the gong with expressions more suited for a battle than speed dating—"have to interact with people."

"I guess we'll have to work together on their antisocial ways."

Leo froze, his eyes wide. "Does that mean you want to do this?"

I wrapped my fingers around his wrist. He was still cupping my face and I leaned into his touch. "I'm still scared, but yeah, I do. I've missed you this week. I don't want to spend more time apart."

"What are you scared of, darling?" The warmth in his eyes, his touch, his scent drew me in until we were wrapped in our own bubble, the chatter in the room fading away.

"What if you change your mind about me? My omega can be . . . a lot. *I* can be a lot."

"It's a good thing my feelings for you aren't small, and I would never want you to make yourself less."

His words would be burned into my brain for the rest of my life. I wanted to embroider them onto a pillow.

"I'm scared, too," he admitted. "It seems so stupid now, but the reason I didn't ask you out the very first time we met was because—well, two reasons, really. The first is I'm a beta and you're way out of my league, but the second is my knee. I was trying to get to where I didn't have to use a cane anymore."

My lips parted. "What? Did you think I would judge you?"

He quickly shook his head. "No, you're too sweet for that. But I've always been told omegas need strong alphas. Not only am I a beta but I'm not strong. Not like I used to be."

My heart ached at the sadness and uncertainty rolling off him, and I couldn't stand the distance between us for a second longer. I dropped out of my chair and crawled under the table.

"What the fuck are you doing?" Leo hissed, but he scooted back to give me enough space to emerge from the table and crawl into his lap. His arms immediately banded around my waist, pulling me tight against his chest.

"Am I hurting your knee?"

"No. And even if you were, I wouldn't let you move." He skimmed his nose along the side of my face. "The prettiest girl in the world is on my lap, and all the alphas in this room are fucking dying of jealousy."

"You're ridiculous." I ran my fingers through his hair, tugging his head back enough for him to meet my gaze. "And the sweetest man I've ever met. I've been obsessed with you from the beginning. Every day with you is brighter. And just so you know"—I leaned in until our lips were almost touching—"you're one of the sexiest, hottest, most attractive men I've ever met. I've never cared about designation. All I've ever wanted is someone who makes me feel safe and seen and . . ." I stopped myself just in time before I said it—*loved*. I cleared my throat. "That's how you make me feel, Leo. And I hope that's how I make you feel, too."

"You do, joonam. Always." His words brushed against my lips. "I love you, Lucy. I think I have for months."

My breath hitched and then I was kissing him. He loved me. *Leo loved me.*

His lips were perfect against mine, soft but commanding as he gripped my jaw. A loud cheer broke out in the room. We broke apart to see all the firefighters standing and cheering for us.

"Huh," I said, turning back to Leo. "I kind of forgot where we were."

"I didn't," he snorted. "But you were the one who crawled under a table to get to me, so who am I to complain?"

I grinned. "It must be because I love you, too."

His lips parted. "Say that again."

"I love you."

"How did I get so fucking lucky?" he murmured. "Let's get out of here."

I nodded my head at King and Wilder, who were striding toward us. "I think we're all on the same wavelength."

"Time to go," Wilder grunted. He carefully lifted me off Leo's lap and into his arms.

I patted his chest. "This feels familiar. At least we're not about to be swept off the mountain."

He scowled. "You are never doing that again."

"You two put on quite a show," King said. He pulled Leo up from his seat, his hand lingering even once Leo was standing.

I hummed. "If we all go back to my place now, we can put on a whole other show."

Their scents exploded. Wilder took off toward the door to more cheers from the firefighters.

"Betting pool ends today, boys!" I shouted right before the door shut behind us.

49

LUCY

This was happening. It was really happening. All four of us were in the golf cart, heading back to my place.

My stomach fluttered with butterflies. This was everything I'd wanted, what I'd dreamed about since I was little. *You've thought that before*, the anxious voice in the back of my mind whispered, but it was easy to brush aside.

My exes had never made me feel like this. Besides, I wasn't the same girl I'd been when I met them. For all the havoc they'd wreaked in my life, they had changed me in some positive ways. I now knew what I deserved and what I wouldn't tolerate. Leo, King, and Wilder had proven themselves over the past two weeks. They hadn't been irritated when I'd pushed them away, and they hadn't treated winning me back like some sort of ego-boosting conquest. It felt genuine, like they actually just wanted me.

None of us was perfect, but our relationship was *real*.

I took a deep breath and Leo tightened his grip on my thigh.

"You doing okay, azizam?"

He was driving much faster than he had on the way to the event, which made me smile. I skimmed my fingers along his arm. "I'm great. That is, *if* we survive the ride back. I think we might be going a whole eight miles an hour. You must be in a hurry for some reason."

King leaned forward, resting his arms on the back of my seat. "He was our getaway driver for our golf cart heist, and I'm pretty sure a snail could have caught us."

"Harry *did* catch us," Wilder said.

A laugh burst from my chest. "Really? What did he say?"

"Nothing," Leo said with a scowl.

"He said Leo was the worst getaway driver he'd ever seen." King grinned. His hand twitched like he wanted to run it through the beta's hair but he stopped himself. I glanced at Wilder and he met my gaze with an arched eyebrow, clearly having noticed it, too. Did Leo and King realize they were attracted to each other? Maybe one of them would make a move tonight. I hoped so. I wanted my guys to be as close to each other as they were to me.

We inched up to the curb outside my shop.

"What do we do with this?" Leo asked. "Return it to Stanley's?"

I shook my head and hopped out of the passenger's side. "He's already in bed, so there's no risk of him discovering it tonight. Summer and I have a deal that anytime I leave the cart here, she moves it back to Stanley's for me when she gets up at the ass crack of the dawn for the bakery."

"Little omega schemers." King's arms encircled me from behind.

"Oohhh, that's a good group chat name. I'll have to write that down."

We moved to the door until we were in the same position we'd been after the Eggstravaganza. I fiddled with my keys. This was it—the fork in the road. Down one path was a safe, boring, romance-free life. Down the other? Possible heartbreak, but also the potential for something incredible.

It was an easy choice. My guys had made it an easy choice.

"Are you coming inside?"

King growled and scooped me up in his arms. "Of fucking course."

Leo took my keys and opened the door, and King carried me straight upstairs. He gently put me down outside my bedroom and caged me against the wall.

"Are you going to let us into your nest, baby girl?"

"What will you do to make it worthwhile for me?" The bratty words were out of my mouth before I could stop them. My omega was at the surface, my instincts taking over.

King let out a low laugh as he collared my throat, giving it a slight squeeze that made me whimper with arousal. "You don't want to test me, little omega. I'll always come out on top."

"But what if I want to come on top?"

Leo snorted and King glared at the beta over his shoulder. I used the distraction to my advantage, ducking under King's arm.

"Just, um, give me a few minutes." I slipped into my bedroom and closed the door behind me. This was my sacred place. My exes had never wanted to come inside my apartment—they said it was too messy and cramped—and my omega had somehow never wanted them in my nest. I shook my head. How had I missed all the obvious red flags? I'd been dreaming of having Leo, King, and Wilder in my nest since the first day I met them, and now it was finally here.

I plugged in my string lights. They crisscrossed the entire ceiling, illuminating the organized mess on the large, low mattress that took up most of the room. The walls and ceilings were painted dark mauve, and there was a plush olive rug on the floor. The nest itself was layered with cozy blankets and pillows in an explosion of earthy jewel tones. And layered underneath everything was my secret stash. My cheeks turned bright pink and I thought about hiding the articles of clothing I'd been slowly stealing from the guys, but then I steeled myself. If they couldn't accept my omega, they didn't deserve me.

I opened the door, letting out a little squeak because King was *right there*, his arm resting above the door frame. Leo was right behind him, and Wilder stood to the side.

"You can come in," I said shyly.

A smile split King's face and I was left momentarily stunned at how gorgeous he was. His dark hair fell lazily over his forehead, and his chest rumbled in a purr as he leaned down to kiss me.

"Thank you, baby."

I stepped aside and held my breath as the three of them squeezed into the room. I crawled to the middle of the nest, my body lined with tension as I ran my hand along an emerald-green velvet pillow. "I know it's a lot..."

"This is so cool," Leo said, eyes wide. "I love it." He propped his cane against the wall and flopped down on the nest, pulling me into his arms.

"Uhh, Leo," Wilder said.

King cringed. "You're not supposed to . . ."

"What?" Leo looked between them. "Why are you just standing there?"

I laughed and snuggled into my beta's chest. "You're supposed to wait until an omega invites you into their nest before getting in."

A strangled choking sound left his throat and he loosened his hold on me. "Shit, should I—"

I wrapped my arms and legs around him. "Don't you dare."

He laughed and rubbed my back. "Thanks, joonam. Now, are you going to invite those two in, or do they just have to watch?" His lips brushed my cheek. "Because I could be down with that."

The two alphas growled, and I giggled. "Maybe another time."

I held my hand out to King and Wilder, and they were beside us immediately. King pulled my hair from behind, and the stinging pain went straight to my clit.

"Our omega likes to tease us, doesn't she?"

I grinned. "So what if I do?"

He chuckled and smacked my ass. "Strip for us, baby girl."

Their eyes were on me, making me feel powerful and vulnerable all at once. I reluctantly released Leo and peeled off my sweater, leaving me in a lacy blue bra. My guys' scents deepened—a mix of cardamom sweetness, orange blossom, and woodsy pine. It was decadent, like I was a forest fairy being hand-fed sweets, and I was greedy for more.

I unbuttoned my skirt and slowly hooked my thumbs into the waistband and pulled it down my thighs, taking my lace thong down with it. I settled back on my knees, my legs spread wide.

My guys swore, their bodies lined with tension and their eyes fixed on my pussy.

I fiddled with my bra clasp, but instead of removing it, I dropped my hands. "Did you not want me to get naked?" At their confused expressions, I added, "Because you seem awfully clothed."

They moved in a blur of limbs, clothes landing everywhere, making my omega wiggle with happiness. After tonight, their scents would be embedded in my nest.

The string lights cast a warm glow on their bare skin, and it was my turn to stare. Leo's golden brown chest was muscular with a dusting of black hair that led straight to his thick, hard cock. He might not have a knot, but my pussy was already desperate for him to stretch me. My eyes flitted to King next. He looked even better than I remembered, with his broad chest and his thick arms that were definitely capable of throwing me around. My mouth practically watered when Wilder finally finished stripping. His build was solid and powerful, even without visibly defined muscles. Everything about him screamed rugged mountain man, from his thick thighs to his . . . thick *everything*. His knot was already bulging at the base of his cock, and precum leaked from the tip, making me pant with need. My eyes trailed up the rest of his body, and my eyebrows furrowed when I saw a layer of scars on his arm.

I reached out to touch them and he flinched away. My heart sank. Was he self-conscious about them?

"Burn scars from a fire years ago. They don't hurt."

I wanted to kiss his scars, wrap my naked body around his, but there was a strange edge to his scent I didn't understand.

Leo gripped my jaw, pulling my gaze away from Wilder as his lips pressed against mine. I couldn't get enough of his sweetness, the way his scent wrapped around me, making me lose track of time. My hands wandered down his body, and he groaned when I encircled his cock and squeezed.

"Fuck. *Fuck*." He cupped my sex and thrust two fingers inside my soaked entrance without warning. I moaned and arched against him. I needed his cock. And King's. And Wilder's. My lip jutted into a pout. Being a greedy omega was hard.

Leo pulled his fingers from me with a loud curse. Before I could complain about losing his touch, he lay down on his back. His cock jutted into the air and he slowly stroked it.

That was *mine*.

King brushed my hair to the side and kissed my shoulder. "Look how good our beta looks. Climb on top of him. Show him what a good girl you are."

Slick dripped down my thighs as I straddled Leo. His large hands squeezed my hips, his fingertips digging into my ass cheeks.

"I'm going to be really fucking pissed when I wake up from this dream," he muttered.

I leaned forward, grinding my pussy along his hard length. "This is one detailed dream."

He captured my nipple in his mouth, sucking hard. "You've featured in all of my dreams these past few months, but none of them were as good as this."

The reverence in his voice took my breath away. I couldn't wait one second longer to have him inside me. I raised my hips, guided his thick cock to my entrance, and let gravity take over as I sank down in one smooth motion. I panted at the stretch and the explosion of electricity rocking my core. Leo tipped his head back with a loud cry, the movement exposing his throat fully to me.

Bite. Claim. Mine.

A sharp pain on my nipple snapped me out of my omega frenzy. King cupped my breasts, squeezing and pinching as I whimpered with a mix of pain and pleasure.

"She clenches down so fucking hard when you do that," Leo said through gritted teeth.

"Our girl likes a bit of pain with her pleasure." His hand came down on my ass and delivered a slapping sting.

"I'm not going to last long," Leo choked out.

That was fine with me. I rolled my hips, my clit grinding against him with each movement. I hovered at the edge of the cliff, my body shaking with desperation. Tears welled in my eyes. I needed to come.

My beta knew exactly what I needed. His thumb slipped between my clit and his stomach, adding the exact pressure I needed. Pleasure crashed down on me as my orgasm washed over me, sharp, perfect, and never-ending.

I slumped against his chest, utterly boneless. His arms banded tight around me as he thrust into me from below, his movements frantic until he came with a shout.

"You're so perfect. I can't believe how fucking lucky I am." Leo pressed a soft kiss to my forehead.

"I'm the lucky one."

I rubbed my cheek against his chest, shocked at the intensity of what I'd just experienced. My skin was so sensitive I was sure I'd come again if someone blew on it.

We stayed there, Leo still inside me, until my need for more was too overwhelming. I wiggled my hips and King got the message, lifting me into his arms.

"That was fucking beautiful," he murmured.

Leo's cum dripped out of me, and King's thick fingers pressed it back inside. I clenched around them, desperate for friction. He maneuvered me so I was lying on my back, my hips spread wide around him. His eyes stayed locked with mine as he collared my throat, squeezing slightly.

"I've been fucking dreaming of this since Boston."

"I need you, Daddy."

He gave me a heartbreaking smile. "You have me. Always."

His cock slipped inside me easily, Leo's cum making my channel slippery and wet. We moved together, our movements slow and gentle. This felt so different from our first time together. I was safe in his arms, cherished and protected. This wasn't a frantic hookup but more like . . . making love.

I wrapped my arms around him and buried my face in his neck, breathing him in. My pleasure built slowly, perfectly. I ran my fingers through his hair, and he leaned into my touch. "Baby girl." His voice was soft, his words just for me. "I'm yours. Forever." He ran his hand up my thigh, gripping the back of my knee to hold me open for him.

I let out a cry as his cock hit a new spot deep inside me, his knot bumping against my clit.

"Forever," I echoed.

Our bodies moved like we were made for each other. Sparks of pleasure built in my core until I came. This orgasm was soft and gentle, reaching into the deepest parts of my body, my soul. King's fingertips dug into my thigh as he came, filling me to the brim.

Tears filled my eyes at the perfection of the moment, and my lips parted when I saw matching ones shine in his.

We were a tangle of limbs and bare skin as we held each other. Everything was perfect except—

I searched out Wilder and found him sitting at the edge of his nest, stroking himself. I whined. Why wasn't he here, touching me? I didn't care how many times I'd already come—I needed him *now*.

King's and Leo's combined cum dripped down my legs and onto the nest as I crawled to Wilder. I reached out my arm. "I need you." My voice cracked with vulnerability. Why was he keeping a distance? Did he not want to be here?

He moved toward me. Slowly. Torturously. And then his hands were on me, which was all I needed to reignite the horrible clenching in my pussy.

"Hold her open for me." Wilder spread my legs wide to accommodate his huge body. King and Leo each slipped a hand behind my knees, pulling my legs up toward my head.

I had never been this exposed. I was completely on display, open to Wilder and at his mercy.

50

WILDER

Lucy's sweet pussy was pink and puffy from her orgasms. Slick and cum dripped from her onto the sheets. A snarl tore through my chest, my alpha furious at the thought of even a drop of her sweetness being wasted.

I'd never done this before—never done *anything* sexual before—but I followed my instincts and dove in to lick her from ass to clit. I would do whatever I could to make this good for her.

I was drunk on her in an instant, addicted after my first taste, and I would never get enough.

Watching her with Leo and King had been enough to drive me fucking insane. My alpha fought against the bounds of my rut suppressants as I struggled to maintain control of my instincts. I had taken two extra pills before entering her nest. Holding myself back from her until they kicked in had been fucking torture. Nothing could have prepared me for what it would feel like to have my omega spread before me, crying out for my cock.

It was heaven and hell, wrapped up in one.

Heaven because she was my everything, my dream come true.

Hell because my diagnosis meant that at any moment, I was seconds away from succumbing to my rut and harming her.

My fear was the only thing grounding me as I continued feasting on her. I was so dizzy from the suppressants that I could barely keep my eyes open, but I didn't stop. A purr rumbled through my chest, and Lucy whimpered as she tightened her hold on my hair.

"Please, Wilder. Please, please. I need you inside me."

My girl was begging for my cock and I couldn't give it to her. I should have slowed things down, stopped her before I entered the nest to tell her everything—how it was too dangerous for me to fuck her, how the safest thing for her would be for me to leave—but I was weak.

I pressed a finger into her tight channel, wishing it was my cock. I added a second fingers and curved them toward me. "Your pussy is fucking strangling me." I added a third finger and curved them toward me. She opened so beautifully at the stretch. My knot fucking ached with desperation to be inside her.

"That's it. Come for me, sweetheart."

She cried out, her pretty little cunt squeezing my fingers as I worked her swollen clit until she came, a fresh burst of slick soaking my beard.

I couldn't stop, couldn't tear myself from her as she rode the waves of her orgasm.

I had never seen perfection like her.

Finally, all the tension seeped out of her, but there was nothing relaxed about the rigid set of my muscles.

I moved over her body with a growl, my fist working my cock so hard it was painful. I came seconds later, splattering her stomach and chest with my release. If I couldn't come inside her, at least I could mark her with my scent.

Her wide eyes met mine as she caressed my jaw. I tempted fate by pressing a soft kiss to her lips. Our first kiss. My heart ached when I forced myself to pull back.

It was too easy to lose myself in her.

"I'll get a cloth," I muttered. I headed to the bathroom down the hall, drawing in big gulps of air as I tried to clear her scent from my lungs. It was useless. Lucy was imprinted on my soul.

When I returned to the nest, my omega was half asleep as Leo and King stroked her hair and kissed her.

I washed my cum off her skin, leaving just enough that my scent would be potent without her feeling sticky. I tossed the towel in the hamper in the corner and moved to the edge of the nest.

I couldn't make myself leave, but I needed to create distance. King met my gaze with narrowed eyes but said nothing. He wrapped Lucy in his arms until her back was plastered to his chest, and I fought my primal urge to howl with jealousy.

51

LEO

YEARS OF WAKING UP EARLY FOR OCEAN RESCUE SHIFTS AND, more recently, flower market days, meant my body woke me at six despite our late night. My lips curved into a smile before my eyes opened. Lucy was sprawled halfway across my chest with King sandwiched on her other side. Everything was perfect . . . except my brow furrowed when I spotted Wilder lying at the very edge of the nest.

He'd seemed off last night. Maybe he just needed more time to get comfortable with all of this. I liked to think I'd gotten to know the reserved alpha pretty well the past couple weeks, and I knew he'd never been with an omega before. This was a lot for all of us to figure out.

"Go back to sleep." King's voice was muffled against Lucy's hair. "We don't have to be at the grand opening until nine thirty." He wrapped his arm around our omega and his hand came to rest on my chest, sending flutters through my stomach. Watching him with Lucy last night had been the hottest thing I'd ever seen, and it only made me want him more. I squeezed my eyes shut. It was too early to navigate my tangled feelings.

I dozed for a little while longer before jolting awake.

Shit.

I had PT this morning and needed to leave now to avoid being late. I was tempted to message Cassie and let her know I'd miss today's appointment, but I was planning to talk to her about getting a referral to pain management. Lucy's acceptance—my entire *pack's* acceptance of my cane—had freed me from the last vestiges of embarrassment. I would always grieve my previous body—its strength, surety, and lack of pain—but I could find a home in my new body.

I smirked. This was the body that had fucked the most gorgeous omega in the world, the one plastered against me as she slept.

I shifted out from underneath her, and King's eyes popped open with a scowl.

"I have PT," I whispered.

"Do you want me to come with you?"

His question knocked me off my axis. He would leave a warm bed, where his *omega* was, to be with me? After years of being told I would add nothing to a pack because of my beta designation, I didn't know how to process this. It was beyond my wildest dreams.

"*Stay*," I mouthed. Maybe I would ask him to come to an appointment in the future, but today I wanted Lucy to have all the attention.

MAIN STREET WAS WAKING up by the time I finished my appointment. I peeked into Beans 'n Bliss and saw Ella was working, so I headed inside to get all of us coffees. King, Wilder, and I were early risers, but Lucy was definitely not. Her morning crankiness, so at odds with her otherwise persistently sunny personality, always made me smile. But I knew she'd want to be especially alert this morning for Summer's grand opening celebration.

"Hi, Leo," Ella said, a mischievous twinkle in her eye. "I heard speed dating had quite the exciting ending."

I shook my head and scanned the space for Carmen and Marisol. They were nowhere to be found, but I'd bet my entire store they'd been here earlier this morning, spreading the news of our dramatic exit.

"I'd like four strawberry field lattes, please."

She squealed and jumped up and down. "Four lattes! Four lattes!" Everyone in the coffee shop was staring at us, and I choked back my laughter.

"Maybe I *really* need caffeine this morning."

Ella wagged her finger at me. "Don't play with me, Leo."

I grinned and handed her my credit card but she shook her head. "It's already paid for."

"By who?"

"King. He has a gift card he refills."

"That's probably just for Lucy, though."

"Nope. He came in here the other day to reload it and said it's for you and Wilder, too."

Warmth trickled through my chest at the alpha taking care of me like this, but I couldn't let it stand. I'd grown up with the Iranian principle of tarof, which was all about hospitality and social etiquette that demanded fighting over the bill.

"Ah, well, I'll pay for today." I held out my card again.

Ella shook her head. "King was very insistent."

I scowled. "King is not here. I am. In fact, I want to pay for a gift card that covers his drinks anytime he comes in."

Ella giggled and took my card. "It's a good thing I love drama."

A few minutes later, I cradled the drink carrier against my chest as I crossed the street. Carrying it up the stairs while maintaining my balance with my cane and my knee, aching after PT, was a challenge, but I managed it. I thought about taking the drinks into Lucy's nest, but I wasn't sure if that was against omega rules. Besides, she needed some sort of incentive to actually get up.

I practically floated back to the nest. How was this my life?

I settled back down beside Lucy and kissed her forehead. "Good morning, azizam. It's time to get up."

Her nose scrunched and she let out the cutest kitten growl.

"I know, mornings are the worst. But there's a latte waiting for you in the kitchen."

Lucy's eyes flew open, but instead of the smile I expected, her expression transformed to one of fury. "Where have you been?"

"I . . . what?" I blinked, totally lost. "I didn't want to wake you before I—"

Lucy sat up and shoved my chest. "Get out! I can't believe you'd come into my nest smelling like that!"

Her shouts woke King and Wilder, who sat up in bed wearing matching confused expressions.

King wrapped his arm around our omega's waist. "What's going on, baby girl?" His voice was low and rough with sleep.

"Leo came in here smelling like another omega." To my complete horror, she burst into tears.

Wilder scowled. "What omega?"

"I don't know what—" Oh shit. Oh fucking *shit*. My brain clicked the pieces together. "Wait, okay, I was at PT this morning and Cassie, my physical therapist, is an omega."

"You let another omega touch you?" she snarled.

"Just for the PT exercises!" I shot King and Wilder a desperate look. I couldn't scent Cassie on my clothes, but omegas had extra sensitive noses. They were also very possessive, something I'd known intellectually but had never experienced.

Thankfully, King took over. "Leo, take off your clothes and put them outside the room. Lucy, settle down. Your beta belongs to you."

I practically ripped off my clothes and threw them down the hallway. I'd put them in the wash in a second . . . or burn them.

When I returned to the nest, she was still struggling against King's hold. The alpha looked utterly unfazed as he flipped her face down over his lap and landed several hard smacks to her ass. She relaxed immediately, the tension in her body melting away.

"That's a good girl," King murmured. "Sometimes you need a little help to settle, don't you?"

"Yes, Daddy," she sniffed.

"I'm going to shower," Wilder said abruptly. He brushed a quick kiss to the top of Lucy's head and left.

Hmm. I definitely need to check in with him, but right now, I had an omega to tend to.

I shifted nervously on my feet. "Lucy, can I enter your nest?"

She nodded and King released her.

I lowered myself to the mattress, wearing only my boxers, and tentatively held out my arms to her. She lunged at me, knocking me on my back. Her arms and legs wrapped around me tight, and she rubbed her cheek against my neck, covering me with her scent.

I stroked my hand up and down her back, wishing I could purr for her. "I'm sorry. I didn't realize I smelled like her."

She let out another growl, and King swiftly smacked her on the ass. "Behave, baby. Now, I need to run home and get dressed. Are you going to be a good girl while I'm gone?"

Lucy nodded.

He brushed her hair to the side and pressed a kiss to her lips, which were just inches from mine. My cock twitched.

"We'll leave for the grand opening once I'm back."

I caught his hand before he could leave. "There's a latte for you in the kitchen."

He nodded, but as he turned away, I swore I saw a blush on his cheeks.

I caressed Lucy's jaw, tilting her face so I could press my lips to the same spot King's were just moments ago. "Can you forgive me?" I murmured.

Her body relaxed around mine. "Yeah, of course. Sorry for overreacting."

"I hate seeing you upset, but I don't hate that you're possessive of me. I love you so much, pretty girl."

Her chest vibrated with a purr. "I love you, too."

We lay there for a few minutes, Lucy's fingers trailing through my hair as I drew patterns down her back. Soon, her scent deepened and she started lightly rocking against my cock. I clenched my jaw. We did *not* have time for any morning shenanigans, plus she had to be sore. Right? Did omegas get sore?

"How're you feeling after last night?"

"Good."

I brushed her hair aside to see her face. Her cheeks were pink, and she was smiling.

"Just good?" I cocked an eyebrow.

She propped herself up on my chest. "*Really* good." I inhaled sharply as she arched against me, grinding her bare pussy against my boxers. The scent of her slick filled the room, and I groaned.

"We have to get ready for the grand opening. We don't want to be late." My words were strained, but I had to stay strong.

A heartbreaking whine escaped her lips.

Fuck it, I was weak.

I sat up so my back was against the wall with Lucy straddling my lap. "My girl is needy this morning."

She nodded. Her pupils were wide, face flushed, hair messy, and she'd never looked more perfect. My lips crashed against hers and my fingers dug in to her ass.

"You can have one orgasm with my fingers to tide you over."

She shook her head, lip jutting out in a petulant pout. "I want your cock."

Fuck. This was every fantasy I'd ever had come true. How was I supposed to resist her? I wanted to thrust inside her, but if I did that, we'd never leave the nest. We needed to show Lucy that we could fit into her life, and that meant winning the approval of her friends.

Besides, I was slightly scared of what Summer would do if we were late to the grand opening.

I shook my head as I sank two fingers into my omega's hot, wet heat, savoring her soft whimpers as I curled them toward me. "Naughty girls don't get to come at all."

"I'm not naughty," she breathed. She was rocking her hips against my hand, taking her pleasure.

"No, you're my perfect girl. So you'll take what I give you." I pinched her nipple and she cried out. "That's it. So fucking beautiful."

We were a flurry of clutched shoulders, fisted hair, and nipped lips.

I pressed my thumb against her slick clit, building her pleasure until she fractured with a loud cry. Slick gushed down my palm and wrist, my mouth watering with the need to taste her again. I brought my fingers to my mouth and licked them, keeping my eyes locked on Lucy's the entire time.

"I refuse to go a single day without your taste on my lips. You ruin me."

Her soft smile was everything. She wiggled proudly over my hard cock. I was seconds from exploding in my underwear.

She licked a line up my throat. "My turn to taste you."

"We really need to get ready," I said feebly, but she was already tugging my boxers down. They were plastered to my skin, soaked by her slick.

Any thoughts of protest died when her lips surrounded my cock.

"Fuck." My jaw ticked, my hands clenched into fists.

Her fingers wrapped around the base of my cock, and in one swift movement, she tightened her hold and took me deeper in her throat.

I swore again, sweat prickling my forehead. "I'm going to come so fast."

She released my cock with a wet pop. "Good. Then we won't be late."

My laugh transformed into a groan when her lips surrounded me again. She gagged slightly when she took me almost all the way to the base of my cock, and that was all it took. I fisted her hair as she sucked me down. I kept my dazed eyes on her as she swallowed my cum and gave my cock a few last long licks.

She sat up with a smile, her rosy nipples matching her cheeks. "Let's start every day like that."

I stared at her, slack-jawed. She had just sucked my soul out of my body and was now just bouncing around, ready for the day?

She kissed me and rolled out of the nest. She stood, and her pussy was eye level with me. I swayed forward as though hypnotized by slick, but she moved to the door.

"Did you say there's a latte for me in the kitchen?"

I nodded.

"Thank you. I'll be ready to go in like ten minutes."

My eyes were glued to her ass as she left. Once she was out of sight, I flopped back onto the bed. My little omega definitely had all the power in this relationship, and I was completely fine with that.

52

LUCY

I skipped to the bathroom. Who knew an orgasm and blow job were the key to putting me in a good mood for the day? A cock would be better. Maybe Wilder would still be in the shower and I could get some...

Especially since he didn't fuck me last night.

I had been overwhelmed by my guys and orgasms and *everything* last night, but now I was awake, alert, and desperate for my alpha's cock.

I opened the bathroom door and pouted when I saw the empty shower. It was probably for the best—today was such an important day for Summer and I didn't want to be late—but my omega was cock-drunk.

It was okay. I could make it until after the grand opening.

Probably.

Maybe.

I chewed my lip as I stood in front of the shower. I was absolutely covered by my guys' scents and dried cum, but I didn't want to wash them off.

I let out an irritated huff, pulled my hair up in a bun to keep it out of the water, and hopped into the shower. I would do a quick rinse. Enough to be out in public, but not enough to fully remove their scents.

I quickly did my hair and makeup and put on the dress I'd sewed especially for the occasion—bright yellow like Summer's bakery, with little embroidered cake slices around the bottom of the skirt.

Now I just needed to get...

Shit.

I needed to dress Felix and Blossom in their grand opening outfits and do a quick photo shoot of them inside the bakery before it opened.

I sprinted down the hall and popped my head into the kitchen. "I'm late! I've gotta go right now."

As I raced down the stairs, Leo's indignant voice followed me. "That's what I've been trying to say!"

I grinned as I spun around the room, trying to remember where I had stashed the outfits. I located them just as my guys joined me in the shop, but then my heart sank. "I didn't make outfits for you."

"Huh?" Wilder looked down at his long-sleeved flannel, jeans, and work boots. "Is there a dress code?"

"No. I just—" *You're being high-maintenance. Stop making such a big fuss.* "You know what, never mind."

King crooked his finger at me, expression stern. I dragged my feet against the floor as I crossed the short distance between us. He lifted my chin so I couldn't avoid his gaze.

"Tell me."

"It's not important."

Oh no. Now he had his spanking face on.

"This is our first time out in town as a pack." I chewed my lip. "I like making matching outfits for my friends for town events."

King and Wilder let out low growls, and all three of their scents intensified.

"You want everyone to know we belong to you," King said. A statement, not a question, but I nodded all the same.

"Sorry if that's weird."

Leo snorted and tugged me into his chest, his body firm against mine. He was using his new cane, the one King gave him, and that made excited little sparks somersault through my chest. "Weird? I fucking love it. Next time we'll all be matching."

I melted against him. My guys were perfect. Except . . . I couldn't smell myself on his skin anymore. My nose wrinkled, my omega turning vicious as my nose scrunched.

My movements were borderline aggressive as I rubbed my cheek against his neck. I might not have made them special outfits, but they sure as fuck weren't going outside without my scent on their skin.

Once I was satisfied Leo was covered in my scent, I moved down the line to King and then Wilder. My chest loosened once they were drenched in my scent. They hadn't argued or rolled their eyes at my possessiveness.

Wilder's scent was a riot of emotion, and his grip on my ass was almost desperate. "Need anything else before we leave?"

I peered into his eyes, but they didn't offer me an explanation for his mood. This would be a lot easier if we were bonded and I could feel his emotions.

My breath hitched. The four of us had been a pack for all of twelve hours and I was already thinking about bonding?

"Lucy?"

Right. This was not the time to have a spiral about our relationship.

"Nope, I don't need anything else. Let's go."

I grabbed Wilder's hand, and we headed out the door.

"What time is it?" I asked as we approached the bakery. Summer had told me to arrive at nine so we'd have plenty of time to set up before the party started at eleven.

"Nine thirteen," King said.

"Wow, only thirteen minutes late. That might be a record." I raised my voice so I could be heard over Summer's music. She had it going so loud we could hear it from the sidewalk.

"I need to get Blossom and Felix dressed and—"

I was interrupted by Lars's truck pulling up beside us. Before it had come to a full stop, Olive threw the door open. She bounced toward me with a squeal, and her enthusiastic hug would have toppled me over if not for Wilder's huge chest keeping me steady.

"Olive! Do not get out of a moving car." Finn exited the truck in a cloud of fury, followed by my brother and Easton—the only one who was smiling.

Olive pursed her lips. "I'm not sure that really counts as moving."

"Unless you want to lose your door-opening privileges, you would do well to listen to me."

Olive just smiled at her alpha's over-the-top protectiveness. "Okay, I promise I won't do that again. Now you should probably leave. I'll see you in a little bit for the opening—" Olive's efforts to shove Finn back to the truck were futile. Her three alphas stood shoulder to shoulder, scowling at my men.

I arched an eyebrow, and Olive mouthed "*Sorry*." Oh god, this was going to be some horrible brother posturing, wasn't it?

"Lars," I said, my voice full of warning. "Be nice."

He grunted.

"Seriously. Don't be obnoxious about this."

"You're my sister. Of course I'm going to be obnoxious."

"I wasn't rude to Olive when you started courting her!"

That got his attention. He stopped scowling long enough to meet my gaze. "Yeah, but that's because Olive is perfect."

The omega in question rolled her eyes. "It's a lost cause, Lucy. Just come over here and let them have their posturing moment. Then we can move on."

Wilder's hands momentarily tightened on my hips before he let go, and I stepped to the side. Olive slung her arm around my shoulder.

Lars opened his mouth and I braced myself for what he was going to say. We didn't get a chance to hear it because Easton spoke up instead.

"Woah, that's a sick cane." He bounded over to where Leo was standing and crouched down to get a better look. "Holy shit, I've never seen anything like that."

King puffed up, clearly proud of the gift he gave his beta. I mean, his *pack mate*. Maybe I needed to figure out a way to force them to admit their feelings for each other.

"Thanks," Leo said, grinning.

I beamed at his easy acceptance of his cane, so different from just a few weeks ago. I dabbed at my eyes and Olive wrapped her arm around my shoulder.

"You okay?" she asked.

"Just happy."

"Good. You deserve all the happiness."

Lars and Finn did not share our happiness.

"Easton, this is *not* what we discussed," Finn said.

But Easton was too far gone. He was sitting on the sidewalk, running his fingers down the cane.

"The carving is pretty straightforward. It's been a while since I've done it, but I'm sure I could pick it back up. I would need to do some research to see how they got this gold veining."

"Easton!" Finn yelled. "What the fuck are you doing?"

"What do you mean?"

"My guys are such idiots." Olive pressed her hand against her mouth to stifle her giggles. "You're not being very intimidating, baby," she called out.

Easton looked completely lost until Lars made an exasperated gesture at my guys.

"Oh. *Oooohhh*." He got off the ground and crossed his arms. "We're supposed to be intimidating you three."

"For fuck's sake," Finn muttered.

Leo was grinning, King looked confused, and Wilder was scowling. Probably because I wasn't within arm's reach.

"Well, the thing is, I'm a friendly guy," Easton said. "So friendly that I make friends wherever I go. My most recent new friend is a pig farmer just west of here."

I glanced at Olive for any clues as to where this was going, but she looked just as lost as I was.

"Lucy and I grew up together. She's like my sister. If you hurt her in any way, I will personally hunt you down, kill you, and deliver you to my new friend's pig farm, where they will eat your corpses, clothes and all, until no one can find even a trace of your DNA."

My jaw was on the ground. Where had this come from? Easton was literal human sunshine in an oversized alpha body.

"He's been reading too many of your mafia romances," I muttered.

"Yeah. But also, that was hot."

I scrunched my nose as Olive perfumed.

"Okay, okay. Enough of this." I stepped in front of Easton and patted his chest. "That was . . . disturbing. But thanks for the sentiment." I turned to Lars and Finn. "I know you two have my back, but the alpha posturing isn't what I need right now. So let's all be friends and go inside."

Wilder snagged me around the waist and pulled me to his side. I stood on my tiptoes and kissed his cheek. "Feel better, big guy?"

He grunted, but his woodsy scent brightened as we headed inside the bakery.

53

WILDER

After a year of living in Starlight Grove, I'd successfully avoided all of their almost weekly festivals. Well, except for last year's Easter egg hunt, when the fire department had been called after Easton brought dozens of plastic swords and organized a battle for the eggs resulting in a small fire, two children stuck in trees, and a number of lacerations requiring first aid.

The alpha in question was currently wearing an apron as he weighed Felix and Blossom in his hands to see if he could juggle them.

"Don't ruin their outfits!" Lucy shouted across the store. She caught my eye and blew me a kiss. My cheeks heated.

Felix and Blossom were both wearing hats in the shape of cakes. When we first got here, Lucy had set up a whole photo shoot with the two of them, using the colorful bakery walls as her backdrop and a tower of desserts as props. Desserts that somehow kept disappearing, although no one would fess up to being the thief.

Lars and I had been given the task of moving picnic tables from the community center basement—an area I was very familiar with after Stanley told us we had to clean it to prepare for speed dating... even though speed dating was not held in the basement—to the street in front of the bakery. I didn't mind the manual labor, but my chest felt like it was caving in every time Lucy was out of sight.

"It's hard to leave them, especially at first," Lars said as we loaded up the final picnic table in the back of his truck.

"What?"

He sighed and pushed the strands of hair that had escaped his bun out of his face—a gesture familiar to me. "When we first started courting Olive, I thought I would lose my mind every time we were apart. It gets easier." He frowned. "Well, maybe not easier, but the bond means I know she's happy and safe right now."

I hadn't known what to expect from Lucy's family, but this was much more welcoming—

"Not that I'm saying you should bond her," he muttered. "And if you hurt her, I will kill you."

Well, that was more of what I was expecting.

His words echoed in my mind as we finished setting up the tables. *The bond means I know she's happy and safe.* My mouth fucking watered, my alpha urging me to pull my omega away from the bakery counter and sink my teeth into her skin.

But Lucy and I would never have that.

I needed to tell her why I would always be on the edge of this pack, no matter how much I wanted her. Fuck, I should have come clean the first time we met. At least if she had rejected me then, I wouldn't know what she felt like in my arms and tasted like on my lips.

She'd already ruined me. I just hoped I wouldn't ruin *us*.

Lars and I were finishing up with the picnic tables when Lucy joined us outside. She'd braided her hair in a crown around her head and looked like a princess.

"It's almost go time." Her eyes sparkled as she curled into my side. "Everything looks good."

"You did an amazing job, sweetheart."

She glowed with pleasure, and I pressed a kiss to the top of her head. Stanley had approved the closure of this section of Main Street so Summer could set up picnic tables in the middle of it, making the area feel like an old-school block party. The bakery itself was an explosion of color, with its yellow awning and the colorful triangle things strung up in the air. A bright flower garland—the one Leo had finished up yesterday before speed dating—hung over the front door.

It wasn't long before a line formed outside the bakery. Surprisingly, Stanley and his husband, Harry, were first in line, both wearing bright yellow Suns Out Bánhs Out T-shirts.

The afternoon flew by in a blur of loud music, laughter, and endless food. For the first time in years, being around people didn't feel like work. The citizens of Starlight Grove were meddling and eccentric but also perfectly happy to accept my quiet, grumpy self.

Leo, King, and I spent most of the party together while Lucy was busy helping her friend. The best part of the afternoon by far was watching Blossom torment King. He'd been thrilled when she'd fallen asleep in his arms . . . until he stood from the picnic table and his button-down shirt fell open. Apparently the naughty bunny had secretly chewed off all of his buttons, leaving his bare chest exposed. Leo and I couldn't stop laughing, especially when an outraged King placed Blossom on top of the table to lecture her on proper decorum. Instead of looking guilty, her expression was smug as she turned her back on him, no matter how many times he turned her to face him.

I'd never understood how a group of strangers could form a pack just because they all wanted the same omega, but somehow it worked.

Leo and I were still laughing when Lucy wrapped her arms around me from behind. Her plush lips kissed my prickly cheek. "What's so funny?"

"Nothing," King muttered as he pulled his shirt together and crossed his arms.

Leo pulled her down between us. "How's it going?"

"Amazing! We're completely sold out. Summer said specifically to thank you three for all your help."

King, Leo, and I shared a smile. I didn't need a bond to know we were all relieved to have Summer's approval.

Blossom hopped over to me and nudged my hand until I put her on my shoulder. She snuggled into the crook of my neck, much to King's outrage. He pointed two fingers at the bunny and mouthed *"I'm watching you."*

"What are you doing, azizam?" Leo kissed Lucy's shoulder as he peered at her phone screen.

"I'm just editing some of the photos from today."

"I think Felix ended up liking his hat," King said. The mayor was sprawled on his back on top of our table, his big belly protruding to the sky. His cake hat was askew, but he'd refused to let anyone remove it. Blossom's matching hat tickled my jaw.

"He always complains about his outfits, but he secretly loves them."

"Do you use the pictures for anything?" King asked.

"Well . . ." She shifted, her slightly bitter scent putting me on full alert.

I gripped the back of her neck, squeezing lightly. My alpha clawed at my chest, desperate to fix whatever was wrong. "What's the matter?"

"Nothing's wrong. I just . . ." Leo nudged her with a reassuring smile, and she took a deep breath. "I have a social media account for Felix. Well, it was originally for Felix, but I've posted a couple pictures of him and Blossom together and people really like them."

"What's the account?" King whipped out his phone.

"The Real Mayor Felix," she mumbled.

I peered at her screen. "What social media is that?"

Leo snorted. "What, no electricity or internet at your cabin?"

I scowled. I had electricity.

Lucy giggled and handed me her phone. I squinted at the tiny squares of Felix dressed in elaborate outfits.

"You have six hundred thousand followers?" King's jaw dropped.

"Shh." Lucy waved her hands. "Don't say it so loud."

Leo tucked her hair behind her ear. "I didn't realize it was a secret. Why don't you want people to know?"

She chewed her lip. "I started it like a year and a half ago just for fun, but it really took off. The first people I told were the guys I was dating at the time."

A loud snarl escaped me before I could stop it. I didn't know much about Lucy's exes except that they were fucking assholes.

She took my hand and squeezed. "I was really excited about making costumes for Felix, but they said it was a silly idea and I should do something more serious."

"What the hell?" King snapped. "Where do they live, baby girl?"

Lucy just shook her head, a small smile tugging at her lips. "It's fine. I shouldn't let what they said bother me, but I just kept going with the account in secret. Now it's been so long I feel weird bringing it up to everyone."

King and I locked eyes, and I knew we were in agreement that nothing about this was *fine*. Those fuckers required sufficient payback for how they'd treated our omega.

"It's not like they were wrong—the account is silly—but I'm finally realizing that maybe it's okay to do something just to make people happy. My followers love giving me outfit ideas, too, which forces me to learn new techniques. I don't have a lot of experience making stuffed animals, for example, but I've learned enough from making these cake hats that I think I can make some now. I thought you might like to have some in your truck to give out to kids." She glanced up at me through her eyelashes.

"That would be amazing." My tone was gruff, my chest aching. The world would be a better place if people had a fraction of her thoughtfulness.

"Show me how to sign up for an account." I held out my phone to her, but before she could take it, the screen lit up with a call from the station. I sighed, wishing I didn't have to answer. Getting a call on my day off was never a good sign.

My fears were confirmed when Ezra told me a large warehouse fire had broken out in Briar's Landing. They needed another engine.

"I have to go in." I gripped Lucy's jaw and pressed a hard kiss to her lips.

"Stay safe." Her wide eyes met mine and she squeezed my hand hard. "Give us an update when you can?"

"I will."

I jogged away, feeling like I was leaving my heart behind.

54

LUCY

I was alone for the first time in days, and I hated it. After the grand opening, Leo, King, and I had spent the rest of the day together. We'd napped, watched a truly horrendous movie at the Hollywood Cinema—a space opera that was a literal opera—and ended the night with some not-so-innocent activities in my nest. But this morning, they'd left for work. Which, honestly, rude. My omega agreed. She firmly believed I should have cuddles and orgasms on tap.

Everything would have been perfect if Wilder had been with us. I'd carried my anxiety for him like a tangible thing as I checked my phone and the news for updates. We didn't hear anything until after midnight, when he'd texted to say he was safe, they'd finally put out the fire, and he was going to crash at the firehouse for the night. His next two-day shift started this morning so I understood him staying there, but I couldn't shake the feeling that something was going on.

Maybe I was being too sensitive, but no amount of convincing could erase the rejection I felt because we hadn't had sex. My brain kept generating all sorts of reasons for it—he was disappointed with my body, he wasn't attracted to me, he regretted his decision. The reasonable thing would be to just *ask* him, but I was scared to hear the truth because that would make it real. Right now, I could hold on to the hope that I was imagining things.

I jumped when my shop phone rang. I excavated it from its spot beneath the dress I was tailoring for Mrs. Cassini.

"Hi, can I speak to Lucy?"

"This is she."

"Hi Lucy. This is Jacqueline Wu. We met at the Boston Children's fundraiser?"

My breath froze in my lungs. Jacqueline Wu had called me. I WAS ON THE PHONE WITH JACQUELINE WU.

"Hello? Are you there?"

"Yes, yes, I'm here. Sorry!" I jumped up from my chair and let out a silent scream. *You're making a bad impression on Jacqueline Wu! Get your shit together!*

"Am I catching you at a bad time?"

"No, absolutely not. You just caught me a bit off guard! What can I do for you?" My words came out all squeaky, but I was just glad I had recovered the ability to form words, period.

"I was talking to my colleague, Fran Soto, and she shared that one of our upcoming fashion interns had to withdraw from our program because she's getting married. We've been going through our waitlist forms and I happened to spot your name, which was quite funny since I had just told Fran about meeting you. I was wondering if you were still interested in applying for the internship? It starts in just one month, so we're in a bit of a time crunch."

"Me?" I looked around my shop as if I'd find a secret camera recording what had to be a prank. Jacqueline Wu had remembered who I was? She wanted me for this internship?

"Yes, you," she said, amusement edging her voice. "Your dress at the event was beautifully designed and constructed. I think you'd be an asset to our program. There would still be a condensed application and interview process, and Fran makes the final determinations, but I'd love to get you the application if you're at all interested."

"Wow, I don't know what to say. Thank you. I'm really honored you thought of me. I just, I mean—" I forced myself to take a breath. "I don't have any formal training. Is that a problem?"

"While our interns are usually recent college grads from various fashion institutes, it's not a strict requirement. I think your real-world experience would be a great addition to the program. The focus of this internship is design, not sewing, although the fact that you can sew will help you, of course." A car honking sounded through the phone. "Listen, I have to go, but I'll have my assistant send you the application, and reach out if you have any questions."

"I will. Thank you so much again."

My hand shook as I hung up. One of my favorite designers in the world had called me and thought I could keep up in a program with college graduates.

"That did *not* just happen."

Blossom just blinked at me with sleepy eyes as if my entire world hadn't just been knocked off its axis.

55

LUCY

My pen tapped aggressively against the desk King set up for me in his rented office space. I'd thought writing on paper might help with my writer's block, but the blank internship application continued to taunt me.

To be fair, it wasn't *completely* blank. I'd written *Artist Statement* at the top. And added a bunch of doodles of Felix and Blossom.

I groaned. Why was this so hard?

The internship was an incredible opportunity. I would spend six months working at a high-end New York City fashion house, getting hands-on experience in design and making connections in the industry. So why had I spent the past two days unable to complete the application? Why did the idea of moving to New York City fill me with dread and terror?

I couldn't let fear hold me back. This was what I wanted.

At least, it was what I *should* want. What kind of person would I be if I passed this up? I'd texted all of my group chats after I got the call from Jacqueline, and everyone was excited for me. But that just made me more stressed, because what if I ended up not even getting accepted after all of this? And what if I did?

"Baby girl?"

King's voice jolted me out of my haze.

"What?"

A sharp line of concern formed between his furrowed brows. "Come here, princess." He held his arms out and I was out of my chair and rounding the desk before I realized what I was doing. He pulled me into his lap, squeezing tightly.

"What's going on?"

A Pack for Spring

I let out a shuddering breath, the tension lining my body easing as I breathed him in. "I'm having a hard time focusing."

"On the application?" I would have missed the slight clench in his jaw if I hadn't been watching so closely.

"Just feeling unsettled, I guess."

Last night at dinner, I asked Leo and King what would happen if I had to move to New York City. *Don't worry, baby. We'll figure it out.* Wilder had been on shift, but I'd texted him and his response had been the same.

But I *was* worried. Leo and Wilder had jobs they couldn't leave, and the thought of being apart from them for six months was agonizing. But if I didn't get the internship, what would happen with my and King's relationship? Would he return to his life in New York? I doubted my protective alpha would be okay being that far away from me, but I also couldn't imagine him being happy leaving the city for Starlight Grove. How long until he got bored with life in a small town . . . bored with me?

King ran his hand down my back, his touch firm and soothing. "You're so tense, baby. Does my girl need me to take care of her?"

My cheeks flushed and my pussy clenched. I nodded. Yes, that was exactly what I needed, what I *craved*. He tugged me closer, his hard cock pressing against my hip.

His lips skimmed my cheek. "Tell me what you need and I'll give it to you."

I squirmed as his question reignited my anxiety. I didn't want to think or make decisions.

King hummed, his eyes locked with mine. "Does my girl want me to take over?"

Relief washed over me. "Yes."

"Okay, sweet girl. I'm going to give you what you need, but I have some calls to make first. Can you be patient and quiet for Daddy until I'm done?"

I nodded, my stomach fluttering with anticipation.

He leaned over and pulled a pillow out of his desk drawer. My lips twitched. "Should I ask why you have that in there?"

His responding smile took my breath away. He was so beautiful like this, carefree and happy. I hoped I had a tiny part in that. "I like to be prepared for whatever my omega might need." He placed the pillow under his desk and guided me down to the floor until I was sitting on my knees, the cushion supporting me.

I would have teased him more about the pillow, but it was like he had pulled this scenario straight out of my fantasies, so I wasn't about to complain.

He cradled my face. "Are you comfortable?"

"Yes, Daddy."

"Good. Take out my cock."

His voice was stern, leaving no room for disobedience. Not that I wanted to disobey. I unzipped his slacks and tugged his boxers down until his half-hard cock sprang free. He scooted his chair forward and his hand collared my throat. "You will keep my cock in your mouth until I'm done with my calls. If you let me fall out of your mouth, you'll be punished."

My eyes widened and I pressed my thighs together as slick trickled from my pussy. I licked up a glistening drop of precum before taking him into my mouth. He was so thick that even just the tip was a stretch as I started to suck.

"That's it, baby girl. If you need to stop, tap my thigh three times. Other than that, I expect you to stay right there until I tell you otherwise."

I moaned and took another inch into my mouth. King stroked my face for a few more minutes before he removed his hand and placed his first call. I held in a whimper when the person on the other end of the line answered and my alpha started talking about the details of a trademark application.

My eyes drifted shut as I gently sucked, losing myself in the feel and taste of him. It was dark and peaceful under the desk. I spent most of my time these days wondering if I was making the right decisions, paralyzed with fear that I was doing the wrong thing. But right now, all I had to do was follow my alpha's instructions.

My omega settled as I fell into an almost trancelike state and King's voice faded in the background. I jolted when he hit the back of my throat. I resisted the urge to pull away, doing my best to swallow him down. King let out a low curse and then his fingers were on my cheek, cupping my head, twisting in my hair. His movements grew harsh and choppy as he fucked my mouth. His scent deepened, all the richness of cedar with a bright burst of citrus that made me lightheaded as I gulped thick breaths—all of them at his mercy.

My fingers surrounded his swollen knot. I squeezed hard, pride filling me when King grunted. He covered up the sound with a cough, and I realized he was still on the phone. Now I was the one who had to fight to stay silent because my alpha needing me so much he couldn't wait until he was done with work made me desperate to come.

His cock grew even thicker and his knot swelled, bumping against my lips with every movement. I hollowed my cheeks, sucking him down harder as he hovered on the edge of coming. My eyes widened in shock as he gripped the back of my head and thrust fully into my throat, his hands like steel. My head spun from lack of air, but then he was coming. Pleasure shot through me like sparks of electricity as I swallowed him down. My panties were soaked, and I had to clutch his legs to stop myself from shoving my fingers into my pussy to ease the ache.

I pulled off King's cock, sucking in deep breaths as I rested my head against his thick thigh, barely noticing when he hung up.

He pushed back enough from his desk to meet my eyes with his hard gaze.

"I guess my girl is getting punished."

My eyes widened. What had I done wrong?

He raised an eyebrow. "Didn't I tell you not to let my cock out of your mouth until I said?"

My lips parted. "But you came," I protested feebly.

He gripped my jaw. "Doesn't matter, baby girl."

"I'm sorry, Daddy." My words came out in a hoarse whisper, and my eyes burned with tears. His expression softened immediately and he pulled me out from under the desk and onto his lap. Was he going to punish me now?

"Shh," he murmured, squeezing me tight to his chest. "I'm just playing, princess. I'm not mad. You did so fucking well."

Oh. *Oh*. This was all part of the game we were playing. Fuck, I was being too sensitive. I slumped in his arms, my eyes drifting shut as he slowly ran his hands down my body.

"Better, baby?"

I hummed. "Yeah."

"Do you want to keep playing?"

If I said no, I knew he would be perfectly content to keep holding me, but I wanted more.

"Yes. But you're not going to punish me, are you?"

His chest rumbled with laughter. "Nice try." He pressed a hard kiss to my lips. "You're definitely still getting punished." His lips brushed against my cheek, soft and warm. "But you'll like it."

My unease subsided now that I knew he wasn't angry with me. After constantly being told what a disappointment I was by *them*, I was still scared of rejection. All I wanted was to please him. And Wilder and Leo.

King arranged me so I was standing between his legs. He reclined in his chair and slowly raked his eyes down my body. My cheeks heated, and my nipples pebbled at his close examination.

"Are you wearing underwear?"

Shit.

I chewed my lip.

"Lucy." His stern voice was almost enough to make my knees buckle.

"Yes. But Daddy . . ."

He ran his hands up the back of my thighs until he got to my lacy panties.

"I was very clear about this."

"But I have to wear them," I protested.

"Why?"

"Because..." My face felt like it was on fire.

He cocked an eyebrow, waiting for my answer.

"It will be too messy if I don't," I finally said.

His chest rumbled and he palmed my core. "But that's not your decision, is it? Your responsibility is to listen to Daddy." He shook his head slowly. "This means more punishment. I don't want to have to do this, but you need to learn a lesson."

I barely contained my eye roll. *Of course* he wanted to punish me... almost as badly as I wanted it.

He sat back in his chair, legs splayed and cock bulging against his pants. "Give me your panties and bend over the desk."

When I didn't move, he said, "Now," injecting his voice with his alpha bark. Another burst of slick gushed from me at his dominance, and his nostrils flared.

I lifted my skirt and slid off my underwear. They were soaked as I handed them to my alpha. He held them to his face and breathed them in. When I didn't move, he barked again. "Over the desk."

I scooted his laptop to the side and lay down on the hard wooden surface. His hands were immediately on me, running up my thighs and flipping the skirt of my dress up so my ass was bare before him. I tensed, expecting him to spank me, but he slid his desk drawer open again and took something out. I turned to get a peek, and that earned me a hard spank.

"No moving."

"Yes, Daddy." I rested my cheek on the cool desk surface.

The click of a cap. The rustle of plastic. And then—

He parted my ass cheeks and cold liquid dripped onto my asshole. I took a sharp breath. King had asked about anal play a few days ago, and I'd said I was interested. I should have known he would move fast.

"Fuck, that's a pretty sight. Take a deep breath for me, baby girl."

I forced my muscles to release their tension. His fingertip slowly entered me, dragging a moan from my lips. My breath caught when he pressed a second finger inside me. I shifted, my body automatically trying to get away from the stinging stretch.

"Shh. It's okay, baby. We'll take it nice and slow."

He pulled almost all the way out and thrust back in again. This time, the stretch was accompanied by a deep, needy ache in my clit.

"That's it. You're doing so fucking well for me. You'll relax and take it."

He continued moving his fingers in and out, stretching me and building my pleasure until I was arching into him.

"Daddy, *please.*"

His hand moved up my body until it settled firmly on the back of my neck. "Naughty girls don't get to come." He thrust a third finger inside me, bringing me to the very brink of orgasm before removing them completely.

I let out a frustrated sob. *"Please please please* let me come. I'll do anything."

He leaned over me, his body flush with mine, and it made me feel owned.

"You must really be desperate to offer me anything."

I nodded shamelessly. I'd never been this turned on. The insides of my thighs were slippery with slick, and the low growl in his voice just added to my arousal.

"Okay, princess. If you can take this last part of your punishment like a good girl, I will consider letting you come."

He stood, keeping a firm hand on my low back as he pressed something hard against my asshole. I whimpered, knowing what was coming. The pressure built against my tight hole as King pushed in the tip of a butt plug. I clenched automatically and then his fingers were on my clit, circling gently. A wave of smooth pleasure rocked through me, allowing me to relax enough to let the rest of the plug slip in.

The moment it was fully seated, an orgasm rocked through me.

My eyes widened and my lips parted in shock at the intensity of it. It stole my breath and left me a sweaty, panting mess.

King swore and leaned his body over mine. "I'm not sure how much of a punishment this is for you."

I wiggled my butt. "No, it's the *worst* punishment. You should definitely stop."

He burst out laughing, wasting no time pulling out the plug and thrusting it back in, hard and fast. A sound somewhere between a moan and a whine escaped my lips. He ran his fingers through my hair, his gentle touch in stark contrast with the harsh way he filled me with the plug.

"Daddy!"

"Yes, baby girl?"

"I need—" Oh god. I was so close to the edge *again*. My clit actually hurt with need.

"Say it."

"I need your cock."

He swore, wasting no time. Lifting my ass, he filled my pussy with one hard thrust.

I screamed. I had never been this full. My nerve endings were on fire, and I was utterly overwhelmed by the pressure.

I never wanted it to stop.

King's knot teased my entrance with every thrust. Each movement shifted the butt plug, but the aching fullness just built my arousal. He moved his hand underneath me and played with my clit, my slick making obscene sounds in the quiet office.

"I'm not going to last long, baby. You need to come again for me."

My breaths were ragged pants as his steady movement and pressure on my clit pushed me over the edge again. I was too tired to do anything but ride it out, the waves of pleasure crashing over me until I was only sensation.

"Can you take my knot, baby? Will you let me stretch that pretty little cunt?"

I couldn't imagine taking more.

I would die if he didn't give it to me.

I was beyond words, but I nodded and arched back against him.

King pressed his thick knot inside me and let out a loud moan. It was the hottest thing I'd ever heard—enough to push me over the edge again. My legs shook and tears spilled down my cheeks, but there was no sadness to them, just release.

I didn't know how much time had passed when King gently gathered me to his chest and sat back in his office chair. His knot shifted with the movement, making me clench around him.

He kept one hand firmly on my thigh and the other caressed my breast. The skirt of my dress was still shoved up, meaning if anyone happened to walk into this office, they would get quite an eyeful.

Not that King would ever let that happen.

A low purr rumbled through his chest. "That was the hottest thing I've seen. Fuck, you're perfect."

I was a relaxed, melted puddle in his arms, but something tugged at the back of my mind. "I'm not perfect."

I rubbed my cheek against his chest. There was something hot about having clothed office sex, but I wanted to feel his skin.

He unbuttoned his shirt for me. My alpha always knew what I needed. "What, baby?"

"I'm not perfect. I'm a mess."

His cheek shook and I scowled when I realized he was *laughing*.

"Yes, I've seen your apartment."

I turned to glare at him. "I don't mean my apartment," I grumbled. "Well, not *just* my apartment."

He quickly stifled his laughter. "I'm sorry. What do you mean?"

Before I could start chewing my lip, his thumb was already there, pressing into my mouth to stop my nervous tic. I sighed and relaxed into his chest.

"The longer we stay in this relationship, the more you'll see all of my flaws. And then you won't want me anymore." The vulnerability of my confession broke through my post-orgasm high, making me want to run away and hide.

King tightened his hold on me, his chest vibrating with an almost aggressive purr. "Maybe you're not perfect, because no one is, but you are perfect for me. Hopefully, with time, it will be easier for you to trust me. To trust us."

I closed my eyes. He was right. Only time would tell. I just wished I had his confidence that this would end happily.

56

WILDER

I walked out of the pharmacy with two bottles of extra strength rut suppressants rattling in my pocket. The pharmacist had given them to me with narrowed eyes and a warning against taking too many, not that they could stop me when rut suppressants were available over the counter.

Lucy's shop taunted me, a beacon of pure temptation across the street. It had been seventy-four hours since I'd last seen her, and I was on the verge of losing my fucking mind. After the warehouse fire, I'd worked my normal two days . . . and then I'd taken an extra shift to cover for one of my guys who was out sick. We were in the process of hiring a new firefighter but were short-staffed until we did.

It was a perfectly logical explanation for why I'd been working so much. Not suspicious at all.

The devil on my shoulder scoffed and crossed his arms. *If you weren't such a coward, you'd be fucking her in her nest right now.*

And *that* was exactly why I needed to stay away.

You could just tell her the truth. Then she can decide if she still wants to be with you.

I'd tried my best to ignore the angel on my shoulder, but I knew my time for secret keeping was up. Lucy deserved to know the truth, even if it meant I lost her.

Before I could talk myself out of it, I jogged across the street and pushed her shop door open. Lucy's bright floral scent saturated the air, but instead of its usual strawberry sweetness, there was a sharp burnt edge to it. I was instantly alert. My heart raced when I didn't see her. Had something happened? Fuck, she needed some sort of alert button attached to her at all times so she could signal us if she ever needed us.

"Lucy?" I called out.

"Back here!"

I sprinted to the back room and stopped short. My brain needed a second to process what I was seeing because my omega was *on top of a ladder*.

"What the fuck?" I hurried to her side, my hands immediately going to her hips to steady her.

"Hi," she said with a defeated sigh. "I hope your day's going better than mine."

"What are you doing?" I growled. Visions of her falling flitted through my mind and I tightened my grip.

"There was a water stain on the ceiling that I've been putting off painting, so I figured I'd get it done. But once I got started, I realized the plaster is crumbling, so I have to patch that and now my arms hurt."

Her face was splattered with bits of joint compound and I reached up to wipe them off. "You need to get down from there."

Her frown deepened. "I have to finish smoothing this before it dries."

"I'll do it for you." I lifted her off the ladder and wrapped my arms around her from behind, but her body was stiff against mine.

"I can do it, Wilder."

"I didn't say you couldn't."

"Didn't you? You don't even think I can stand on a ladder correctly."

"Sweetheart, that's—"

She shrugged out of my hold, leaving me cold. "I'm really busy, and I know you are, too," she said in a clear dismissal.

My sleep-deprived brain sluggishly tried to piece together what had just happened. "Time-out. What's wrong?"

"Nothing. I just have a lot to get done." She sniffed and wiped at her face.

Fuck, that sound was enough to destroy me. I closed the gap between us, my chest pressing against her back. "Tell me what I did wrong so I can fix it."

"I'm just tired of everyone treating me like I can't do anything. Just because I'm an omega and like girly things doesn't mean I'm dumb."

I spun her around to face me. "Who said you're dumb?"

She shrugged.

I cupped her jaw with one hand. "Give me names. I'll take care of them." I suspected it was her exes. The little she'd told us about them the other day had fucking killed me.

"I don't know. Everyone, I guess. You don't even think I can stand on a ladder."

I let out a slow breath, trying to find the right words to say. Expressing myself had never been my strong suit, but Lucy made me want to try. "Just because I want to do things for you doesn't mean I don't think you're capable. How could I think that when you run this shop and are good at everything you do?"

"I'm not good at camping." She arched a haughty eyebrow.

My lips twitched. "What are you talking about? You're a total pro on the mountain."

Surprised laughter burst from her chest, and it was the best fucking sound I'd ever heard. She wrapped her arms around me, and I returned her embrace, holding her tight. Her fingers twisted in my shirt, but I stayed silent, waiting. This was what I was good at. I could stand and hold her all day until she was ready to share what was bothering her.

"I got an email from Fran Soto," she said in an almost whisper. "She invited me for an interview the day after tomorrow."

Ahh. There it was.

"That's amazing, sweetheart," I said gently, even as dread and pride rocked through me in equal measure. I would never admit it, would never do *anything* to hold Lucy back from her dreams, but I didn't want her to go. There was no way I could handle being hundreds of miles away from her, but the sensory overload of big cities made it hard for me to function. Even Starlight Grove could be a lot for me. "Are you nervous?"

She nodded. "Nervous to get it. Nervous to not get it."

What did I say to that? I wished Leo was here. He was so much better at this stuff than me. The only thing I knew how to do was hold her tighter, as if my body could shield her from the world.

"You only submitted your application last night, right? They must really want you."

"Yeah, maybe." She pulled away enough to wipe her cheeks with her shirtsleeve. "I'm sorry for snapping. I panicked when I got the email so I decided to spackle the ceiling. Using those healthy coping skills."

"You get to be grumpy sometimes. I just want you to be happy."

"I've missed you." Her whispered confession destroyed me. I grabbed her hand and she entwined our fingers with a squeeze.

"I've missed you, too, sweetheart."

"Do you think I should take the internship if they offer it to me?" Her bright blue eyes stared up at me, beautiful and vulnerable.

No.

"It sounds like an amazing opportunity to advance your career," I hedged.

"Yeah, you're right." She smiled, but there was a strained edge to it that I hated. Was it nerves around the interview or something else?

"Are you still on shift? Or can we get lunch?" she asked.

I grimaced. "Still on shift, unfortunately. I have a few minutes before I have to head back, though, so you better finish your spackling."

I resisted my possessive urges and took a step back. I wanted to fix the ceiling for her, but if this was what she needed from me, I would give that to her.

Lucy's lips parted before transforming into a wide smile. "I think it just needs one more layer." She pressed a kiss to the corner of my mouth before grabbing the knife and stepping back onto the ladder.

I immediately moved behind her, my hands going to her ass.

For stability.

She glanced down at me but didn't protest as she finished up patching the ceiling.

"Now I just have to wait for it to dry before I sand it. At least that's what the online article said."

My hands hovered around her as she climbed down from the ladder.

"You did such a good job, sweetheart."

Her sweet "Thank you" was the best gift in the world.

As I headed back to the firehouse a little while later, I realized I had once again failed to tell her the truth about me.

57

KING

I GOT WILDER'S SOS TEXT WHILE IN A MEETING WITH BLACKthorne Ventures. Lucy had been invited to schedule her internship interview, but according to Wilder, she was stressed about it. Leo was making an out-of-town flower delivery and Wilder was on shift, so it was up to me to support our girl.

I tuned back in to the argument happening around me. My lawyer and Blackthorne's lawyer had been going back and forth on negotiating a specific *something something* . . . I hadn't been paying attention because I truly couldn't give a fuck. Everything I'd placed in the center of my life—work, image, others' approval—had somehow been stripped of all its importance. I'd even found myself online shopping for custom nest pillows *during a finance board meeting*.

I stood and the room fell silent. "Excuse me, gentlemen. I have to leave for a family emergency, but I trust you have this under control."

I didn't look back as I strode out of the room to my car, each step lifting the weight I'd carried on my shoulders for the past decade.

THE BELL ABOVE THE door chimed as I stepped into Spring in Your Stitch. The mere sound of it was enough to get my heart pounding because it signaled I was about to have my omega in my arms.

Lucy was deep in conversation with someone on the phone and didn't notice me. I took the opportunity to just look at her. Would I ever get used to her beauty, or would she always steal my breath? Her gold hair was down today, held back by a pink headband that matched the pink embroidered flowers on her denim jumpsuit. She was half hidden by bolts of fabric haphazardly stacked beside her, teetering precariously like they were seconds away from joining the piles of fabric on the floor.

It was a testament to how much I loved her that I found her messiness endearing instead of aggravating.

Holy shit.

I loved her.

Of fucking course I did. Lucy was the center of my world. Joy filled my chest like a balloon and I wanted to blurt it out, announce it to the entire town.

She must have caught my scent, because she looked up and gave me a little wave. My heart fucking fluttered as I crossed the space between us and pulled her into my arms, not caring that she was still on the phone.

"Okay, I see. Right, well then, I guess I'll see you soon. Thanks, Kat." She hung up and leaned her face against my chest with a groan.

"What's wrong, baby girl?" My hand trailed a path up her back until I got to her neck. I dug my fingers in, gently massaging away the tension.

"I special-ordered a fabric for a client's custom dress order, but the fabric shop in Briar's Landing called this morning to let me know it's back-ordered for another six weeks. They thought they might be able to get it from a different supplier, but they just called back and said they can't get it. The only thing they could recommend was that I come in and see if they have a different fabric in stock that I could use as a substitute. And the timing is especially tricky because now I have to go to New York." She glanced up at me, her teeth digging into her lip. "Did Wilder tell you?"

"About the interview? He did. And it's *amazing* news. You're incredible."

Lucy's smile and murmured thanks seemed strained, and I understood why Wilder had been concerned.

"Do you think you can take time off to come with me to New York?" she asked.

A Pack for Spring

How did she not understand that I would do fucking anything for her? "Of course. Especially since I'm supposed to be on leave from work right now, anyway. Not that anyone seems to remember that."

Lucy grinned and I curled a lock of her hair around my finger.

"I can make some reservations. Show you my favorite spots in the city."

Fuck, I'd have to ask Caroline where to take my pack. Ten years in New York City and my daily routine consisted of going to the gym, the office, and back home to eat my take-out order and fall asleep on the couch. How was it that my life in Starlight Grove was so much more full and vibrant after only a few weeks? At least I could take a picture of a hot dog stand to show Ivy's class, who had fully decided that my job was a fish protection / hot dog vending combo.

"That sounds really fun," Lucy said, but then her face fell. "In the meantime, I have to figure out this fabric situation. Summer texted me earlier that Harry has to go to Briar's Landing and can give me a ride. But he's leaving in a few minutes and I don't want to leave Blossom alone."

My eyes widened when the bunny in question popped her head out of the collar of Lucy's sweatshirt.

"Has she been in there the whole time?"

"Huh?" She glanced down. "Oh yeah. She's been fussing if she's not against my skin, so I added a bit of fabric to an old bralette so she could hang out in there. I would just bring her to the fabric shop with me, but Kat is super allergic to basically all animals."

The bunny in question turned so she could glare at me.

Yes, she was *glaring*. There was no other way to describe her narrowed eyes and twitching nose.

I kept my expression neutral, but I was tempted to scowl back. What the fuck did she have to be mad about? *She* was the one who had bitten off all of my buttons at the bakery opening.

"Maybe Lars could watch her." Lucy pulled out her cell and I held in a snarl at the idea of another alpha helping her. I didn't give a fuck if it was her brother.

"I can do it."

Lucy froze before slowly looking up from her phone. "You want to watch Blossom?"

I would probably regret this . . . but I would do anything to make Lucy happy and she loved that evil little bunny.

"Of course. She can keep me company until you're back from the store."

"Are you sure you'll get along?" She covered Blossom's ears. "She can be a little temperamental."

"I'll behave if she does," I muttered under my breath.

"What?"

"Nothing. We will be totally fine."

This tiny bunny would not defeat me.

To my horror, Lucy started to tear up. "God, sorry, I don't know what's wrong with me today. Must be hormonal or something. It'd be great if you could watch her. I just don't want to be an inconvenience if you have more work you have to get done."

"Baby." I pulled her into my arms, being careful not to crush the bunny. "You could *never* be an inconvenience, and even if you were, that's what I'm here for." My chest rumbled with a purr and she relaxed against me.

Was it time? Should I say it? What if she didn't feel the same way?

I pulled back and cupped her face with both hands. Lucy still looked unsure, but a profound certainty had taken hold in my chest.

"I love you, Lucy. Maybe it sounds cheesy to say, but my heart is yours. There's nothing I wouldn't do for you."

Her lower lip trembled and a couple of devastating tears spilled down her cheeks. I wiped them with my thumb, my heart pounding as I waited for her to say something.

"I love you, too," she whispered. "I can't believe how lucky I am."

I captured her lips in a gentle kiss. She felt perfect in my arms. I'd never dreamed love could feel like this.

As much as I wanted to carry Lucy up to her nest and fuck her for the rest of the day, that wasn't what she needed from me. So I fought all my instincts and let her go. I carefully fished Blossom out of her hiding spot. *I swear if this bunny bites me while Lucy is watching...*

She sat quietly in my hand. Thank god.

"See? We'll be okay."

Lucy still looked a little dazed from my declaration and kiss.

"Thank you. I'll be fast, promise. And if you need help or get busy and need someone else to watch her, Lars and Olive should be home so you could bring her to the lighthouse."

"You will not rush. Blossom and I will be fine."

Her shoulders relaxed and I was treated to her gorgeous smile. She stood on her tiptoes and pulled me in for a kiss. "Thank you." She broke away too quickly and kissed Blossom on the forehead before heading out the door.

"Why the fuck do you get a goodbye kiss?" I muttered. Blossom whipped her head around to glare at me once more. I lifted her so we were eye-to-eye. "We are not going to add to Lucy's worries. You are going to cooperate. No mischief, no drama."

Blossom twitched her nose at me before giving me her back.

This was going to be fine.

58

WILDER

I PULLED THE PAN OF ENCHILADAS OUT OF THE OVEN AT THE firehouse and set it on top of the stove, joining the pan I'd already pulled out. The cheese was still bubbling, but I grabbed a plate to serve up my portion, anyway. In a few seconds, my guys would descend upon the kitchen like ravenous beasts. I wasn't a gourmet cook or anything, but I liked feeding people. It made me feel good. Useful.

Like when I made Lucy a grilled cheese in my cabin. For the first time since I started firefighting, I wished I had a job with normal hours. Being away from her for these long stretches was torture, although being on this shift meant I could put off telling her the truth of my diagnosis for a bit longer.

It wasn't fair to her, or the guys, for that matter. They all deserved to know.

My phone rang and my heart raced when I saw it was King calling. I'd texted him a couple hours ago about Lucy, and my mind immediately imagined the worst.

"Hello?"

"Wilder. I need your help." King was always annoyingly calm and businesslike, but right now, he sounded like he was seconds away from losing it.

I gripped the counter, my knuckles turning white. "Is Lucy okay?"

"What? Yes, she's totally fine. She had to go to Briar's Landing and I'm watching the demon for her."

A Pack for Spring

"Demon? What the fuck are you talking about?"

"The bunny! The little demon bunny from hell who has it out for me! But she likes you. So you need to come here and talk some sense into her."

My guys stampeded into the kitchen, and I stepped out into the hall so I could hear King. "You're calling me because you can't handle a tiny bunny that's literally smaller than your fist?"

"You can judge me all you want as long as you get over here," he hissed.

"I'm in the middle of a shift. I can't just leave."

"Wilder, I swear to god, if you don't get over here, I will set fire to my house just so I can call 911 and get dispatch to send you over."

What the fuck was happening at that house?

"I guess arson prevention is part of my job," I said dryly.

"You have five minutes to get here before it's no longer prevention." He hung up the phone.

I stared at my uneaten plate of enchiladas, my stomach rumbling. Fuck. I had to go over there, didn't I? We were a pack now.

I picked up my plate and headed back into the kitchen.

"This is great, boss," Ezra said around a mouthful of food.

I grunted. It might be immature, but I still held a grudge against him for flirting with *my* girl. I transferred my lunch into a plastic container before adding two more helpings to it, against my better judgment.

"I have to respond to a call. I'll be back soon. Noah, you're in charge while I'm gone. Call me right away if any other calls come in."

Silence descended on the kitchen. I put the lid on the Tupperware and turned around to find all of my guys' eyes on me.

Yousef sat back in his chair with a shit-eating grin. "Could this important call have something to do with a cute little omega?"

"No," I snapped.

The guys cheered. Assholes.

"Boss, if you can wait three months before you bond her, that would be appreciated," Noah said with a glint in his eye.

"No, no. Lucy is amazing. You definitely need to bond her in the next nine days," Ezra said.

I scrubbed my hand over my face with a long-suffering sigh. *"An-other* fucking betting pool?"

Noah winked. My fucking captain *winked* at me.

I flipped them all off before grabbing my food and stalking out of the kitchen to my truck.

KING

SHE IS DOING THAT FOOT STOMP THING

SHE IS PLOTTING MY DEMISE

I snorted and pulled out of the parking lot. I headed down Main Street, slowing when I saw Leo's car in front of his shop. Looked like he was back from his flower delivery.

I pulled over and headed into his shop, leaving the truck running. Leo was sitting in an armchair with his laptop.

His eyes widened when he spotted me. "Lucy?"

"Is fine. But King needs to be rescued. Let's go."

The beta grabbed his cane. "Rescued? From what?"

I smirked. "Blossom."

"Huh?"

I held the door open for him. "No fucking clue, but he sounded desperate."

A loud *meow* had me looking up just in time to see Felix scamper down the big tree outside the shop with the agility of an Olympic gymnast. The same tree I'd fucking rescued him from. He landed nimbly on his feet and trotted over to my truck.

"Do you ever get the sense that Felix is an evil mastermind?" I asked Leo.

"Yes. And seeing how he somehow materializes inside my house whenever he wants, he has greater powers than we could ever know."

THE FRONT DOOR TO King's rental was unlocked, so I pushed it open. "King? You here?"

A loud crash from the other room greeted us, and Leo looked at me with an arched eyebrow. "I feel like we're walking into a horror movie."

My lips twitched. "Stay behind me. I'll protect you."

"Big manly alpha is going to protect me? At least *I* have a weapon." Leo lifted his cane in the air.

I snorted. "I guess you should go first, then, so you can defend me."

The beta grinned as he took the lead.

I'd never been inside King's place before, but I assumed it didn't always look like this. A lamp in the living room had crashed to the ground, and toilet paper covered the entire floor. We followed the paper trail into the kitchen and found a frazzled King standing in a pile of flour, in a standoff with Blossom.

"Umm, hello?"

The alpha whipped around. His button-down shirt was completely undone and his hair was ruffled and sticking up.

"Thank fuck. Talk sense into her!" He pointed at the tiny bunny sitting on top of the kitchen counter.

I frowned. "It's not safe for her to be up there." I walked over to Blossom and scooped her up in my hand. She let out a happy squeak.

"No. No. You can't pretend to be all cute and reasonable now!" King's voice was bordering on hysterical.

I put Blossom on my shoulder and crossed my arms. "Don't yell at her."

King snarled and tore at his hair. Leo chuckled and patted him on the back. "We'll get this cleaned up, don't worry. By the way, I like the new look." He gestured at King's bare chest.

"She chewed the buttons off my shirt *again*. This time she got my hair, too!" He pointed at a chunk of his hair that did, in fact, look shorter than the rest.

Leo and I couldn't contain our laughter. I put my hand on Blossom to make sure she wasn't jostled as my shoulders shook. King glared at us as he scrubbed his hand down his face, but I was pretty sure I saw a hidden smile.

"I think this is yours," Leo said. He started to bend over to pick something up off the floor, but King beat him to it. Leo was clearly sensitive about his leg, and King went out of his way to make things easier for the beta without making him feel self-conscious. I wasn't the most in-tune person when it came to romance, but anyone could see that these two were into each other.

King held up a small button and made an *I'm watching you* gesture at Blossom.

I grabbed the Tupperware I'd set on the counter and dished up the enchiladas, popping them in the microwave. "What did you do to anger her?"

"I think it's because I said her ears were lopsided that one time! It wasn't an insult!" He slumped down on a barstool, his head in his hands.

"Well, have you apologized?" Leo asked seriously.

"Apologized? To the *bunny*?"

Blossom nudged me and I gently set her down on the counter in front of King, who let out an aggrieved sigh.

"Blossom, I apologize for this grave insult. Your ears are perfect." He glanced at us, eyes wide. Leo made a gesture for him to continue.

"You are very pretty, and your fur is soft, and . . ." He groaned and put his head down on his arms. "Please forgive me."

Blossom slowly hopped over to him. We all held our breath. She leaned in, snuggling the side of his head, and then . . .

She bit off a chunk of his hair and hopped back to Leo, depositing her stolen goods in his hand.

King groaned, Leo laughed, and I just slid a plate of enchiladas across the island. "You'll just have to keep working to win her over."

He muttered something under his breath and dug into his food. I passed a plate to Leo.

"Damn, Wilder. This is really good," he said. "I didn't know you could cook."

"I *would* offer you some food," King said bitterly, "but Blossom ate my meal prep salads."

There was a beat of silence, and then the three of us burst out laughing.

"Don't tell Lucy," he said, covering his face.

Leo grinned. "Your secret is safe with us."

If this was what pack life was like, maybe we would be okay.

59

LUCY

> **HOROSCOPE PISCES**
>
> Going through your Saturn return is like walking through an endless tunnel. There's pain in that darkness, but sometimes the most worthwhile things in life require disintegration before they can be rebuilt on solid ground. Keep going.

KING'S HAND DIDN'T LEAVE MY THIGH THE ENTIRE DRIVE TO New York, even once we got into Manhattan traffic. Something about his one-handed driving turned me on, which would have been a bit embarrassing, but at least it distracted me from my inner turmoil.

My guys had chalked up my mood the past few days to my pre-interview anxiety, and that was definitely part of it. The only interview I'd done was for a part-time job at La Dolce Vita's seasonal gelato stand on the beach when I was fifteen. Somehow I thought this interview might serve up harder-hitting questions than, "What's your favorite ice-cream flavor?"

But my uneasiness ran deeper than interview jitters. This was the opportunity I'd dreamed of since I made collages of my favorite outfits from Mormor's fashion magazines. This internship would be an affirmation of all the hard work I'd put in through the years, and maybe it would finally make me feel worthy of calling myself a designer, artist, and seamstress. I'd wanted to prove to myself that I could do something meaningful with my life . . . but I wasn't sure that's what I needed anymore. Maybe the life I'd created, and the work I did, was already worthwhile.

"You ready?" Leo opened my car door and I blinked. I'd been so out of it I hadn't realized we'd arrived.

I glanced at King and he leaned over the console for a kiss. "I'm going to park the car. You'll do amazing. I love you, baby. No matter what."

I swallowed the lump in my throat. "I love you, too."

I took Leo's hand and smoothed my skirt before we walked into the lobby, Wilder flanking my other side. He'd been quiet the entire drive, too, saying he was tired from his long shift, but his scent gave him away. Something more was going on, and it was not helping soothe my anxiety.

The lobby was gorgeous—huge vaulted ceilings, plush furniture, marble floors, and a cafe off to the side. Everyone here was scurrying around in designer clothes, laptop and coffee in hand. I tugged on my dress again. Should I have worn something different? I'd made it last summer—a fitted number with long sleeves and a short skirt covered in bright floral appliqué that stood out painfully in the sea of black pencil skirts.

My guys half propelled me to the front desk, where I checked in and was told my interviewer, Fran, would be down soon. We took a seat on the lobby couch.

"Do you want coffee?" Leo stroked the back of my hand. "Or a snack? It looks like the cafe has pastries."

I shook my head. My stomach was churning too much to eat and I was too wired for caffeine.

"You'll do great, azizam. I have no doubt." Leo pressed a gentle kiss to my forehead.

Wilder stared straight ahead with a blank expression. I leaned into his side and was about to demand he tell me what was going on when a woman with sleek black hair and an impeccably tailored black pinstriped suit got off the elevator and walked straight for us.

"Hi, Lucy." She held out a confident hand and I stood to shake it. "I'm Fran Soto, director of our internship program. If you're ready, we'll head upstairs."

Wilder seemed to snap out of his haze and pulled me into a quick hug. "You've got this, sweetheart. We'll be here when you're done."

I felt lighter as I followed Fran into the elevator.

"Thanks for making the time to come with such short notice," she said as she led me into her office—a window-lined room with sketches and magazines covering the walls and a haphazard stack of fabric samples on her desk. I grinned. It was exactly what I'd imagined a fashion designer's office to look like, and not too far removed from the chaos of my shop.

"I really appreciate you inviting me to interview. It means a lot to me."

Fran smiled as she sat down across from me and jumped right in. Her sharp wit and sense of humor shone through during the interview. She seemed genuinely interested in my store and even asked questions about my grandma from the artist's statement I'd finally written.

I held my breath while she flipped through my portfolio.

"You have a fun sense of style, and it's great that you have experience designing for diverse bodies. We've been focusing on expanding our line of plus-sized clothing. If that's something you're interested in, you could develop that as a focus during your internship."

"Does everyone pick a focus?"

Fran hummed. "Our program is designed to give our interns broad exposure to different career opportunities within fashion, with a focus on design. You would assist with sketches and sewing, creating mood boards, researching trends for our winter line, and assisting during fittings and shows. But there's some room within our program to develop an area of focus. What are your career goals?"

Shit. This was quite possibly the most straightforward question she could ask, and I'd practiced my answer in the mirror last night. But now that I was sitting here, my rehearsed answer felt trite.

"To be honest, I didn't think working in a big fashion house would ever be in the cards for me since I didn't go to college, so the past week has definitely been a bit of a whirlwind." I took a deep breath to steady myself. "I guess what I really want is to expand my skills and confidence in designing and sewing couture. I love working

A Pack for Spring

individually with clients to design something unique to them." I clenched my hands on my lap to keep myself from fidgeting, but Fran just nodded thoughtfully. She asked a few more specific questions about my portfolio pieces before ushering me out of her office for a building tour.

Fran led me through the maze of hallways, introducing me to anyone we came across. "You'll love what's on the next floor." We took a turn out of the elevator and she swept her arm out in front of her. "This is our sewing room."

I peeked through the door. An enormous cutting table sat against the back wall, corkboards displayed fabric samples, and lining the tables in the middle of the room were a dozen different sewing machines.

This was *heaven*.

"Is sewing a big part of this internship?" I asked.

"Not a big part, no. Mainly you'd hand-sew to make small repairs or adjustments on shoots or behind the scenes at shows. The focus of this internship is more heavily weighted on designing clothes for larger-scale manufacturing versus couture, but you would still gain invaluable experience to reach your goals."

My heart twisted. The internship would require me to work long hours. I doubted it would leave me much time to sew for myself.

I reluctantly left the sewing room behind, and we emerged into a small coworking space where two beta women my age were working on their laptops.

"Oh, good. I was hoping you'd be here. Lucy, this is Brooklyn and Ellie. Brooklyn was actually an intern in the design program a couple of years ago. Lucy is interviewing for the internship today."

I gave the two women a wave as a man in a dark purple suit jogged into the room.

"Fran, sorry to interrupt, but Patrick is on the phone for you."

"Ah, okay. Can you girls hang out with Lucy while I take this call? You can convince her to come work with us."

"Sure. Come in, Lucy. We'll spill all of Fran's secrets," Ellie said.

I grinned and sat down at the table. It would be nice to have coworkers my age to collaborate with.

Brooklyn stared intently at my face. "You look so familiar to me, but I'm not sure why."

I cocked my head. "I don't know. I rarely come to the city so . . ."

She snapped her fingers. "I got it! You sew for Mayor Felix, right?"

Oh shit.

My mouth gaped like an unattractive fish as Brooklyn continued. "This is so embarrassing—for me, not you! I'm obviously obsessed. I took a screenshot of the selfie you posted on your birthday because your dress was really pretty and I was trying to figure out how you made it."

I'd broken my rule to remain faceless on Felix's account when I posted our birthday selfie. It was one thing to know intellectually that I had over half a million followers, but it was another to actually meet a stranger in the wild who followed me.

"Your work is incredible. And Blossom? I am obsessed. I can't wait to see their outfits for Midsummer! I was even thinking about going to Starlight Grove for the festival."

"Okay," Ellie interjected. "Now you sound like a stalker who wants to wear Lucy's skin like a suit."

Brooklyn wrinkled her nose. "Well, that's a disgusting image. I promise I don't want to wear your skin. Mostly, I just wish I was as cool and talented as you."

My stunned fish face continued. This woman worked in a huge fashion house in New York and she thought I was *cool and talented*?

"You're considering taking the design internship here?" Ellie asked.

I shrugged, my cheeks pink. "I'm just interviewing today. I don't know if I'll even get the offer."

"Of course you'll get it," Brooklyn said. "They'd be stupid not to snap you up."

My face was seconds from going up in flames. "Do you like working here?"

"Yeah," Brooklyn said. "The fashion world can be brutal. After my internship here, I got an entry-level position at another fashion house and hated it. My manager was awful. But Fran is a really solid boss, and I've definitely learned a lot."

"The hours can be rough," Ellie added. "Lots of weekends and stuff. But I think it's worth the sacrifice if you're working toward your goals."

"Do you want to transition away from sewing to design?" Brooklyn asked.

I chewed my lip. "I'm not sure."

"Of course, you already *are* a designer. Ellie, she's the one who made that strawberry dress I was telling you about."

"That was *you*? I swear we studied that outfit for ages trying to figure out the pattern!"

"Really? I could send it to you."

"Lucy, you can't just be handing out your patterns for free!" Brooklyn said. "Besides, the most I've ever sewn was curtains for my house, and by the end of it, I was ready to throw the machine out the window."

"If you ever ran a sewing class, I would take it in a heartbeat," Ellie added.

"Yes! There's this seamstress I love who has this whole online program with her patterns and tutorials and stuff. You would kill at that! You could do a whole separate class on pet clothing. I made my cat a bandana and I swear she looked at me like *This is the best you can do?*" She shook her hand. "I never should have shown Princess Whiskers your Instagram."

Had I entered an alternate reality? My friends and family had been complimenting my sewing for years, but they *had* to say nice things. These were two strangers. "I really just do it for fun."

"Well, if you ever want to set up an education site, my girlfriend could totally help. She's a computer person," Brooklyn said.

"A computer person? For the love of god. You live together and you still can't remember her job title?"

She shrugged. "I mean, I moved in with her after three dates, so I'm not sure that's saying much. When you know, you know."

Ellie looked at me, shaking her head, but I grinned. It wasn't like I could say anything. My guys were practically living in my nest already.

"Let's exchange numbers so we can keep in touch," Brooklyn said.

Ellie muttered that her friend was a stalker under her breath, but they both put their numbers into my phone.

"You'd be welcome to come to Midsummer, by the way," I said. "Although my guys might not approve of your whole skin-suit plot."

Brooklyn gasped. "Your *guys*? I didn't realize you were bonded."

My cheeks heated at my slip. "Not yet. We're still courting."

"I don't know who I'm more excited to meet—Felix or your pack." She tapped her pencil against her lips. "Let's be real, it's Felix. Unless you're also making costumes for your pack?"

"Oh, I'm definitely going to sew something for them."

"I can't wait to see."

60

LUCY

I HEADED BACK TO THE LOBBY ONCE THE INTERVIEW HAD wrapped up. My chest was a swirl of tangled emotions, but there was a blanket of happiness over it all. Deep down, I'd expected to be told I had no business being here, but everyone I'd met had made me feel the opposite. I couldn't wait to tell my guys all about it, but they weren't on the couch where I'd left them. I scanned the lobby but still nothing, and the high-powered air-filtration system made it so I couldn't catch their scents, either.

My heart pounded and my skin felt tight and itchy as I circled the room and peered into the cafe. They wouldn't just leave me, right? I pulled out my phone, but there were no missed calls. They'd probably gone to the bathroom or something...

I waited a few more minutes, but when they still didn't show, I dialed King—the one out of all of us most likely to have his phone on. I jolted as a burst of static came through the speaker.

"Hello? King?"

There was no response except for the honking of a horn, muffled shouts, and more static. My heart raced and anxious sweat dripped down my back.

"Lucy? Can you hear me?"

I drew in a ragged breath at King's voice. "Barely. Where are you?"

"Shit, sorry, baby. I—interview—hospital."

Most of his words were incomprehensible. I pressed my phone hard to my ear, trying to hear him over the cacophony of background noise. "Did you say *hospital*?"

More static, and then Leo's muffled voice broke through. My ear hurt from the loud noises coming from the speaker, but I didn't turn down the volume as I tried to catch his words.

"We're almost—once we—checked in—will take a taxi—pick up."

"What? Leo, I can't hear you."

"Shit. Fuck."

Of course those words came through crystal clear. There was a loud clattering sound and then the call cut off.

I called back right away, but all I got was an endless series of rings and King's curt voicemail message.

Waves of hot and cold crashed over me, and I felt like I was about to throw up. Maybe I'd heard wrong and King hadn't said hospital. He could have said *Broadway show*.

Yep. That seemed likely.

A text from King came through and I fumbled to open it.

KING

> Wilder passed out. We just got to NYGH. Stay there.
> Leo or I will come get you

LUCY

> What's wrong with him? Is he going to be ok??

Waiting for a response was agony. My eyes stayed fixed on the screen until it came through.

KING

> In the ER, running tests.

> Don't panic. I'm sure he'll be fine

That was *not* reassuring.

I pulled up my maps app and typed in *NYGH*. New York General Hospital. Two miles away.

I sprinted through the lobby and out the front door. I had no idea if you could actually hail a taxi like they did in the movies, but I wasn't about to wait for my guys to come get me.

I stepped off the sidewalk and held out my hand, feeling like the main character from *Knots and the City*. A few torturous seconds ticked by and then a bright yellow taxi pulled up beside me.

I SPRINTED INTO THE ER, spinning around when I hit the waiting room and still didn't see my guys.

I half collapsed on the check-in desk, startling the woman sitting there.

"Just enter your Social Security number—"

"I'm not a patient. My alpha is here. Wilder Everett?"

The woman pursed her lips and typed something on her computer. I clenched my jaw and my fists to stop myself from shouting at her to hurry. My omega was seconds away from a complete meltdown, and that would not endear me to the hospital staff.

Before the woman finished typing, the door at the back of the waiting room opened, revealing Leo.

I choked out a sob and sprinted toward him, slowing just enough so I didn't take him to the floor when I crashed into him. His arms wrapped tight around me and I pressed my face to the exposed skin of his neck.

"Azizam, I was coming to get you," he said in stern disapproval. "How did you get here?"

I ignored his question and forced myself to pull away. "How's Wilder? What happened?"

He kept one arm tight around me as he led me to the back. "We were waiting in the lobby and everything seemed fine until he said he had to go to the bathroom. He got up and then just dropped to the floor."

I whimpered and he kissed the top of my head.

"We called for an ambulance and they brought him back right away. They've got him in a room and are drawing labs. He's still unconscious, but they said he's stable."

My head spun and my scent was a riot of stress and bitterness as Leo guided me down the hall until we got to a small room where King was sitting. He jumped up and immediately pulled me into his arms.

"How the fuck did you get here?"

I whined and twisted my fingers in his shirt. Leo pressed against my back. Having them surround me helped, but I needed Wilder.

"Where is he?"

"They took him down to get a CT scan. They won't tell us much since we're not legally a pack, but they've reiterated that he's stable."

My skin crawled and my omega rose to the surface. "They can't keep us separated. I need to see him."

King grunted and pulled me back to his chest, holding me tight even as I struggled against him. "They won't keep you separated. I will make sure of it. But right now, you need to take a breath and calm down. It won't be good for him if you're stressed."

He moved back to the chair and sat down, pulling me onto his lap. Leo sat down beside us. "Want to tell us about the interview?"

I shook my head. I couldn't focus on anything right now.

"You can tell us all about it once Wilder is back." He caressed my face, and I leaned in to his touch.

"In the meantime," King said, "you can tell us how you got here."

The corner of Leo's lips twitched. "*You're in trouble*," he mouthed.

I barely held in my eye roll. "I took a taxi."

King's jaw twitched. "You got in a car with a stranger?"

For some inexplicable reason, his disapproval eased my tension. I snuggled into him and entwined my fingers with Leo's.

"They had their name on a piece of paper inside the taxi."

A loud growl ripped through his chest, and Leo and I both laughed.

"Nothing fucking funny about this," King muttered. His voice was deep and low in my ear, and I just squeezed him tighter.

61

WILDER

One time during Mountain Rescue training, I slipped during a practice climb up a rock face. I'd been wearing a harness, but I'd lost all control in the air and smacked my body against the rocks. By the time I got oriented and back to the ground, I was sporting bloody cuts and bruises. The next day, I'd barely been able to get out of bed.

Whatever was going on with me right now was more fucking painful than that.

I cracked my eyes open, getting a brief flash of a hospital room, but even the dim light made my head feel like it was splitting open. I shut them again and tried to catalog my injuries. My limbs were heavy and aching, but nothing felt broken. Even more concerning than my pain and exhaustion of unknown origin was the fact that I had no memory of what had happened or where I was.

I breathed in slowly, and the most delicious scent in the world flooded in.

Omega.

Memories flooded back. Sitting in the lobby waiting for Lucy to be done with her interview. Feeling so on edge being separated from her, I popped another suppressant. The room spinning around me before everything turned black.

My alpha clawed at my chest. *Omega. I need my omega.*

Mixed in with the astringent hospital room smells was Lucy's mouthwatering strawberry garden scent.

I opened my eyes and the room slowly came into focus. I turned my head and there was my girl, asleep in a hard plastic chair, her brow furrowed even in her sleep.

"Lucy." My voice was a ragged croak, but her eyes flew open immediately.

"Oh my god, you're awake. How're you feeling? I should call the nurse." Her movements were fast and jerky as she looked around the room, clearly disoriented.

"Come here, sweetheart."

"Where is the nurse button?" Her voice rose with panic. "It's okay, I'll just run and get her."

She turned, but I snagged her hand before she could leave.

"If you leave this room, I'll chase you down."

"What? You can't do that." She was all indignation, but she moved back to my side at my weak tug.

I scowled. "Why are you here alone?" Why the fuck would Leo and King leave her here alone to sleep in a chair?

"They tried to kick us all out when visiting hours ended since we're not a bonded pack. I might have, uhh, kicked up a bit of a fuss and King threatened to call a lawyer, so they finally let me stay. King and Leo are waiting in the lobby. They didn't want to leave you, either."

She pulled her hand from my grasp and I was too weak to stop her. Instead of leaving, she poured me a glass of water from the jug next to the bed and stuck a straw in it, holding it up to my lips. I took a sip. This was a fucking humbling experience. I should be the one taking care of my omega, not the other way around.

"What happened?" I asked, my voice clearer now.

"You passed out in the lobby and wouldn't wake back up." Lucy's lip trembled and she pressed them tight together. "King and Leo called an ambulance. They ran a bunch of tests, but they wouldn't tell us anything about the results since we're not family."

Fury radiated through me. Lucy, King, and Leo were the best family I ever could have found. They didn't deserve to be treated like this.

"Oh." Lucy leaned forward and snagged a plastic button attached to a thick cable from under the pillow. "Here's the call button." She pressed it before I could stop her. I didn't want anyone else in the room. I just wanted her, preferably curled up on top of me. I needed her touch, her scent, her everything.

The door opened and an older woman in light blue scrubs entered.

"Oh, you're awake! Great. My name is Gloria and I'm your nurse this evening. Let me call the doctor and check your vitals. How are you feeling?"

Lucy started to move away from my side, but I growled and tightened my hold on her.

Gloria grinned. "Don't worry, Lucy. I'll work around you. We know how alphas can be."

Hmm. She definitely earned some points for being kind to my omega.

"How're you feeling?"

Like I've been hit by a car. "Fine."

She was taking my vitals when the doctor walked in—a tall beta woman with a short pixie cut.

"Mr. Everett, it's good to see you awake. I'm Dr. Sinclair." Her eyes flicked to Lucy. "Would you prefer to talk about your medical care in private?"

"No."

Lucy shot me a look, but I didn't care about being rude. No one was separating me from my omega.

Dr. Sinclair was unbothered. "That's fine. Do you know what caused you to pass out?"

I had a guess. "No."

She hummed. "Based on your lab work, it was a rut suppressant overdose."

"What?" Lucy's eyes searched my face. "You're on rut suppressants?"

"Yeah. I took an extra dose this morning."

Dr. Sinclair cocked her head. "How much extra is extra? The level of suppressant in your blood would indicate you've been taking double or triple the typical dose for quite a while."

Fuck. All the times I'd planned to tell Lucy everything, and it came to this. It was time to face the consequences of being a fucking coward.

"Probably something like that for the past few weeks," I muttered.

"Why?" Lucy whispered.

"I have HA," I told the doctor, who nodded.

"I assumed based on your lab work." Her eyes flicked to Lucy and back to me. "Your CT scan was clear and your blood work is fine except that your liver values are out of range. We want to keep you overnight to monitor you, give you fluids, and repeat the blood work in the morning. If your lab work shows improvement in liver function, which I expect, you can be discharged tomorrow. But it is very important that you cease all rut suppressant use. I know I can't stop you since they're available over the counter, but after an overdose like this, there is no safe dosage. Next time, you might not be so lucky."

The pain in my body was nothing compared to what was happening in my heart as her words landed. I'd held on to the fantasy for too long—that the rut suppressants would be enough to dampen my alpha and make myself safe for Lucy.

Now I knew what I had to do, and I hated myself for it.

"I see you live in Starlight Grove. We'll set up a follow-up appointment with a local designation doctor, and you can discuss managing without suppressants going forward. If you don't have any questions now, we'll let you get some rest and check in on morning rounds."

Silence descended on the room once the doctor and nurse left.

"What's going on?" Lucy's voice sounded so fucking small. I loosened my hold on her and pushed myself up to a more seated position. She slipped off the bed, returning to the chair she'd vacated.

It's for the best.

She shouldn't even be in the same room as you.

Rip off the Band-Aid.

"Have you heard of hyper alphosferone?"

An adorable little crinkle appeared between her eyebrows. "Is that like hyper omestrogen?"

"Um, I'm not sure. But HA means I have over double the amount of alpha hormones as usual. I revealed as an alpha at fourteen." Normally, alphas didn't come into their designation until they were eighteen, and some not even until their early twenties. "High school was a shit show. I went from being a pretty laid-back kid to being an aggressive asshole. My parents tried to support me, but I kept coming home covered in bruises from the fights I would pick with the older kids. They took me to the doctor, and that's when I was diagnosed."

"That's why you're on suppressants?"

"Yeah." My voice was hoarse, like my body didn't want to release these words. "I settled down after I started them, but the parents at the school still felt I was too dangerous to be around their kids. They gathered a whole petition with signatures of everyone who wanted me kicked out. My parents tried to fight it, but in the end, I finished school online."

"That's horrible," Lucy said. She reached forward to grab my hand, but I moved it away.

Her face fell and my stomach churned with sick nausea. The high school parents' faces, twisted in anger, flashed before my eyes and then transformed to that alpha's face—the one from the court case that haunted my nightmares.

"I thought if I took extra suppressants and we didn't have sex, I could safely be around you. But I was wrong."

"Is that why you wouldn't have sex with me the other night?" she asked softly.

I nodded. "I'm sorry I didn't tell you everything sooner. I was being selfish. The reality is, if I can't be on suppressants, we can't be around each other. Ever."

She stayed frozen, but her scent was twisted and bitter, like a field of dead flowers. "No. I—what are you talking about? We're together now."

I shook my head. "We shouldn't be. You need to go to the waiting room and leave with King and Leo."

She shook her head, her eyes glassy with tears. "I don't understand what's happening. Why is it a problem if you're not on suppressants? We can figure this out."

She reached for my hand again, and panic surged through me. I was probably too weak right now to hurt her, but what if I snapped? I flinched away from her touch and she froze, tears dripping down her face.

"I'm sorry it's ending like this, but that's just how it is. You need to leave now. Do not contact me again."

She crossed her arms. "I don't know what is going on, but I'm not leaving until you explain yourself!"

Tension roiled through my body and I could practically feel my alphosferone levels rising. She had to get out of here *now*.

So I did the only thing I could think of to protect her.

"Leave now with King and Leo." The force of my alpha bark hit her like a tangible thing. She lurched back, eyes wide, and let out a heartbreaking whimper. She shook her head, but her omega couldn't resist the force of the command. She tripped over the chair and I lurched forward, but she righted herself, opened the door, and then was gone.

Taking all the goodness in the world with her and leaving me alone.

Like I always knew I would be.

62

LEO

King's knee bounced furiously inches from mine in the hospital waiting room until I finally broke and rested my hand on it.

"Everything will be okay."

He made a very Wilder-esque grunt, but his leg stilled.

"I don't like being away from her," he said. "Actually, I don't like being separated from either of them."

"Who knew the grouchy mountain alpha would win over the grumpy business alpha?"

"Grumpy business alpha?" His glare made me laugh.

"Seems like an accurate description to me." I searched for something else to say to fill the silence. "How's the property sale going?"

He shifted in his seat. "I don't know. I'm feeling kind of . . . conflicted. My parents bought the coastal land decades ago. I guess they were considering building a vacation home there, but it never happened."

As a beta, I wasn't particularly sensitive to scents, but the more I was around King, the more attuned I grew to his, which had now grown bitter.

"Why is that?"

I realized my hand was still on his leg. My cheeks burned and I went to move it, but he stopped me. A rough palm surrounded mine and I shuddered at the heat of it, at this hint that King might be interested in me the same way I was him.

"They bought the property before my brother got sick. He died of cancer when I was little, and after that, the only thing my parents had time for was work. They never did anything with the property, and I just wanted to sell it as fast as I could, but . . ."

He shrugged, trailing off.

My thumb brushed along the back of his hand. "But what?"

"The development company wants to build all these high-end vacation homes without caring about the environmental impact. There aren't many stretches of untouched coast like that anymore."

"You could always hang on to it."

He shrugged. "I thought seeing the property would be a reminder of everything I lost. A brother . . . parents who actually wanted to spend time with me. But being in Starlight Grove has brought me a new family."

I wanted to wrap my arms around the huge alpha, brush my hand through his hair, and kiss his forehead. But before I could do any of that, King's body went on full alert. I followed his gaze to find Lucy standing in the doorway across the waiting room. A haunted, devastated Lucy, who took one look at us and started sobbing.

"WE SHOULD JUST GO to his house once he gets back to town and force him to talk to us," I whispered. Lucy was sandwiched between us in her nest and I didn't want to risk waking her. She'd sobbed the entire drive home, falling asleep only after King carried her into her nest. All she'd managed to tell us was that Wilder had rejected her, which made no sense, but he hadn't answered any of my one million calls.

"Talk, murder, either one," King said with a low growl.

I shot him a look of disapproval, even though my protective instincts were also surging. I didn't want to kill Wilder, but the idea of putting some rose stems on his chair so the thorns poked him in the ass was rather appealing.

"He loves her. There's something more going on."

King shook his head. "What could be worth rejecting her? Devastating her like this?"

I didn't respond because I couldn't think of a good reason, either. What I did know was that Wilder was intensely loyal, deeply in love with Lucy, and part of our family. I wasn't going to give up on us.

63

LUCY

> **HOROSCOPE PISCES**
>
> Pisces, you beautiful, sensitive romantic. Your love and empathy are your strengths, but don't forget, there's a whole world out there.

THE MATTRESS SHIFTED BENEATH ME AND I WHINED, TIGHTening my hold on King, who was trying to get away from me.

"I have to get to my meeting, baby girl," he murmured.

I shook my head and pressed my face into the hollow of his neck.

He cupped the back of my head. "You can come with me."

I growled in frustration. It had been five days since Leo and King had carried me out of the hospital and driven me home. I'd stayed in my nest ever since.

I needed to pull it together. Wilder and I weren't bonded. Hell, he'd only come into my life a month ago. So why did it feel like there was a gaping hole in my heart? Like the loss of him was destroying me from the inside out?

Leo shifted on my other side, and a bolt of panic shot through me. He had to leave to fulfill a large flower order, and my arms weren't strong enough to keep both of them in bed.

"Come into the shop with me, jigaram. We can set up a little nest for you in the back room."

I shook my head. I didn't want them to go, but the thought of leaving my nest was worse. My omega was sad and bruised, the blankets and pillows around me my only shield.

A Pack for Spring

Leo groaned and squeezed me to his chest. "I'm worried about you. Maybe we should go to the fire station—"

"No." They'd gently suggested we call Wilder or even track him down and force him to talk to us, but I'd refused. If Wilder didn't want me, I wasn't going to try to convince him to love me.

I'd spent the entirety of my last relationship doing that.

I knew if I really wanted Leo and King to back down, all I had to do was tell them Wilder had used his bark on me. I didn't quite understand why I hadn't, except that I knew it would turn them against Wilder, and for some inexplicable reason, I didn't want that.

I released Leo and King. "I'll be fine on my own."

"Lucy," King's voice was devastatingly tender.

"I promise. Just come back as soon as you can."

He pressed a soft kiss to my forehead. "Always."

I STOOD IN FRONT of the open fridge with unseeing eyes. My layers of clothing—Leo's sweatpants, King's T-shirt . . . and Wilder's flannel—kept me from feeling the cold air.

With Leo and King gone, there was nothing to distract me from how much I missed Wilder. I didn't know if I wanted to run across town to scream at him or hug him.

I was a good multitasker. I could do both.

My phone vibrated on the counter, but I ignored it. It was probably a text from my friends. Or my moms. They'd all come over when they found out the news, but I'd refused to see them.

Once again, I was the failure omega who couldn't keep a pack together.

I closed the fridge without taking anything out. I'd been repeating this dance for the past few minutes. Getting Blossom her lunch was the only thing that had dragged me from my nest. She was happily munching away at her salad while I wandered aimlessly around the kitchen. It was stocked with premade meals and snacks, dropped off by Summer, Tara, my moms, Carmen, and Harry, but nothing sounded good.

I rested my forehead against the closed refrigerator door. I didn't know how long I'd stayed standing there, eyes closed, when the downstairs doorbell rang.

I didn't move.

It rang again.

And *again*.

I lifted my head with a scowl. The shop was closed, so I was guessing this was a meddling friend visiting and not a tailoring emergency.

Ding. Ding. Ding.

Blossom nudged my ankle and I picked her up. "Should we go back to the nest and hide, or see who's at the door?"

Ding. Ding. Ding.

I let out a frustrated screech and stomped down the stairs, stopping short when I glimpsed Parisa through the window.

Shit. I was a mess—eyes red and puffy from crying, tangled hair, drowning in men's clothing—and was tempted to ignore her and head back to my nest. But that felt too rude and probably wouldn't work, anyway, since she was *still ringing the doorbell*.

Parisa smiled when I opened the door, pulling me into a tight hug. "I've missed you. Ready to go? My mom made lunch, so I hope you're hungry."

I ran my hand through my hair, my fingers catching on the tangles. "What? Did we have plans?"

"For lunch, yes."

I racked my brain, trying to remember, but came up with nothing. "I'm sorry, I don't remember—"

"Oh, I made the plans like twenty minutes ago. I texted to let you know."

"I don't think that's how plans work. And I'm not really feeling up to being social. Sorry you wasted your time."

A Pack for Spring

"It wasn't a waste," she said easily. Before I knew it, she had taken my hand, pulled me out of my store, and closed the door behind me.

Parisa's alpha Amir opened the car door for us. "Nice to see you again, Lucy."

"I think I'm being kidnapped." I said as Parisa half shoved me into the car. "I could have you arrested."

She cocked an amused eyebrow. "Who's going to arrest me? Blossom?" She scooted in next to me, leaning over to stroke Blossom's ears from her spot in my arms. "And don't worry, today's a girls' day. Amir is just here as a chauffeur."

"I know my place." He grinned, his tender eyes meeting his omega's in the rearview mirror, and it made my heart hurt. I wanted to demand we turn back around, but fighting Parisa would take too much energy. I took a deep breath. I could pull my shit together, if only for this afternoon.

THE SUN WARMED MY FACE as I curled up on the comfortable outdoor sofa on the Azad family patio. We'd moved out here after eating one of the best lunches I'd ever had. Parisa was sprawled out beside me, Bibi reclined on the sun lounger smoking hookah from an elaborate copper pipe, and Tara was deep in conversation with Blossom. It was a bit of a one-sided conversation, but Blossom looked riveted all the same.

"Blossom and I need to learn Farsi." I wanted to know what Tara was saying and to communicate better with Bibi. She spoke English, but it was clear she wasn't nearly as comfortable speaking it as the rest of her family.

"I'll practice with you," Parisa said. Her eyes were shut, the sunlight turning her skin golden.

Tara beamed. "Moosh bokhoratet. We'll all help you. Won't we?" she cooed at Blossom.

"What does that mean?"

"It's something you say when you think someone is cute," Tara responded.

Parisa snorted. "That's what it means, but the literal translation is *may a mouse eat you.*"

My eyebrows flew up. "What?"

She shrugged. "No clue. Farsi has lots of weird little sayings that don't really translate to English."

Hmm. Leo had called me something new this morning, but I hadn't been in the right mind frame to ask what it meant. "What does... jeeg... uhh, I can't remember what it was."

"Jigaram?" Parisa asked.

"Yes, that's it."

Tara's hand went to her heart and she sighed. "Leo said that to you?"

My omega preened at her reaction. "What does it mean?"

"Listen," Parisa started. "I promise it's actually very meaningful. But technically, it means *my liver.*"

"Did you say *liver*?"

"You cannot live without liver," Bibi said.

Tara and Parisa nodded sagely.

"Leo called me his liver? And that's romantic?"

"Yes, of course," Tara said. "You should tell him jigareto bokhoram."

Oh god. The phrase was pronounced with that back-of-the-throat sound I had no idea how to make. "What does that mean?"

"I love you," Tara responded at the same time Parisa said, "I would eat your liver."

A laugh burst from my chest, and it felt warm and strange after the hollowness I'd carried with me the last few days. "I guess I can't judge too harshly. Swedish has some phrases like that. Sötnos is like sweetheart, but the literal translation is sweet nose."

"Eh," Bibi said as she got up from her seat. "Liver more important than noses."

Blossom squeaked and jumped off Tara's lap, her nose twitching as she landed softly in the grass.

"Blossom might disagree." Parisa grinned.

"Azizam, come with me." Bibi gestured for me to follow as she headed toward the greenhouse, my little bunny on her heels.

64

LUCY

I FOLLOWED BIBI AND BLOSSOM THROUGH THE GARDEN UNTIL we emerged around the back of the greenhouse. My breath caught at the riot of flowers in neat rows on the ground in front of us. It was vibrant and stunning and so *Leo*. His fingerprints were so clear over all of this beauty, and it made me want to cry.

"It's so beautiful."

Bibi put her arm around me, her grip strong and sure. We stood in silence and watched a delighted Blossom zoom around the garden.

Bibi patted my cheek and gestured at the field. "You pick flowers."

"Me? Are you sure?"

She nodded and walked into the greenhouse, leaving me alone. Except I wasn't really alone. The garden was bursting with life. Bees buzzed around me as I selected my favorite blooms, cutting them with the shears I found on top of an old tree stump.

The breeze washed the scents of flowers and pine trees over me, making my soul ache for my alphas. My chest still hurt with Wilder's rejection, but I drew strength from the beauty around me and didn't collapse.

It wouldn't be long before the summer veggies and berries would be ready. I bet Blossom would love to go blueberry picking with me. I usually went several times a season—once with my moms, once with my friends, and once with Felix for his annual blueberry-picking costume. It was actually the first picture I'd ever posted to his account—Felix wearing a bow tie I'd embroidered with little blueberries. The second year, our audience had grown and I'd embroidered him a vest to go with his tie. Everyone was excited to see what I'd add to his outfit this year. I hadn't decided yet on a blueberry hat or pants, but I definitely wanted to make Blossom a costume that turned her round little body into a blueberry.

I added a couple of gorgeous ranunculus to finish my bouquet, spinning it carefully in my hand to make sure I liked all the angles. "Blossom, let's go check out the greenhouse."

She zoomed ahead of me and my lips curved into a real smile. Even in the midst of heartache, the world was still out here, ready to greet me.

A wall of humid air hit me as I entered the greenhouse. Blossom was already seated on Bibi's lap, enjoying copious head scratches.

"What do you think?" I asked, holding out my bouquet. "It's not as good as what you or Leo would make, but your flowers are so pretty it's impossible for them to look bad."

She smiled. "Very beautiful." She stood from her chair, tucking Blossom to her chest, and gestured me over to a side table with vases. "This one." She pointed at a beautiful black metal vase with curved handles.

I arranged the flowers, frequently glancing at Bibi for approval as I adjusted them. When she gave me a nod, my insides filled with warmth.

"What's your favorite flower?" I asked.

She looked around the greenhouse. She held up two fingers and pointed at a beautiful pink rose. "Gol-e roz."

I repeated the phrase. "Does that mean rose?"

She nodded and moved to sit on a bench, patting the spot beside her. Her fingers were gnarled from age and hard work, but they were strong as she took my hand.

"What's your other favorite?"

She raised our joined hands and pointed at a delicate row of red poppies growing in a waist-high raised bed.

"They're lovely."

"Blossom cannot eat."

My eyes widened and I scooped Blossom up from where she was sniffing a potted plant. "Oh, of course. I'll keep her away. I don't want her ruining your garden."

Bibi shook her head. "No, it . . ." She paused, trying to find the right word, and I grew even more determined to learn Farsi. "Poison."

"Oohhh, oh my goodness, thank you for letting me know. They're so beautiful, though. Poppies, right?"

"Yes. From Iran. Leo find seeds for me."

"He talks about you all the time. You matter so much to him."

"Leo is good boy." She patted my hand, and I smiled.

"He is a good boy. I'm glad you're all so close."

"We part once only. When my family move here."

I squeezed her hand. "Leo told me when they first moved, you had to stay in Iran because of your husband." I hoped I wasn't bringing up bad memories or speaking out of turn, but a gentle smile stayed on her lips.

"He was bad man. But strong women do not let man ruin them." She cocked an eyebrow and my breath hitched at her intense, knowing gaze.

"Did you hear what happened with Wilder?" I asked.

She nodded, but her warm brown eyes weren't pitying, and I drew strength from that. I let out a shuddering breath.

"I don't know what to do. Maybe I just need to let him go." I turned my head to hide my glassy eyes, but she caught my chin.

"Destiny demands action."

Her words were like electricity through my body, making my skin tingle and my spine straighten. My mind spun as I tried to make sense of their meaning, but she didn't offer further explanation. I cherished them all the same.

"I'm glad you were able to move here after your husband died."

Bibi cupped my face and gently patted my cheek. "Poppies not good for man, either." She smiled widely, a twinkle in her eye as she stood from the bench, said something to Blossom in Farsi, and headed out of the greenhouse.

Leaving me frozen on the bench.

Holy. Shit.

Did she just say what I thought she did?

I glanced at the poppies, seeing them in a whole new light.

I stroked Blossom's velvet ears. "So, um, either she's telling me I should kill Wilder or she's telling me to take my destiny in my own hands and not let him go." Blossom stretched her little body as she tried to reach a leaf dangling down from the plant beside me. I snatched her around the waist, pulling her away. "That's not yours. Also, now I'm a tiny bit worried about what other dangerous plants might be in here." I let out a strangled laugh at the absurdity of it all.

Destiny demands action.

Was I being too passive, expecting the universe to just hand me the perfect romance?

"I just want a pack who will fight for me, Blossom." I brushed a tear from my cheek.

Wilder hadn't fought for me. He'd rejected me so fast, barely offering an explanation. Maybe he didn't deserve another chance . . . but could I let him go? What if he was part of my destiny and I needed to fight for him, for us, for our new family?

I forced myself to peel away the layers of hurt that had blanketed me since that night in the hospital and replayed the memory. Wilder's blank expression. His harsh words. His *bark*. It was one of the cruelest things you could do as an alpha, abuse your power against an omega like that.

And yet, Wilder had only ever shown me care and gentleness.

I played through the memory of the hospital room again.

His bitter, twisted scent had saturated the air like decaying leaves on the forest floor. The scent of his fear.

Wilder had been *terrified*.

I didn't know how long I sat there, but the brightness of the greenhouse and the gentle spring breeze brought clarity. If Bibi could survive her husband and create her own future, maybe I could find it in myself to be brave, too. Rejection might feel like dying, but it was survivable. And on the other side of rejection was the possibility of love, family, and the pack I always dreamed of.

Blossom was a heavy weight on my lap as she fell asleep. I adjusted my hold on her and stood.

No matter what, I wasn't alone. I had King, Leo, Felix, Blossom, my friends, my moms, and this town behind me. And maybe I even had the backing of the universe as I seized my destiny.

On my way out of the greenhouse, I trailed my hand over the delicate poppies and smiled.

65

WILDER

> **HOROSCOPE TAURUS**
>
> Taurus, you're usually so steady and levelheaded in love. Draw on those traits today and stop being a complete and total idiot!

THE STARLIGHT GROVE CLINIC'S LOBBY WAS QUIET. A HOME improvement show played on the TV, and every staff person had been friendly and helpful.

I still fucking hated being here.

I'd done my best to avoid doctors my entire adult life. Before this past week, the last time I'd seen a doctor was when I had to be hospitalized with my burns. Fuck, that was ten years ago. If it weren't for the multiple semi-threatening calls I'd gotten from the hospital telling me to get new labs done so I didn't drop dead, I wouldn't be here at all.

I'd thrown myself into work the second I got back from New York. Everyone at the firehouse had given me a wide berth, clearly sensing my dark mood. I'd finished an entire shift without being pranked once, something that had never happened since I'd started working here. I never thought I'd miss the guys' asinine pranks, but they were preferable to the dirty looks everyone had been giving me. Things only got worse when Lucy came by *twice* to see me in the past two days, and I'd hidden in my office like a coward.

I needed to get the fuck out of this town. There was no way for me to live this close to Lucy without losing my mind. Every moment without her felt like slowly being ripped apart. Distance wouldn't make it easier—my heart would forever be a gouged, shredded lump—but it would at least make Lucy safer. That was all that mattered.

This was always how our relationship was going to end, wasn't it? My hopes that we could make this work had been pure delusion. There had always been a countdown timer looming over us.

After this doctor's appointment, I would notify the regional fire chief I was resigning. Maybe I'd move out to the West Coast.

I was jolted out of my spiral of self-loathing when a nurse called my name. I stood, still surprised when a wave of dizziness didn't wash over me. I hadn't realized how much the suppressants were messing with me, but I felt stronger and more clearheaded than I had in weeks.

And I couldn't even find it within myself to care.

Nothing mattered without Lucy. I even missed King and Leo. The video game Leo liked came out yesterday, and I'd been tempted to get it for him. I was sure they both hated me now. I was a risk to their omega.

The nurse—Annie—made chipper small talk as she led me down the hallway. My only response was a grunt, and that made me think about King's exasperation with my nonverbal responses. Riling him up had been one of the best parts of working together on Stanley's projects.

"You'll be in here today. I'll get your vitals and Dr. Finch will be right in."

I'd expected the clinic to be white and sterile, but the hallway had a huge rainbow painted on the walls and no scent of antiseptic hung in the air—likely because of the hum of the heavy de-scenter machines running in the background. Dr. Finch was the only designation medicine specialist in town, which meant Lucy probably came here for medical care, too. I bet she liked the mural. It was as bright and vibrant as her.

Once the nurse finished with me, she left me alone in the room. I groaned and rested my head in my hands. This appointment was useless. It wasn't like this doctor could tell me anything new. I couldn't take suppressants anymore, which meant I couldn't be around any omegas, especially not the one my alpha was fixated on.

The door opened and an omega with curly black hair entered. "Hi, Wilder. I'm Dr. Finch. How're you doing today?" She sat down on a rolling stool in front of me and opened up her laptop.

"Fine."

She hummed to herself as she typed something on her computer. "I've reviewed your records from the hospital. Your lab work showed some very troubling levels. You were diagnosed with hyper alphosferone at fourteen?"

I nodded.

"And you've just taken suppressants for treatment?"

My brow furrowed. She asked as if there were other options. Before I could respond, there was a knock on the door.

"Come in," Dr. Finch called out.

Annie popped her head in. "Sorry for the interruption. Mr. Everett's omega has arrived." She turned to me. "I didn't realize you were waiting for someone when I brought you back. You should have said something!"

My heart raced as the nurse stepped aside, allowing Lucy to slip inside.

"Sorry I'm late," she said, slightly out of breath. "Hi, Dr. Finch."

"Hey, Lucy." The doctor looked between the two of us, her eyes wide. "I didn't realize you were together."

I opened my mouth, but Lucy spoke first. "It's new, but yes, we are." She sat in the chair next to me, so close our arms brushed. I clenched my fists tight, fighting my screaming instincts that urged me to pull her into my lap.

Dr. Finch glanced at the computer. "You're not bonded, right? Your discharge paperwork listed you as single, but maybe they just meant unbonded?"

Her devastated face in the hospital room. Her twisted scent. Tears dripping down her cheeks.

Lucy brushed her fingers over my wrist, gently unfurling my fist and entwining her fingers with mine. My chest felt tight and expansive at the same time. This was the first time I'd been around her without any suppressants in my system, let alone the extra doses I'd been popping since we met. I breathed slowly through my mouth, fighting the temptation to drag her onto my lap and scent-mark her.

"Not bonded yet," Lucy answered easily. I didn't have it in me to argue, because what the fuck was happening? Why wasn't she demanding I leave town forever? She should hate me.

"Do you have others in your pack?"

"Yes. King, another alpha, and Leo, a beta."

Dr. Finch nodded. "That's good. I don't quite understand why you were taking such high doses of rut suppressants when you're courting Lucy."

Had I landed in an alternate universe? Nothing about her question made sense.

"I could hurt her." It hated speaking the truth out loud, but it had to be done. I moved my hand out of Lucy's reach and shifted to create space between us.

She crossed her arms with an adorable little huff. "He won't have sex with me. Apparently, his cock is just too powerful."

I choked on my spit and Dr. Finch's lips twitched.

"Pretty sure I never said that," I sputtered.

"He's convinced we can't be together unless he's taking unsafe doses of suppressants." Nothing in Lucy's expression of body language betrayed how she was feeling, but her scent was sharp and bitter, like she was in pain. My chest tightened until I could barely drag in a breath. Before I realized what I was doing, I'd pulled her onto my lap and buried my face in her hair.

"It's not that I don't want to be with you, sweetheart. It's that I can't," I murmured.

She twisted in my arms and cupped my chin, running her fingers through my beard. Fuck. How was I supposed to live without this? The universe was cruel to dangle this in front of me, only to rip it away.

"But why? I don't understand. Most alphas go into rut."

Why the fuck didn't Lucy have better self-preservation instincts? She should be scared of me, not clinging to me.

I looked at the doctor for help. She fixed me with a pensive expression before speaking. "You're right. It is common for alphas to experience ruts when their omega is in heat, but HA is more than that. I'm assuming you're concerned about violating Lucy's consent?"

My jaw clenched and I nodded. I worked up the courage to glance at Lucy, but the expression of shock and horror I expected to see on her face didn't materialize.

"Violate my consent? You've never been remotely aggressive with me. Even when I wish you would be." She muttered that last bit under her breath, but I was close enough to hear her. My cock surged to life, but mixed with my arousal was soul-destroying fear.

"I would never do something intentionally to hurt you, but—" I cleared my throat. I should move her back into her own chair, but my arms wouldn't release her.

"HA makes me unpredictable. I've been taking daily rut suppressants since I was a teenager. When I first revealed as an alpha, I became violent at school, especially toward other alphas. Rut suppressants made me feel almost normal again, and I stopped fighting." I tried to keep my tone even, but my chest was a riot of emotion. "My parents never treated me any differently, even when everyone was telling them to kick me out of the house before I went into an alpha rage and hurt them. They died soon after I graduated."

"They'd been older when they had me. My mom passed of a heart attack, and my dads followed shortly from broken hearts."

"I had to figure out what to do with my life, and I knew I wasn't cut out for sitting in classrooms, so I became a firefighter. It worked. I'm stronger than most alphas, and heavy labor is one of the things that levels out my hormones."

I wished I could stop the story here, but I had to keep going. "I dreamed of being part of a pack and having an omega, but then the *Turner* court case happened."

Dr. Finch made a noise of recognition, but Lucy looked confused. "What is that?"

I clenched and unclenched my fists as my mind was transported back to that day as a nineteen-year-old in my shitty apartment. My throat tightened, and sweat prickled my forehead. I couldn't do this.

"Is it okay if I tell her?" Dr. Finch's voice was gentle.

I nodded.

"It was a huge televised trial at the time. It must be almost twenty years ago now, but back then, everyone was watching. The alpha in the case was part of a bonded pack with two other alphas and an omega. One night, he grew so possessive of their omega that he attacked his pack members. He killed one of them, and when the omega tried to interfere, he turned on her and she ended up having to be hospitalized."

"That's horrible," Lucy said. "But I don't understand . . ."

"The alpha, Turner, had HA," Dr. Finch said. "Doctors testified at trial that he couldn't be held accountable for his actions because, according to them, HA-induced rut is a form of insanity. People were furious when he was acquitted, and there were petitions to make it illegal for alphas with HA to bond with omegas."

"Because we're not safe for them," I said, my voice hoarse. "I've known since then I could never be a part of a pack."

I jolted when Lucy's fingers brushed against my cheek. "But you are a part of a pack. Our pack." Her voice was soft and tender.

"I shouldn't be," I said harshly. "I tried to stay away, but I obviously failed. I thought maybe it would be okay if I took extra suppressants and avoided touching you too much. Even with all of that, I almost lost it that night after speed dating." My cheeks flushed. I didn't want to have this conversation with an audience, but it was safer for Dr. Finch to be here. She could at least call security if I lost control.

"I can't ever get that close to you again. I can never knot you or bond you." Fuck, my cock ached at just the mention of it. "I don't add anything of value to this pack. You're better off without me."

Lucy scowled and turned to the doctor. "What do you think?"

Here it was. Dr. Finch would tell Lucy the truth, and we would part forever.

"I think the two doctors who testified at the trial were full of shit."

Wait, what?

"They based their testimony on a study that was later withdrawn from the *Journal of Designation Sciences* because the data was falsified. There's no evidence that alphas with HA are more dangerous than the average alpha. It's become a whole political thing—alphas want to use an HA defense in court so they don't face consequences of their bad behavior while also maintaining their rights to bond and be part of packs. It's ridiculous."

Lucy fixed me with a triumphant expression as I tried to make sense of the doctor's words.

"Many alphas struggle to deal with the new surge of hormones when they first come into their designations," she continued. "We often see an increase in physical aggression in alpha teenagers and young adults, whether or not they have HA. Suppressants can be one form of treatment, but other things can help, too. Physical activity is one of them, so I'm not surprised firefighting is a good fit for you. But there are actually a lot of other things that can help young alphas regulate themselves, like dance, art, and meditation. For some *shocking* reason, those aren't promoted as often." The doctor's voice was drenched with sarcasm. "No matter what, there is no excuse for abusive behavior, no matter your designation."

Lucy wiggled happily on my lap, a satisfied smile on her face. "I'm the perfect omega for you, then. I love crafts. We can do them together."

My mouth was open, but no words came out as my entire perspective of myself shifted.

"In addition to the lack of evidence around HA being a cause of abuse or violence, there's another reason I'm not concerned about you and Lucy being together," Dr. Finch said. "Do I have permission to share about your medical history, Lucy?"

"Yeah, of course."

"Lucy has a condition called HO, or hyper omestrogen. It means she has higher levels of the hormone omestrogen than the average omega, making her instincts more prominent."

I tightened my hold on Lucy. "Does it hurt you?"

"No, not at all," she said, leaning into my chest. "I'm on suppressants—a *safe* dose, since I can't get mine over the counter like you can." She rolled her eyes. "They help keep things even. But . . ." She chewed her lip, her cheeks heating. "I'm still kind of a lot, even for an omega."

Dr. Finch made a disgruntled noise, and I was in complete agreement.

"Who fucking said you're a lot?"

Lucy's scent instantly lost its bitter edge, transforming into a deep, floral sweetness that did not help my hard-on.

"I'm really needy," she whispered. "And instead of getting better as the relationship goes on, it gets worse."

My lips twitched. "I think I can handle that."

Dr. Finch seemed completely unfazed by the drama unfolding before her, but maybe she was used to it, working in designation medicine.

Before I made any promises to Lucy, I had to be sure. "How can you guarantee I won't hurt Lucy?"

"I can't."

My heart stopped, my chest seized, and even though it made no sense, I tightened my hold on Lucy when I should be letting go.

"But," she continued, "I am very confident that if you hurt her, it won't be because of your condition."

A sigh escaped me and I buried my face in the crook of my omega's neck.

"I'm going to step out for a few minutes, but I'll be back to address any lingering concerns." The door shut softly behind her.

Lucy rubbed her cheek against mine, scent-marking me. And then something happened I never expected to experience in my life—she started purring. The sweet vibration filled me from the top of my head to the tips of my toes. I was undone and remade in an instant, belonging completely to her.

"I'm so fucking sorry for the pain I've caused you this week. I promise I'll do whatever I can to earn your forgiveness. I'll host a million speed dating nights if it means I get to go home with you."

"You won't leave?" Her voice was vulnerable and unsure, the confidence and bravado she'd brought into the appointment melting away.

A responding purr rumbled through my chest. "Never. I don't deserve you, but I won't ever let you go. I love you."

She cupped my face with both hands, and her big blue eyes scanned my face like she was peering into my soul. "I love you, too."

Our lips met in a tender kiss, and it was almost enough to make me cry. "I never thought I'd get this again," I murmured between kisses. "To hold you, taste your sweetness."

She held me tighter, fingers twisting in my hair, and our kiss soon turned hungry. She nipped my lip, I dipped my tongue into her mouth. My fingers dug into her hip and she arched against me.

I groaned when she pulled away.

"We should maybe not do this here," she said with a giggle.

I snorted. "Yeah, maybe not." I ran my thumb across her cheek. "You're mine, sweetheart. And I am completely yours. I could never belong to anyone else."

She leaned into my touch, her eyes soft.

A knock at the door signaled Dr. Finch's return. "Everything sorted?"

"Yep," Lucy said, wiggling happily on my lap.

"Glad to hear it. Wilder, Annie's going to come in and draw some blood so we can check your labs, but things were trending in a good direction by the time you were discharged from the hospital, so I don't expect any surprises. You'll get a call if we need to follow up on anything."

"Wait, before we go, I have a question," Lucy said.

Dr. Finch sat back down on the rolling chair.

"I'm thinking about going off my suppressants."

A growl ripped through my chest and my scent surged at my omega's words. All sound ceased, and I was consumed by the image of her in heat, her slick dripping onto the soft blankets and pillows I'd gifted her for her nest.

Knotting her and refusing to pull out for fucking hours.

Making her come over and over until she was sobbing from pleasure.

The doctor cleared her throat and pressed a button on her desk. The whirring sound in the room grew louder as the de-scenter machine kicked into high gear. Lucy laughed and patted my chest in what was supposed to be a soothing gesture but did nothing to bank my intense need to claim her.

"You haven't had a heat before, is that right?" The doctor kept her attention on Lucy, both omegas ignoring my reaction.

"Correct. I wanted to check if there was anything I needed to do to prepare for going off my suppressants."

"I'll prescribe you some supplements and I recommend focusing on eating nutrient-dense and high-calorie meals. Many omegas find it hard to eat during heats, and putting on some extra weight ahead of time can be helpful."

"Will it be a problem that I'm practically *ancient* for a first-time heat?"

It was Dr. Finch's turn to laugh. "I'm not sure twenty-nine counts as ancient quite yet. It's hard to tell how each omega will react. As you're going off the suppressants, you are at risk for breakthrough heats and surges, which usually last for a few hours at a time. It's a good idea to make sure you stick close to your pack during that time, just to prevent being caught by surprise. There's no reason your full heat wouldn't be normal, although omegas with HO usually have heats that are one day longer than average."

"That sounds good."

Lucy moved off my lap as the nurse came back in the room to draw my blood, but my eyes never left her. I vibrated with energy, my alpha and I finally unified in a desperate need for my omega.

And for the first time, that didn't scare me.

66

WILDER

My hands gripped the steering wheel as I drove up the mountain to my cabin, Lucy in the passenger seat.

She was quiet. *Why was she so quiet?*

I took a deep breath, gathering my strength to break the silence, but I lost my nerve and released it in a noisy exhale. Why the fuck was my house so far away? Maybe if I concentrated hard enough, I could move it closer with the power of my mind just to end this awkwardness.

Finally, *finally*, my driveway came into view.

I threw my truck into park. Not that long ago, we had been in this same exact spot. Except this time, the woman beside me wasn't a stranger.

She was the love of my life. My omega.

Lucy unbuckled her seat belt and turned to face me, expression fierce.

"If you ever use your bark on me without my consent again, this is over."

Shame burned through my body, dark and heavy. I swallowed, trying to find the words, but nothing could undo what I'd done. "I'm so fucking sorry, sweetheart. I never will again, I promise you."

She nodded slowly, her expression giving nothing away. Fuck, telepathy would come in handy right about now.

"I know." She let out a slow breath. "I know how scared you were, and you were disoriented from the medication. I just . . . I can't handle that again."

"I promise I'll do whatever I can to earn your forgiveness." My chest swelled with emotion, making it hard to breathe. "I'll spend my life doing everything I can to make you feel happy and loved. You deserve it. You deserve everything."

I reached up to touch her face but pulled back. I didn't deserve to touch her. But she took my hand and kissed my palm. "So do you, Wilder. You deserve all the happiness in the world, and I've already forgiven you. You don't have to earn it."

Her bright blue eyes met mine, and I couldn't deny the sincerity I found there. She was choosing to be here with me . . . choosing to touch me. She wasn't afraid of me. Emotion welled in my throat. "Thank you," I choked out. I ran my thumb along the curve of her perfect cheek. She had new little freckles on her nose from the sun and I wondered how many would pop up in the summer. And I would be here to see them.

She shifted to her knees and leaned over the console until her lips were almost touching mine. The most tempting forbidden fruit. I moved to kiss her, but she leaned away, her eyes sparkling with mischief.

"But just so we're clear, alpha, I have no problem with you using your bark on me consensually. And right now? You have my full consent to do *anything*, unless I say red."

"What do you—"

She moved like lightning. Her hand was on the door before I realized what she was doing, and then she was out of the truck, running into the woods. A roar ripped from me as my instincts rose to the surface. Without the suppressants in my system, my alpha took full control.

For the first time in my life, I let it.

I jumped out of the truck. A slow smile spread across my face as I glimpsed her golden hair before she disappeared down the trail. The woods were dense here—thick with trees and vegetation, the earthy scent of pine filling the air, but nothing could mask my omega's scent. It was sweet like strawberry sugar, thick with arousal, and carrying a sharp edge of anticipation.

Fucking perfect.

I kept a slow, steady pace as I followed her, imagining the thrill she'd feel when thinking she'd gotten away, all to be erased when I caught up to her, pinned her on the ground, and fucked her hard. My cock strained against my jeans, my knot already half inflated and desperate to be surrounded by her snug little cunt. Once I knotted her, she could fight as hard as she wanted, but she wouldn't be able to escape me.

I picked up my pace, heat pulsing through my veins, following her scent until . . .

I stopped short at a piece of fabric on the ground. My chest rumbled as I picked it up and pressed it to my face. It was my omega's sweater, but her scent was too strong for her to have only worn it.

She had wiped her slick on it to distract me.

Dark satisfaction pumped through my veins. My little omega was toying with me.

I picked up my pace, my body tense and on full alert. Next, I found her bra. Leggings. Last was a scrap of lace. I pressed her panties to my face, breathing in her intoxicating scent.

The world faded away as my rut took hold.

I broke out in a sprint. Clever little omega leading me on a chase, but she couldn't hide forever. She would never be able to hide from me.

The world was a blur of green leaves as I hunted her, and it wasn't long before I caught a hint of gold. I whirled around, my chest heaving.

"Where are you, little omega? If you come out now, your punishment won't be as severe."

Nothing.

A smile split my face as I slowly prowled through the trees, my body poised to strike at every snapping twig. My cock strained against my crotch, but at least the pain of it cleared my head. I cupped myself through my pants. "Come out, come out, wherever you are."

A sharp inhale of breath.

"You can't hide from me, omega."

I lunged to my left, swinging my arm around the base of a tree. My fingers brushed her hair, but she escaped my grasp and took off running. I was momentarily frozen, mesmerized by the bounce of her bare ass.

My heartbeat pulsed in my ears as I gave chase. She was tired, her pace faltering as heaving breaths escaped her lungs. She'd been a good girl and kept her shoes on, but I didn't want her legs to get scratched up, so I closed the distance between us.

She looked over her shoulder, her eyes wide as I lunged. My arms snagged her waist and I turned in the air to ensure my body cushioned our fall.

She whined, and the sound had the power to end me.

I rolled us over so I was on top of her. "A little omega, all alone in the forest. Whatever will I do with my prize?"

She let out a kitten snarl and lashed out, kicking and scratching at my legs and chest. "Let me go!"

I encircled her wrists with one hand and pinned them to the forest floor above her head. "Finders keepers, kitten. I found you, so now I'm going to fucking keep you."

"No, you can't do this!" She twisted and tugged her hands, but my hold on her was iron. "Who is going to stop me? You're mine, and before this is over, your little cunt will be sore and puffy from being stretched on my knot." I rubbed my beard against her cheek, scent-marking her. "I'll keep you as my little pet. That pretty, creamy skin will be all marked up and your pussy will be stuffed so full of my cum it will drip out of you for days."

Her chest arched, offering her pretty little tits to me on a platter. I leaned down and sucked them hard, savoring her cries. When I stopped, her nipples were swollen, but it wasn't enough. I needed my marks covering her entire body.

"Stop." Her weak arms tried to push me away. "I'm not your pet."

I sucked a patch of skin on her neck, not stopping until I was sure it would leave a mark. "You can protest all you want. It won't matter. If my pet can't learn to be obedient, I'll just have to put my collar and leash around her neck." I pressed my hand behind her knee, spreading her wide as she soaked my pants with her arousal. "Or maybe I'll put you in a harness and carry you around, attached to my knot until you're a good, obedient pet."

Her body grew limp as she gave up fighting. I loosened my hold as she softened in my arms. I trailed my fingers along her hip, the curve of her waist, and her breast.

Then her knee shot up, trying to strike my balls, but I shifted back just in time. The distraction worked—she managed to free one hand, but her victory was short-lived as I regained control.

"Naughty omega. You're going to pay for that." My hand came down on the side of her thigh in a stinging slap. "Present for your alpha." I injected my voice with the full power of my bark. I released my hold on her, leaving her free to run away if it weren't for my bark keeping her in place. Her pupils expanded until they took up almost the entirety of her blue eyes. Her chest heaved and her scent filled the air as she slowly got on her hands and knees. Her round ass waved in the air, pure temptation, and I slapped my hand down on it. I'd nearly lost it when King spanked her in her nest. Now it was my turn.

I pressed a firm hand to her back, forcing her to drop her chest to the ground. Her whimper told me the forest floor was rough against her sensitized nipples. I grinned as I started spanking her. I kept a steady pace, alternating between her ass cheeks and the tops of her thighs. "Good thing I don't mind training my pet." I leaned over her, pressing my chest to her back until she was completely pinned. "You're never going to escape me, even if I have to knot your ass to keep you by my side."

She cried out as I pressed a thick finger inside her asshole, which was already dripping with slick.

"Are you going to be a good pet for me?"

"Yes, alpha."

"Then flip over."

This time I didn't bark the command, waiting to see if she could obey on her own. I could practically hear her thoughts as she struggled with her decision. Finally, slowly, she rolled onto her back. Bits of dirt and pine needles stuck to her skin. Her hair was a wild mess, and her thighs were drenched.

She'd never looked so fucking perfect.

"Very nice, kitten. Now, spread your legs and show me that pretty pink cunt."

She parted her legs, but it wasn't enough. I forced them wider.

"Hold them open." I moved her hands to the backs of her knees. "Don't release them without permission."

She moaned, and her chest heaved with her fast breaths. "Alpha, please."

I trailed my finger through her sex, gathering up her slick and sucking it off my finger. "Does my omega need my cock?"

She nodded, and my chest rumbled as I braced my hands on either side of her head, lowering down until our lips were almost touching. "Then *beg*."

She thrust her hips up, grinding against my rock-hard cock, but I shifted away so she couldn't get any friction. She thrashed until she tired herself out.

"Please, alpha. I feel so empty. I need your cock inside me." Tears brimmed in her eyes, and it was enough to make me almost lose my mind.

Almost.

I gritted my teeth to keep control.

"If you want my cock, you'll have to take the rest of your punishment."

Her lip jutted out in the cutest pout. "I don't need punishment."

My teeth grazed her neck. "Then no knot for you."

She fought against me again until tears spilled down her cheeks.

"Poor kitten. So empty without her alpha's cock. That naughty little cunt clenching around nothing." I circled her entrance with my finger but didn't give her what she craved.

She let out a strangled scream. "Okay! I'll do it. Punish me, alpha."

"That's my good girl." I didn't give her a chance to think before my hand came down on her pussy with a wet slap. She moaned and I spanked her cunt again. Her arms shook, but she didn't release her knees, keeping herself open and exposed until her clit was red and swollen. Her slick dripped onto the ground beneath her.

I couldn't hold off anymore. I ripped off my belt, unbuttoned my jeans, and pulled out my cock.

Her breath hitched and she licked her lips. "I want to taste you."

I replaced one of her hands with mine, holding her leg open. "Next time, kitten. I need to be in that tight pussy when I come."

The head of my cock pressed against her entrance, and reality crashed back, harsh and cold. I shut my eyes and tried to take a deep breath, but anxiety squeezed my chest.

A gentle hand cupped my jaw. "Wilder?"

Her sweet voice grounded me, and after a few more breaths, I opened my eyes. "I've never done this before." My gruff admission made her eyes widen.

"Really?"

I nodded. My cock was too large for most betas or alphas to take, so without an omega, I'd resigned myself to a life of celibacy.

Lucy's perfume deepened and her grin was pure satisfaction. "I like that."

"Yeah?" I worried I wouldn't make it as good for her as she deserved, but my omega was practically vibrating with excitement.

"I love that I'm your first." Her entrance caught my tip. "Please don't keep me waiting, alpha."

My chest rumbled with a growl and I surrendered to my instincts once more. They dragged me under until my entire world narrowed to the omega caged beneath my body.

I worked my cock inside her with short thrusts as I played with her clit to keep her relaxed. Her pussy strangled my cock—hot and tight and perfect. In all my fantasies, I'd never imagined it would feel like this—like finding the missing piece of myself.

Like coming home.

"Wilder," she whispered, and I knew she felt it, too.

Our limbs trembled as they tangled together, our movements growing more and more frantic. She arched her hips each time I thrust inside her, like she was trying to pull me even deeper.

"This is heaven."

She dug her fingers into my back, and I snarled. I wanted her marks on me. Permanently.

I maneuvered my hand between us, my thumb pressing hard against her clit again until her pussy contracted around me. She threw her head back as she came, lips parted, hair a messy halo around her, and she'd never looking so fucking beautiful.

Omega. Knot. Now.

Even with her soft and pliant after her orgasm, it was a tight fit to get my knot—which was almost completely inflated—inside her.

She whimpered as she struggled to take me.

"Just breathe, sweetheart. You were made for me."

I gently circled her clit, soothing her through the incredible stretch as my baseball-sized knot forced its way inside her.

She screamed with her orgasm when I finally locked inside, and I buried my face in her neck as I came at the same time. Endless hot cum spurted inside her, filling her up so completely I could practically feel the bulge in her abdomen.

The world faded around me until all that was left was *her*.

I kissed her, dipping my tongue into her mouth and nipping her swollen lips. "You're mine, forever."

"Forever." She pulled out my hair tie and ran her fingers through my hair. "Bond me."

I jolted back, and we both groaned as the movement tugged on my knot.

"What did you just say?"

She caressed my cheek, her eyes bright and lucid. "Bond me, Wilder. Please."

My rut receded, allowing me to think at least a bit more clearly. "We don't have to rush it, Lucy."

"You don't want to?"

"Of course I want to, sweetheart. I would be the luckiest bastard in the world to be bonded with you." I brushed her hair out of her eyes. "But I need to earn back your trust."

She shook her head. "I've spent the past year believing I couldn't trust myself. I've been looking outside of myself to find direction, hoping I would get a sign from the universe that would tell me what to do, who I should be. But I finally feel like maybe I can trust what I want." She wrapped her arms around my neck in a tight hug. "*Who* I want. And I want you."

I shuddered, my throat tight with emotion. "You are my everything."

My mouth watered as I kissed the spot where her neck met her shoulder. I hesitated for a heartbeat. A few hours ago I'd been ready to leave Starlight Grove because I could never be with this omega, and now she was begging me to bond her.

"I love you," I murmured.

She ran her fingers through my hair. "I love you, too."

Her words ripped apart my world and put it back together, the painful cracks of my past now gilded with gold. I scraped my teeth against her skin and then—

I bit down, entwining our souls together forever. The second her blood hit my tongue, the frenzy of rut returned.

I drew back, staring at my mark.

More.

She needed more.

So everyone would know she was claimed.

She squealed as I sat up, taking her with me so she was straddling my hips.

Yes, perfect. Now she was in the right position.

I curved forward and bit her breast, my chest rumbling with

satisfaction to see another bond mark on her. She inhaled sharply, her fingers trailing along her second mark. I honed in on her hand and then my teeth dug into her palm. My chest rumbled with a satisfied purr.

A peal of laughter broke through my haze, and a sting on my neck cracked me wide open. Lucy sank her teeth into my skin, and her emotions flooded through me, light and vibrant. And if Lucy was part of me—living in my soul, *loving* me—I might not be a monster after all.

67
LUCY

I'D NEVER BEEN THIS CONTENT IN MY LIFE, WHICH WAS strange since I was outside, completely naked, and covered in dirt and twigs.

But none of that mattered because I was snuggled against my alpha's chest with his vibrating purr against my cheek, his soul entwined with mine, and his marks on my body. I'd never heard of an alpha leaving multiple bond marks on their omega, but after years of being unsure if I was wanted, this was exactly the reassurance I needed.

I inhaled, drawing in his scent—smoky leather and pine, as wild as the alpha holding me. We clung to each other, breathing through the tempest of sensations, a storm of love soothing away our fears and anxiety.

"I never knew it could feel like this." Wilder's voice hitched, and a tear rolled down his cheek.

I kissed it away, hoping I was stealing all of his pain with it.

"Me, either," I murmured.

He eventually sat up, keeping me in the protective circle of his embrace. His knot was still lodged inside me, giving no indication that it was going down anytime soon. I looked down at where we were connected, fascinated by how stretched I was around him. There was a slight sting and a feeling of fullness, but mostly there was pleasure and a deep sense of security.

I whimpered when he trailed his finger over my multiple bond marks.

"I'm sorry, sweetheart. I lost control."

His expression was contrite, but I burst out laughing because the main emotion I felt through the bond was pride.

I rolled my hips against him and he swore, his huge palms cupping my ass.

"You don't seem very sorry to me."

He shrugged with a grin. "Yeah, you're right." His expression sobered and he ran his hands slowly up and down my body in careful inspection. "But you're okay? I didn't hurt you?"

"You didn't hurt me." My fingers ran through his hair. It looked as wild as I was sure mine did. I definitely needed a bath, and I had some scrapes and bruises from being fucked on the forest floor, but even in the midst of his rut, he'd been achingly careful with me.

He let out a shuddering breath, relief rushing down the bond like gentle waves cresting against the beach. When I shivered, he took his shirt off and pulled it over my head, revealing the scars on his chest. I traced them with my finger.

"My second year as a firefighter," he said, answering my unspoken question. "It was a house fire and there was a kid trapped upstairs. I tossed him out the window to my crew on the ground, but a beam fell on me before I could get out. Spent a month in the hospital, which fucking sucked. The kid was okay, though, and he visited me several times with his parents."

As much as I hated the idea of him risking his life, my heart swelled. I skimmed my lips along his scars. "How could you ever see yourself as harmful or dangerous?"

His cheeks flushed, and I grinned. My grumpy mountain-man alpha was *blushing*.

"Let's get you inside." He stood, his hand palming my ass to keep his knot from pulling at me. Sparks of intense pleasure ran through me as I wrapped my arms and legs around him. Every step he took brought me closer to an orgasm until I came with a loud cry. Wilder cursed, bracing himself against a tree for balance as he thrust as much as he could when he was locked in me.

"Greedy girl," he murmured, voice full of affection.

I traced his bond mark on my hand, making him groan. "Yeah, I'm the greedy one."

He grumbled something, but we were both pure joy flowing in the bond.

He kept walking, but his unbuttoned jeans kept sliding down his legs as he headed back to the cabin. He was a swearing mess as he held me with one hand and his jeans with the other, as I laughed hysterically.

"Who knew outdoor sex was so undignified?" I snorted as he gave up on his jeans, kicking them off and leaving them on the forest floor.

He just grunted. "I'll come back for the clothes after I take care of you."

By the time his cozy cabin came into view, I was half asleep, but I pried my eyelids open at Wilder's growl.

King and Leo were sitting on the cabin's porch, waiting for us.

"You're going to be nice and share, right?" My words were slurred as my eyes drifted shut. "I'm yours, but I'm theirs, too."

Wilder's chest heaved as he fought through his alpha's waves of possessiveness, but his growl subsided and his shoulders softened.

"Yeah, sweetheart. I'll be nice."

King and Leo met us in the driveway, and my omega wiggled happily at having all of my guys together.

"You doing okay, baby girl?" King pressed against my back, his heat welcome against my cooling skin.

"Yes, Daddy."

A burst of amusement shot through the bond, and I pinched Wilder's side.

Leo kissed my cheek. "Seems like you have a new mark." His fingers trailed over Wilder's bite on my hand.

King let out a strangled noise as he brushed my hair aside, finding another bond mark on my neck. "What the fuck? She's not a chew toy."

"Don't worry. I still have plenty of open spots for yours, Daddy."

He gripped my chin. "Good. Because I won't last long without my mark on my girl."

I could no longer keep my eyes open, but I flailed my arm out toward him. "Want to do it now?"

King's laugh ghosted against my skin. "I think I'll wait until my baby girl is conscious."

"Good plan," I mumbled.

The moments that followed were all a haze—being lowered into a deep tub of hot water, my frustrated whines when my alpha's cock slipped out of me, followed by firm hands pulling me out of the bath, drying me off, and settling me on a soft bed.

Wilder's low voice floated through my dream. "I don't know how much you know, but I'm sorry for the past week."

"Lucy told us everything," King said. "If we're going to be a pack, you can't just leave when things get hard."

"I never will again," Wilder vowed, and I felt the truth of his words through the bond.

Leo gently rolled me onto my stomach and started brushing out my wet hair. "We're family, which means we lean on each other."

"You're not worried about me being a threat to her?"

My brow furrowed at the vulnerability in Wilder's voice, but it settled back down at his gentle purr.

"Lucy is sure," King said.

Wilder's shock jolted through the bond, and my lips curved up in my half-asleep state.

"We'll figure everything else out as we go." Leo ran his fingers through my damp hair. "As long as we keep her at the center, we'll be okay."

"I see that now. Our perfect girl."

Their heat surrounded me as they laid down around me in a tangle of limbs, and the last broken pieces of my heart knitted together.

68

LUCY

"This is the life," Leo murmured. "My omega on my lap." He trailed his fingers up my bare leg. "Her cute little pussy all bare." His hand slipped under the shirt I'd pulled on this morning—one of Wilder's—and cupped my sex. "Our alphas making us breakfast while I make her come."

We were tangled up together on the couch while King and Wilder made blueberry pancakes, scrambled eggs, and bacon. I whined and arched into Leo's touch, greedy for more even though I'd already come several times this morning. Wilder had woken me up by licking me to an orgasm. The moment I came, he'd bitten my hip, adding another bond mark on my skin. King had woken up at my cry, muttered something under his breath when he saw the new mark, and had fucked me until I screamed.

And now, Leo's fingers plunged inside me as his thumb circled my clit, quickly pushing me to another orgasm, all before ten in the morning.

"That's my good girl. Look at you, taking your pleasure."

"If you're done fucking, breakfast is ready," King shouted.

Leo chuckled and lifted me off his lap before adjusting his hard-on. "Greedy girl. You've got to eat your breakfast first, darling, and then you can have your dessert."

My cheeks heated at the realization that I'd been perfuming while staring at the outline of his cock through his gray sweatpants. I tore my eyes away and handed him his cane before we walked into the kitchen.

King winked as he flipped the last few pancakes onto a plate and Wilder wrapped me in his arms. I probed our new bond, trying to sense any jealousy, but all I got was a thread of amusement and a huge wave of arousal. His eyes were soft as he tucked my hair behind my ear. "I was worried bonding you would make my alpha even more aggressive, but it's helped put me at ease."

I put my arms around his neck, but even on my tiptoes, I couldn't reach his lips. He took pity on me and leaned down so we could kiss. "Thank you for taking a chance on me," I whispered. "And you can mark me as much as you want. I love it." I didn't care how unusual it was—I would be happy for Wilder to mark me a hundred times, and King, too, because each silvery scar was a symbol of their love for me. I wished Leo could mark me, but I would just have to make up for it by putting my bond mark on him.

"You never have to thank me, sweetheart. I'm the one who's been given more than I ever dreamed."

He picked me up and sat me on a stool. We were crammed around the counter, my elbows bumping against Leo and Wilder as I ate, and I loved every moment. The pancakes were amazing, but I actually gasped when I took a sip of my coffee. "This tastes like a strawberry cardamom latte."

Leo grinned. "I may have bribed Ella to sell me a bottle of their syrup."

I squealed and launched myself at him, peppering his stubble-covered cheeks with kisses. "This is the best morning ever."

He grinned. "You're easy to please."

It was just a passing, throwaway comment, but it made my breath hitch and eyes water.

"Fuck, what's wrong? I didn't mean it. You're very hard to please." Leo ran a panicked hand up and down my back in what I imagined was supposed to be a soothing gesture.

I choked out a watery laugh. "I'm fine, promise. Sorry for being silly. It's just, my exes always said I was impossible to please and I needed to stop being such a spoiled, materialistic omega."

The energy in the kitchen turned dark with fury.

A Pack for Spring

"They said *what*?" King's voice was ice.

I chewed my lip. I hadn't meant to reveal all that. I'd learned that people expected social, happy Lucy, so I was used to hiding when I was upset and returning once I'd pulled myself together again. My guys weren't going to let that happen.

Wilder lifted me onto the counter and gripped my chin so I couldn't look away. "We will hunt them down and feed them to the pigs that Easton's friend owns. You are *so* fucking easy, sweetheart."

I cocked my head and Leo made a strangled noise. "He means easy *to please*."

I saw the moment Wilder realized what he'd said, and his look of horror made me burst out laughing. "I mean it's true." I winked. "I'm *very* easy around you three."

King shot me a heated look, and the tension in the room broke. I moved back to my stool and squeezed Leo's hand. "Thank you."

"Just telling the truth. Although I certainly don't mind if you want to be difficult and make us work for it." His lips brushed my cheek. "Dealing with our bratty omega is fun, too."

He returned to his breakfast while I squirmed uncomfortably and hoped my T-shirt was enough to stop my slick from leaking onto my chair.

King placed a fresh cup of strawberry cardamom coffee in front of me. "Finish your breakfast, princess."

I took another bite, blushing at his murmured, "Good girl."

Leo and King asked Wilder questions about the cabin, giving me a chance to process my feelings as they gave me casual, reassuring touches. When we finished, we decided to move to the porch. The day was warming up, the sun was shining, and the forest smelled alive. Porch-sitting was such a better way to experience nature than camping.

Wilder stole me onto his lap, his hand gently rubbing over the bond mark he'd put on my palm. "I never heard how your interview went. I'm sorry I didn't ask before now. I hope I didn't ruin it."

I'd been in such a funk the past few days that I hadn't told King or Leo about the interview, either . . . or about the email I'd received yesterday.

"You didn't ruin anything. The interview was done by the time I realized you'd gone to the hospital. It went well."

The guys waited for me to elaborate. When I didn't, Leo carefully asked, "Did they tell you when they'll let you know if you got it?"

I nodded slowly. "I actually got an email from them yesterday morning, just a few minutes before I walked in to the doctor's appointment. That was the reason I was late." I took a deep breath. "They offered me the internship. It would start July first."

Wilder's hold on me tightened, and he kissed my forehead. "Congratulations, sweetheart."

"Thanks," I almost-whispered.

King moved to my side, his hand firm on my thigh. "What are you thinking, baby girl?"

I played with the edge of my T-shirt. "I should take it, right?"

Leo snagged my hand and squeezed it. "You don't want to? Did something happen that upset you?"

I shook my head. "Nothing happened, which is part of the problem, I guess. Everyone was really nice. I got a tour, talked to a couple of former interns, and saw their sewing room, which was amazing. But . . . the focus of the internship is design, not sewing, and most of the interns have goals of designing for wide-scale production."

"And that's not what you're interested in," King said. "You want to make high-end couture."

My eyebrows shot up. "You remember that?"

"Of course." He looked almost insulted that I'd even asked. "You shouldn't take the internship if it's not the right fit."

"But it's a really prestigious fashion house. The things I learn and connections I make could help me succeed as a designer. It's not like I'll get an opportunity like this again. If I turn it down, what's the alternative? Staying in my hometown and running my little store?"

"You say that like it's a bad thing," Wilder said.

"Isn't it?"

"Why?" Leo looked legitimately confused.

"How could you believe people won't take your designs seriously when you have a million people obsessed with what you're making?" King asked.

"They're obsessed with Felix, not me."

"Yes, all the people complimenting the outfits and asking for sewing tips because you are, quote, 'the best sewist I've ever seen,' are just there for Felix."

Leo cupped my face, forcing me to meet his gaze. "Why does a career have to be serious? You are the most fun, playful, sunshiny person I've ever known. Why not bring that into your work?"

"And you don't just sew pet costumes, not that it'd be a bad thing if you did," King said. "All it took was you going to a single event wearing one of your dresses to catch the attention of Jacqueline Wu and have people falling over themselves to get a slot for a custom dress."

My lip twitched. "Not sure one person qualifies as a crowd of people."

"There would have been a crowd if I hadn't swept you away, desperate to get you alone." He captured my lips with his, not caring that I was on Wilder's lap or that Leo was cupping my cheek.

It was too much—their support, their confidence in me. My chest swelled with happiness.

King pressed a last gentle kiss to my lips before pulling away. "We just want you to be happy. I gave up everything I wanted out of desperation for my parents' love and approval. I wasted the past decade of my life on people who didn't even care about me. I can't regret it because it brought me here, to you, but that doesn't mean you have to make the same choices."

I moved off Wilder's lap and put my arms around King. My heart hurt for how little love he'd gotten in life—how little love both of my alphas had received. It was good Leo and I were here now.

"I love you," I murmured. "I'm glad you made your way here."

69

LUCY

I used a lint roller to catch any loose strings on Leo's baba's custom suit before slipping a garment bag over it. I couldn't wait for him to see it. He had already promised to model it for us when we went over for family dinner.

I slumped down on my rolling chair, my eyes drifting shut. My guys all had to wake up early this morning—Leo and Wilder at the crack of dawn to get to the flower market and firehouse, and King not too long after for some sort of work meeting. Since I didn't drive, I had to get up with them. Well, *get up* was maybe a bit of an exaggeration since Wilder had ended up rolling me in a blanket and carrying me to his truck. Not much could convince me they really loved me as much as them finding my morning grumpiness cute instead of annoying.

I wanted to be back in bed with all of my guys, sleeping and fucking the day away, but since napping in my nest alone held no appeal, I had started my work day. "If these guys think they're going to turn me into a morning person, they are sorely mistaken," I muttered.

The shop phone made me jump, and I realized I'd fallen asleep at my desk. It should be illegal for people to make phone calls before noon.

I rolled my chair over to the checkout desk, where my phone was sitting on the new shelf King had gotten Easton to install.

"Spring in Your Stitch, this is Lucy."

"Hi Lucy. It's Jaqueline."

My heart pounded and my stomach lurched with nausea. My guys hadn't pushed me about my internship decision, but when I told them at dinner that I'd emailed Fran to turn it down, they'd said they were proud of me.

"I heard you decided to pass on the internship," she continued.

I braced for her disappointment or anger. "I hope you don't think I'm ungrateful or not appreciative—"

"What? No, of course I don't think that. I was hoping we could snap you up, but I'm not surprised you turned it down."

"You're not?"

"I knew it would take a lot to steal you away from that gorgeous shop of yours, and then Fran showed me your social media account—I started following Felix, by the way, and voted in the Midsummer outfit poll."

My jaw dropped. What?

"You're so talented," she continued. "Never feel bad for turning down opportunities that aren't right for you. It means you'll be free to say yes down the line when the right offer presents itself. Besides, this serves my selfish interests. I'm already planning my trip to Starlight Grove so I can hire you to design a custom dress for me."

I gripped my phone harder. "But I . . . what?"

"I hope if nothing else, this interview experience gives you more confidence. You're very talented. Don't belittle what you've accomplished."

I swallowed hard. "Thank you. That means more than you know."

"I'll be in touch once I know my travel dates. Take care, Lucy."

After we hung up, I stared at my phone, stunned.

I TOOK DEEP BREATHS as I turned my Razor scooter down my moms' street.

Well, it might not be exactly *my* scooter. I'd found it in the garage of King's rental, but it wasn't like Ms. Ito needed it right now.

Lala was in the front yard, kneeling as she pulled weeds coming up around the bright pastel tulips lining the walkway. The tension in my chest eased. Of all my moms, Lala understood me the best.

She waved as I parked the scooter in their driveway.

"Hey, love, I didn't know you were coming over."

"Just a spur-of-the-moment thing. I wrapped up work early, so I figured I'd come say hello."

Her cocked eyebrow told me she didn't quite buy my nonchalance, but she didn't push it as she pulled me into a tight hug. "Where's the bun-bun today?"

"Blossom is hanging out with Wilder at the firehouse." We'd picked her up from Summer this morning. King had pouted because even after he'd meticulously prepared her morning salad, she had still chosen to go to work with Wilder instead of him.

She pursed her lips. "And when are you bringing these guys over for us to meet?"

"You mean interrogate?"

"It's our job as your moms." Her tone was light, but her scent turned bitter. She averted her gaze, busying herself with brushing the dirt off her hands.

"What's wrong?" I asked.

"I just . . . I'm so sorry, honey. We failed you with your exes."

"What do you mean?"

She swallowed hard. "It was obvious pretty early on that they didn't make you happy. Every time we saw you, it was like they'd chipped away a little bit more of your sunshine. I should have done more to protect you from them."

My throat tightened with emotion as I grasped her hand. "You did try. I just wasn't ready to listen." All of my moms had made little comments questioning my exes, which had felt like personal attacks at the time. "I was the one who reacted defensively whenever you brought it up. It's my fault. I should have known better."

She shook her head, expression fierce. "Don't say that. Their treatment of you is not your fault. Some lessons we can only learn by living them. I just wish you could have been spared a broken heart."

I blinked quickly to keep my tears from falling. "Love you."

"Love you, too." She squeezed my hand and I jumped, still

not used to the strange sensations when someone touched my bond mark.

Lala's mouth gaped when she flipped my hand over. "Lucy Bluebell Andersson-Spring!"

"Ahh, yeah, surprise! There have been some recent developments."

"You're the reason for my gray hairs." She scowled, but I just laughed.

"You don't have gray hair."

"Well, if I did, it would be all your fault." She huffed. "Come inside so you can tell everyone else."

I dug my heels in. "Or you can just deliver the news. That sounds good to me. *Okaybye!*"

She rolled her eyes, keeping a surprisingly firm grip on my arm as she half dragged me across the yard. "Nice try."

I gave up the struggle once we were inside and followed Lala into the kitchen. Jojo and Mamma were on their laptops at the counter, and Mom was making cardamom buns that smelled just like Leo. My cheeks heated as I almost perfumed at the smell of baked goods.

"Hey, honey." Mamma held out her arm to me without looking up from her computer screen.

I shook my head but walked over and gave her a hug. Her nose crinkled as she sniffed me. That was enough for her to peel her eyes away from the computer screen.

"Why do you smell like alphas?"

"I don't think you want me to answer that," I said dryly.

Jojo and Mom burst out laughing, and Mamma shook her head, lips pursed against a smile. "Is it getting serious?"

"Umm, well—"

Lala poked me in the back.

"I bonded Wilder yesterday."

Jojo gasped and moved my hair to the side to expose the bond mark there. "Congratulations, baby. Although it would have been nice for us to actually meet him first."

"Wait," Lala said. "Did you bond King, too?"

"Not yet."

She lifted my hand, showing my second mark to the room. "Then what is this?"

I shrugged, but I couldn't stop my huge smile. "He was feeling a bit possessive."

Mamma's jaw dropped, but before she could make a comment that would inevitably set me on edge, I forged ahead. "I also found out I got offered the fashion internship, but—"

"Wait, really? Congratulations!" Lala said.

"Of course you did," Mamma said. "That's incredible."

"Well, the thing is, I think I might—"

Fuck. No. Be confident, Lucy.

"I mean, I've turned it down."

"Oh." Mamma tucked her white-blond hair behind her ear. "Why's that?"

"The internship is more focused on design and large-scale manufacturing, which isn't necessarily my interest. I don't want to take the spot away from someone who would use the internship as a stepping stone to their dreams."

"Are you sure you're not doing this because you want to stay in town with your men?" Mamma asked.

Defensiveness flared inside me like it often did when I was explaining my decisions to my moms. I took a deep, slow breath and let it out. "You say that like it's a bad thing to want to be with my pack."

"No, honey, that's not what she's saying," Lala said, her words doing nothing to soothe my prickly frustration at once again feeling misunderstood by them. "We just don't want you to give up on your dreams for them."

My jaw clenched and my omega snarled at their critique of *my* guys. "They wouldn't want that, either. I made this decision for me."

"Okay, everyone take a breath." Mom set a plate of cardamom buns on the table and nudged me toward a chair. "Let's all sit down and listen to what Lucy has to say."

I took my time spreading butter onto a cardamom bun. "I'm sorry I haven't brought King, Leo, and Wilder over yet. Things have been pretty chaotic, and I wasn't sure we would work out for a while there. But I am sure now. They've shown me what real love feels like. They make me happy."

"That's all we want," Lala said. "For you to be happy."

I slowly shook my head, swallowing around the lump in my throat. "I guess I thought my courting record would make you doubt my judgment, and I've been carrying around enough doubt for myself."

Mom entwined her fingers with mine, squeezing tightly.

"I know you didn't like my exes, but I never told you how bad things got," I said, forging ahead. "Partially because I was ashamed, but also because I blamed myself for a long time. They put me down all the time, but they were so good at keeping it subtle or masking it with concern. I realized that if I said yes to the internship, I'd be doing it because I want to prove to them that I'm not worthless and untalented. Not because I actually wanted it."

"Oh, honey," Jojo said, leaning forward to squeeze my shoulder.

"Saying no feels like freedom. It feels like finally choosing myself and what I want for life." I brushed away the tear rolling down my cheek.

"Have we made you feel pressured?" Mamma asked.

Mamma was a classic alpha—confident, protective, and no-nonsense. She'd always been successful in her field and instilled in me values of perseverance and hard work, which I was grateful for. She'd advocated for Lars and me in school when he was diagnosed with dyslexia and I struggled to pay attention in class, but I had also gone through life secretly scared I was disappointing her.

"I know you didn't mean to, but sometimes it feels like nobody in this family really sees me. I know you love me and are proud of me, which is why this is so hard to say out loud because I don't want to make you feel bad or think that I'm not grateful for growing up in this home and . . ."

"Shh." Lala pulled me into her arms. "You don't have to qualify anything or spare our feelings. No parent is perfect, and we can't fix what we don't realize we're doing."

I kept my eyes fixed on my cardamom bun. My mouth was too dry and my stomach too tangled to enjoy it.

"Sometimes the things you say make me feel like you see me as weak and unserious. Like when I said I was going camping, you acted like it was the most ridiculous thing in the world." *Just because they were right didn't change how I felt about it.* "And when I opened up my shop, I overheard Jojo and Mamma talking about how I didn't have any business skills. It feels like if I fail, I'll just prove everyone right."

"Oh, love." Jojo sighed. "I'm so sorry I said that and that you overheard." She moved around the table and pulled me into a hug. "You proved me wrong within about five seconds of being open, and I'm so ridiculously proud of you."

"I'm so sorry, too," Mamma said, her scent bitter. "You moved so fast when the shop space became available and I was scared it wouldn't work out, leaving you crushed. But in the end, I was the one who made you feel that way. I should have done better expressing how much confidence I have in everything you do."

"Thanks, Mamma." I sniffed.

"Oh, baby." She rounded the table, pulled me to my feet, and all of them crowded around me, squishing me in their arms.

"We're going to do better," Jojo said, her voice thick. "I promise."

"I'm so proud of you," Mamma said.

When we finally broke apart, we were all wiping our tears, which was truly shocking since none of my moms besides Lala ever cried.

"Here, you take these home." Mom handed me a glass container filled with the rest of the cardamom buns. She was never one for sappy words, but I felt her love in the way she took care of me. "You can share them with your guys if you want," she added.

I scoffed. "Fat chance. These are mine. But maybe you can make some more when I bring them over."

She beamed. "You got it."

A Pack for Spring

More hugs and heaps of reassurance later, I rode away from my moms' house on the scooter. The shining sun warmed my skin even as the windy day blew salty ocean air over me. If I were in an animated movie, this would be the scene where I broke out into song. My mind was still reeling from how quickly my life had changed. Everything was falling into perfect place. There was just one thing left for me to do.

70

KING

I pulled into a parking space near the Red Lantern and flopped back in my seat. I'd spent all day in miserable meetings, missing my omega... missing my pack. Why did this keep happening? I was supposed to be on leave, but I kept being pulled into emergency meetings. To be fair, I'd told everyone I would be back at work within a week. Two months later, I was still in Starlight Grove.

And I never wanted to leave.

All the things I thought would annoy me about small-town life—the small talk, ridiculous festivals, and nosy neighbors—were somehow *endearing*. I'd come to enjoy Marisol replacing things in my shopping cart because *you'll like this better* (she was correct), talking with Ella as she made my morning latte about the newest episode of *Rut Island* that Leo had forced us all to watch, and the town's children chanting "Fish King" anytime they saw me.

Starlight Grove felt like home.

The past few months had flipped my entire life upside down. My parents would be horrified to see me neglecting work like this. They'd spent the past few decades shutting themselves off from their humanity after my brother died, but that wasn't how I wanted to live. I wanted to build a life with my pack at the center.

I got out of the car and headed toward the restaurant. Leo waved from his spot on the bench outside. His rust-red suit was perfectly tailored to his broad frame, and the wind tousled his dark curls as he fidgeted with his cane—the one I'd gotten him. My alpha rumbled with satisfaction.

"Hey," he said as I got closer. "How's it going?"

I sat down beside him. The small bench made it so our legs were pressed together, and the heat of him against my skin sent a strange sensation through me.

"Long day of meetings," I grumbled. "Lucy isn't here yet?"

I'd offered to pick my pack up on the way back from my rented office space, but Wilder was on shift and couldn't get away, Leo's physical therapist had told him to incorporate light walking into his routine, and Lucy was on her way back from a networking event she'd attended with Summer in Briar's Landing.

My alpha had been desperate to go after her all afternoon, but I didn't want to be too overbearing, so I'd settled on texting her hourly and tracking her through the app I'd installed on her phone. It was hard to imagine a safer area than Starlight Grove and the surrounding towns, but apparently my protectiveness had no limits.

"She texted me not too long ago. The networking meeting went long so she's running late."

The night was quiet, so different from the honking cars and sirens I was used to. Silence stretched between us, but Leo's presence was soothing. His light cardamom scent settled the tension I'd been carrying all day.

"Have you eaten here before?" he asked.

I shook my head. "I don't eat out much."

Leo groaned, and my eyebrows shot up.

"I've suspected this for a while now," he said.

"Suspected what?"

"That you're one of those healthy gym-bro alphas who meal-preps chicken and spinach to eat every day."

Actually, it was arugula this week, but I wasn't about to admit that.

"Nothing wrong with eating healthy," I muttered.

Leo grinned, the expression transforming his face into something breathtaking. "You ordered a salad at the diner the other day. A *salad*." He said the word with the same inflection someone would use to describe drugs or cannibalism. "I'm going to have so much fun corrupting you."

His tone made my cheeks heat, and I looked away, disoriented. My phone vibrated and I fumbled as I pulled it out of my pocket, grateful for the distraction. Leo looked at his phone, too, because Lucy had texted the group chat—the one she'd named Blossom's Daddies.

LUCY

> Hey so sorry! We are stuck in traffic and are going to be late. You two go ahead and eat!

LEO

> We don't mind waiting for you

LUCY

> No seriously please go ahead! I'll feel so bad if you don't

Leo met my gaze and shrugged. "What do you think?"

What I thought was that I was fucking starving, but I wasn't about to admit that my grilled chicken and arugula lunch hadn't quite hit the spot today.

When I didn't respond, he patted my thigh. "Let's eat. We'll order something for her."

He leaned on his cane and slowly pushed to standing, perfectly positioning his ass right at eye level. My crotch tightened as I followed him inside.

I had *never* had such a strong reaction to another man. The other day, Lucy had made pointed comments suggesting she knew about my attraction to Leo. She hadn't seemed upset . . . but that didn't mean she would be okay with Leo and me getting together. Forming a pack was hard as it was. Wouldn't this just complicate it? Besides, I didn't even know if I wanted him like that.

My cock fucking twitched. Well, maybe I *did* know.

I was so preoccupied with my tangle of confused emotions, I barely realized that the hostess had already seated us in a booth.

"You doing okay?" Leo asked.

"Yeah, sorry. Just a long day."

Our server came over with menus and waters. I recognized him from Summer's bakery grand opening.

"Hey, Alvin," Leo said, reaching out to grasp his hand. "You're a busy man. Still saving up for a car?"

The teenager grinned. "Yeah. I'm getting close. Hopefully, I'll have enough by my birthday."

"Hell, yeah."

The few times I'd seen Alvin at the bakery or around town, he seemed pretty reserved and introverted, but Leo effortlessly brought him out of the shell. He'd only lived in town for a few months, but the way he talked to people, it was like he'd been here his whole life. I'd learned to wear a serious, professional mask in all social settings, but maybe I wouldn't have to with Leo around. He and Lucy were the definition of social butterflies, dragging a reserved Wilder and me through life with them.

We put in our orders, letting Alvin know we would put in a to-go order for Lucy if she didn't arrive in time to eat with us.

"How was your day?" I stretched out my legs under the table, accidentally brushing against Leo. He didn't move his leg and neither did I.

"It was good. I had PT this morning and headed over to my parents' house to harvest some flowers from my grandma's greenhouse."

"How's PT going?"

Leo's eyes were fixed on his water glass. "It's fine."

Should I press him? Make him talk about it? I was no stranger to avoiding the shit I didn't want to deal with, which meant I knew what an unhealthy coping mechanism it was.

"You go several times a week, right?" I risked asking.

"I have been. But Cassie said I can start coming in just once a week."

"That's good, isn't it?"

His jaw clenched, and I had the urge to pull him into my arms.

"It means she doesn't think I'll see much more significant

improvement. At this point, it's just about maintenance and preventing further damage."

Immediately, my mind started whirring with ways to problem-solve. "Have you gotten a second opinion? What about a different specialist?"

It wasn't like Starlight Grove was some hub for medical care. Maybe there were experimental treatments or trials I could get him into in New York or Boston. I didn't give a fuck if he used a cane, but I hated that he was in pain—both mental and physical.

Leo's face shuttered and I caught a slightly burnt edge to his scent that put me on edge. "I've already gotten a second opinion."

"I'm sure you have. It's just I have some connections that could be helpful—"

"It's fine. I'm fine."

Shit. I took a deep breath, doing my best to push down my alpha's need to take control. I'd come on too strong.

This time, the silence that descended on us was stilted and awkward.

If I couldn't fix his leg right now, I at least needed to fix this between us. "I'm sorry. I didn't mean to upset you."

His shoulders loosened. "No, I'm sorry for being defensive. I fought my prognosis for a long time, and I'm doing better at accepting things, but it's still hard."

Before I could second-guess, my hand surrounded his. His skin was warm and rough as he entwined our fingers.

"Actually, I have my first appointment with pain management coming up and I was wondering if you'd come with me. If you're not busy—"

"Yes," I said, cutting him off. "I'll be there."

His smile was radiant, and I noticed the tiniest dimple on his right cheek.

"Thanks," he said softly.

I nodded, feeling dazed. It was hard to keep my train of thought when I looked at Leo.

A Pack for Spring

"How are the greenhouse flowers looking?" I finally asked.

"Really good. I think in the next year or two, I'll be able to supply the majority of the flowers I need at my shop. I'll have to give you a greenhouse tour when we go to family dinner."

"I'd love that." I had very briefly met Bibi when we'd picked up goat's milk for Blossom. She'd given me a thorough once-over, said something to Leo in Farsi that made him blush, and told me she looked forward to getting to know me. I hadn't realized what she'd meant at the time, but now I thought she'd known we were going to be a pack before we did.

I kept hold of Leo's hand until Alvin brought out our food.

Our conversation flowed easily as we ate, but I was on edge with the anxious excitement coursing through my body. Was I just imagining the way he pressed his leg against mine? The way his scent deepened? Glances that could only be described as heated?

By the time Alvin dropped off a plate of fortune cookies, I was a flustered, aroused mess.

"Should we see what's in our future?" Leo asked.

We each grabbed one and cracked them open. I squinted at the small slip of paper. Fuck, I really needed to start bringing readers with me. I was getting old. Finally, I managed to decipher the fortune.

The man across from you is hot. You should kiss him.

I almost choked. What the fuck?

Leo stared intently at his fortune, and I could have sworn that his face was red. He popped the cookie into his mouth and my gaze lingered on his lips.

"What does yours say?" I asked before I could stop myself.

He cleared his throat. "I'm going to the restroom." He was out of his seat before I could say anything, his fortune crumpled in his hand.

I sat back in my seat, my heart beating like I'd just sprinted a mile. It was still racing when Leo returned to the table, a to-go bag of food for Lucy in hand.

"You ready?"

I nodded and stood. "I'll get the check."

He waved. "Don't worry. I already paid."

"Excuse me?" My voice deepened, my alpha surging. He wanted to take care of my beta, not the other way around.

Leo gave me a devastating wink. "Better luck next time."

What. The. *Fuck*.

I sputtered as I followed him to the exit, snagging the to-go bag out of his hand.

"Did you even have to go to the bathroom?"

Leo laughed at my outrage. "Nah."

"We could have split the check."

He threw me a knowing look. Yeah, as if I would ever agree to splitting the check. I rolled my shoulders, irritated that I had been bested by his plan, when I caught the light floral scent of my omega. I stopped abruptly and spun around, looking for her. Why hadn't she called us to say she was here?

"What is it?" Leo asked.

"I can scent Lucy."

He pulled out his phone. "Huh. She didn't text."

"Maybe she came in through the back with Summer?"

Leo shrugged. "Let's go check."

I followed him back the way we came. No one stopped us, so we walked down the hallway toward the kitchen. Even with the scent of food in the air, my alpha detected Lucy right away. I jerked my head at one of the office doors and pushed it open.

I didn't know what I expected to find inside, but it wasn't Lucy and Summer sitting at a desk, giggling, a pile of fortune cookies and empty food containers in front of them.

"What do we have here?" I crossed my arms.

Lucy whipped her head up with a gasp.

Leo grinned as he cocked his head. "Are you getting into trouble, pretty girl?"

She shook her head, looking decidedly guilty.

Summer snorted. "That's my cue to go." She stopped on her way to the door. "Actually, no. The three of you should go because I don't even want to think about what's going to happen in here if you stay."

Lucy's cheeks heated, and she shoved her friend. "We're going, we're going. Thanks for your assistance. You ready, boys?" She breezed by us, providing no explanation for why she had been hiding in the office and not stuck in traffic.

I glanced at Leo and he just shook his head. "I think we've been played."

We followed Lucy back through the restaurant. "What did your fortune cookie say?" I asked.

"I'll show you mine if you show me yours."

My cheeks heated at his words. Fuck, my mind was in the gutter.

We exchanged small crumpled slips of paper.

Kiss him. No context. No reason. Just do it. See what happens.

Leo's sharp inhale and deepening scent went straight to my cock. We locked eyes, and his cheeky smile and cocked eyebrow told me we were on the same wavelength. Giddy nerves sparked through me as I reached out and took his hand, feeling like a teenager again.

The cool night air washed over us as we stepped outside, but it did little to clear my head. He ushered Lucy and me to a small cove on the side of the building, hidden from the sidewalk by a leafy tree.

We crowded around our omega, her body pressed between ours, and I gripped her jaw. "Were you ever stuck in Briar's Landing?"

Lucy bit her lip to stop from smiling as she shook her head.

Leo's fingers twisted in her hair. "Our fortune cookies were weirdly pointed. You wouldn't have had anything to do with that, would you?"

"The fortune cookies here are always very unique," Lucy said.

"I think the fortunes had some help this time around," I growled.

Leo hummed as he reached up to run his fingers through my

hair. "It seems like our omega wanted to make sure we got a certain message."

My breath hitched, heart skipped.

Message fucking received.

"Too bad she decided to be naughty and lie to us instead of just talking to us." I shook my head with mock sadness. "Then she could have avoided her punishment."

Lucy's lips parted in outrage. "I wouldn't have had to scheme if you two weren't being so slow about it."

"Oh, pretty girl, that's no excuse." Leo's low voice went straight to my cock, and I knew Lucy could feel it with the way I was pressed against her.

"No excuse at all." I moved my hands slowly down her body until I was cupping her ass. I hadn't been thinking clearly, though, because it meant my hands were level with Leo's crotch. I breathed in sharply when the beta shifted his hips forward until his hard cock pressed against my hand. Lucy perfumed, and Leo's scent deepened. Fuck, they smelled so perfect together.

Leo arched an eyebrow, keeping full eye contact as he slowly took my hand and turned it so I was cupping his erection. My chest fluttered with anticipation. Were we really doing this? Lucy practically trembled with excitement as I ran my other hand up Leo's body, skimming along his muscular chest until I reached his face and cupped it.

I shifted forward. He met me halfway and then—

A brush of lips. Eyes drifting closed.

He was sweetness and spice on my tongue, his lips soft but firm as they moved confidently against mine.

I was panting once we pulled apart, and Leo's expression was all lazy satisfaction as he brushed his thumb along his lower lip.

Lucy squealed, her body practically vibrating as she bounced on her toes. "Okay, looks like you have this under control. I'm going to get going and you two have the best night. Bye!"

I snorted and snagged her around the waist, pinning her back to my chest. "Leo, what do you think about our omega trying to run off?"

He shook his head as he ran a slow hand up her body, skimming her breasts until he collared her neck. "I think it's cute she thinks she's not coming with us."

My breath caught at the way he emphasized *coming*, and his satisfied smirk told me he knew exactly what he was doing.

The beta might just be my undoing.

71

LEO

I'd been fantasizing about King since the first moment he stepped into my shop, but I never expected this—to be standing naked, in my omega's nest, with the hot-as-fuck alpha raking his heated gaze down my body.

And I was doing the same damn thing. I'd seen him naked before, but this time, I felt like I had full permission to look my fill. His body was lean and muscular, his abs forming a V that pointed to his thick, long cock. I'd never been with an alpha before, and seeing his knot—already slightly swollen—made me shiver.

I took a small step toward him, the plush mattress squishing beneath my feet. "Is this happening?"

King swallowed and I swore his cheeks were pink in the dim light. I'd never seen him like this—vulnerable and unsure. "Yeah, this is happening."

Lucy squeaked with excitement, and we turned to look at her. She slapped her hand over her mouth. "Sorry." The word was muffled. "I promise I'll be quiet."

I cocked my eyebrow at King, and he shook his head with a slow smirk. "I think it's time to punish our girl, don't you think?"

I nodded. "Oh yeah. She needs to know we'll always follow through."

"Come here." King pointed at the spot in front of him.

Lucy chewed her lip, shifting her weight until she slowly bridged the space between us. Once she was within reach, we quickly stripped her off. I wound her long, gold hair around my hand and crashed into her lips with a hard kiss. The moment I released her, King's lips replaced mine. There was something about watching him devour our girl that set me on fire.

"You're going to do as I say, aren't you?" King's voice was a growl as he pinched her rosy nipples.

Her pupils were blown, her scent was so thick it coated my tongue.

She nodded.

"How do you respond to me?"

Slick dripped down her inner thighs. "Yes, Daddy. I'll do what you say."

"That's right, you will. Now, present." His voice was infused with a slight bark. I wasn't compelled to respond to it like an omega would, but it still made my cock twitch.

She didn't hesitate before moving, pressing her chest to the mattress and her ass in the air. Was it possible to come without touching myself?

King and I knelt, and I ran my hand down her back. Her skin was so fucking pretty—soft and freckled. King roughly cupped her sex, and she moaned as she ground her pussy against him. "Naughty girls who try to manipulate their men don't get to come," he said with mock sadness. "They get their asses spanked."

"No, Daddy, *please*. I need to come."

Good thing King was here because I would have given in to her little cries immediately, but this was all part of our game. Our girl craved dominance, and we would always give her what she needed.

"What do you think, Leo?"

"Hmm." I drew out the sound, savoring her desperation.

She whimpered. "Please, Leo."

"Maybe there's a way she can earn an orgasm by the end of the night," I said.

King wrapped her hair around his fist and tugged her head up from behind. Her back arched, pushing her ass up even higher. "Be grateful your beta is in the mood to be merciful. If you take your spanking like a good girl—no moving, no complaining—we might let you come. Understand?"

"Yes, Daddy."

He moved without hesitating—his hand swiftly coming down on her ass, leaving a pink handprint. I swore under my breath and gripped the base of my cock to keep myself from coming. I hadn't known if punishment would be my thing, and maybe it wouldn't be when I was alone with Lucy, but seeing King spank her? Fuck. I would watch that all day long.

Lucy curled her fingers around a blanket as she did her best to stay still. By the time King finished, her ass was bright pink and her inner thighs were drenched with slick.

He gripped the back of my neck. "Your turn."

I ran my palm up Lucy's back.

"How're you feeling, pretty girl?"

"Like I've been punished enough." She glanced back at me with a pout, but there was a twinkle of mischief in her eyes.

I grinned, any tension in my chest easing. She was enjoying this.

"Too bad you don't make that decision. Ten more from me." I spanked her butt cheek, the stinging slap echoing through the room. My cock twitched with each slap, especially as her perfume deepened. I gave her the last spank and couldn't resist dipping my fingers into her cunt just so I could lick it up.

"I don't understand how you taste this good, but *fuck*."

I gathered up her slick again, but this time, I offered my fingers to King. He grabbed my wrist and sucked them deep into his mouth before kissing me, sharing her sweetness as his tongue thrust into my mouth.

Lucy's breath caught and we broke apart.

"Seems like a ridiculous question at this point, but you're okay with this, baby girl?" King asked.

"You eating my slick? Yes."

He slapped her ass, hard, and Lucy rolled onto her back with a squeal to shield herself from him.

I covered my face, shoulders shaking with laughter. "You're such a brat."

She giggled. "Yes, I am totally fine with *this*." She pointed between the two of us.

King leaned over and kissed her forehead. "As long as you know that you're the center of our world, of our pack. Nothing is going to change that."

She ran her fingers down his cheek and nodded. "I just want you two to be happy. And maybe to see you fuck. You know, if that's something you're interested in." She batted her eyes, a picture of innocence.

My lips twitched. She was so full of shit. But also . . . how could I refuse her?

I turned to King, and his molten eyes met mine. Tension crackled in the air, and I ran my fingers through his hair. There was just enough length for me to grip it.

"Are you mine?" I asked. We were kneeling, chest to chest, the energy between us electric.

"Fuck yes."

Our lips crashed together in a fight for dominance. I plunged my tongue deeper into his mouth, trying to lap up as much of his sweet orange blossom taste.

When we finally broke apart, chests heaving, I gripped his jaw. "As long as you know I'm not calling you *Daddy*." My hands caressed his muscle-corded back until I got to his firm ass cheeks. I palmed them and squeezed hard. King grunted as he thrust his hips forward, grinding his cock against mine.

I skimmed my lips up his jaw until they brushed the shell of his ear. "Now, are you going to be a good boy for me and give me that ass?"

I held my breath, waiting to see how he'd respond to me taking the lead. He was frozen, and I was sure he'd refuse, but then he slowly lowered himself onto his back.

His eyes were dark and heated as they raked down my chest. "Have your way with me, beta."

I leaned over him, and we both groaned when our cocks touched.

"Wait." He touched my chest and I froze. "Is this hurting your knee?"

It took a second for my arousal-muddled brain to catch up to his question, but once it did, I smiled. This time, there was none of the insecurity or defensiveness I'd held since my injury, just tremendous love and gratitude for my new family.

"What have I been doing all that physical therapy for if not to fuck my alpha?" I collared his throat as we kissed. I wanted to drag this out, make it last forever, but I was also desperate to be inside him, to fill him with my cum.

The scrape of a drawer opening pulled my attention. Lucy took a bottle of lube from her nightstand and tossed it to me.

"What a good girl. I think that earns you an orgasm." I winked and she wiggled happily.

I turned my attention back to King. I popped the lube open, coating my fingers and pressing them to his asshole, just holding them there. The alpha groaned and his ass twitched until I took mercy on both of us, pressing one finger in and then the other. I clenched my jaw, keeping my breaths steady as I tried to maintain control. He was hot and tight and would squeeze my cock so fucking well.

I worked my fingers in and out until he relaxed around me. "That's it. One more." I slipped in another finger.

King reached for his cock, but I grabbed his hand and pressed it to the mattress. "Your pleasure is mine tonight." His scent grew even more potent, but he didn't fight my hold. Having my alpha submit to me was the biggest fucking thrill.

My cock fucking ached, and my precum dripped onto King's stomach. I wanted to drag this out, make it last forever, but I was on the verge of losing control.

I pulled my fingers out, dragging a cry of protest from my alpha. His cock was red and ruddy, his knot already starting to swell.

"Lucy, I think our alpha needs you to suck him down that hot little mouth of yours."

She wiggled happily and crawled over, wasting no time licking a long line from his knot to his tip. The tendons in King's throat strained as he threw his fist over his eyes.

I couldn't hold off any longer. I covered my cock with lube before gripping his leg, using my hold as leverage as I pressed the tip of my cock to his asshole. Low moans and sharp breaths echoed in the room as I slowly pushed inside him. Sweat prickled my skin as I forced myself to keep my thrusts slow, letting him adjust to me.

By the time my cock was buried completely in his ass, our chests were heaving. I cupped his face, savoring the feel of him even as electric pleasure shot sparks through my body, urging me to *move*.

When Lucy wrapped her sweet lips around King's cock and sucked him down, he threw his head back with a loud cry and my control snapped. I pulled out almost all the way before thrusting back in hard. Curses spilled from his lips as he writhed with pleasure. I rested one hand on the back of Lucy's neck and the other on King's chest as I kept a fast pace. Lucy took King deep, choking occasionally as my hard thrusts forced him deeper into her mouth.

"I'm going to come," King warned.

I was almost there as well. I pressed his leg up to his chest and thrust in even deeper. King shouted as he came, his lips parted in ecstasy. That, in combination with the sounds of Lucy's gags, took me over the edge. I came with a shout, pushing deep inside him as Lucy drank him down, not spilling a single drop.

I collapsed on the mattress. Our ragged breaths filled the room as twinges of pleasure rocked through my sensitized body.

King turned to face me. "Fuck. That was . . ."

I cut his words off with a kiss, our swollen lips tenderly moving against each other. The sensation of overwhelming weightlessness filled my chest until I couldn't stop myself from blurting out what I was feeling. "I love you."

King cradled my jaw, his touch tender. "I love you, too. I never thought—" he cleared his throat. "I never thought I'd be this lucky." He rubbed his cheek against mine, scent-marking me.

I grinned and held my arm out to Lucy, who was practically bouncing on the bed with happiness. She curled into my side.

"You're practically drooling, darling."

"Yeah, well, sorry not sorry, but that was freaking hot."

"Fuck yeah it was." I kissed the top of her head, so fucking grateful for her easy acceptance of King's and my relationship.

I wanted to stay here forever, but I pushed myself up with a groan. "I have to clean up."

King's hand went to my chest, stopping me. "I'll take care of it." His tone was low and firm, the dominant alpha snapping back in place.

He gave Lucy a gentle kiss before leaving, returning moments later with a damp cloth. He cleaned me up, his touch and the rough washcloth making me half hard again, before lying down next to our omega, sandwiching her tight between us.

We were a tangle of limbs, hot and slightly sticky, our scents deep and perfect as they blended together. I must have dosed off for a few minutes, because I woke up to Lucy squirming against me until her cunt brushed against my hard cock. I grabbed her hips, trying to keep her still, but she let out a protesting whine.

King palmed her ass, ignoring her cries of protest as he dug his fingers into her sore, reddened skin. "Is our baby girl feeling needy?"

"You said I could come."

I cocked an eyebrow. "So we did."

King grinned, meeting my gaze as he got on his knees. In one smooth move, he rolled Lucy so she was on top of me, her legs spread on either side of my hips and her drenched pussy parting around my cock as she rocked forward.

"Take your beta's cock in that sweet cunt," King growled. He kissed a line up her spine. "And once he's all settled in there, nice and snug, I'm going to press my cock inside your pussy, too, until you're so fucking full you can't even think about getting away."

72

LUCY

Yes yes yes.

This was everything I'd dreamed of. I straddled Leo and positioned his cock at my entrance, but instead of taking him slowly, I let gravity pull me down in one swift movement. I trembled with pleasure, already on the verge of coming. Leo swore and tightened his hold on my hips, his fingertips digging into my skin. I burned with arousal, but before I could move, King pushed me down flush on our beta's chest and pressed his cock to my entrance.

I'd never done double penetration and was *slightly* concerned they were about to break me. Good thing I was too aroused and desperate for an orgasm to care.

King pulled me off of Leo's cock just enough to inch inside me, and they both thrust in together. My fingertips dug into Leo's arms as I tried to take them both.

"Take a deep breath for me, baby girl. You're all tense." King's hand stroked firmly up my back and I let out a slow breath. The pressure eased, and their slow rocking movements transformed to pleasure.

"That's it. That's our good girl, taking us both in her sweet omega pussy."

"*Fuck fuck fuck,*" Leo chanted to a little musical tune. "*Don't come. Don't come.*"

I choked on a laugh and both of my guys swore at how I tightened around them.

"That's not helping," Leo gritted out.

"Sorry." I giggled. "Maybe try a different jingle."

"Spank her," he said to King.

My mouth fell open in indignation, but before I could say anything, Daddy's hand slapped down on my butt cheek.

"Be nice to your beta," he said sternly.

I scowled and intentionally tightened around them, making them both shout. I grinned at my victory, even as King's hand came down on my other ass cheek, the sting propelling me even closer to my orgasm.

He leaned down, his chest pressed to my back until I was completely immobilized between them. I'd never been this full before and I panted through the overwhelming sensation of it, all the while wanting more.

"I love you, baby girl." King's teeth scraped against my neck, and I trembled with anticipation.

"I love you, too. So much." King's eyes shone with pure joy. My alpha, who had experienced so little love in his life but was deserving of it all. "Bond me, King. Make me yours."

"You're already mine," King said. "Both of you. Forever."

"Forever," Leo whispered.

King bit down, and the initial sting quickly replaced with intense pleasure of my orgasm as he crashed into my soul. The gold strands of his bond were solid, confidently taking up space inside me. The very core of his being wrapped around my insecurities and replaced them with his strength and love.

Happy tears streamed down my face.

"You were made for me, baby. I would have waited forever for you." My alpha's voice was low and reverent, the words spoken between soft kisses to my new bond mark.

I was beyond words, but if I could have spoken, I would have said every moment of loneliness and waiting was worth it for this moment.

Leo's and King's movements became frantic as they thrust inside me. Each movement stretched my pussy, the stinging pleasure sending me over the edge again as the three of us came at the same time. They spilled inside me with loud cries, their murmured praise lost in a haze of pleasure. The hard press of their bodies was the only thing tethering me to reality.

We stayed like that, neither of them pulling out, until I could no longer ignore the urge to complete my bond with King. I whined, desperate to bite him but unable to move. But of course my alpha knew what I needed. He offered me his hand, and I bit down on the fleshy skin of his palm with a happy sigh. Our emotions intensified as the bond flared, burning hot and pure.

"Fuck, baby. That's . . . you feel . . ." He trailed off, but I didn't need words. I felt everything—his awe, his love, his *devotion* toward me.

There was just one thing missing.

I pressed my lips to my beta's neck. "Will you be mine, Leo?"

"*Ours*," King corrected.

Leo's smile was radiant. "I already am."

It took a little maneuvering for King and me to get into position, but clearly none of us could stand any space between us.

My lips brushed the right side of his neck as King took the left, and we bit down at the same time. Leo flared into my soul like a key finally clicking into place when you come home at the end of the day. His presence was sweet and gentle, enveloping me in his tender care.

"Fuck. I can feel you both. You're right here," he gasped. A tear trickled down his cheek and I kissed it, the salt lingering on my lips.

"Forever and ever," I murmured. My eyes drifted shut and I felt a surge of Wilder's happiness through the bond. I'd stopped by the firehouse earlier to tell him what I was planning. He'd laughed and said I deserved to get my ass spanked for manipulating Leo and King, but he was just as impatient as I was for the two of them to admit their feelings for each other.

Now the four of us were entwined forever.

73

LUCY

"Baby girl." King stroked my back, his skin slightly rough against mine. "It's time to wake up."

No. It was sleep time.

"I know you don't like the morning, princess. If you get up, I'll go get you a latte and pastry."

Tempting, but no.

I rubbed my cheek against my pillow, and it let out a low purr. *Hmm. Did it usually do that?* Thick arms surrounded me, smelling like pine and home. I sighed happily as I pressed my face to Wilder's throat. I didn't know when he'd snuck into the nest or how long I'd been sprawled on top of him, but everything felt complete now. His purr intensified, and his thigh slipped between mine. The pressure against my bare pussy made me squirm.

King kissed a line up my spine, his lips ending on the bond mark he'd placed on my neck. Mmm, the morning was no time for conversation, but it was the perfect time for fucking.

He palmed my ass but didn't move his fingers toward my core.

"Your bottle of suppressants on the bathroom counter is empty, baby. Do you have more somewhere?"

I let out a frustrated growl. "No, I haven't refilled them." My words were muffled against Wilder's skin. If he could just slip his cock...

"Do you want me to swing by the pharmacy while I'm out?" King asked.

"No. I want you to cuddle me while *sleeping in*."

Leo chuckled as he returned from the bathroom. He flopped onto the bed and threw his arm across Wilder and me. "Joonam, I'm sorry

A Pack for Spring

to tell you that most of the world considers nine in the morning sleeping in."

"What do they know?" I muttered. He was all floral cardamom, and it made me hungry for him. "Wilder knows it's sleeping time."

The chest underneath me shook with laughter. "I've been up since six, sweetheart. But I'm happy to hold you all morning."

"Our precious grumpy girl." Leo's kiss on my cheek was sweet and tender, but his wandering hands palming my ass were anything but. I arched against him, my nipples hardening as they rubbed against Wilder's bare chest.

"We love our grumpy morning omega," King said. "But she still needs to answer Daddy about her medication."

His low voice made me shiver and I whined, hating how empty I was. I jolted when King pinched my nipple. My eyes popped open as I turned toward him in outrage. "What was that for?"

"What are you supposed to be doing?"

I jutted my lip out in a pout. "Sleeping?"

His lips twitched, but he didn't relent as he gripped my jaw.

I let out a long sigh. "I don't need my suppressants refilled because I'm not taking them." My cheeks burned and my stomach fluttered, bracing for their reactions.

His grip tightened. "Why is that?"

"Because I want to have a heat."

Wilder turned to stone beneath me, and waves of shock and arousal flooded me from all directions through the bonds.

"When did you stop taking suppressants?" King's voice was strangled.

"I just skipped last night."

"How long until you go into heat?" Leo asked.

"I don't know. A couple days maybe?" I chewed my lip. "Are you guys mad?"

The tension in the room dissipated.

"Not at all," Leo said. "Just surprised."

"It feels a little sudden," King added. "I don't want you to think there's any pressure, baby girl. You can take as much time as you need to feel ready."

The lump in my throat was all gratitude. "I know. I genuinely forgot I was out, but I'd been putting off refilling it because I feel ready for a heat. If we wait any longer, it will be too close to the Midsummer festival. I guess I could wait until after Midsummer, but that's when I was planning to start working on my online sewing course and officially open up orders for custom clothing."

I finally braved a glance at Wilder. His reaction was the one I was most worried about. Even alphas with regular hormone levels often went into rut during heats. I hoped the whole chasing-me-through-the-woods thing had eased his anxiety about hurting me, but this was still a big step. His expression was unreadable, and he was shielding his emotions from me in the bond.

I didn't like it.

I scowled and prodded at the golden strands joining us on the deepest level possible. He let out a shuddering laugh and hugged me tight to his chest, his face pressed to my hair.

"You're such trouble."

"Don't hide from me," I grumbled back.

He opened the bond, releasing a floodgate of love, fear, and anxiety. He shifted so he was sitting up, keeping me straddling his lap.

He locked eyes with King and Leo. "I'm going to get an injectable tranquilizer that you can use on me in case I lose control."

I tightened my hold on him. "You won't—"

"Nonnegotiable, sweetheart. I'm not willing to risk your safety."

I narrowed my eyes. I could feel his resoluteness in the bond, so I let out a little huff of defeat. "Fine. But you won't need it." I pressed a kiss to his jaw. "My omega can handle you just fine."

He grinned, chest rumbling. "I'm sure she can."

"Have you had a heat before?" Leo asked. "I don't know a ton about them."

I shook my head. "I thought about it with my exes, but it never happened."

King and Wilder growled, but Leo kept a cool head as he stroked my hair. "Why is that? You were with them for a while, right?"

"Almost a year." God, it was so embarrassing to think how long I stayed with them. "They wanted me to have one. Well, that's an understatement. They said I couldn't move in or have a nest at their house until I had a heat with them." I'd never told anyone the full story of what happened, and now that I'd started, the words spilled out.

"They said it wasn't natural for omegas to be on suppressants, but I was really busy with my shop. At least, that's the excuse I gave them for not going into heat, but after we broke up, I realized the real reason was that my omega didn't trust them. The longer I went without having a heat, the more distant they became until they were withholding pretty much all affection, although they still acted like perfect alphas when we were in public. I was actually relieved when I found the proof that they were cheating because it gave me the courage to end it."

"Oh, baby girl. They didn't deserve you," King murmured.

My friends had said the same thing for months, but it finally felt like the truth of it was sinking in.

"I think I know that now. But if you think it's too soon for me to have a heat, I totally get it. I can refill my suppressants, and if I take a double dose today, I should be fine."

"I don't want to wait," Leo blurted out.

I smiled up at him. "Yeah?"

He cupped my cheek and gave me a sweet kiss. "Fucking my girl for days? Sounds like a dream come true."

"I don't want to wait, either," King said. His deep scent swirled around me, all bright citrus.

"Wilder?" I whispered his name and trailed my fingers through his short beard. "Will you see me through my heat?"

A surge of possessive arousal shot down our bond so strong I swore I had a mini orgasm.

"Yes, I will," he said roughly.

I captured his lips, winding my fingers through his hair as I dipped my tongue in his mouth. He palmed my ass, pulling me tighter against his hard cock, concealed by his boxers. Since we were all here, and I was already naked...

"Oh shit," Leo said, making Wilder freeze.

I groaned. Could women get blue balls?

"King and I are signed up to chaperone Ivy's class trip to the New England Aquarium tomorrow. I'll text her to say we can't go."

"Oh no. How tragic," King said dryly.

"No, wait, you can't cancel," I said. "My heat shouldn't start for a couple of days. Ivy said the kids are so excited for more of King's fish facts."

The alpha in question grumbled, but I saw through him. He was excited about the field trip, too.

"I don't want to leave you," he said, his anxiety and uncertainty reaching me through the bond.

"You have the next four days off, right?" I asked Wilder.

"Yes. I'll also put in a request for heat leave, which I think is up to ten additional days."

"See, Wilder will be with me, and Boston isn't that far away if something happens."

King ran a harried hand through his hair. "I don't know."

"Fish King cannot disappoint the children," Leo said.

"I'll take care of our girl," Wilder added.

Any more sweetness and I'd burst into tears.

"I see I'm overruled." King kissed the tip of my nose. "If you're sure, princess."

I ran my fingers down his cheek, rough with stubble in contrast to his usually clean-shaven self. "I'm sure."

74

LUCY

I'D ALWAYS KNOWN MY HORMONAL CONDITION MEANT MY omega was more intense than average, but I hadn't realized how much since I'd been on suppressants for so long.

Now, as I whined when Wilder walked three feet away from me to the kitchen pantry, there was no hiding it. I hopped off the counter and plastered myself against his back.

"Sweetheart." He gently turned me so I was hugging his chest. "I'm not leaving."

I knew that, but my omega wasn't as reasonable.

"I'm sorry. I know I'm being crazy."

He lifted me against his chest, one hand supporting my ass while the other grabbed the ingredients he needed. "You're not crazy. I always want to be touching you. I just need to figure out how to do that while still taking care of you."

"It's fine. You can put me down on the counter."

He chuckled. "Oh yeah?" He released his hold on me and I stayed exactly where I was, my arms and legs wrapped around him.

"I'll let go," I said. "Anytime now."

His arms were around me again, squeezing me tight to his chest. "I have an idea."

I kept my face buried in his neck as he carried me outside to his truck, grabbed something, and headed back to his bedroom.

"You'll have to let go of me, but just for a few minutes." He laid me down on the bed and I reluctantly loosened my hold.

"What is that?"

He was holding a tangle of . . . something.

"These are rock-climbing harnesses. I keep them in my truck for Mountain Rescue."

I scrunched my nose. "Umm . . . do you not remember how we met? Me and the outdoors don't get along."

He grinned. "It's not for rock climbing."

"What's it for?"

He stripped off my clothes—not that there was much to take off since I was just wearing one of his sweatshirts like a dress. "I'm going to put you in this harness and attach it to straps around my body so I can stay inside you all day long while still having my hands free."

His fingers dug into my ass, the slight sting grounding me because *what the fuck had he just said?*

He cocked an eyebrow, waiting for my response. This was unhinged. Excessive. Ridiculous.

"Yes, let's do that."

He grinned, but there was a slight thread of anxiety in the bond. My alpha was still a little hesitant around me, but I didn't take it personally. Every day he grew more confident that he would never hurt me. But sometimes, he needed a little push.

I stood and took the smaller harness from him. "What do I do with this?" The straps were black and in a complicated configuration, and I had no idea how to put it on. Luckily, I didn't have to figure it out because a loud growl tore through Wilder's chest.

He cupped my pussy, using his grip to lift me off the ground. I let out a cry at the delicious pressure.

"You are pure temptation. You want to be strapped to my chest, sweetheart? Split open on my cock as I go about my day, unable to get down until I decide I'm done with you?"

Slick gushed from me, drenching his hand and my inner thigh.

"I want it. I want *you*. I trust you, alpha."

"My good girl," he murmured against my hair before he lowered me to the floor. In a frantic rush, he stripped off his shirt and unbuttoned his jeans so his cock sprang free.

He stepped into the large harness. The straps encircled his thighs and wrapped across his chest. Once he was done, he dropped to his knees in front of me.

"You're so fucking pretty." He pressed a kiss to my pussy. "So sweet. So perfect."

He guided my feet through two loops, adjusting the nylon straps around my waist. I was so turned on I could barely stay standing, especially when he tightened straps around my chest that framed my breasts. I could still move freely, but each strap pressing against my skin was a tantalizing reminder of how much he owned me.

"Anything pinching?" He tugged on the harness, checking the fit.

I shook my head.

He ran a thick finger through my pussy lips, gathering up slick before he sucked it off. "I fucking love seeing you tied up for me. I should keep this on you always as a reminder of who you belong to."

I rocked forward, desperate for friction. My skin felt electric.

"Except I'll add a crotch rope. It will go straight through your pretty little cunt lips, rubbing against your clit every time you move. The perfect reminder to be a good girl for me when we can't be together. But today"—his huge hands gripped my thighs and lifted me so I was pressed against his chest—"we have other plans."

He sat on the bed and moved me so I was straddling him. He used a series of carabiners to attach various points of our harnesses together until I could barely move. My front was plastered to his bare chest, my legs wrapped around him. I clutched at his shoulders when he stood, but we were securely attached together.

I felt like a doll, completely at his mercy. My pussy clenched, aching with how empty I felt. "I need you. Please, alpha, please."

"I fucking love hearing you beg. Are you desperate for my cock, little omega?"

"Yes." I wiggled, trying to maneuver him inside me, but I was helpless. He chuckled but finally had mercy on me.

He grabbed my ass, pulling me away from him just enough to press his cock to my entrance. He loosened his hold on my hips, and gravity did the rest. I dug my fingers into his shoulders as I cried out at the way his thick cock stretched me. My breaths came fast as I tried to adjust to the pressure and sting. I couldn't shift, couldn't move. All I could do was take him.

Wilder wrapped my hair around his hand and pulled, the spark of pain intensifying my need. His eyes were black as rut creeped over him. I ground myself against him, trying to get the friction I needed to come.

"Look at you, struggling to take my cock. Think of how much fuller you'll be when I stuff that tight pussy with my knot, too."

Oh god. I couldn't take more, but I *needed* more.

"Relax your sweet little cunt for me." He started gently bouncing me, each movement rubbing against my clit. I was crying and babbling nonsense as his knot pressed against my entrance.

"That's it. My little toy. You're so fucking perfect." His hand came down on my ass and it pushed me over the edge.

I buried my face in the crook of his neck as I screamed my release, battered by waves of pleasure. He thrust up and his knot slipped inside me, immediately swelling beyond anything I'd experienced. It pressed against all my pleasure spots until I was coming again. By the time the haze cleared, Wilder was rubbing my back as he murmured soothing words.

"Such a good girl for me. Letting your alpha use you how he needs." He pressed a kiss to the top of my head. At least he was breathing hard, or I would have been insulted that he wasn't as wrecked as I was.

When he started walking, I tensed at the new sensations rocking through me. His knot shifted inside me with every movement, and I sobbed from the intense pleasure.

He patted my ass as he headed into the kitchen. "Now it's time to make my girl breakfast."

75

LEO

Bringing a horde of elementary school children who were riding the end-of-the-school-year high to the New England Aquarium was as chaotic as I'd imagined, but it was fucking fun, too.

The best part was seeing King in his element. I wasn't sure what the serious businessman would be like around kids, but they were obsessed with him. He was a fount of obscure marine animal facts in his T-shirt with *rainbow dolphins* on it. Seeing this other side of him—the man he might have been in his twenties before he became a bigshot CEO—made me fall in love with him even more.

He'd shocked me when he tugged me into a dark corner of the aquarium for a hurried make-out session while the group was distracted by otters. When he pulled away, a brilliant smile on his face, I felt like a giddy teenager all over again.

King was busy sharing fun facts about stingrays at the touch tank when my phone vibrated.

WILDER

Lucy's heat is starting

Temp is 103

She's crying because she wants her nest

King locked eyes with me, clearly sensing my panic through the bond. He pulled out his phone and swore loudly.

"Ms. Winter! Mr. King said a bad word!" Tanner shouted. Ivy was on the other side of the touch tank, and she looked up, brow furrowed with worry when she spotted King jogging to my side. His jaw was clenched, his body practically vibrating with tension.

"We shouldn't have left her."

I gripped the back of his neck. "Focus. Everything will be okay. Wilder is with her and we're only a couple hours from home." I was just as upset that we weren't with our omega, but I needed to keep it together for my alpha.

He grabbed my shoulders. "The field trip doesn't end for another two hours."

"Right, we can rent—"

"We must steal the school bus."

I scrunched my nose. "What?"

King aggressively turned his head from side to side, looking like a cartoon. "You create a distraction, and I will slip the keys from the driver's back pocket."

"Huh. I'd heard that alphas lost their minds during heats, but seeing it is a whole other thing."

Ivy joined us and I kept a firm grip on King's arm in case he decided to follow through with grand theft auto.

"Wilder just texted. Lucy's gone into heat," I said.

"Oh my gosh! That's so exciting." She took in King's grazed eyes. "Oh, right. I see the problem."

"We need to rent a car and drive back now. Will you be okay here without us?"

Ivy waved her hand. "We'll be totally fine. We have plenty of chaperones. Do you need help getting a rental car?"

"Plenty of cars in the parking lot," King muttered.

I slapped my hand over his mouth. "I saw a rental place around the corner."

Ivy's lips twitched. "Please drive safely and call me if you need anything. And Leo? I'm glad Lucy has you. James takes such good care of us while we're all"—she gestured at King—"well, like *that*."

"Thanks, Ivy," I shouted over my shoulder as King half dragged me away.

A few moments later, we were on the road in a rented minivan. King maintained a white-knuckled grip on the door as I pushed the van five miles over the speed limit—faster than I ever drove. Between my worry for Lucy and the strong pulses of arousal hitting me through our bond, I struggled to focus. I couldn't imagine how much worse it was for the alphas.

By the time I took the exit for Starlight Grove, I was a bundle of nerves. What if I couldn't give Lucy what she needed during her heat? I wished I'd had time to do more research, but I clung to Ivy's words, desperate to believe I might have something to contribute besides being the chauffeur.

When I finally pulled up to the shop, King was out of the car before I put it in park. I expected him to run straight inside to get to Lucy, but he waited for me. My heart ached as I rounded the car, and I pulled him in for a kiss. "Go take care of our girl. I'll be right there."

His chest rumbled as he gave me another hard kiss before running inside. I headed into the shop, checking to make sure everything was locked up and flipping the sign on the door to *Closed*.

As I ascended the stairs, Lucy's scent hit me like a wall. It was so intense I staggered backward, my cock instantly standing at attention. Holy shit. The most delicious floral strawberry taste settled on my tongue, sweet and intoxicating. I paused outside her nest, taking a deep breath to center myself before pushing the door open. The moment she saw me, Lucy wiggled out from where King was eating her out.

"Leo." She threw her arms around me. "You're here."

"I'm here, sweet girl. How're you feeling?"

She ignored my question, tugging off my T-shirt with a snarl before starting with my belt. Her foot shifted on the mattress and she lost her balance, bumping my cane and making it fly out of my hand. I let out a panicked noise as we fell onto the huge bed. Luckily, the many layers of blankets, pillows, and stolen pieces of clothing cushioned our fall. I was filled with smug satisfaction when I spotted my sweatshirt that I'd been looking for yesterday.

"Sorry. Did I hurt your leg?" Lucy's voice carried a panicked edge. I couldn't believe that even in the midst of her heat she was still checking on *me*.

"Fuck, I love you." I licked her throat, wishing I could put a bond mark there. She tasted like candy, so mouthwateringly sweet I would never get enough. "You didn't hurt me, azizam." Being on top of her like this strained my knee a bit, but the pain meds I'd taken earlier were helping.

She arched against my chest, her hard nipples like little diamonds against my skin. "I need you."

I groaned and cupped her pussy. It was drenched with slick and I plunged three fingers inside her. "You need a knot stretching your pussy?" I glanced up at Wilder and King, expecting them to meet me with jealousy or impatience, but all I saw was heat in their eyes.

Lucy squirmed and clenched around my fingers. "Need *you*." Her movements became more frantic. I let out a startled shock as her hand wrapped around my cock and squeezed.

King ran his thumb across his lower lip. "Looks like she knows what she wants."

"Fuck, fuck, fuck." I clenched my teeth, trying to hold off my orgasm. I grabbed her hips and rolled so she was on top, which only made it worse because now she was rubbing her sweet pussy along my length, her breasts swaying tantalizingly.

"Too empty," she whined.

I palmed her ass, digging my fingers into her skin. "Are you going to be a good girl for us and let us fill all your tight little holes?"

"Yes," she gasped. Her breathing sped up as she gazed down at me with wide, glassy eyes. From all the articles I'd read, she'd soon fall completely into her heat and become less responsive and more driven by her hormones.

"Good thing you're in the perfect position for Wilder to take your ass while Daddy takes your mouth and I fuck your sweet little cunt."

Wilder swore loudly. "I'm right on the edge of rut," he gritted out. "Once I fall into it, I'm not sure how long I'll be like that. If I do anything to hurt her—"

King clasped him on the shoulder. "You won't, but we have the meds and we'll be here to stop anything from happening."

Wilder's shoulders softened. "Thanks. I'm—" He cleared his throat. "I'm glad you're here."

My heart swelled with how much I loved my new family. How did I get so fucking lucky?

Lucy let out a loud, exasperated sigh. "Yay, family. We all love each other. Now can someone fuck me?"

76
LUCY

Wilder chuckled. "What our omega wants, she gets." I shivered when his huge hands palmed my butt, pulling my cheeks apart. My needy whines transformed to moans when he spit on my asshole and pressed a thick finger inside me.

The emotions in the bond were pure *possession*. I was theirs and they had full permission to do whatever they wanted to me.

I didn't want to make decisions.

Didn't want to think.

I just wanted to *feel*.

My head was forced back as Daddy used my hair as a leash. "That bratty mouth needs a cock filling it."

I parted my lips to answer, but he used the opening to push himself inside my mouth. He hit the back of my throat, but he didn't stop until his full length was inside me. His cock cut off my air, making my stomach contract as I gagged on him.

"Look at how fucking filthy you are, desperate for Daddy's cock." He pulled back just enough to let me take a ragged breath, but then Wilder and Leo thrust inside me at the same time. My scream was cut off as I was pushed forward, forced to take Daddy's cock until my lips bumped against his knot.

I'd never been this full. My ass, pussy, and mouth were split open, the stretch of it overwhelming and yet somehow not enough.

Then they started moving. Pleasure shot through me—hot, electric, and all-consuming. I surrendered to my instincts, feeling wildly out of control and completely safe at the same time.

The outside world drifted away as I sank into my heat.

Time ceased to have any meaning as my men passed me around. I was a doll, under their control, only protesting when they stopped.

Like now.

I kneeled on the bed, my pussy clenching with emptiness.

"You need to eat," Leo said.

A straw was pressed to my lips and I clenched my jaw, shaking my head. There was only one thing I wanted in my mouth right now.

"You're not the one in charge here, omega." Something wrapped around my wrists, and my hands were forced behind my back. I realized too late that they had put leather cuffs on my wrists and ankles and were now hooking them together. I was trapped, stuck in a kneeling position with my back arched and tits pushed out. I fought until I exhausted my strength, but they weren't done with me. Sharp teeth bit into my nipples and I squirmed, trying to dislodge them.

"These nipple clamps are staying on until you drink this entire protein shake." Daddy's stern voice filtered through my lust-drenched brain. His lips brushed against my ear. "And you won't come until you've swallowed every last drop."

He toyed lazily with my nipples, sending sparks of intense pain and pleasure straight to my clit. Tears of frustration trickled down my cheeks. My lips parted in defeat, and I sucked down the shake as fast as I could, scrunching my nose when he finally pulled the straw away.

"Good girl," Wilder murmured. "Taking every last drop."

Fuck. Slick bathed my thighs. I couldn't even close my legs with the way I was bound, leaving me wide open for my guys' hot glances.

Daddy kissed me, swallowing my scream when he removed the nipple clamps without warning. Another orgasm rocked through me, and I sobbed. All I could do was take what they gave me.

"You need to learn to obey us the first time we tell you to do something." Daddy's arm banded around my waist and he pulled me tight to his chest. "Our omega needs more training."

I shook my head. "No, Daddy." My hazy mind barely understood his words, but his erection was taunting me as it pressed against my back. No matter how many times they'd filled me, it was never enough.

"Present for us. I want to see that pretty little ass in the air, aching and dripping with slick."

I glanced at Leo to see if he'd save me, but he just cocked an eyebrow. A low growl rumbled in Wilder's chest as his fingers wrapped around his huge knot, his eyes fixed on my pussy.

"Fine," I huffed.

King released my ankle cuffs but left the chain connecting my wrists. He held the chain as I leaned forward, ensuring I didn't fall on my face as I lowered my chest to the bed, my ass in the air. I moaned as my sore nipples pressed against the mattress. King just chuckled as his hand came down on my butt cheek. I blushed as my scent thickened, drenching the air in flowers and strawberries and making it crystal clear how much I craved this. With each slap, I relaxed farther into the blankets.

Leo stroked my hair. "Look at how well you're taking your spanking. I think it's only fair for all of us to take turns punishing our omega. Except I have a different idea." He pulled my hair, forcing my head back until my mouth was inches from his cock.

"Take your beta's cock in that pretty little mouth," King commanded as a particularly hard smack propelled me forward.

I had no idea how this was a punishment, but I happily parted my lips and sucked Leo down. His tip was huge, already stretching my mouth as I took him deeper. He hit the back of my throat and we both moaned. My eyelids drifted shut as my inner omega took over, drowning me in a haze of pheromones. Leo cupped my jaw, using his grip as leverage as he thrust. I'd barely registered that King had stopped spanking me until he thrust inside me, his cock stretching my greedy pussy. I was tired and sore but desperate for more.

"Fuck. Fuck, your pussy is heaven."

Leo's cock muted my cries as King stretched me. He played with my clit and I was so close to coming it barely took anything for my

A Pack for Spring

orgasm to crash over me. I was in a haze, my skin electrified as I rode the waves of pleasure. It was almost too much, but then King cupped my core with his hand, keeping firm pressure as his thrusts grew more frantic.

Leo's grip on my jaw tightened, the only warning I had before he spilled into my mouth and King pumped me full of his cum. See, this was what I needed, not stupid *food*.

Leo's chest heaved as he lay beside me, maintaining his stinging grip on my hair. "Good girl, taking Daddy and me at the same time. Your other alpha is next, and I can't fucking wait to see how he trains you."

Daddy was still buried deep inside me except for his knot. He ran a firm hand down my back. "Look at our girl. She still thinks she's in charge here, even in the middle of her punishment. Let's see if your other alpha can get you in line."

Daddy pulled out without knotting me. I was on the verge of cussing him out when Wilder took his place behind me and parted my ass cheeks. Cum and slick dripped from me, and my omega was furious I wasn't filled anymore.

"Don't worry. I know how to keep our omega in line."

I shivered at the deep rumble in his voice. He leaned down over my back, pressing me farther to the bed. "You desperate for my knot, kitten?"

Alarm bells rang in the back of my mind but were overridden by my lust and arousal. "Yes, alpha."

In one swift movement, he thrust inside me—but not into my pussy, into my asshole. I cried out in shock, panting through the unexpected stretch. They'd taken me in the ass several times over the past few days, but I had never been knotted there. I squirmed, but fighting was futile with my bound hands and Wilder's vise grip.

"Just relax, kitten," Wilder said. "I know you can take it."

King leaned down so his lips brushed against my cheek. "What do you say if you need to stop?"

I scowled. Why was he talking about *stopping*?

He chuckled. "I'm glad you don't want to stop, baby girl. But what do you say if it gets to be too much?"

"Red."

"Good girl."

I gasped as Wilder thrust so deeply his knot pressed against my asshole.

"Good girls get knotted in their pussies. Bad girls get knotted in the ass," Wilder snarled as he teased my entrance.

I shuddered, the heavy heat haze settling on me again until I was floating. The pressure against my asshole built until I was sure I would break. Just when I was about to say it was too much, Wilder bit down on my shoulder. I screamed at the sting of yet another bonding bite, at the orgasm that seized me with pleasure, and at his knot slipping fully inside my ass.

Tears streamed down my face as my orgasms kept coming, transforming me until I could do nothing but ride the waves of pleasure.

"That's my good girl. So perfect for me, for all of us."

He arranged me so I was lying on my side with my alpha wrapped around me, kissing my shoulder, soothing his hands down my front even as his knot stayed firmly locked inside me.

"I love you. Forever and ever. My sweetheart. My omega."

I sighed as sleep took me, perfectly content and exhausted by my men.

A SMALL CHAIN CONNECTED my wrist cuffs, keeping my hands pressed together at the small of my back as someone lifted me onto Daddy's face. My pussy lips parted, and his tongue speared inside me. I screamed at the pleasure, but my beta's thick cock cut off the sound as he thrust into my mouth. My jaw ached from how I'd been used, but if he pulled out now, I would beg him to keep going.

Daddy kept sucking my clit until the pleasure turned to pain. My pussy burned at the continued stimulation and I sobbed, trying to shift away. Fingers dug into my thighs, followed by a sharp bite on my shoulder. My bond with Wilder flared as he slipped his cock inside me. I was pinned, held immobile as Daddy pulled me back to his relentless mouth.

"Shh, I know it's a lot, but you're doing so well." Gentle fingers brushed away my tears. "Look at how beautiful you are. My dream come true."

The pain in my clit slowly transformed back to pleasure. My orgasm caught me off guard—so sharp and all-consuming I barely registered my men coming with me, filling me to the brim.

Cum dripped down my chin, and my vision turned dark. My alpha pulled me back against his chest, his knot stuffing my sore pussy.

"That had to have exhausted her, right? I swear to god my cock is chafed."

There was a rumble of laughter.

A groan.

And a murmured "Don't count on it."

I WAS CURLED UP on my side, coming in and out of lucidity. I was sticky, sore, and exhausted, but somehow I still needed more.

"Shh." Wilder's deep voice rumbled against my back, and I realized I'd been whining. "You need your alpha, kitten?"

Rough hands parted my legs and he pressed inside. I let out a shuddering sigh of relief. I writhed against him, but he tightened his hold. "You need to sleep." He stroked his hands down my front. "I'll stay inside you, sweetheart, and keep this greedy little pussy stretched while you rest."

I struggled against my exhaustion, but he kept his touch firm and soothing. The tension in my muscles slowly released and I finally drifted off.

77

LUCY

I HAD NO IDEA WHAT IT WAS LIKE FOR A FREE DIVER TO COME back to the surface, but I wouldn't be shocked if it felt like this.

"Are you back with me, sweetheart?"

The low voice lulled me back to that sweet place that was all sensation and pleasure. My limbs were warm, my body floating. I liked it here.

My nose crinkled when something was pressed to my mouth that wasn't a cock. I turned my head, trying to get away, but it followed me.

"You need to hydrate. Drink this for me."

I pressed my lips together.

The earth beneath me shook. "Where's that sweet, compliant omega who kept presenting her sweet little cunt to me?"

Something gripped my jaw.

"Do you need me to be strict with you? Because I can do that. *Open*."

My lips parted and I gulped down the water trickling into my mouth.

"That's my good girl."

Slowly, reality trickled in. "I'm in a bathtub."

"Someone got a bit messy." Wilder tightened his arms around me and kissed my cheek. He was sitting behind me in the tub, our limbs entwined, his fingers soothing my skin.

"My heat's over." A lump rose in my throat at the realization.

A Pack for Spring

"Are you in pain, sweetheart?" The concern in Wilder's voice was evident. He must have sensed my sadness through the bond.

I shook my head.

His chest rumbled with a purr, and he ran his thumb along his bond mark on my breast. "It can be intense to come down from the rush of hormones. You take as much time as you need."

My eyes drifted shut. Time lost all meaning, tracked only by the number of times Wilder refilled the tub with hot water.

When I woke again, I was much more lucid. I turned against Wilder's chest so I could see my alpha. His hair was tied back in two short braids, and I had a vague memory of Leo braiding his hair to keep it from getting tangled.

"Hi."

A slow smile spread across his face. "Hi, beautiful."

"How long did my heat last?"

"Eight days."

I jolted. "*What?*"

His chest shook with laughter. "I'm pretty sure you fucked King and Leo into a coma. They're asleep in the nest."

"No coma for you?" I asked, feeling oddly perturbed at the idea that I hadn't worn him out.

"Nah, but that's only because my alpha is as fucking desperate for you as your omega is for me. For us."

I supposed that was acceptable. I pressed a tender kiss to the bond mark on his neck. "How was it for you?"

"The best fucking week of my life." His strong hands massaged the knots out of my exhausted limbs. "I was scared I would hurt you, but even in rut, I can't bear the idea of you being in pain."

I pressed my smile to his damp skin. "I could have told you that."

"I shouldn't have doubted."

I was a relaxed rag doll as Wilder finished washing my body, got me out of the tub, and wrapped me in a huge towel. He brought me back to the nest, where he fed me a cinnamon roll and fruit smoothie—both courtesy of Summer, who had apparently dropped off heat snacks for all of us.

King and Leo moved closer to me in their sleep until I was curled up among all three of my guys. All those years of waiting and hoping for my pack were worth it.

I drifted off with a smile on my lips.

78

LUCY

HOROSCOPE PISCES

Pisces, after a season of self-discovery, summer invites you to flirt with your newfound confidence, knowing that the groundwork of spring will guide you toward lasting security for you and the ones you love.

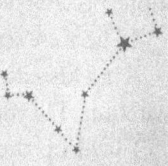

"Drumroll please!"

My guys, Felix, and Blossom sat at the large table in my shop, staring at me expectantly.

"Umm, I don't hear any drumroll sounds." I raised my eyebrows.

King furrowed his brow. "Oh, I thought that was just a thing people said."

I let out an impatient huff, my hands on my hips.

Leo elbowed both alphas. "Cue us again, azizam."

"All right! Drumroll please."

Wilder tapped on the table, King made a noise no one would ever mistake for a drum, and Leo made a barely passable *ba-da-ba-da* sound. Felix, on the other hand, flicked his tail like he couldn't believe I'd suggested he do something so undignified, and Blossom flopped over on the table, fast asleep.

I snorted. "That was terrible. Let's not do that again. But here's the grand reveal!" I zipped open the garment bag and pulled out three button-down shirts.

"Woah." Leo got up from his chair to get a closer look, King and Wilder following close behind. "Those are amazing."

Today was the Swedish Midsummer Festival—a celebration of the first day of summer and one of my favorite days of the year. Once

I'd recovered from my heat, I'd jumped into making everyone's Midsummer outfits. I sewed my guys a pair of slacks and a matching button-down—Wilder's was dark burgundy, King's was navy, and Leo's was olive green. That had been the easy part. The delicate floral embroidery on the collars and down the sides of each pant leg was what had kept me at my shop late at night, my guys blowing up my phone because it was "cuddling time"—King's words, not mine.

"These are seriously amazing," Wilder said.

King kissed the top of my head. "I can't wait for all of us to be matching. Do you like your outfit, Felix?"

I held up the floral embroidered vest I'd made for him, and he gave me a *meow* of approval. Blossom was fully conked out beside him, but I felt pretty confident she'd love her matching mini vest when she woke up.

I leaned in to King. "Were they worth my late nights?"

He made a very Wilder-like grunt that made me laugh. I loved that my guys matched my neediness, missing me when I was working, even if we'd spent the entire day together.

"Okay, we need to get moving. After you get dressed, I'll check if I need to make any adjustments," I said.

I skipped to the back room where I'd stashed my dress. I'd opted for pale blue fabric with gold embroidered flowers scattered across the voluminous skirt. I glanced in the mirror. An omega with bright eyes and pink cheeks stared back at me, a huge smile on her face. How was my birthday only three months ago? Spring had certainly fulfilled its promise of transformation and new life.

"What do you think?" I returned to the front room, giving my guys a spin so my skirt flared around me, but stuttered to a stop because my guys were ... well, *sexy* was an understatement. Their outfits fit perfectly, highlighting their broad chests and muscular arms and thighs.

"Baby girl ..." King trailed off.

I bounced over. "You like it, Daddy?"

"Fucking love it." He gripped my chin, holding me at his mercy as his lips crashed against mine. I dragged my tongue along his, nipping at his bottom lip. We were right next to the table. He could bend me over, lift my skirt, and . . .

A sharp smack on my ass startled me out of my fantasy. My mouth fell open when I realized Leo was the one who had spanked me. "What was that for?"

"You'll be upset if your hair and makeup get all messed up."

I stuck my tongue out at him, but he just smirked as he pulled me away from my sulking alpha. "It's time for your flower crown."

"I'll get it," King snapped. "Leo, you need to sit down."

Leo huffed with mock annoyance, but his flushed cheeks gave away how much he loved his alpha's overprotectiveness.

"Come on." I tugged him over to the closest chair. "Daddy says."

I went to sit beside him, but Wilder snagged the seat first and pulled me onto his lap.

I snuggled into his chest. This would be my happy place forever.

"Are you excited to dance around the maypole?" I asked.

Wilder grimaced. "Is that a requirement?"

"Only if you want to make me happy."

I caught his muttered "Brat" as Leo snorted.

King returned with two large cardboard boxes. He set them down on the table in front of me, but instead of the single flower crown I'd expected, there were six—four large ones and two miniature ones.

"While you were busy with our outfits, we made these," Leo said. "A flower crown for each of us, and for Felix and Blossom, of course."

I looked between King and Wilder. "You made flower crowns?"

"Leo's a good instructor," King said. He leaned down to kiss our beta.

My chest squeezed at their thoughtfulness. They knew how important it was to me that we all matched, and instead of dismissing it as silly, they did *this*. I blinked quickly because Leo was right—I was not about to burst into tears and ruin my makeup.

I helped pin on everyone's flower crowns—including Felix's and Blossom's—and was about to head out when I remembered one last surprise I'd prepared.

"Wait! I almost forgot." I ran to the storage room and returned with Leo's present.

He burst out laughing when I handed him the cane-shaped package. "What could this be?"

I grinned. "I couldn't find a box big enough for it."

He tore the brown paper off, revealing a see-through Lucite cane I'd covered with pressed flowers. I'd recruited Felix to help me steal flowers from Leo's shop. After I'd dried and glued them onto the cane, I'd covered everything with a clear coat to seal them.

Leo was quiet as he took it in. When he looked up at me, there were tears in his eyes. "Jigareto bokhoram. This is amazing."

He used his cane to stand and pulled me tight against his body.

"You're welcome. You can eat my liver anytime."

JAUNTY FOLK MUSIC PLAYED by our local band, The Light Rovers, filled the air as the residents of Starlight Grove danced and sang around the maypole.

My guys had gone to get us food and drinks, leaving me with my moms, who were all sporting flower crowns and outfits I'd sewn for them through the years. Mamma wrapped her arm around me. She was wearing the first blazer I'd ever made in high school—the one with wonky, puckered seams and the interior pocket I'd embroidered with *I love you* in Swedish. I'd made her much better outfits in the years since, but she said this one was her favorite because of how hard I'd worked on it.

"How're you doing, love?"

I rested my head against her shoulder. "I'm happy."

She squeezed my shoulder. "Good."

"Uh-oh," Mom said. "We might be waiting on food for a while."

I followed her gaze to see an intense Stanley cornering Wilder.

"Should we rescue him?" Lala asked as Stanley frantically waved his clipboard.

Jojo snorted as she wrapped her arm around her omega. "*You* can, but I'm not about to get roped into another Stanley lecture."

"So..." I fidgeted with my skirt. "What do you think of my guys?" Between my heat and time-intensive Midsummer prep, we'd only gotten together with my moms once for dinner at the Azad house. It had gone really well—all of our parents had gotten along right away—but I hadn't had time to really talk to my moms about everything that had happened over the past couple of months.

"I was worried they'd be like your exes, but our new sons are wonderful," Lala said.

"Your *sons*? When did you get so close?"

"You've been busy at night, darling, so we've spent some time together." Mamma patted my arm as if she hadn't dropped a huge bombshell.

"Doing *what*?"

"Just mother/son things," Jojo said.

"Nothing bonds you like a trip to Newburyport," Mom added.

"Newburyport? What are you talking about?"

"I was worried about a New York City CEO," Jojo continued. "I thought he might be too uptight and not really *get* you. But he has a diabolical mind, and I fully approve."

"Agreed," Mamma said. "I never would have thought to mist fabric furniture and rugs with milk."

"And his tech connections are impressive. He even let me be the one to send the intel."

"What intel?" I asked loudly.

"Not that I was surprised they're cheating again," Mom said, fully ignoring my question. "But they won't be able to get away with that again."

"What are—"

"Oh, I love this song!" Lala said. "Let's go." My moms joined hands and ran to the maypole, grabbing Tara and Mahmoud on the way. Leo's parents had fully embraced the Midsummer spirit with their yellow and blue outfits and flower crowns.

I scanned the crowd and spotted Leo heading toward me with a slice of cake. I jogged over to him.

"I'm going to pretend you couldn't stand being away from me for a minute longer, and not that you ran over for cake," he said with a grin.

I narrowed my eyes. "Actually, I ran over because my moms were telling me something very interesting about a trip to Newburyport." I glanced down at the slice of strawberry cake. "Also for this." I stole it from him and took a huge bite. *Serves him right for keeping things from me.*

"Hmm? Great town, or so I hear." His expression was all innocence, and I scowled.

"Uh-huh. It just so happens to be the city my exes moved to."

"Oh yeah?"

"Leo."

He laughed, his deep brown eyes sparkling as he played with the ends of my hair. "I don't know what you're talking about, azizam. It would be really weird if your pack drove to your ex-pack's home with your moms, broke in while they were out, misted all their furniture with milk, and sent proof that they're cheating on their current omega to her apartment."

My jaw dropped. "You *didn't*."

He used my distracted state to steal a huge bite of cake. "There's nothing we wouldn't do for you."

I didn't know what it said about me that instead of indignation, all I felt was warm, gooey gratitude toward my guys and my moms.

For seeing me.

A bolt of anxiety shot through the bond, and Leo and I lurched. King sprinted over to us, his hair sticking up and eyes wild.

"Have you seen Blossom?"

"What do you mean? I thought she was with you." We'd all been shocked when Blossom had stuck close to King's side all day, choosing him to carry her to the festival.

"She was! I swear I was paying attention to her the whole time!"

I squeezed his arm. "It's okay. She probably got distracted by something and hopped off."

Wilder jogged over. "What's wrong?"

"Blossom is missing," Leo said.

"Shit." Wilder went to run his hand through his hair but was stopped by his flower crown. "She was hanging out with Felix, but I don't see him, either."

King looked on the verge of tears. I squeezed his arm.

"It's okay. Let's just spread out and look for her."

At least she was bigger now than she'd been at the Eggstravaganza. She was much less likely to be stepped on, and her little body was about ninety-seven percent sass, so she would certainly give a kidnapper a run for their money.

We spread out and just a few minutes later, King shouted. "I see her!" He sprinted to a food booth and let out a frantic noise. "Help! We need an ambulance!" He turned around with Blossom in his arms. She was flopped on her back, her paws and chest drenched in red.

We all ran over, but when I got a closer look, my heart rate returned to normal. King, however, did not share my relief.

"Why aren't you moving!? Where is the vet? James!"

I covered my mouth to suppress my laughter. "Umm, King?" But he couldn't hear me over his shouts.

Leo wrapped his arms around me from behind and rested his chin on the top of my head. "He's a lost cause."

James jogged over, eyes wide. "What? What is it? Did Felix get into the meatballs?"

"No, it's Blossom! She's dying!" King held out the bunny to James, who pressed his lips together.

"I think she'll pull through. Besides maybe having a tummy ache from the amount of strawberries she's consumed."

King's jaw dropped, and he lifted Blossom under her little arms until they were face-to-face. "You did this on purpose."

Blossom's nose twitched.

"No, you can't fool me with that innocent act. I know how your diabolical mind works!"

"He's lost it," Wilder said.

Leo and I nodded.

"I am the only one who sees the truth!"

"Of course you are, baby." I took Blossom from King, keeping her in the crook of my arm as I kissed his cheek. "Let's go get a slice of cake. That will make you feel better."

I handed Blossom to Wilder as I led a still-grumbling King to the dessert table.

"I apologized for the ear comment," he said. "And I made her that castle play area in the cabin."

I patted his arm. "I know, Daddy. You're doing great. She's pranking you because she likes you."

"You think so?"

It was hard work to suppress my smile. My real answer was that Blossom pranked King because he was so easily flustered, but I wasn't about to tell him that.

"Absolutely. And why wouldn't she? You're the best Daddy I could dream of."

He wrapped me in a tight hug. "I know you're bullshitting me."

I shook my head. "No, you really are the best."

He snorted a laugh and kissed my forehead. "I love you."

79
FELIX

I trotted through my domain, flower crown perched on my head, enjoying the quiet of Main Street since everyone was still at the Midsummer festival.

I savored the rare moment of peace. Few people understood the true pressures of being the mayor.

The stores were closed, but I still cast my discerning eye over them to ensure nothing was out of place. My tail flicked as I passed the sunshine omega's bakery. I licked my lips, dreaming of another bánh mì. It was times like these that I wished I had pockets. Maybe I would ask the smiley flower omega to add some to my next outfit.

The sidewalk past Suns Out Bánhs Out was an obstacle course of construction. I pressed my face to the dark glass of the empty shop to check the renovation progress. The interior looked almost complete—the crew had even removed the protective paper from the floor. All that was left was the final touches on the exterior and installing the sign.

A purr strummed through my chest. This summer would be very interesting indeed. There was just one thing left for me to do.

The Beaufort House wasn't far from Main Street. I'd never met its original inhabitants, but I was certainly familiar with the revolving door of inhabitants who had darkened its doorway these past years.

I slipped inside. It was time to break the curse.

King of Midsummer, curse breaker, matchmaker... the work of a mayor was never done.

My paws silently glided across the floors until I got to the kitchen, where I'd already stored the supplies I'd gotten from Bibi—esfand, or rue seeds, and a metal esfand burner.

Hmm. My apprentice should have been here by now. Maybe her prank was taking longer than expected. The strawberry massacre had been the perfect distraction for me to slip away. Besides, any opportunity to enact psychological warfare against the town's alphas was worth taking.

Finally, the front door creaked open and my apprentice hopped inside... but she wasn't alone. I narrowed my eyes at the firefighter alpha.

"Why did you bring me here?" He scanned the space and did a double take when he saw me sitting on the kitchen counter by the stove. "Fuck, no. All I wanted was a quiet day with my pack, and now I have to deal with *this*?"

I rolled my eyes. Alphas were so dramatic.

Blossom hopped over to me and I narrowed my eyes. Did she really think I would do something as ridiculous as burn down the house?

I mean, I'd considered it, but decided to try curse-breaking first. Arson could follow if this didn't do the trick.

To get started, I lifted the small metal lid off the burner with my teeth. I knocked the bag over and about half landed inside the metal container. Good enough.

Now... how to turn the stove on? While cats were superior to humans in all ways, there was the rare moment when opposable thumbs would come in handy.

Alas, I would manage.

"Listen, Felix, I don't know what you're doing, but this is not your house... I don't think. Let's just go back to the festival."

I placed both paws on the stovetop's knob. It clicked, but no flame erupted.

"What the fuck? You're going to burn down the kitchen."

Eh, that could be repaired.

"Or singe your hair."

Huh. He had a point. Fire safety was very important.

Wilder muttered something under his breath and picked up the esfand burner. "Is this incense or something? And you want to burn it?"

Finally he got it. Took him long enough.

"I must be going crazy." The firefighter alpha turned the knob, and this time the flame caught. Excellent. I grabbed the wooden handle again and held it over the flame. Before long, the smell of burnt popcorn wrinkled my nose. Maybe the idea was that whatever dark spirits lurked in the house would be put off by the smell so they'd leave.

Now I just needed to make sure all of the rooms were purified. I hopped off the counter and carried the burner through each room. Blossom and Wilder followed me throughout the house until we returned to the living room.

I sniffed. Something felt different in the air, although only time would tell if it had truly worked.

Wilder muttered something as he snagged the burner and ushered us out of the house. It was good for alphas to feel useful every once in a while. Maybe that's why Blossom had brought him along. Clever little apprentice.

Wilder closed the door to the Beaufort House behind us and I stretched luxuriously on the front porch. Blossom gave a little squeak and I rubbed my face against her head. I needed to groom her ears and then it was nap time.

There was an extra pep in my step as we headed back to Main Street. The sun was shining, the air had finally warmed, and my girls were happy.

Three down. One to go.

80

KING

The festival was winding down, and I couldn't keep my eyes off my girl. The omegas were sprawled across a large quilt, oblivious to the flurry of activity around them as Stanley directed the volunteers on the proper event teardown procedure.

I shifted my weight, feeling antsy. I had a surprise for my pack, but we couldn't go until Wilder returned. He'd wandered off somewhere a little while ago and wasn't answering my texts.

"It's pretty much impossible to stop them once they get going," Lars said, nodding at the omegas as he joined me at the edge of the field.

I grinned as Lucy did a spot-on impression of Stanley waving his clipboard in the air. "Lucy said they're having a movie night at the lighthouse this Friday?"

Lars lifted his chin. "Just a heads-up—movie night often ends with them scheming up some sort of prank against us."

Somehow that wasn't hard to imagine. I didn't mind harmless pranks as long as my little brat knew it would earn her a post-movie-night spanking.

"To comply with their no-boys-allowed rule, we usually meet up with Logan, Rome, and James for dinner." Lars rubbed the back of his neck. "You, Wilder, and Leo would be welcome to join us. If you wanted to."

My breath caught, but I tamped down my excitement. I needed to play this cool. "Have you decided to spare us from Easton's pig farming revenge?"

Lars muttered something under his breath. "As long as you don't hurt my sister. I guess you're part of the family now." He said it so begrudgingly I had to laugh. I couldn't blame him—I was sure I'd feel just as protective if I had a sister—but winning over my omega's brother felt like a genuine victory.

"I appreciate the invite. We'd love to—"

A shrill scream broke the air and my body tensed, ready to spring into action, until I realized Stanley had made the noise. I cocked my head at the scene playing out before us. Summer was running around the field, waving Stanley's clipboard in her hand as he chased her and the other three omegas cheered her on.

Lars shook his head, but he was smiling. "I'll see you Friday." And with that, he strode over to his omega, threw her over his shoulder, and headed toward the lighthouse while Lucy and Ivy booed him for spoiling their fun.

"Summer better be careful or Stanley's going to write a new town ordinance that prohibits the stealing of clipboards." My heart skipped a beat as Leo joined me.

His curls fell down his forehead and I brushed them to the side. He pressed a kiss to my palm before entwining our fingers.

"Lucy's moms invited us over tomorrow for dinner and said to bring my family, too," he said. "I have a feeling our parents are entering some sort of competition for who can be the most hospitable."

I grinned. "We're the real winners in that competition."

We'd had our first big family dinner at the Azad house last week, and it had been pure chaos . . . and completely wonderful. It was everything I'd wished I'd had growing up—loving parents, loud siblings, warmth, hugs, and endless good food. We'd all ended up in their backyard, where Lucy had explained her precise technique for roasting the perfect marshmallow, resulting in all of us presenting copious marshmallows to her for judging. Honestly, it was impressive how she'd managed to get an endless supply of s'mores without lifting a finger.

"Lars invited us to get dinner with his and Ivy's pack while the girls are having their movie night."

"Look at you." Leo grinned and nudged my side. "Making friends all around town."

I snorted, but our bond meant I couldn't hide my warm, syrupy feelings.

Leo briefly let go of my hand to adjust his hold on his cane.

"How's your knee? Are you in pain?"

He pulled me close and kissed the corner of my mouth. "I'm fine." His lips skimmed my cheek until they brushed the shell of my ear. "Are you jealous I'm not using the cane you got me?" His voice was low and sultry, making my cock twitch.

I gripped the back of his neck, making sure my thumb rubbed the bond mark I'd put there. His pupils dilated and breath hitched.

"Am I interrupting?" Wilder's voice jolted us back to reality.

"Where have you been?" I asked.

"You seriously don't want to know." He shook his head. "Blossom is hanging out with Felix. Are we ready to go?"

"I have something I want to show you all," I said.

I tugged on my bond with Lucy and she spun around, eyes scanning until she spotted the three of us. She skipped over, her floral skirt catching in the wind with each bounce.

"Hey!" She half crashed into me with a wide smile. "You ready to go?"

Leo tugged her into his arms. "King has something to show us, apparently."

"Oohhh, what is it?"

"It's a surprise," I responded.

Lucy jutted her lip out in a pout. "Or you could tell me now."

I shook my head. "I'm going to grab my car." We weren't going far at all, but the fastest way to get there was walking along the beach, and I didn't want the sand aggravating Leo's leg. "I'll pick you all up at the road in a minute." I gripped Lucy's chin and gave her a hard kiss. "Behave." I did the same to Leo. "You, too."

Lucy leaned against Wilder and he wrapped his arms around her waist. "He didn't tell you to behave," she said. "So it's your job to cause all the chaos."

I shook my head but couldn't stop my smile.

I'd smiled more the past couple of weeks than in my entire life.

"Oooh, the surprise is the beach?" Lucy asked as we got out of the car.

"We were literally just by the beach. This *same* beach," Wilder said.

"No grumpiness allowed today." Lucy poked his side and squealed when he swooped her up into his arms.

"Lead the way, King," he said, grinning.

I kept my arm around Leo as we headed down the sandy path to the water, helping him stay balanced as his cane sank into the sand with every step.

I stopped before we'd gone too far. "You know I've been working on that commercial real estate deal? Well, this is the property."

"Wait, you're selling this land?" Lucy's face fell and a pang of sadness reached me through the bond. "When you said commercial property, I was expecting an office building or warehouse. This is beautiful."

"Seems a shame to let this area be developed," Wilder said.

I turned to Leo, waiting for his opinion, but he just smirked and met my eyes with a knowing gaze. Our bond was filled with amusement, not disappointment. I brushed my hand through my hair. Being this *seen* was . . . unsettling but also wonderful.

"I'm glad you feel that way because I've decided not to sell it to the developer."

Lucy perked up. "Yeah? What are you going to do with it?"

"Most of the land will be put in a permanent trust for wildlife and land conservation, with the exception of the section we're standing on now. I was thinking we could build a house on it."

"A house?" Lucy breathed.

"We don't have to if there's a location you like better. I was just thinking we need a real pack house, one that's secluded enough for the mountain grump"—I jerked my head at Wilder, who rolled his eyes—"while still being an easy commute to town."

Lucy let out an excited squeal and hopped out of Wilder's arms. "I love this idea." Then her face fell. "But wait, what will you do? Can you permanently work remotely, or will you still have to travel into New York?"

Fuck. I had been so deep in my head planning this surprise that I hadn't actually *communicated* with my pack. "Well, I may have already handed in my resignation to the board," I said sheepishly. I'd told them last week and recommended Caroline to replace me as CEO.

My three packmates stared at me in stunned silence until Leo cleared his throat.

"Any other major life changes we should know about?" he asked dryly.

"No. Well, okay, I started a nonprofit for ocean conservation, but I haven't mailed in the paperwork, so it's not final or anything," I muttered.

"You are ridiculous." Leo pulled me into a hug, and before I knew it, all three of them had their arms around me, squeezing.

"It's a good plan," Wilder said.

"It's a *great* plan," Lucy emphasized as she bounced in my arms. "How soon can we get the house built? Can I design my nest? What if we have a whole floor for my nest? The Nest Wonderland catalog from March had this huge attic room nest with vaulted ceilings and exposed beams, and I've been dreaming about it ever since."

I chuckled and kissed her forehead. "Of course you can, baby girl. We can make it whatever you want. I have an architect lined up, and I talked to the construction crew working on that new shop beside Summer's place. They're available to start construction right away. We're still looking at a six-month wait at the earliest, but probably closer to a year." I ran my fingers through her hair. "If you still want to have a heat this fall, we can make it work in your apartment again, or we can rent a nest. There are some really nice heat clinics in Boston."

She cupped my face with both hands and pulled me down to her level. "We'll figure it out. As long as we're together."

Her lips were plush and soft as she kissed me, her sweetness settling into my soul.

81

LUCY

"I can't believe we're going to live here." I sighed and rested my head against Leo's shoulder. The two of us were sitting on the sandy embankment while King and Wilder walked the area that would become our home's foundation.

He kissed the top of my head. "Dream come true."

I breathed deep, letting the salty sea air wash over me as the sun's final golden rays touched my skin. For all my stress and indecision since my birthday, everything about my life felt *right*.

I was getting ready to launch my first two online sewing courses—one for making dresses and one for pet clothing—and I even had a waitlist for custom clothing orders. I'd been braced for snide comments and critique when I'd announced the classes on Felix's Instagram, but not a single person online or in real life had questioned my qualifications. And if they didn't, maybe I shouldn't, either.

My alphas finally finished their conversation about construction something or other and joined us. I held my hands out and Wilder pulled me up while King helped Leo.

"We should probably head out before it gets too dark," Wilder said.

"Wait, before we do, there's one more Midsummer tradition we can't miss."

The three of them narrowed their eyes, clearly sensing my mischief through the bond. Their faces momentarily disappeared as I pulled my dress off over my head. When I emerged in just my panties and bra, they were all staring at me, mouths agape as they not-so-subtly adjusted their crotches. I undid my bra and pulled down my panties.

"Skinny-dipping." I threw my underwear at King and laughed as

I sprinted down the beach, arms extended to the side as I embraced the world.

The waves hit my legs and stole my breath away. The summer sun hadn't had the chance to warm the water yet, but I ran farther into the icy spray before turning around. My guys had stripped off their clothes and were heading toward the water—King and Wilder carrying Leo between them. His arms were slung over their shoulders and they each had one of his legs as he shouted commands. "Faster! We must catch the mermaid!"

Laughter filled the air as they crashed into me, all of us tumbling into the shallow waves. The candy-colored sky cast a glow on us as we swam and kissed in the water I'd wake up to everyday once our house was built.

Wilder wrapped his arms around me. I snuggled into his chest, soaking up his heat as the water and evening breeze made me shiver.

"You sleepy, sweetheart?" he murmured.

"Just a little. Don't worry, I'll get my second wind."

His chest rumbled with a purr. "I don't doubt it, kitten."

I pressed my smile to his salty skin. So far, year twenty-nine was my favorite year yet, and it was just getting started.

The end.

Introducing our newest family member, Blossom! The mayor has already taken her under his paw.

Felix and Blossom at their new favorite lunch spot! Suns Out Bahns Out is officially open!

Every day is a good day to surprise someone with a bouquet of flowers (extra large!)

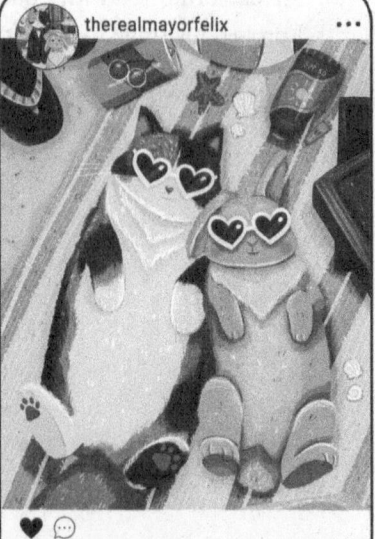

It's almost summer! Grab your favorite sunnies and a romance book for a perfect beach day.

ACKNOWLEDGMENTS

Eliana!!! (I'm shouting your name really loudly so you can hear me all the way in Australia.) We did it!!! We had big dreams when we met up in New Zealand, but I don't think either of us could have imagined where the following months would lead. This journey has been wild, hectic, and challenging, and I don't think I would have made it without you by my side. I'm so grateful for you—your humor, support, and occasional petty snark. I will forever treasure our friendship and this world we've built together. What an absolute gift.

Also . . . remember when we first started talking about writing cozy omegaverse and thought we could only handle writing one cozy book each before returning to our angsty roots? Joke's on us! We wrote *two* cozy books each . . . and who knows what the future holds.

To Patrice—being an author is a lot less scary knowing you're in my corner! Thank you for wholeheartedly championing this series, for your love of cats and Felix, and for the ways you support me as a person and an author.

To Kate—for taking a chance on the first-ever traditionally published Why Choose Omegaverse! Your enthusiasm and support for this series have been life-changing (and, dare I say, industry-changing). Thanks for loving this world (and your man Wilder) so much!

Thank you to our entire team at Putnam—Tarini, Katie, Jazmin, Regina, and so many more, who have been such amazing champions of Cozyverse.

To Rachel—for always being a safe place for me to complain, celebrate, and everything in between. Here's to many more chaotic writing retreats together!

To Darcy—I'm writing this in the Boston Public Library after we finally got to meet in person for the first time. I feel so lucky our virtual paths crossed four years ago.

To my amazing beta readers—Aimee, Blair, James, Jenny, and Robyn—and my sensitivity readers, Mina and Melissa. Your encouragement gave me the boost I needed to finish this book, and your invaluable feedback helped shape it into the best possible version of itself.

To Ella, whose name I stole for our Beans 'n Bliss barista—for being one of my favorite people.

To Celina—for seeing me and loving me. And for your hatred of going on family hikes, which inspired the start of Lucy's story.

To Kara—for your astrology wisdom and horoscope writing!

When I started writing Cozyverse, I didn't plan for grandparents to play such a big role. But as *A Pack for Autumn* and *A Pack for Spring* unfolded, it became clear how important these relationships were for many of my characters. From Finn being raised by his grandparents in *A Pack for Autumn*, to Lucy being inspired to sew by her mormor, and Leo's tender relationship with Bibi, grandparents have shaped the lives of some of my favorite Starlight Grove residents. It makes sense because my grandparents have played a huge role in my life.

To my Pappaw—for all the mornings making pancakes together, countless Tarzan stories, for driving all the way to Cleveland to help me move, and for planting roses at my house.

To my Bibi—for all the sing-alongs on the piano, for encouraging my writing, and for your consistent support. I'm so grateful for these extra years we've gotten together.

And to my Iranian grandmother, who I never got to meet—you were in my heart the entire time I was writing. I hate that the only thing I know about you is the suffering that ultimately ended your life. Through Leo's Bibi, I got to imagine a different story for you—

Acknowledgments

one where you got away and lived the life you deserved—surrounded by love and joy and flowers.

Last but never least—to my readers. You continue to amaze me with your love and support. The way you've embraced Cozyverse and supported Eliana and me in our transition to being traditionally published honestly makes me emotional. Thank you!

He just wanted a decent book to read ...

Not too much to ask, is it? It was in 1935 when Allen Lane, Managing Director of Bodley Head Publishers, stood on a platform at Exeter railway station looking for something good to read on his journey back to London. His choice was limited to popular magazines and poor-quality paperbacks – the same choice faced every day by the vast majority of readers, few of whom could afford hardbacks. Lane's disappointment and subsequent anger at the range of books generally available led him to found a company – and change the world.

'We believed in the existence in this country of a vast reading public for intelligent books at a low price, and staked everything on it'
Sir Allen Lane, 1902–1970, founder of Penguin Books

The quality paperback had arrived – and not just in bookshops. Lane was adamant that his Penguins should appear in chain stores and tobacconists, and should cost no more than a packet of cigarettes.

Reading habits (and cigarette prices) have changed since 1935, but Penguin still believes in publishing the best books for everybody to enjoy. We still believe that good design costs no more than bad design, and we still believe that quality books published passionately and responsibly make the world a better place.

So wherever you see the little bird – whether it's on a piece of prize-winning literary fiction or a celebrity autobiography, political tour de force or historical masterpiece, a serial-killer thriller, reference book, world classic or a piece of pure escapism – you can bet that it represents the very best that the genre has to offer.

Whatever you like to read – trust Penguin.